BONE HUNTER

❖
❖
❖

BONE HUNTER

◆
◆
◆

Sarah Andrews

ST. MARTIN'S MINOTAUR / NEW YORK

Library of Congress Cataloging-in-Publication Data

Andrews, Sarah.
    Bone hunter / Sarah Andrews.—1st St. Martin's Minotaur ed.
        p.   cm.
    ISBN 0-312-20381-0
    I. Title.
    PS3551.N4526B66   1999
    813'.54—dc21   99-23850
                                                    CIP

10 9 8 7 6 5 4 3 2

For Duncan,
who knows about dinosaurs.
May my love support you in continuing to
reach beyond my limitations.

Acknowledgments

My thanks to M. Lee Allison, Utah State Geologist, for exhorting me to write this book. I am indebted also to the following geologists and paleontologists for their technical assistance and insights: David D. Gillette and Janet Whitmore Gillette, Museum of Northern Arizona; Marjorie Chan, University of Utah; Michael Leschin, Cleveland-Lloyd Quarry, Bureau of Land Management; John Horner, Museum of the Rockies; John Bolt, the Field Museum; Robert Bakker; Sarah George, Utah Museum of Natural History; Donald Rasmussen, consulting geologist; Debra Mickelsen, University of Colorado; Matthew James, Sonoma State University; Christine Turner and Pete Peterson, U.S. Geological Survey; Vincent Santucci, U. S. National Park Service; Louis L. Jacobs, Southern Methodist University; and Brooks B. Britt, Museum of Western Colorado.

I wish to thank Doris E. Andrews, Hayward State University; Maria Titze, Salt Lake City *Observer;* Deborah Bodner; and Carol Mapes for assisting me in better understanding the history, faith, and practice of the Church of Jesus Christ of the Latter-day Saints.

For their technical contributions toward the greater accuracy of this text, my thanks to Sonoma County Assistant District Attorney Greg Jacobs; Eddie Fryer, Federal Bureau of Investigation; Chris Kappler, Sonoma County Sheriff's Department; Sarah Davis; and Priscilla Kapel, Bioenergy Balancing Center.

I am grateful to Jon Gunnar Howe, Thea Castleman, Mary Madsen Hallock, and Kenneth Dalton (a.k.a. the Golden Machete Critique Group); and to Eileen M. Clegg, Clint Smith, Marjorie Chan, Marilyn Wessel, and David Gillette for their spirited and insightful critiques of the completed draft.

My thanks to my editor, Kelley Ragland, for her usual excellent editing and to all the folks at St. Martin's Press for championing this book through the publishing and marketing process.

My thanks to my son, Duncan Brown, for reminding me that the ossified brains of grown-ups can get them stuck in intellectual ruts. And, as always, my thanks to my husband, Damon Brown, for his unstinting support and good humor while being the artist's husband.

BONE HUNTER

◇
◇
◇

$\diamond$
$\diamond$
$\diamond$

1

$\diamond$
$\diamond$
$\diamond$

IT'S ALL TRUE. WHEN THE SQUAD CAR ROLLED UP BEHIND me and the loudspeaker blared, "Hold it, right there!" I was, in fact, trying to break into George Dishey's house. But I had an excuse. Really.

It's true that I had chosen to attack a window at the back of the house so I would not be seen, but think about it: If I'd thought I was doing something wrong, I would have at least waited until dark. I wasn't standing there in those shrubberies, hurrying the job, jamming that knife blade into that window sash that recklessly because I was afraid anyone would think I was breaking in, which I of course was; no, I was hiding in the backyard because I was afraid the neighbors would see me and make unpleasant presumptions about my social life.

It was that kind of neighborhood. George had taken pains to let me know that. "They're good Mormons," he'd told me the evening before, lowering his voice as if they could hear him, even with the doors and windows locked, in the so-called privacy of his own living room. "You know how it is," he had continued, with a dramatic sigh. "Here I am, the eligible bachelor, making a decent living. Those good Mormon mommas watch me like a hawk." He'd lifted an index finger to one eye, demonstrating the look with all the dramatic flair for which he was famous. "Guess they think I'd make a good catch for one of their umpty-jillion daughters to breed with." He had laughed, throwing his unlovely head back so that his grizzled beard stuck out like a shelf, and had cast a sidelong glance at me to see how I was taking his bait. "Hah! They think there's still hope of converting me!" Here he'd smacked his lips, as if he'd just consumed an especially rich morsel of food.

I hadn't replied. I couldn't imagine any self-respecting Mormon targeting a "Gentile" with a grizzled beard. And even as un–politically correct as I am, I don't like that judgmental kind of talk; it always leaves me cold. And I know that George Dishey had a reputation for being outspoken, even argumentative, for the sake of the publicity that picking a fight would bring him, so why argue? Give me a break; he was the internationally famous Dr. Dishey, and I was just Em Hansen, the barely-made-it-through-undergrad hack geologist from Chugwater, Wyoming. Besides, he was at least twenty years my senior and paunchy, so my candid reaction to his implied overture would have been downright rude. And I was, in fact, in the delicate circumstance of being his houseguest, he was an unmarried man and I an unmarried woman, neighbors do talk, and, well, even in my moments of greatest self-confidence, I hate engaging in controversies or otherwise attracting attention to myself.

So. So I fell for his line and did my best to pretty much sneak in and out of his house, sneaking my bags out of my rental car in the dark as if there was something wrong with my being there. Which there wasn't. Okay, so I wasn't proud of the fact that I was taking lodgings with this peculiar man in Salt Lake City rather than coughing up the money to stay at the posh ski resort of Snowbird with the rest of the conference attendees. You see, that's why I was there, to speak at a symposium on forensic paleontology at the annual conference of the Society of Vertebrate Paleontology. Or at least that's what George Dishey had told me I was there to do.

But back to that highly embarrassing moment when I was caught trying to break back into his house. It was a Sunday morning, the first day of the conference, and George had left early, without telling me where he was going or why. I wouldn't even have known he was gone, except that when the phone rang, it woke me up, and even through two closed doors and the veil of sleep, I could hear him hollering into it, and then I heard the door slam and the sound of his vehicle starting up and pulling away from the parking slip. The forensics symposium wasn't scheduled until the afternoon, so I'd gone back to sleep for a while, then later had gotten myself up and showered and stumbled around until I found an iron and an ironing board, and had pressed the creases out of my best blouse and slacks and gotten dressed. As I helped myself to a breakfast of prefab frozen burritos, which the microwave had rendered scalding on the outside and still hard on the inside, I had wondered idly where he had gone and when he might return. By eight o'clock, I had grown restless. By 9:00, I'd begun to worry. By 9:30, it had occurred to me that I could leave any time I wanted, and I had complimented myself on having had the foresight to rent a car at the airport so I'd have my own transportation. George had argued hard against this, saying we would of course go and come from the conference at the same times anyway, but I had learned too often that when working with men, independence of motion is essential.

On top of everything, I was supposed to deliver that speech at the symposium, and I was a bit nervous about it. Okay, I was scared stiff, and pacing up and back in George Dishey's kitchen, wondering where he'd gone, wasn't exactly soothing. I decided to drive around town awhile before heading up into the mountains to the east, where the conference was convening. It was a nice sunny autumn day, the city had a smile on, and I had not seen it since I was too young to remember. So I wrote George a brief note saying I'd see him at Snowbird, gave my hair a last brush, cussed under my breath that it still didn't look quite right, walked up to the front door, and then stopped.

What if the neighbors saw me leaving? What, in fact, would they think? Was this town still so conservative that having a woman in his house without benefit of wedlock might compromise his career? And worse, might I draw an unwelcome opinion-fest from some self-righteous church lady?

In the end, I had waited until I saw the neighbors file out to their minivans in their Sunday finest, gave them ten extra minutes to make sure they didn't double back for their prayer books or something, and all but dashed out to my car, slamming the front door behind me. That was silly, I know, but there you have it. I was sprinting down the sidewalk, thinking nothing more clever than, *Will some tardy church lady see my slacks and know I'm not heading to church?* when I realized I had left the keys to my rental car in the house. As I skidded to a halt, that realization collided with the next, which was that I had no key to George Dishey's house, either. He had not offered me one. Good old George had managed to exert some control over my comings and goings after all.

So you see, it was all very innocent, and, in fact, it was with the best intentions that I was breaking into George Dishey's house. And if I was acting a mite covert, it was because I was worried about his honor, not my albeit felonious-looking activity. Honest.

When I heard that loudspeaker go off behind me, I about jumped out of my skin. The pocketknife I was using to jimmy the lock on the bedroom window jerked free of my grip and gouged deeply into my left thumb. That left me stunned for a moment, and of course an instant later my thumb began to hurt like fury, but at least that gave me something to squeal about while I tried to organize my thoughts.

Imagine the scene. Baritone voice through loudspeaker: "You there! Drop your weapon!"

I: "Hey, no problem!" I tossed the knife onto the lawn and clutched the wound shut with my right hand. It was starting to bleed, fast.

Voice: "Now back away from the building, slow and easy."

I: "Okay, I'm—this hurts!" I stumbled out of the bushes and turned gingerly to see what was behind me. The lights on the top of the car were wheeling about. My heart began to race, and sounds seemed to recede from my head.

The cop, who was by then out of his car and halfway up the lawn, moving toward me with one hand hovering over his now-unlatched holster, eased in toward the window and with one foot kicked my old beat-up two-blade Buck knife farther away from me. "Kneel down and put your hands apart on the ground!" he ordered.

I knelt.

"Hands on the ground!"

Blood began to drip from between my fingers. "I . . . I can't. I'm, ah, bleeding." The blood was escaping my grip now, plop, plop, plop. I didn't want to get it on my slacks. They were the only really good pair I owned, and they fit well, and when you don't really have a waist and you're a bit thick through the thighs like I am, a fit like that is hard to find.

The cop noted the blood as he quickly surveyed the scene. "What are you doing here?" he asked brusquely.

I opened my mouth to tell him but couldn't think of a good answer.

"What are you doing here?" he repeated. His hand still hovered above his holster.

I wondered thickly what all the excitement was. Sure, he had caught me outside a man's house on a Sunday morning with no church to go to, but was that a capital offense? What if this were my house? Was this how Salt Lake City's finest approached well-dressed home owners who chose to fiddle with their window locks on Sunday mornings? Or was there an all-points bulletin out for a female cat burglar of medium height, brown hair, sort of forgettable-looking, who liked the challenge of broad-daylight theft? "I'm . . . um . . ."

The moment was so unreal that I found myself watching him as if he were a movie. That impression was amplified by the fact that he was movie-star good-looking and very fit. Sharp blue eyes with heavy black lashes. Black hair. A ruddy, healthy pallor, roses and cream, like the best of the Irish. His uniform was perfectly pressed, and it fit him like something in a clothing ad.

In an effort to make sense of what was happening, my mind decided that if I were watching a movie, I must be on a date. Yes, that fit, because I was, after all, wearing some of my best clothing, and I'd just showered and done what I could for my face. I felt embarrassed that my date had caught me kneeling on the lawn, and I hoped he wouldn't think I was some kind of slob. Here he'd been so kind to invite me to his movie, and I'd gone and knelt in the dirt. I didn't want to disappoint him. He seemed so . . . authoritative.

I shook my head, trying to clear it. My mind was going. For a moment, I wondered if it were loss of blood, but I hadn't lost that much, not yet. Then I remembered that with any injury, no matter how slight, there is some measure of shock.

With some effort, I cleared my throat. Try it sometime, when you're on your knees in front of a policeman while bleeding from a fresh knife wound. The old pipe can grow tight. Finally, I managed to say, "I'm a guest of Dr. Dishey's," and tipped my head toward the house. "I have to get to this conference I'm attending, and I got out here to my car and realized that I'd forgotten my keys. They're right in there, on the um—" I peered up toward the window. My stomach was beginning to flutter. I'm usually tougher at the sight of blood, having done my share of ranch chores in my day, but I began to feel the need to put my head between my knees. "Can this wait?" I mumbled.

The cop unclipped his microphone and called his station. "Central, this is Raymond. Got a female Caucasian here, medium height, brown hair, gray eyes, early thirties. She's cut and bleeding. Request backup to take her to the hospital."

He needed a backup to take me to the hospital? What? "Listen," I said, "if there's any problem, you can talk to Dr. Dishey about it. I don't know where he went, but I'm sure he'll be back any time now. We're supposed to be at the conference by noon, so I mean . . ." A wave of nausea swept over me. "Please?"

Another police car pulled up at the curb, siren bawling to a stop. My head was beginning to ping. I looked up into the firm, handsome face of my non–guardian angel, or at least this angel who appeared to be guarding the world from me, and found him studying me with a mixture of detachment and concern. He neither looked away nor met my eyes, but gazed at me steadily, as if watching for signs that would alert him if I was about to attempt flight. I felt a growing need to lie down on the grass.

With an effort, I stared up into his eyes. They were like a mountain lake at dusk, almost indigo, very deep. "My car keys are inside," I said softly. "My luggage is inside. George will be back, I swear it. He can explain everything."

Still he did not make eye contact. I looked away—at the ground, at the grass stains on my knees, at the sticky blood that was accumulating between them. Then, as the legs and feet of two more policemen hove into my darkening view, he said, "That's not hardly likely, is it, ma'am? Because we found George Dishey an hour ago, and he's dead. But you already know that, *don't* you?"

2

I HAD NEVER BEEN HANDCUFFED BEFORE, LET ALONE TO A hospital gurney. I lay staring at the texture of the ceiling tiles, feeling the constriction of that cold steel bracelet, wondering what could possibly have happened to George Dishey that the police would react this strongly. But I didn't ask. Murder is an ugly thing however it is done, and all the fight was gone out of me for the time being. I waited only for the anesthetic the intern had injected into my thumb to take effect so that the pain would stop. After that, I didn't care what happened. They could stitch my thumb to the floor as long as they kept it numbed.

I shook my head, trying again to clear it. Being welded to a floor—or to a murder investigation—would not do at all. I had a job to return to in Denver, where I was working as a petroleum geologist for a boss who had not been amused at the thought of releasing me for three days for an activity that would not directly add to the stuffing in his wallet. "A conference on forensic geology?" he had snorted, showing me yellowed teeth around the remnants of his spent cigar. His shrewd eyes had danced thoughtfully as he chewed ruminantly on the tattered roll of tobacco. "What kinda bullshit is that?"

"Um, it's a sideline of mine. You see, I use what I know

about geology and geological industries to help solve crimes. I've acted as a consultant to the police a few times," I'd said, as the palms of my hands grew moist. I had waited until the last minute to ask for leave, even though I'd known about the conference for months.

"Crap," he'd replied. "You find me some oil. You gotta scratch this itch, fine; take your vacation time. But I wanna see you back here by Thursday with nuttin on your mind but 'Drill here.' "

Before I could get another word in edgewise, he'd plugged a fresh cigar into his mouth and flicked his fingers at me, his way of announcing to his underlings that their audience with the king was over.

My heart had fallen. In the tradition of many oil-patch entrepreneurs, my cigar-chewing employer granted two weeks' leave each year, and he wanted to talk to the employee who took the second week. I had shuffled down to the personnel office to sign away three-fifths of my annual vacation, thoughts of rebellion thoroughly buried under the weight of reality. Petroleum jobs were rare as hen's teeth. My previous boss, J. C. Menken, had called in a lot of favors to get me this one after his company folded. With recent mergers of the giant companies, Mr. Cigar could have his pick of lackeys like me, and I suspected that he had at length only approved my leave on the basis that he could brag to his buddies in the steam room that one of his slaves had been invited somewhere by the famous George Dishey—you know, da dinosaur guy you see on da TV programs.

So as I lay on that gurney, I was less worried about my thumb than the fact that I had to be at my desk by Thursday morning at 8:00. With George dead, the fizz had all gone out of this whole junket, and it would have suited me fine to give my damned talk and catch an evening flight home and be at work on Monday. Unfortunately, I already had too good an idea what involvement in a murder investigation could do to my chances of getting home on time.

Time. The second hand on a large, impersonal clock swept slowly around its smooth white face. I stared at it, trying not to look into the eyes of Officer Raymond. That, I did not want to do. Looking at Officer Raymond made me want to cry, and as long as I didn't understand why I felt that way, I wasn't going to let it happen.

Presently, the intern slipped back in through the door from some other job she was doing and probed at the fleshy part of my thumb. "Do you feel that?" she inquired.

"No."

"Good. Now just hold still, and I'll have you sewn up in a jiffy."

"Fine." Stoic was a role I knew how to play.

Clink, clack went the stainless-steel hemostats she was about to clamp onto my flesh. She opened a suturing packet and laid out the prethreaded needles on a sterile cloth. She selected a weapon. I turned my head to look away, but there stood Officer Raymond. I looked back. She irrigated the wound, probed for foreign objects, irrigated again. Lifted a needle. At the precise moment she lowered it to my thumb, a new man walked into the emergency room. The intern paused, looking up at him. He smiled at her, at me, at the scene—flashed a big juicy grin that only amplified the unnervingly bright light in his eyes—and flipped open a wallet to show me his badge. "Go right on with your work, Grace," he said to the intern. "I'm just going to ask your patient a few questions."

Sadist, I thought.

"Fine, Bert," said the intern. "Just keep out of my light."

"Your name is Emily *B* for Bradstreet Hansen," the man named Bert informed me, "and you *say* you're a guest of the deceased."

"Yes." I concentrated on his face, which was only a little

less daunting than the sight of the intern preparing to suture my thumb. A pressure hit my left thumb. That was all, just pressure, but I knew what it was. I closed my eyes and breathed deeply, remembering the half-dozen other times I'd had stitches in my life, remembered the horses I'd fallen off on the way to getting hurt badly enough to need them. Remembered—

Tug. She fiddled, tying the first knot.

"So that's your story. Okay," Bert said lightly, as if that was all just fine and settled now. "So we have a homicide on our hands, and maybe you can help us with it, then."

My arm rocked slightly with the intern's ministrations. "Fine," I said. "Just ask your questions. I'm not going anywhere." *Nice, Em. Make it sound defensive.*

"Why don't you just take it from the top?"

Tug. "Certainly. I am a geologist. I am in town for a conference on vertebrate paleontology. Dr. Dishey invited me. I'm supposed to deliver a short speech this afternoon at one of the symposia," I said, being somewhat snotty about my Latin plurals for the occasion. "I had never met him before last night, when I drove in from the airport. I had only spoken with him on the phone. My plane was late, delayed by weather coming out of Denver. I'd give you the flight number, but it's with my luggage in Dr. Dishey's house."

Tug.

"When I got in, Dr. Dishey offered me a drink, but I said I was tired and just wanted to go to bed. I did just that. Alone. In a separate room from Dr. Dishey. That was at about nine. This morning early, I heard the phone ring. I heard Dr. Dishey answer it. He was shouting. Quite abruptly, the conversation ended, and half a minute later, I heard him go out. He slammed the door. I heard his vehicle start. Big engine. Sounded like a truck. I heard it leave. I went back to sleep. I stayed asleep until about seven."

Pressure. Tug.

My stomach was starting to swim again. I swallowed hard and told myself it was the anesthetic. Tried not to think about the fact that I was lying on my back, and that this man was leaning over me. "I got up, showered, ate breakfast, waited around for a while, and then headed for my rental car. Halfway there, I realized I didn't have my keys. I thought about waiting awhile longer for Dr. Dishey to show up, but I didn't like sitting around on his front porch waiting, so I looked at the window, realized what an old-fashioned latch it had, and thought I'd give it a go. That was when Officer, ah, Raymond showed up."

The intern made a fifth and last stitch, finishing her embroidery, and began dressing the wound. I dared open my eyes. The man Bert, obviously a police detective—he was in civvies, after all, and had that kind of cozy "tell me everything" attitude some of them affect—smiled at me, a kind of ghoulish attagirl. I blinked, hoping he was some narcotic-induced dream bubble that would pop and disappear, but he only swayed slightly, further unseating my stomach. He was somewhere in his forties, with thinning hair combed back in strings, and possessed of rather opaque pale greenish eyes, like two cabuchons of Persian turquoise. Abstract thoughts like that occur to geologists—comparisons between animate and inanimate objects—and they throw us off sometimes. With the stress of being questioned and the local anesthetic confusing the million nerve endings in my beleaguered thumb, the thought upset my mental filing system, putting Detective Bert geographically under *P* for Persia, rather than under *U* for Utah.

"You could not see this telephone." He leaned farther over me. The ceiling seemed to crawl.

"No. It was in another room. I did not see the telephone, Dr. Dishey, or anything else."

"Why?"

"Because it was not yet light out. There were streetlights,

but my bedroom was in the back of the house. The blinds are heavy. There was no clock. I did not look at my watch."

"So you do not, in fact, know what time this telephone rang." His tone was still light, but I could feel the pressure of his choice of words, the subtle assertions that said, You don't know what you're talking about, or, You're lying.

Straining to keep my voice level, I said, "No. If I had to guess, I'd say about five."

"What exactly did Dr. Dishey shout into this telephone you did not see?"

I took a long, deep breath, mentally counted to ten, and reminded myself that I had nothing to hide. Wondered if I should ask to have a lawyer present. Tried to remember if he or Officer Raymond had read me my rights. Wished the anesthesia had been general. "I couldn't hear much. He just sounded angry."

"Nothing at all?"

"Well . . . okay, I remember a few choice epithets, the kind of thing you'd know anywhere, just by the rhythm of the words." I paused, squeezed my eyes shut again. Would Officer Raymond be shocked that I knew the rhythms of four-letter words? And what in hell did I care for? "There was something that sounded like 'You can't!' and, 'You'll bust the thing to pieces,' but I could be wrong. I was more asleep than awake."

"Ah. So then you went back to sleep."

"Yes."

"And you awoke about seven."

"Yes."

"Do you always sleep ten hours at night, Em?" He sounded incredulous, like I was having him on and he felt it was time to tell the little girly that the Man knew better.

The sting of his insinuation landed right on top of the realization that he had guessed my nickname correctly. Em is what my friends call me, and much as I hate being called Emily, it rankled me that he should presume to be so familiar. Had he made a lucky guess, or had I told him? No, I was certain I had not. I had, in fact, only offered my driver's license as explanation of who I was, had given it to Officer Raymond before he loaded me up and brought me to the hospital. Which meant he still had it now. Which meant I couldn't drive, even if I could retrieve my keys.

Rather than feel fear, I chose anger, and it swept through me like fire. I opened my eyes and fixed a glare on the detective. "Listen, *Bert*. I know you have a job to do here, and I know it's a tough one. Really. You'll find *this* statement a little hard to believe, too, but I have some experience with police investigations. I am a geologist, but I have been involved with four separate homicide investigations as a special witness. I can present my bona fides. Call the Denver PD and ask for Carlos Ortega in Homicide. In fact, I have worked so closely with him that I can give you his direct number. Would you do that for me? Hmm? Would you call him?"

The intern, having finished her chore and cleaned up her utensils, hopped up off her stool and left the room. The detective spread his lips and cheeks into a wide smile that left his pale eyes looking like they'd been painted on as an afterthought. "Sure," he said. "All in due time. Tell me about this conference you *say* you are attending."

I tried to shift my mental gears into neutral. Tried to be Em Hansen the professional, the person who had her game face together to attend a conference outside of her specialty. "It's the annual meeting of the Society of Vertebrate Paleontology. Up in Snowbird."

"*You're* a paleontologist?"

"I am a geologist, like I said. My specialty is in oil and gas."

"But you're going to a paleontology conference."

"Yes. Dr. Dishey is a vertebrate paleontologist. A dinosaur specialist."

"Dinosaurs," he echoed.

"Carnivorous dinosaurs, in fact," I said nastily. "He invited me to the conference to speak on my other, ah, specialty."

"Which is?"

"Forensic geology. That's why I've been involved with murder investigations," I asserted levelly. "It is sometimes necessary to understand geology in order to solve a crime. And I'm supposed to speak there this afternoon," I added, looking pointedly at the clock.

The detective smiled obnoxiously, raising his eyebrows in a mockery of looking impressed. "Ah, a latter-day Sherlock Holmes. You look at the dirt on the victim's shoes and know he was down by the quarry."

At first, I did not favor his jest with a reply. Then I said, "That's just part of it. More often, it's a matter of having inside knowledge of the profession. Goes to motivation," I said importantly.

With elaborate condescension, the detective said, "And Dr. Dishey thought you should tell his friends all about it."

"I suppose he thought it would add a little *spice*," I hissed.

Angry as I was, I had hoped I'd badgered him into offering a heated rejoinder, but instead, the detective said coolly, "You could go on one of those TV shows. 'Dead Bodies and the Women Who Love Them.' Now, about that nice long sleep you had."

"That what?"

"You were in the nice carnivorous dinosaur man's house, and—"

"Fine. I slept only seven hours. I don't sleep well in strange places, so I read for a while."

He raised his eyebrows in happy interest. "Wonderful. What ya reading?"

"*The Refiner's Fire.*"

"What?"

I heard Officer Raymond shift suddenly. I rolled my head toward him and looked at him. His lips had parted. He was surprised, and looked into my eyes for the first time, looked deep inside, as if he expected to find someone he knew in there, someone who'd been missing for years. Recovering himself, he looked away and spoke to the detective. "*Refiner's Fire.* By John L. Brooke."

Now it was my turn to gape. *The Refiner's Fire* was a thick scholarly tome on the roots of Mormon cosmology. I had found it on the bookshelf in my room. I had selected it expressly because it had looked dry and brainy enough to put me to sleep. What was a rank-and-file cop doing reading it?

Now the detective smiled his geek smile at Officer Raymond. "One of your church books. Ah." He turned back to me. "So you read until midnight, woke up when the phone rang at you think five, went back to sleep until seven. Then you took a shower and ate. What did you eat, Em?"

I took another deep breath, closed my eyes. "Burritos. From the freezer. I don't recommend them; in fact, I'd love it if someone could rustle up a decent doughnut for me. But I ate them, and there you have it. I waited for Dr. Dishey to return. He did not. I got restless. I decided to do some sight-seeing."

"And yet you waited until ten-thirty?"

Now I colored, a nice red blush from collarbone to scalp. If Officer Raymond knew about books on Mormon cosmology, he was sure as hell going to have an opinion about my reasons for tarrying another hour before setting out to my car. "I just waited," I said firmly.

"You *waited*," the detective said, his voice edging on accusation. "You *waited*."

"That's enough!" I said. "Are you charging me with a crime, or am I free to go?" I jerked my right hand into a fist, clanging the bracelet of the handcuff as it tightened against the frame of the gurney. "You call Carlos Ortega! You do it *now!*"

Interestingly, it was Officer Raymond who moved to bring things to a conclusion. He stepped halfway out into the hall and signaled to a nurse. "We done here?" he called.

The detective looked at him with an expression bordering on disgust. Then he looked back at me and grinned almost maniacally. "Don't leave town," he said, like he thought the line funny.

◆
◆
◆

3

◆
◆
◆

THE RIDE UP TO SNOWBIRD WAS PURE MISERY. ABOUT THE
last thing I would have chosen for my grand entrance to the
annual meeting of the Society of Vertebrate Paleontology was
to arrive by gleaming white squad car labeled POLICE in ten-
inch blue letters and be escorted in by a cop. I felt nauseated
enough at the thought of walking into that conference, presuming, as I was, to speak to them about my work in forensic
geology. Imagine standing up in front of seven or eight hundred of the brightest, best-trained observers on the planet and
saying something that they might find laughably naïve. Now
imagine doing that with gauze an inch thick all around your
thumb and grass and blood stains all down your slacks, accompanied by a drop-dead good-looking cop in navy blue uniform, badge, gun belt, and nifty little radio that has a habit of
gargling at him intermittently. You can't hardly suggest that
the car is some rental you picked up at the airport, or that
what's-his-name is a paleontologist who's just a wee bit eccentric in his choice of attire.

I sat miserably in the front seat of Officer Raymond's prowl
car, ruing the day I'd been born. Detective Bert had allowed
as how he wasn't ready yet to let me back into George
Dishey's house to get my car keys—his crew was still busy

there—and decided it was to his advantage to have me go on to the conference with Officer Raymond. *This is what I get for making a stink about going on about my business*, I'd told myself, but I'd been around enough police investigations to know I was getting off easy. They could have delayed me well into the next day.

I could just imagine the conversation up at Snowbird: "So, Ms. Hansen, we missed you at the conference Sunday afternoon. Might you tell us why you failed to present your talk?"

Answer: "I was in the jug."

Little that I now felt mentally or emotionally prepared to give my forensics speech, being kept from doing so would have been the final humiliation. In that moment, I hated Detective Bert so much that I wanted *him* to come, wanted the pleasure of watching him sit stupefied in the audience as I addressed the multitude on the wisdom gleaned from four previous murder investigations. *Yes, Bert, four! Four separate cases I have solved in my short career as an accidental detective. And come to think of it, this George Dishey murder smells like another one you need my help with. You need someone who understands the profession and the professionals, an insider who can spot the flaw in the picture, pierce the veil of mystery around the murder of your dead paleontologist there.*

Bert had seemed to think it riotously amusing to assign Officer Raymond to drive me up to Snowbird. "So you want to make detective," Bert had sneered at him. "Yeah, I saw your application there in the stack. Big aspirations for the homeboy. Big break for you—you found the corpse, and then, momma bar the door, you race right over to the home of the deceased to see what else you can find. You ever hear of procedures, cowboy? Once the case is handed over to us, *we* do the house and family stuff. *You* go back to checking Dumpsters for lost dogs. Well, hotshot, here's your big chance. You take little Emily up there to her rock-jockey conference at the cushy ski resort and make sure she plays nicely with the other boys and girls."

As he drove me up through the spectacular glacier-cut valley of Little Cottonwood Canyon toward Snowbird, Officer Raymond kept his eyes on the road. He didn't appear to find any more humor in baby-sitting me than I did, but I could see where big Bert's mind was going. By sending me to the meeting with a police escort, he could call attention to the matter of George Dishey's death in a suitably imposing manner; unless I missed my guess, a few of Bert's colleagues would be there ahead of us, working the crowd, blending in with the gathered paleontological faithful, digging for motives among George Dishey's brethren.

When we reached Snowbird, Officer Raymond turned off the highway and parked that squad car right in front of the conference center—the soaring eleven-story glass face of the Cliff Lodge—nudging it in next to the short-term loading and unloading position at the curb by the main entrance.

I stumped inside, rode the escalator up one level to the registration desk, and identified myself. "Em Hansen," I said. "I'm a speaker. This is Officer Raymond of the Salt Lake City Police Department. He wishes to speak with the general chair of the conference."

The cushiony middle-aged lady who was passing out registration packages took one look at Officer Raymond and gaped. I don't think it was his looks that got her. I think she just didn't know what to say. I supposed her job orientation had lacked instruction regarding the handling of miscellaneous visiting police officers.

Finally, she pulled herself together and got to digging for my registration card. When she found it, she frowned. "I have an Emily Hansen, but there's no speaker's ribbon with it," she said apologetically.

"Let me see the schedule," I said. "I'm supposed to speak in a symposium this afternoon."

She dealt me a program. I dug through the Sunday list. Nothing. No Em Hansen speaking on forensic geology at the forensic paleontology symposium. In fact, no symposium on forensic paleontology altogether. I checked Monday. I checked Tuesday. I checked the luncheon-speaker slots, the dinner speakers. Nothing. The carpet and floorboards under my feet seemed increasingly insubstantial, as if they were about to give way and send me plummeting into the bowels of the earth.

Officer Raymond peered over my shoulder. "No talk?" he asked bluntly.

"Must be some sort of misprint," I mumbled, but I could feel his eyes burning into me, knew he was thinking that I'd made the whole thing up.

I reopened the registration package, scanned it for the names of the prime movers of the conference. "It says here that Daniel J. Sherbrooke is the conference 'Host Committee Chair.' That's who you want to see." To the lady, I said, "Where can we find him?"

She got up from the registration table and led us across a dizzying series of Persian carpets toward a flight of stairs that led down to a sumptuous reception area in front of the ballrooms. I glanced quickly around the sea of conferees, searching for anyone who looked familiar, but saw only strangers. They ranged from starving graduate students in their mid-twenties to established, if well-worn, academics to crumpling white-haired geezers who intended to go out with their professional boots on. They were geoscientists, to be sure; save for a few who were camouflaged in suits, they all had that hearty, weathered, abstracted look of the intellectual who prefers to be outdoors. Most were what you'd have to call casually dressed. Some were neatly but pragmatically groomed and decked out in slacks and sweaters, and a few had affected swanky, if some-what eccentric, styles reminiscent of riverboat gamblers. A large faction wore T-shirts with pictures of dinosaurs on them, blue jeans, and cowboy boots. These seemed blissfully at ease with hair that had grown out and out and out without benefit of barbering; men with beards and ponytails, women with dull hair that drooped. They all sucked abstractedly at cups of coffee, some talking with colleagues, others staring unself-consciously into inner space. I began to feel less con-spicuous.

The registration lady took us halfway down the stairs and pointed to a group of men and women who were chatting boisterously. "Dan Sherbrooke's over there. The large man in the brown pants."

"Thanks," I said. As I descended the rest of the thickly carpeted staircase past a stunningly large Chinese folding screen, I made a show of clipping my name badge in place on my left breast pocket, as much as to tell Officer Raymond, *I am legitimate. I am a geologist, damn it, I am registered at this conference, and I did not kill George Dishey.*

The first line of the name badge read EMILY HANSEN. The second line read, in big letters, EM, and the third line, in small type, had the name of my employer and port of call: *Cathcart Oil & Gas, Denver, Colorado.* The badge was about three by five inches, was encased in heavy plastic, and the clip was metal. The combined weight thereof made the whole left side of my blouse sag as if I'd slept in it. So much for looking sharp; I was now grass-stained, trussed in gauze, and listing to port. I marched quickly over toward the gathering of bone men, leaving Officer Raymond to scramble along in my wake. "Dr. Sherbrooke," I said, presenting my right hand to be shaken, as if I shambled into conferences looking like hell every day of the week. "I'm Em Hansen. Dr. Dishey invited me to speak at the symposium on forensic paleontology."

Sherbrooke reflexively scanned my name badge, which meant he was staring at my breast, something that always leaves me feeling a little crawly. He was tall and globular, with long, plump arms that tapered down to smooth fingers. An easy smile. Curling hair in need of a trim, with long leftover strands hovering in disarray over a shining scalp. Breath that smelled like a late breakfast rich in coffee and bacon. Metal-framed glasses repaired with monofilament fishing line passed round and round through one hinge and sloppily knotted. A real brown pants kind of guy. He looked uncomfortable, even visibly annoyed. "Ah, yes . . . you're with George Dishey, you say?"

"Yes. He invited me to speak."

Sherbrooke examined my face as if evaluating the bones that lay a quarter inch beneath its surface. "Hansen, you say?"

We were interrupted by the appearance, at Sherbrooke's left elbow, of a weaselly young man with drooping yellow mustaches, a long, messy ponytail, and the kind of beet-red skin that looks perennially sunburned. By weaselly, I mean he was short and slender and cave-chested, the kind of rat man with wire-rimmed glasses who shows up to paint your house as someone's assistant and leaves cigarette butts in your sink. He looked so emotionally high-mileage that it took me a moment to realize that he was only somewhere in his twenties. "Dan," he said through his narrow, nicotine-stained teeth.

Sherbrooke rotated around to peer down on him. "What, ah, Verne?"

"Vance!" hissed the weasel.

"Um, Vance," Sherbrooke said with elaborate patience. "What is it . . . Vance?"

"The jackasses who run this place left the ends off the events tent last night, and a bunch of the posters blew over." He sniffed indignantly, a sour little self-appointed god judging the mishaps of contemptible mortals.

I found him annoying on sight, a self-pitying little pocket of poison who sickens the air around him. He made my skin itch. That description may sound just as judgmental as I've just accused him of being, but what goes around comes around. Besides, I was by that time in the mood to get petty. I'd been having the granddaddy of all hard days, by all appearances, the shit hadn't stopped raining in on me yet, and I had no need of duking it out with some banty rooster attitude case. I cocked a shoulder toward him so I wouldn't have to make eye contact and tapped one foot in impatience.

Sherbrooke tilted his nose a few degrees higher, as if avoiding an unpleasant smell. "Tell them to put the ends on the tent."

"I did."

"Then go back there now and make sure it happens. Really, isn't this something you can handle on your own?"

Vance slunk away.

I reasserted my place at Sherbrooke's elbow and repeated, "My name is Em Hansen, and George Dishey invited me to—"

"Oh, yes. Hmm. I'm sorry, but I don't recall seeing your abstract submittal. Which symposium did you say are you in?"

"My abstract . . ."

"Yes, your abstract. The summary of your proposed talk. Even the invited speakers submit abstracts." He placed a hand paternally on my shoulder, as if to say, You're being foolish in public, darling, but there, there.

The floor had now completely dissolved, I was indeed falling, and the earth was eating me for lunch. I had asked George if I needed to send an abstract, but he'd said no, he'd take care of everything, just show up. Well, he'd taken care of things, all right. "Did George even have a symposium scheduled?" I asked, the words clotting in my mouth. My ears began to ring with the small panic of humiliation, and the odor I was smelling was rat, a great big one.

"George? No." He laughed derisively. "When has George ever opened himself to the direct scrutiny of his colleagues?" Sherbrooke lifted his hand off my shoulder to wave at a colleague, gliding over my obvious upset with an attitude that suggested, We'll just ignore your discomfort and perhaps it will go away. I saw his lips moving, but his words flowed past me like clouds, pale and empty. I blinked, strained to listen, focused in just in time to hear him say, "And just where is our dear George today, ah"—he looked at my badge again— "Em?"

I snapped free of my shock. "Officer Raymond can tell you better than I," I said, and stepped aside.

Sherbrooke shifted his interest to my uniformed escort, who motioned for him to step away from the throng for a moment. It was done subtly, yet with authority. For all his comparative youth, Officer Raymond had the better moves of the two as he fetched the older man to the edge of the room. They communicated in low voices. Raymond watched intently for signs of guilt. Sherbrooke turned gray. His smile went slack and his arms dropped to his sides, giving him the aspect of a life-size doll, gape-mouthed and limp, a jelly man who'd been propped up with a stainless-steel rod up his butt to keep him stiff. As he asked questions, only his lips moved.

Presently, Sherbrooke turned to face the room. His eyes were wide and glassy.

Heads had begun to turn. Sherbrooke's assembled colleagues observed him with the intense curiosity that only people with twenty-four years of schooling and decades of intense devotion to an investigative profession can generate.

Sherbrooke took a deep breath, lifted his chest like a thespian about to spew Shakespeare, and announced in a booming yet unsteady voice, "George Dishey is dead!"

Officer Raymond glanced quickly from face to face through the crowd, recording reactions like a high-speed camera. People turned from Sherbrooke to us. "Dead?" they gasped, like a many-headed creature with a hundred shuffling feet and two hundred voices, "He can't be dead. I just saw him yesterday," and "Was he ill?" and "What did he die of?"

I wanted to know that myself.

The crowd churned toward Sherbrooke, splitting around the tables laid with coffee to get a closer look at what was happening, their babbled questioning growing to an information-hungry growl. One man stood still, budding off the back of the flowing throng like a new creature coming into life, his behavior so singularly different that he drew my focus. He opened his mouth and barked, "About time you got that son of a bitch!"

The crowd turned to see who had spoken, opening a corridor down the middle of the room like the Red Sea parting for Moses. I peered sharply toward the man, trying to see his eyes past the glare of overhead lights reflected on a pair of glasses as thick as Coke bottle bottoms. He was built like a truck tire, with shoulders any footballer would be proud of and graying hair cut so short it was almost invisible. He wore a faded pine green T-shirt and chino pants so old they would no longer hold a crease. I slithered around the back of the crowd until I was close enough to read his name badge. MAGRITTE, it read—just the one name in smaller print—and in large type below it, EARTHWORM. His port of call—a junior college somewhere in California—had been struck out with a ballpoint pen, and handwritten below that was simply "Unaffiliated, God Damn It."

Matching the dramatic flair of Earthworm Magritte, Dan Sherbrooke boomed, "It figures you'd say something like that, *Worm!*"

Earthworm Magritte jabbed his glasses up his broad nose

with one short, thick finger. "Aw, hell, Dan, it's a bummer when someone leaves the game. But shock-shock, he lived, he died. Move on. It's not the end of the universe; it's just one less thorn in your hide. More room for you to win the Golden Jawbone Award next time. But I suppose you gotta get dramatic and give us some homily on what a great man he was. That's cool. Get on with it." He offered these comments with no apparent contempt, only bald, if somewhat loud, statement of opinion.

In the ensuing silence, Sherbrooke rolled his head back until he could sight Magritte down his nose. Slowly, he spread one hand across his rubbery chest. When all eyes were on him, he uttered, "I am in a state of grief. A colleague has fallen."

Magritte shrugged his thick shoulders. "Aw, the hell you say. A bullshit artist has gone splot in his own manure."

Now Sherbrooke evinced anger. "I don't think you know what you're *saying*," he tolled, his voice rounding like a southern preacher's. "We're talking about a man who has been *murdered!*"

The sharp, inquisitive eyes of two or three hundred paleontologists flicked from Sherbrooke back to Magritte, and I swung my head back too, just one more member of the Greek chorus playing Ping-Pong tournament spectator as the two major actors volleyed lines. I was thinking, *This is getting ludicrous,* but the look on Magritte's face stopped me. His large, thick-lipped mouth hung wide, and his sandy eyebrows had flown up above his impenetrable glasses. "It actually *happened?*" he gasped.

Sherbrooke pointed to me. "Ask *her*," he intoned. All heads swiveled my way.

I glanced desperately around for Officer Raymond, but he had faded back into the crowd. "Me?" I blurted. "Well, sure, I stayed at his house last night, but—"

"You see?" Sherbrooke bellowed, then turned and walked

away. On that nonsensical note, the Greek chorus mercifully broke up into a gaggle of clacking tongues and scanning eyes. Leaving good old me turning in the breeze, caught being unusual in a roomful of people who have made their life's work that of studying—nay, *scrutinizing*—the unusual.

This is perhaps the place where I should emphasize this fact about paleontologists, so you will understand exactly how naked I felt. Half of them begin as geologists and half as biologists, but the point where they meet is in decoding evolution, and the study of evolution is all about spotting trends and divergences from those trends. And here I was a rank newcomer with a bandaged thumb, grass stains, and the hideous luck of having slept at a dead man's house. They observed me clinically, watching to see what I would do and what would happen to me next. I couldn't help but wonder if they had me pegged as an endangered species.

Grimly determined to look like the innocent bystander I was, I shifted my shoulders in line with the crowd and did some scanning of my own, recognizing some faces from television specials on dinosaurs, some names from the registration packet, others from the spines of my old geology textbooks. This was a gathering of the elite among vertebrate paleontologists, a rare, intense festival of note swapping and antenna touching among scientists, persons who as a class spent the grand bulk of their time working—by preference—in solitude. A moment ago, the atmosphere had been jolly and convivial; now, it was electric and edgy.

I noticed the scent of pine and turned to find out where it was coming from. Earthworm Magritte was standing about five feet to my left, staring at me with frank interest. He had his thick hands spread out on his sturdy hips.

"What's the Golden Jawbone Award?" I asked.

"It's the booby prize," he answered. "A bronze cast of the holotype of *Allosaurus fragilis*'s left mandible, mounted on a walnut plaque. We hold a kegger each year and give it to the guy who claims the most from the least evidence. They make a speech and gas away all they want while their audience gets stone-cold drunk. George won it the last three years running."

"How charming. Just the thing I want for my ego wall. I'd put it right next to my diploma."

Magritte recorded my quip without smiling. "You ought to see George's ego wall. Or I guess you have. He took the jaw off the plaque two years ago and started carrying it to meetings, kind of brandishing the thing like a scepter. The king of fools."

"Is that how you see yourselves?"

Magritte ignored my question. "He'd have it sticking out of his back pack on field trips to let the new recruits know he was *the* George Dishey. A real wise guy, our George."

"So he thrived on being called a bullshitter."

Magritte pushed at his glasses again. "In yo' face—his favorite place to be."

Officer Raymond reappeared at my side. "Who's that guy?" he asked, gesturing toward an elderly man with an aquiline nose. "And that woman, and—"

I glanced back at Magritte. He had vanished. To Officer Raymond, I said, "One at a time. The nose is a famous Brit. Analyzes dinosaur tracks; you've seen him running down beaches on TV, prattling about the rate at which the big leaf-eaters could trot. Don't know the woman." She was petite and sharklike, with a sharp nose and fashion glasses. She was doing the same thing I was, looking from person to person to gauge reactions, her jaws rhythmically working at a wad of gum. "That guy," I said, acknowledging the next person Raymond nodded toward, "is Jack Horner, out of Montana. He's a Mac-Arthur fellow. You know, the genius award. Crichton modeled the paleontologist in *Jurassic Park* after him. The guy next to him is Dave Gillette, another biggie; he did the *Seismosaurus* dig. That next guy I don't know. Probably studies fossil shrews or something unsexy like that."

Raymond gave me a sharp look.

"Big vertebrates are where it's at in paleontology if you want to catch the public's interest," I said, the wild nervousness of the moment loosening my tongue. "I don't know much about bones, never been to a meeting like this before, but just look at how many of the players I recognize, and they're all big-bone guys. Shrews are probably in some obscure way more important to keeping the earth turning on its axis, but it's the dinosaurs, those big dead reptiles, that capture the hearts and minds of the TV-watching public. Myself included. So if you're a big-bone paleontologist, TV interviews are where it's at, and PBS or the Discovery Channel or someone's gonna beat a path to your field location and photograph you expounding on your incredible find, with fabulous western scenery in the background and your hair blowing away from your bald spot. Unless you're Robert Bakker; that guy always wears a hat." I looked around. "I don't see him here."

Raymond's eyes had taken on the slight glaze of someone doing some high-speed fact filing. "And George Dishey was a dinosaur paleontologist," he said.

"Exactly," I said.

"Specialized in carnivores," said Earthworm Magritte.

I spun around. He was right behind me.

He said, "Carnivores—that's where the really big money is."

Raymond's eyes snapped toward him.

Magritte said, "It's not just the books and T-shirts and the lunch boxes and the little plastic action models you get with your burger at McDonald's. Dinosaurs themselves are worth a lot of money. The bones. It used to be potsherds; now it's dino bones. Everybody wants some for their museum, or coffee table, or maybe slabbed open to use as bookends."

A bit unhinged to find him behind me like that, I opened my big yap and said, "I suppose the Chinese think they're a tonic when ground up and served just before—" I was about to say "sex." My tongue was running away with me. It's an arrogant little trap that always lurks about a step in front of fools like me who have trained our brains more fully than our wits. Worse yet, I was falling into it right in front of this police officer, this man who had been assigned to ride herd on me through this conference, this man who had the odd intimacy of thinking that I might be a murderess. There was an electricity to the moment, of standing there that close to a man who held that much potential power over my future, feeling the heat of his breath as he bent to hear me over the din of the room. I caught myself examining the way the soft fabric of his off-duty shirt draped the firm muscles of his chest. I caught the scent of maleness and good soap, imagined that I would feel a pleasant humidity in the cloth. I looked away. I had been showing off, trying to impress him. I was making an ass of myself. "I need to settle this business about my talk," I said abruptly, and walked away.

4

WHEN I HAD AT LAST FULLY CONVINCED MYSELF THAT THE
talk I had taken great pains to prepare was not going to occur,
I set to work pumping people for information about George
Dishey. I didn't ask Officer Raymond if he wanted my help.
I did not in fact care whether he wanted it or not. Beside the
obvious reason of needing to get off the suspect list and on
with my life, I knew that there would be no better time to pry
into these other people's lives than when they were still interested in mine.

As I circulated through the crowd, sliding in and out of
conversations with the astonished conferees, I watched Officer
Raymond work. Something more than his good looks kept
drawing my eyes to him. There was an intensity to him. His
work was clearly important to him, more so than was called
for by mere attention to detail and correctness, or by the am-
bition of wanting a promotion. He consumed each person just
as he had consumed me when our eyes had finally met in the
hospital. He seemed to be searching for something essential,
something he craved. As I watched him, I thought, *An appetite
for truth is something I can understand.*

I worked through the obligatory gaggle of people who
wanted to hear the scant nothing I knew about the murder of

George Dishey. More important, they wanted to gush away about how shocking they found the situation, and speculate wildly about who might have done it. Smart money assured me it must have been a mugger, or some crazy from the hills, but just a few others wanted me to know that George was not universally liked, don't ya know. These bolder souls would quickly catch on that Officer Raymond was listening a little too intently, suddenly realize that I was with him and not them, and clam up. The talkativeness that comes with a sudden shock like hearing that one of your colleagues has been kakked was beginning to wear off, and they were returning to a more normal, more wary state. I figured I'd have to wait until I returned the next day without my police escort to get down to any meaningful gossip. And by then I knew that, even if Detective Bert told me I was free to go, I would return. I was bitten. The chase was on, and I wanted to know which one of these sons of bitches had gotten hot enough to murder my manipulative, shit-stirring little host.

At length, the coffee break we'd interrupted broke up and people confusedly meandered back into the symposium that actually *was* scheduled for that afternoon, something about predator-prey ratios in the Mesozoic. I tried to listen to one of the talks, but I realized that, for the moment, the revised cladistics of early Triassic diapsid quadrupeds and its relationship to a hot lunch was a bit too abstract for my overstimulated mind to grasp.

Officer Raymond drove me back to George Dishey's house after first phoning ahead to the police station to confirm that I was free to go home. Except, of course, that George Dishey's house was not my home.

On the way down the mountain, Officer Raymond began to pick my brains. "No one appeared to be withholding evidence," he said.

"Scientists specialize in evidence," I replied with no small pride. "And we know all about coughing it up when the time is right. Professional ethics require that we make a clean presentation of the facts. Or at least what we consider the facts to be."

"What do you mean by that?"

"We're talking about a bunch of people whose careers depend on being the first with the latest," I replied, "And think about it: They're dealing with scanty records of animals who've been dead a long time. At least you cops get a fresh corpse."

"Can you enlarge on that?" he asked, his voice tightening.

I stared at his handsome profile, wondering for the sixth or seventh time what condition George Dishey's corpse must have been found in to warrant such sensitivity. Police officers saw the results of violent death as frequently as anybody. They grew inured to it. What could have gotten them so stirred up about this one? I considered asking him, but it didn't take a genius to know that the police weren't going to budge with the information. The more distinctive the mode of death, the more carefully they would conceal it from the public, and that public included me. That way, they could weed through the crank calls and nutcase confessions that would soon be finding their ways through the police switchboard, and if they found someone who could accurately describe the techniques required to create the gruesome evidence, they would know they had a winner.

I knew that for the moment, I had to content myself with being forthcoming, in hopes of convincing the professionals of my innocence. I fell back into being a fountain of wisdom. "Back at college, I took a class in paleontology, and the dinosaur stuff was pretty interesting," I began, already embellishing the truth. My undergraduate course had covered fossils from *A*, for algal mounds, to *Z*, for—well, not for dinosaurs. We had spent a few days on dinosaurs, but I had read a little since—Jack Horner's *Dinosaur Lives*, Dave Gillette's *Seismosaurus*, and a few others—and had seen a few television specials. "The thing is that in order to fossilize a dinosaur, you have to bury it really quickly. Otherwise, all the other dinosaurs—or at least, the carnivorous ones—will eat it and scatter its bones. In order to bury something that big that quickly, the best bet is to have it die in a river; say, by drowning. That happened a lot."

Officer Raymond brought his squad car expertly down the wide turns that carried the highway past the red and gold foliage that would soon be a dead brown litter underneath the winter's snows, past the myriad avalanche chutes that would soon be laden with deadly slabs of white death, and out of the mountains, his shoulders and arms moving with hypnotic grace. Now he merged onto a belt of highway that rushed us along the ancient broad lake terraces that formed the upper reaches of Salt Lake City. I couldn't tell if he was listening to me or not.

Filling the loneliness I was beginning to feel, I continued anyway. "Just think of modern elk herds crossing a river. The waters are swollen from a sudden storm. Something makes them stampede, perhaps a lightning bolt. They panic, push one dino brother into deeper water. Too deep, he loses his footing, can't swim. *Bam*, drowned quadruped. So anyway, your dinosaur dies in the water where it has a chance of getting buried in the sand that's being carried down the river, but then the water itself starts working on the corpse. It takes a lot of sand to bury one of these guys. Some of them weighed ten, twenty tons. So anyway, the carcass starts to rot, and the first thing that happens is the big joints start to come apart. The first thing that usually comes off is the head, then a leg. Particularly with some of the big brontosaurus-type herbivores. Their heads weren't on all that tightly, and *boing!* Off it goes downstream. The flood's over and the water level drops, and *whang*, some scavenger chews off another haunch. Maybe all that gets buried was part of one foreleg and a chunk of the backbone, and the rest gets eaten or ground up by rocks saltating downstream. Then you've got to wait a few hundred million years, hope what's left isn't so deeply buried that you'll never find it or that it didn't erode away a few hundred thousand years before you were born, and then *wham*, you're out on your horse one day looking for a lost calf and maybe you get lucky and happen to spot it because the sun angle is just right. Then you've got to hope you know what a dinosaur bone actually is, and not confuse it with some old cow bone, or with the surrounding rock."

"Why would that happen?" he asked.

"You mean, why would someone think it's a cow bone?"

"No, rock."

"It's often the same color. The bone gets mineralized."

"Oh." His gaze stayed trained on the roadway.

I'd been making some pretty wild gestures as I spoke, typical of geologists and other geoscientists, like paleontologists. People make jokes about us. They say, If you want to make a room full of geologists shut up, tie their hands to their sides. Now my hands dropped to my lap and I cleared my throat. "I'm just saying that most of the time, here in human time, you find your corpse in one piece, and—" I stopped. Was that it? Had some fool dismembered George Dishey? My mind slipped out of intellectual mode and my stomach tightened. "Hey, just what happened to George, anyway?"

We had exited onto city streets, still following the contours of the shores of Lake Bonneville, the Pleistocene inland sea that had drained and evaporated into the present-day shallow ghost of a sea called Great Salt Lake. We passed the University of Utah and maneuvered into the quiet old residential neighborhood beyond it where George Dishey had until this morning lived. Officer Raymond's eyes were on a truck in front of us, his expression unreadable. "The house is down here on the right," he said softly.

I looked down the street. Two cars besides my own were parked in front of George Dishey's house. We pulled up to the curb, got out, and walked up to the front door, which stood open in the early-evening warmth. I stepped inside. The evidence team was just finishing the task of searching the interior.

I was blasted by a voice from one corner of the room. "Ah, the girl geologist, back from the bone conference!" I turned. Detective Bert straightened up from an examination of one of the many bookcases, and said, "How'd it go, Sherlock?"

Ignoring his question, I hurried into the room where I had slept the night before. My suitcase was open, and my belongings, from blue jeans and sweaters down to the most intimate bits of flimsy, were laid out none too tidily on the bed. I opened my mouth to complain, then snapped it shut.

"Oh, were those yours?" Bert asked unctuously from beyond the doorway.

I gave him a look but kept my mouth shut. He had taken advantage of his mandate of searching the dead man's house to go through my things, too.

"Well, here's your keys," Bert said, dangling them from a finger. He oozed up to the doorjamb and draped his body insolently against the wood. "And here's a spare key to the front door. Or do you plan to stay?"

My back molars nearly cracked under the compression of my jaw muscles. I wasn't going anywhere, not if this man wanted me to leave.

He said, "You keep in touch, hear?"

I advanced on him, determined to back him out of my room and out of that house. And he did leave, grinning all the way with that sick way of his that had no heart behind it. I had slammed the front door before I realized that Officer Raymond was still inside with me. "Excuse me," I said, yanking the door open again. "I'm, um, sorry." I needed him to leave—immediately. It had been a gruelling day, I was a long way from home and anyone I could call a friend, and my cut thumb was beginning to throb like someone was hitting it with a hammer. If he didn't leave fast, he was going to have to watch me cry.

"You okay here?" he asked.

"Fine. Just fine."

He handed me a card. It read "Salt Lake City Police," had a logo, his full name, Officer Thomas B. Raymond, and a phone number. "You call me if . . . well, you know, if you think of anything else that would help the investigation, or if you . . . you know, need anything."

"Sure," I said. I knew he was trying to be chivalrous, but knowing that his real reason to stay in touch with me was something else again—to solve a crime and maybe get a promotion out of it—left me feeling deflated, like I was somebody's kid sister whose company was more a chore than a pleasure.

"You got food in the house?"

"I . . . I'll go out if I need anything."

"You—"

"I'm *fine*, damn it!"

Officer Raymond observed me for some seconds, then turned, nodded good-bye, and left. The door closed slowly behind him.

Through the windows, I saw him walk down the lawn toward the street. His lean, limber body flexed gracefully with the unconscious motion of walking. When he reached his squad car, he paused for a while with his hand on the handle of the door, his eyes closed, his face set in an expression of solemnity. I thought I saw his lips move, as if he were speaking to someone who was standing quite near to him. After a moment, he climbed into the car and drove away.

I watched the empty parking space for seconds that stretched into minutes, feeling more lonely than I'm used to feeling when I'm alone. I considered getting into my rental car and driving back up to Snowbird. They would be having dinner now, listening to someone blather away about something of great interest to bone junkies. What had been on the menu? I shook myself. Prime rib. I couldn't stand the idea of eating, much less of putting a knife to freshly killed flesh.

5

Sgt. Carlos Ortega answered the phone at his mother's house, where I caught him in the middle of dinner. "Em," he murmured, "Mama has made *menudo*. Can I call you back?"

My heart sank. "Sure," I said, in a voice that must have sounded like a condemned prisoner acquiescing from the top step of the gallows.

I heard his sigh in return. "*Momentito, amiga*, while I stretch the phone cord to the table here. Okay. That's good." To his littlest brother, he said, "*Oye*, Salvador, *pasame las tortillas, por favor*," and then back to me: "Okay. Okay. So what is wrong in your life, my friend?"

"Is it that obvious something's wrong?"

With an ironic tone, Ortega said, "These many years I know you, *amiga*. You think yourself awkward, but in fact you consider my feelings at most times, *como una señora muy fina*. But here you are calling at my dinner hour. I am a detective, no? It is my job to notice things." He took a noisy slurp of his stew, pacing out this dissertation. "And you have many ways you express yourself. Tonight, it is what you are *not* saying. You are not saying that you are calling *larga distancia*, something you have done only when your heart has found trouble. But no, this is not even deduction. I know you are not home because I saw your landlady today, and she informs me you are out of town. *¿Verdad?*"

"*Verdad.*" In the four years I had known Carlos Ortega, our conversation had developed its own pattern and pace and had increasingly become studded with Spanish. Moreover, he was within the bliss of his mother's cooking, and at such times he reverted to the mannerly, elegant language of his childhood. My landlady Betty would have been his source of lunch. Much to my growing discomfort, she and Carlos had become . . . ah, friends. "Yes, I am calling from Salt Lake City."

"And the weather is nice?"

"Lovely."

"But you are sad." His voice wrapped me in sympathy.

My vision began to swim. I fought to hold back the tears that wanted to flow. "Yes," I whispered. *Yes, I am sad. And it's not just what's happened today. It's whom I've met.*

"So speak to me. Tell me what makes *tu corazon* to ache."

A drop rolled down my cheek. Another. To stanch the downpour, I said something that would raise my anger. "I've been arrested."

I heard his spoon hit the table. "*¿Que? ¡Amiga! ¿Por qué!*"

"Well, I don't mean arrested, exactly; they didn't have enough to hold me on. No, that's not right. I'm saying this all wrong, but I'm their prime suspect. I mean—*they didn't call you?*" It hit me all at once: This was news to him. Now I really *was* angry.

"*¡Pare! ¡Pare! ¿Por qué es su*—*" With an effort, he shook himself back out of Spanish. "What were the charges?"

"Um. Ah. Murder."

"*¡Ay, caramba!* No, this a joke. *¿Verdad?*"

"No. I was staying at this guy's house and now he's dead, and they caught me—well . . ." I took a deep breath and told him the whole weird story about locking myself out of the house.

Carlos hammered me with questions, rapid-fire, until he was satisfied that he had the essentials. "Name of the deceased."

"George Dishey."

"How did you know him?"

"I didn't. I'd just met him. Well, you see, he'd heard about me. About the work I—you and I—had done together. About me helping your police investigations with my geology. I don't know who told him, but I begin to be known, you know? I mean, petroleum geologists are a dime a dozen, but forensic geologists are really something—or that's what he said. And I wanted to hear that. So I'm just a bachelor's degree with only a few years' experience. So I'm no one from nowhere. I thought it would be nice just once—"

Carlos interrupted. "*No es importante, querida.* Just tell me how he contacted you."

"He just called me up out of a clear blue sky one day and told me about this conference, and of course I knew who he was, and at first I thought it must be someone playing a prank, because he's like on TV and in the magazines and all."

"But it was him, and you were honored."

"Flattered," I said bitterly. How easily I had let George convince me to come. I knew that big names don't necessarily mean big hearts, but by the time I'd arrived in Salt Lake, I'd built George up into a secretly nice guy whom no one but me could really understand. Hah. And now here I was deciding that this cop was the next solution to all my longings. When was I going to learn?

Carlos smacked his lips over another spoonful of his *menudo.* "Continue."

"So he told me about how he was going to have a session on forensic geology at this conference, because part of what a paleontologist does is he figures out how the fossil died. Because you see, they're all dead. The animals a paleontologist works with. And plants. That's what distinguishes paleontologists from biologists, I guess." I had seen Carlos only last Wednesday but hadn't told him about the conference, or the talk. Why had I held out on him? Had I on some level smelled a rat?

"So you hadn't met him before you arrived for the conference."

"Right."

"You saw the body?"

"No. And thank God. It must have been a mess."

"How do you know this?"

"The cops are really upset. These guys are taking this one personally."

"*Ayii*," Carlos whined, signifying the depth of trouble I was in. Then, finally calming down enough to start eating again, he asked, "Where are you now?"

"At his house."

"This dead person's?"

"*Sí.*"

"This George Dishey's?"

"*Corecto.*"

"*Aiyii. No es bueno. Aiyii.*"

"*Aiyii* what?"

Carlos muttered under his breath for a moment. "Forget I said anything. You go and have a good life."

"Carlos, what kind of *mierda*—"

"No! I offer no advice! Each time I try to help you, you do the opposite! I take no responsibility!"

"Yes, but this time—"

"You don't know who killed this man. What if—"

"Don't worry, Carlos. If you were trying to get away with murder, would you drop by your victim's house to make sure you got noticed? No. It's probably the safest place I could be.

No te preocupe. Besides, the police are all over me. They even assigned a guy to take me up to the conference." I was overstating this, I knew, but I wanted to convince myself as well as Carlos. "He and two or ten of his pals are probably down the block right now, waiting for me to make a move, sitting there in their unmarked cars, drinking Postum."

"Postum?"

"Yeah, this is a Mormon town. Try getting a decent cup of coffee around here. Most places it's no caffeine, no smokes, no liquor harder than three-two beer."

Carlos slurped his *cerveza* obnoxiously.

I said, "This prime suspect thing totally sucks."

"Wash your mouth."

"You try getting arrested sometime! So nobody called you. That's interesting."

"*¿Por qué?*"

"*Por qué* something made them decide to let me go about my business. I had assumed it was talking to you." I laughed mirthlessly. "You know, like I thought you'd vouched for me and they'd taken your word for it, or at least that your word was good enough to get them to take the handcuffs off, but here you say this conversation never occurred. So why'd they let me go?"

◇

ORTEGA WAS RIGHT, of course. Prudence would have dictated that I find myself another place to stay, but fatigue, frugality, and fatheadedness made me dig in my heels and stay put. I told myself that it could be a week or weeks before I was cleared of any suspicion in this investigation, and that by then I'd be out of a job and wouldn't have the means to pay off the plane flight out here that I'd jacked onto my credit card, let alone cover an extended stay at a hotel. I agreed to call Carlos if anything else happened. He agreed to phone the Salt

Lake City Homicide Squad and find out what he could. I hung up the phone no more comforted than when I'd dialed it.

I sat staring numbly around George Dishey's living room. It was more library than living room, chockablock with book-shelf after bookshelf, each crammed to the gills with academic tomes and scholarly texts on matters paleontological. I spotted the titles of a few popular books, like Crichton's *Jurassic Park* and Bakker's *Dinosaur Heresies*. Some of the more technical books were old, original monographs. These had to be worth a mint, and George must have known it, as some were turned cover out and proudly displayed on little holders that kept their spines from cracking. George's writings—almost all of which gleamed from the glossy pages of popular books and maga-zines, rather than from scholarly texts—were also on display, some even with little spotlights trained on them, the banality of their hyped-up titles and illustrations standing in stark con-trast to the more staid productions of the monographs. His covers were brightly colored, even lurid, and there he was on the dust jacket of the latest, flourishing that bronze jawbone, grinning into the camera. "As seen on TV," the jacket blurb read. I marveled at his cheek, using a bullshit award as a trademark to impress the masses.

I examined it closely. It really was a showpiece, a good eighteen inches long and laden with teeth. He gripped it by the posterior end and had planted it flat across his chest, his other arm bent at the elbow and fist rammed against his hip, like a pirate brandishing his knife.

In one corner of the room stood a four-drawer filing cabinet. The drawers were labeled EENY, MEENY, MINEY, and MOE. I smiled at the thought of Detective Bert trying to make sense of them. Next to the filing cabinet stood a hollow-core door turned horizontally and set up on cinder blocks to serve as a desk. The hole through which a doorknob would have reached held a glass jar full of pens and pencils. A swanky ergonomic chair faced George's computer, which was a gutsy state-of-the-art job from which the police detectives had extracted the hard drive. The rest of the surface of the desk was stacked high with papers that threatened to advance on the room like so many glaciers. The evidence team had gone through these too; I had seen a man working them when I returned. I glanced at the couch and the overstuffed chairs, a grubby grotto of garage-sale modern furnishings in which the police had taken no interest. George had been at heart an academic, placing his love and value in his books and the tools of his trade.

Speaking of his tools, I thought, *where's his field equipment?* I assayed the room again, looking for the obligatory Brunton compass, field notebooks, and rock hammer any geologist would own, and the fine collection of brushes, dental picks, and pry bars one specializing in paleontology would have amassed. They were not in evidence. I wandered over to the basement door, opened it, and took a look. There was nothing down there but house guts and the scent of mildew; a wet basement even in this dry climate. I meandered into the kitchen and surveyed the backyard in hopes of a garage or storage shed. Nothing but the carport in which he had parked his truck, which now stood near wherever it was he had gone in such a hurry.

Confused by this lack of field equipment, I wandered back into the living room and got to studying a collection of framed photographs on the wall above George's desk, the ego wall of which Earthworm Magritte had spoken. They hung interspersed with George's Yale sheepskin, a thank-you plaque from a public television station, something from the Cub Scouts of America, a very dear childish drawing from "Mrs. Gearhart's Second Grade Class, thank you Dr. Dishey," and the empty walnut Golden Jawbone plaque. There were two snaps of George in younger days. One was of George as a young boy, precociously posed in front of the *Tyrannosaurus rex* mount at some cavernous museum, his hands up in predatory claw-creature mode, his lips retracted to display dentition made comical by the lack of one front tooth and the oversized appearance of one new one. Another showed George in Vietnam-issue jungle fatigues, lounging against a helicopter with several of his mates, all grinning and making obscene gestures except the pilot, a weirdly handsome young man who gave me the shivers. He had jutting cheekbones and regarded the camera with eyes as dark and menacing as a crypt. I wondered what the war had done to him, wondered for that matter how George Dishey and all the others in the photograph had fared.

The other photographs were publicity photos, the kind some photographer with a big-format camera snaps to publicize one event or another. Here, the dedication of a new museum display; there, a group of Cub Scouts visiting dino land; down here, a pose with a big find in the prep room of a museum, everyone in lab coats but him. From the middle of each picture, George Dishey mugged shamelessly toward the camera. No matter how formal or casual the occasion, he wore a T-shirt, baggy pants, and a bandanna around his neck and sported a ponytail so big and bushy that it had to be a parody of those I had just seen at the conference. He was a plain-looking man with a lumpy nose, lively eyes, a quick smile, and an unkempt beard. Just the sort of man to play the hokey prospector in the amateur theatrical of some gold rush play. In several shots, he wielded the Golden Jawbone in a corny impression of the run-amok madman from a horror flick. The sight of that awful prop reminded me of meat, which in turn reminded me of dinner.

My stomach tightened with hunger. Few things, even being arrested for murder, can dissuade me from eating for long. I wandered into the kitchen but stopped on the threshold. The idea of going through a dead man's refrigerator seemed indecent. Moreover, the house was beginning to get on my nerves; it had a bad case of bacheloritis, from its unkempt furniture to the threadbare towels haphazardly strewn across the floor of the bathroom. The place screamed for a little housekeeping. I felt drained and depressed, and I needed something more cheerful to rest my eyes on than the disordered wreckage of a dead man's life. I resolved to go out somewhere and find myself a meal worth eating.

Out on the streets, the sun's rays were slanting low, transforming the thin Rocky Mountain air into liquid gold. Folks were beginning to switch on their headlights as they scurried here and there to their homes and pastimes. For once in my life, I was glad to be driving a car with an automatic shift, as I was able to do most of the steering with my right hand and spare my wounded thumb. I aimed my rental car downtown, following the residential streets downhill to a main artery and then turning toward the tall buildings that marked the city center.

Salt Lake is a clean sort of city, a showpiece reflecting the industriousness of the insular, highly productive Mormon society. The gilded evening light bounced cleanly off of ice-cream-pale buildings, dodging down sidewalks and through alleyways that smacked of cleanliness and pride. The only disruption in an almost overwhelming display of civic orderliness were the places, here and there through the downtown streets and skyline, where heavy construction was hurriedly under way to spruce up and expand the streets and lodgings in anticipation of the winter Olympic Games due to grace the city in 2002, a little scandal notwithstanding. I bumped over a newly laid section of track that would carry a pristine downtown light-rail transit system, then dodged around a lane closed off to accommodate a huge crane that was tossing new hotel space skyward. During the few short weeks of Olympic frenzy, Salt Lake City planned to throw a party worth strutting over, even if its resident populace had to suffer for it for years in advance.

Downtown, there was little traffic, and I got to poking along in my search for a restaurant. There would be eateries in each of the massive hotels, I was certain, but I wanted something more eclectic, something more local, something that would distract me from my mood. I headed west on South Temple until I reached Temple Square, then indulged myself in a brief bit of tourism, turning north on West Temple and then east on North Temple (the streets are named for their positions relative to the Temple building, rather than to the directions they head) in order to get a rolling glimpse of the gilded angel that trumpets from the top of the highest spire. As I turned south onto Main Street and slowed to gawk, I noticed a car in my rearview mirror that was likewise slowing to match my pace. What was strange about its movement was that it was half a block back and slowing down even though there was no intervening traffic. It had been in my mirror all the way into downtown, but I'd been following a major route, so that hadn't seemed strange until now. Now I cursed aloud and said, as if Sergeant Ortega were in the car with me, "You see, Carlos? Like flies on shit. The boys in blue have stuck a tail on me. They think I'm pretty stupid, like I won't notice an unmarked car."

I sped up. So did the car. I turned west again on South Temple and headed toward the Delta Center. After a moment, I noticed the car again, still following along behind me. It was a nondescript car, the sort of midsize sedan with smooth streamlining and little character that one rents at the airport, not unlike my own.

I continued down into the plaza that fronted the Delta Center and found myself boxed into a cul-de-sac. I slammed my right hand against the steering wheel in frustration.

I considered spinning a quick U-turn around the plaza but then stopped to think the situation through. What if it was not, in fact, a police detective who was following me? *What if—*

That particular what if I did not care to consider.

The twilight was fading fast, but I was in a wide-open place, surrounded by crowds of people who were heading into the

Center for some event, so I was, for the moment, relatively safe. I stopped, double-parked, and looked around. The plaza was closed on three sides by the Delta Center and its voluminous parking lots, a Victorian mansion that had been retrofitted into a Chart House restaurant, and the grand old edifice of the local Union Pacific Railway Station. I thought, *I'll just park here and head into this nice public restaurant and see who follows me, if anyone. If it's the God Almighty police, they can cool their heels while I eat dinner.*

I looked in the rearview mirror. The car that was following me had also stopped. Something in the tightness that was my stomach told me that the car did not belong to the police. *This is how a deer feels when it's being stalked by a hunter,* I thought grimly. *Well, it ain't hunting season out here in the open, fellah.*

The car had double-parked, just as I had. The owner of the truck it was blocking arrived and flagged it away. I saw it cruise past, turn around the plaza, and pull to the curb down near the crossing through which I'd have to make my exit. Now I truly was boxed.

I took a squint at the driver. He looked familiar, not like someone I knew, but like someone I'd seen somewhere. High cheekbones, a beard. Thick fingers on the wheel. Conscious that I was now looking at him, he drew sharply into the shadows, away from his window.

It's just the cops keeping an eye on their flimsy excuse for a suspect, I told myself. *Relax.* I looked around for another exit, but every one headed into a parking lot, all of which were packed by the rivers of people flowing into the Delta Center to cry and swoon over the country and western recording star whose grinning mug loomed two stories high across the Center's enormous face. I put my car into drive and rolled slowly forward, praying for a place to park. My day's tiny ration of luck found me a place to park in the lot beside the restaurant. Hurrying out of my car, I scurried inside, where I hove to at the maître d's desk and waited nervously to be seated. A young man glided up and asked if I had a reservation.

"No," I said, mechanically producing a smile. "Just one for dinner, please." I glanced over my shoulder, checking to see if anyone was coming in the door behind me.

"Oh, I'm sorry, miss, but we're completely full just now. If you'd like to wait . . ." His eyes fell to my bandaged thumb. He tried to glance away, but the thickness of the gauze drew his gaze like a moth to the flame.

"How long might it be?" I asked, falling into my starchiest English.

The young man looked perturbed on my behalf. "It might be as much as forty minutes. We're usually not open on Sundays, but there's a special event across the way there, and well, you know." Then, with a teasing smile, he added, "If you'd like to tour the house while you wait, you might even meet one of our resident ghosts to pass the time with. We have a history of the mansion here in the menu."

Ghosts. That was all I needed. The clinking of glassware and odd riffs of laughter that issued from the rooms full of jolly diners all around me began to further fray my nerves. "You got a phone I could use?"

The maitre d' directed me farther back into the mansion. I dialed the number on the card Officer Raymond had given me and waited. When a dispatcher came on, I said, "This is Em Hansen. Officer Raymond gave me this number to call if I needed help. I'm a law-abiding citizen who's gotten balled up in the George Dishey murder investigation, and I'd like to know if that's your guy who's tailing me."

"Hold, please."

I held for three minutes and was about to hang up when I heard not Raymond's calm baritone but the caustic drawl of Detective Bert. "Emmy! What's up?"

I breathed hotly into the phone. I had prepared to say that

someone was following me, but this creep would delight in letting me know just how melodramatic that sounded. So instead, I said, "What's up? Not me. You want to pull your tail off me? Why don't I just call in and tell you where I'm going, so you don't have to follow me around like a goddamned criminal. You know, maybe save the poor taxpayer a buck."

Bert's reply dripped with sarcasm. "You have a *tail*? What's it look like, tiger? Black-and-yellow stripes?"

"Listen, cut the shit," I said, before I got a grip on myself. He had asked what the tail looked like. That meant it might not be his. "He's driving a tan sedan, late model, midsize American make. Don't know exactly what kind—they all look alike. It was too far away to read the plates, except that they were Utah. One guy on board, couldn't see him clearly. White male with a long beard and high cheekbones." *Kind of like the helicopter pilot in the Vietnam picture. Except not really. And it wasn't just the beard. This man was just not as handsome. Something different in the brow* . . . "Wearing gloves, maybe," I added, remembering the thick fingers on the steering wheel. *Gloves? In this weather? Wait a minute—is that to cover evidence?* "He yours?" I demanded, trying to sound more angry than frightened.

"And you are calling from the Chart House restaurant," he said.

"Yes, but I'm not staying. Got any recommendations for a place that's open on a Sunday night that doesn't have a half-hour wait?" I asked, trying to sound cool.

He laughed softly. "I don't get out half enough. But drive around, enjoy yourself. In a town this big, you're bound to find something open."

"Great." I volleyed. "Hope your guy has a full tank." *As in, This is your guy, right?*

I hung up and stalked back out the door to my car, cranked the engine, tore around the plaza, and waved to the driver of the tan sedan as I sped past him. My shadow fell in behind me, half a block back. He wasn't even trying to stay out of sight. *So that means he's a cop, right? Or it means he's not a cop, and not altogether bright, which is a truly scary thought, because stupid people can be more dangerous sometimes than smart people, and—*

It was time to get rid of him. I led him around downtown Salt Lake City, back up to Temple Square and down past the Salt Palace with its spinning windmills. I finally got a good lead on him when I took a hot pass through the long parking lot behind the Little America Hotel and then zipped through a light just as it turned red. He hesitated and I kept going, slipping through an alley that fortunately was not blocked. As I swerved around yet one more construction barrier, the car jumped on a bit of uneven pavement and banged my aching thumb hard on the steering wheel, but it had been worth it. I didn't care if that man had been foe or friend, I was one fox who could not stand the breath of dogs.

Once free of my doppelgänger, I had no stomach left for dinner. The events of the day had finally overwhelmed me, leaving me for once lacking in appetite and tense to the point of physical pain. I resolved to go back to George Dishey's house, gather up my belongings, and move to a motel—a nice, obscure concrete-block special with ugly carpets and a policy of forgetting faces.

It was now fully dark, and the streetlights competed with the heavy foliage of the mature trees that studded the residential lots of the neighborhood where George Dishey had lived, and read about dead reptiles, and apparently annoyed most people with whom he came in contact.

I couldn't find a parking space in front of the house, so I pulled up to the curb around the corner and backtracked along the sidewalk and up the walkway toward the front door. I was in such a rush to get my gear and leave that house that I had the key in the lock and the door halfway open before I noticed that I was not alone.

6

SOMEBODY WAS IN GEORGE DISHEY'S HOUSE, SOMEBODY who didn't care what he tore or broke or shattered as he careened noisily through the far rooms. I didn't see him. I saw only the living room, a quick camera-shutter glimpse; saw books dumped out onto the floor, illuminated only by the dancing reflected light of the intruder's flashlight and the glowing blank screen of the computer. It hummed eerily, struck stupid by its lack of a hard drive.

I jerked backward, slamming the door in my hurry to get away. I raced across the lawn, hell-bent for the shortest route to my car. *He didn't see me,* I told myself. *Get to the car. Get to—*

The deafening crack of a rifle shot concussed the air, followed instantaneously by the sounds of falling glass and a car accelerating toward the house. I lurched forward, stumbled, got my footing again, gathered speed, and flew forward and down as a great weight crashed against my back. Another shot rang out, this one closer, and I saw the car that had been following me whiz by. I struggled but could not move. A warm, firm body pressed me into the earth, clutching me, now rolling, tumbling me into the low bushes that crouched beneath the front windows of the house. I gasped, coughed, spat earth out of my mouth, tried to drag myself out from under the weight above me.

"It's me!" a voice whispered harshly next to my ear. "Ray. Hold still!"

"Officer—"

"Yes! Keep your voice down. The shot came from the car, but there's someone else in the house!"

The frantic pulse of blood rushing through my ears was matched by the heartbeat that cannoned against my back. Officer Raymond's strong hands clasped my arms, and his heaving breath flooded my cheek. He had me pinned, facedown. As I tried to shift to take the pressure off my chin, he pressed me even harder, wrapping one leg around mine so I could not struggle.

A door slammed at the back of the house. The sound of someone running faded into the gathering night.

Officer Raymond loosed one hand and unclipped the microphone that had begun to dig into my back. "Raymond reporting gunfire, Fourth North at H. Suspect in tan Chevy sedan, Utah license *F* as in Frank two seven seven two one, heading east on Fourth. Carrying shotgun. B and E suspect escaping on foot northbound; check the alleys. I have Hansen, front yard. Approach premises with caution; there may be others watching or in the house."

"It was a rifle," I whispered, spitting grass from my trembling lips.

"What?"

The flash of rotating lights blinded me. Police cruisers were arriving, fast and hot, sirens off. "The firearm. It was—"

"How do you know?" Raymond asked, still pressing me to the ground. I could not tell whether he was holding me once again as a suspect, or to protect me.

"My father had one. Shot coyotes. We had a ranch—"

"Firearms sound alike," he said suspiciously.

Adrenaline now had my mouth running a mile a minute. "No, they don't. A rifle makes a cracking sound above the *pow*. A shotgun or a pistol, just the *pow*. Physics. The rifle bullet breaks the sound barrier, makes the crack, but you hear it right on top of the *pow* because you're so close to it. My dad explained it to me."

"Why?" he asked, incredulous.

"I don't know. Because I asked. I stood beside him enough times when he was shooting. His shotgun had a kind of thud when it went off, because he carried a heavy load—big Wingmaster, pounds you in the heart, but he was afraid of mountain lions—but his rifle was like a knock in the head. The idiot didn't give me any earplugs. Made 'em ring for days sometimes. There's a little muscle in your ear that—aw hell, you let me up and we'll be picking two slugs out of the wall, not a bunch of shot."

I could hear other cars arriving, footfalls as men hurried to the doors, the sound of the front door rending as someone worked it with a pry bar. I sighed. "I have the key right here in my hand."

Officer Raymond rolled off me abruptly. "Over here!" he called as he took the key and pitched it to the policeman who was ripping at the door. Twisting my neck around to watch, I saw the key follow a perfect arc that ended squarely in the fellow's outstretched hand. A portion of my mind noted the perfection of that throw, made from a prone position no less, and decided, with the odd detachment that adrenaline can produce at moments of crisis, *He must have played baseball.*

The man at the door wrestled it open, stood aside, pulled his pistol, nodded to a second officer, who had now joined him on the doorstep, and slipped in. A long minute later, I heard, "All clear!"

Officer Raymond snatched me up to a standing position as if I were a doll. "You okay?" he asked, still holding my arms.

"Define okay," I said jerkily.

In the light that now filtered through the holes shot through the curtain of the front window, I thought I saw him smile. "No bones broken?"

"No."

"No fresh blood?"

I checked the bandage on my thumb. Our little roll on the lawn had peppered it with dirt, but the wound had stayed closed. "Just good old American red, type A-positive, usual volume all present and accounted for."

"Good," he said, now smiling broadly. "You keep it that way, tough girl."

7

ONCE AGAIN, THE HOUSE WAS ALIVE WITH POLICE DETEC-
tives, who were sifting through every disturbed book and paper
in search of evidence. I'd done my best to describe the man
I'd none-too-clearly seen driving the tan Chevy to an Identikit
specialist (Officer Raymond corroborated my take) while I
watched a detective dust the house for prints, then had managed to hold myself together as another detective took my
second statement of the day. I sat in the kitchen, head propped
up in my good right hand, occasionally taking a sip from the
cup of coffee I had scrounged. My adrenaline shakes had settled into a nervous fatigue.

Whoever had dumped George Dishey's files and books out
onto the floor had made a clean getaway—save for a clumsy-
looking old walkie-talkie he had left behind—and it soon became apparent that both men—presuming whoever had been
in the house was male—had cleared the neighborhood without
a trace. I overheard police calls from officers' radios that said
they had found the car abandoned five blocks away, complete
with two spent Wetherby .300-caliber rifle shells—belted Mag-
nums, the kind of load you use for elk, or other large animals
you want to stop with one shot—and a search was continuing
throughout the neighborhood for pedestrians. "It's as if they

just vanished," one voice said. "No one saw anyone running. No one at all."

Officer Raymond slipped into the room and leaned against the refrigerator. I blearily realized that he was dressed in civvies—a nice pair of jeans, white leather running shoes, and a dark indigo shirt that matched his eyes. But even dressed in casual clothes, he was extraordinarily neat and tidy, as if those jeans had never seen real dirt and those running shoes had never contacted anything messier than dry pavement, or perhaps the well-groomed turf of a ball field. I looked down at my own battered clothes. He was a city boy, and I was a country girl. I thought of how homespun I must look to him, and felt slightly nauseated. I felt an urge to find a comb and a fresh shirt. "Can I get into the guest bedroom now and pack my bag, Officer?" I asked.

"Not just yet. The detectives are still working. And you can call me Ray," he said, coloring slightly.

"Seeing as how we're getting so well acquainted," I replied dryly.

He pulled his mouth up into a tight smile. "Well, and seeing as how we're going to be seeing even more of each other."

I shook my head. "No. They haven't sicced you on me again, have they?"

"Looks like it."

"Lucky you. Don't you ever get to go home?"

"You'd think. My current assignment is to help you find other—safer—accommodations."

I rolled my eyes. "Well, at least they picked someone who likes to keep his suspects in one piece. I want to thank you for that tackle you put on me."

"You're welcome."

"Football, too, then."

"Excuse me?"

"I'm trying to figure out all the sports you've played. Never mind. My brain is bouncing off its own walls. Happens every time I get shot at." When Ray's eyes widened, I added, "That's a joke." I turned away from him and took a sip of my coffee, trying not to stare. It was one thing that he was good-looking—anyone would notice that—but I now knew what it felt like to have his body full on top of mine, and as hair-raising as that moment had been, it had produced a bond, at least in me, one I wasn't ready to acknowledge. He was kind, he was warm, he was drop-dead handsome, and I literally owed him my life. "So how did you just happen to be in the right place at the right time?" I asked.

"I'd been following you."

I set the cup down, startled. "You were?"

He shrugged his shoulders unself-consciously. "Sure. It's my job."

"But I didn't see you."

He smiled wryly.

This time, I allowed myself to look him up and down, from his glossy black hair to his well-proportioned feet and back again. "You're pretty good," I said, then felt my face flush with embarrassment. I immediately wished I'd chosen different words.

He blushed again too, this time deeply, and with all the glory that men with ruddy complexions can muster. And he didn't look away. But neither did he smile.

I said, "So you were following me. And you saw him pull up."

"I saw you shake him by Little America; then lost you in that alley trick. I . . . guessed you'd be heading back here, and I picked you up again on South Temple."

"And Mr. Tan Chevy made a dash here. So what do you make of him following me while the house was getting tossed? Had his walkie-talkie gone out? Like maybe they're working together?"

"I'm supposed to ask *you* that."

I stared into my coffee again. We were back to cop and suspect once more. "These guys are smart, or at least one of them is, but they're amateurs. Here's my evidence: They have enough intelligence to send one to keep an eye on me so I don't interrupt the other one's search. But Mr. Chevy is a rank beginner at tailing, doesn't know he isn't supposed to get noticed, or just doesn't care. Likewise Mr. Toss, or he's a bit too emotional or maybe he got to crashing things about so much that he couldn't hear Mr. Chevy warning him over the radio. So Mr. Chevy finds me already here and he does the dumbest thing in the books: He takes a shot at not only me but also a police officer."

"I'm out of uniform."

"What kind of car you driving this time?"

"Unmarked."

"Okay, so let's give him back ten points on the IQ scale for thinking he's aiming at open game. But shooting is patently stupid. It's overkill. It's panic."

"I won't argue there."

"So maybe these guys did whatever they did to George in a moment of panic, too."

I was expecting another rejoinder, such as, *We don't know these are the guys who did George,* but instead Ray drew himself inward. He closed his eyes and stiffened, shutting down outside stimulus.

"I'm sorry," I muttered. "I forgot. There's something really bad about the way George was killed."

His eyes snapped open again, wide, alarmed. "How do you know that?"

I straightened up and pushed the coffee away in disgust. I was more than tired of this suspect business; I was all the way to irritated. "Because it's written all over you. I recommend you keep with the sports, but do not—I repeat, *do not*—take up poker. You're as guileless as I am."

Just then, Detective Bert popped into the room and slathered us both with one of his impertinent grins. "So, you two love-birds, we're all done in here. I'll be seeing you. You have a nice night's sleep, okay?" With that, he showed me his first bit of mercy of the day by simply leaving. Which was lucky for him, because I now knew that he knew that the man in the Chevy wasn't one of his, and I have been known, when that angry, to kick. Not that I condone violence, but when you ride horses, you learn to defend yourself when they pull dirty tricks that might endanger you.

Steadying my breath, I got up and headed into the bedroom to try once again to pick my clothes up off the floor. Mr. Toss had had himself a party. From the doorway, Ray said, "I'm going out to my car for a moment. I'll lock the door behind me. Don't open it for anyone but me."

I nodded and knelt down to sort underwear from once-pressed shirts, folded them, and laid them back in my suitcase. It took me several moments to find my toilet kit; Mr. Toss had kicked it underneath the bed. As I picked it up, it sloshed. Opening it, I found that he had also stepped on it, rupturing both my tube of toothpaste and my shampoo. "That's why I know it was a man in the house," I grumbled aloud. "A woman would've had more respect."

Holding the dripping kit away from my clothes so I wouldn't get them any messier than they already were, I carried it into the kitchen to clean it out in the sink. As I ran water into it, I saw a dark form slip across the backyard. In the half second it took me to assemble data and react, I thought first that it must be Ray coming back, but as the shape slipped briefly out of deep shadow into the dull remnants of the light from the window, it was entirely too small.

I dropped from the window and scuttled across the floor, fetching up in the narrow space between the refrigerator and the stove. It smelled as if it must usually be home to the garbage can. Sticky residues stuck my shoes to the floor as I squeezed farther back into the nook. Something tickled the top of my head. I looked up, saw the dangling cord of the kitchen phone. I jumped quickly up and grabbed the receiver, and was relieved to find that the buttons were on the handset. Falling back to the floor, I dialed 911.

"State your emergency," said a voice.

"This is Em Hansen," I whispered, not bothering to give the location I knew would already be illuminated on the dispatcher's desk set. "Please radio Officer Raymond in his car." My mind sped ahead, worrying that the dispatcher wouldn't know which car he had.

"Can you speak louder?"

My throat tightened as if an invisible hand were clutching it. "Please radio Officer Raymond. He should be in his car. It's right *outside* here, for crap's sake!"

"Please repeat your . . ."

My attention shifted from the dispatcher's voice to the door that led to the backyard as I heard the small sound of metal striking metal, a key rolling the tumblers of the lock. The knob turned. It was too late to dash out of the kitchen. Instead, I squeezed farther in between the counter and the refrigerator, trying in vain to hide myself from whoever was now opening the door, now stepping inside the house. . . .

I heard soft footfalls. A voice, light and cheery. "Hell-*ooo!*" it called.

The telephone crackled in my ear. "Miss? Are you there?"

The door closed, and the source of the cheery greeting stepped into my line of view. It was a small woman, barely more than a girl—petite, almost fragile. An elf, a fair wisp of a person, covered in a dark cloak that looked like it had been cut from an army-surplus blanket. She knocked back its hood and peered at me. She was plain, not pretty. Twentyish, but so diminutive and work-worn that I could not tell exactly. She could have been eighteen or even younger. She had pale, washed-out blond hair, but her skin was dry and cracked from long and early exposure to the sun. Her gray eyes were bright behind thick, unattractive glasses, and her lips were bowed in a tentative smile. I knew in a flash that there was nothing to fear from this person, except—

Into the phone, I said levelly, "Please just ask him to come," and hung up. To the little female staniding in front of me, I said, "Hello yourself," more confidently than I felt.

Her smile bloomed, bringing roses to her cheeks, a surprise from one so otherwise indistinct. "Ooooo," she cooed, then jubilantly cried, "Stand up! Stand up!" When I did, she closed the remaining few feet between us, swept my hands into hers, and clutched them to her waifish breast. "We meet at last," she said, sighing passionately.

"We—"

"I'm just so glad! I can't tell you. George promised me a birthday treat, but I had no idea it could be you! He's been so silly about this, really, thinking we shouldn't meet, but now we *have* met, and it's just perfect, isn't it? Have you been here long?"

"I—"

"Oh, I've dreamt of this day. We shall all be in the Celestial Kingdom together, at the highest level of heaven, I know it! We shall—"

"No, wait! Let me talk. Who *are* you?"

Her smile tightened into a pucker. She bowed her head slightly and looked up at me from underneath her almost colorless eyelashes, as if I were having a very funny little joke with her. "Oh, come now, silly. I'm Nina. You can't tell me George hasn't told his wife my *name.* . . ."

"I'm not—" I stopped myself. Whoever this creature was, she thought I was George Dishey's wife. But George hadn't had a wife, had he? No, I was certain of that; he had been a known bachelor. I'd heard that fact advanced as an explanation for his eccentricities, his rather unusual public persona. *And he stood right there and called himself an eligible bachelor not twenty-four hours ago, back when he was . . . alive. So who is this creature? His daughter? Had he, in fact, been married but separated, or divorced? Surely there's no trace of female habitation in this house, no evidence of a wife. . . .*

Nina was still holding my hands, at waist level now, and had begun to sway back and forth, as if we had just been dancing and the music had ended before she was ready to let me go. Her cloak parted, showing a drab, shapeless frock made of cheap, faded broadcloth. She seemed oblivious to the oddity of her dress, and was still waiting for a welcome of which she felt confident.

I took a breath, noting that it came shallowly. My abdomen had grown tight with that weird little fear that says, *Something's happening here, and it doesn't look* good. . . . I said, "Okay, Nina. I see you have a key to this house, so, ah . . . welcome. Now, excuse me, but I'm still not tumbling to who you are." About there, my mind prompted me that I had not yet corrected her, not told her that I was not George Dishey's wife. Did she think I was her stepmother?

Nina raised her arms exultantly and strung them around my neck. "Oh, Heddie, I'm Nina!" she sang, "Nina Dishey, George's *other* wife!"

8

NINA LET GO OF ME AND GLANCED EXCITEDLY ABOUT THE room. "Where is George, anyway?"

"Um . . ." Before I could say anything, I heard Ray's knock at the front door. I hurried to open it, babbling nonsensical things, like "Who could that be at this hour?"

I yanked the door open but saw no one. I tensed and began to step back, grabbing for the door handle as I went. Then the shadow to the left of the door moved, and Ray stepped toward me, eyes wide with concern. He held his right hand behind his back, no doubt concealing his drawn pistol. He stopped short when he saw Nina.

I stepped out of his way. "Ray, this is Nina. She's ah . . . George's wife."

Ray froze.

I turned around just in time to see Nina twist her hands up in front of her face like a little girl who didn't want to be seen by a grown-up she didn't know. She seemed to shrink several inches, and I began to wonder if she was in fact a child I had mistaken for an adult.

I reached out and put a hand on her shoulder. She huddled up against me and whispered something I couldn't quite hear.

Playing the adult to her child, I said, "Can you speak a little louder please, Nina?"

She tugged at my blouse, drawing me toward the kitchen. I signaled Ray to wait where he was and followed her.

In the kitchen, she whispered loudly enough that I could understand her. "I wasn't supposed to let him see me."

I whispered back, "Who? Ray?"

Urgent whisper: "Anybody!"

"But Ray's okay. He's my friend."

She looked doubtful. "George will be angry."

"Don't worry about—" I stopped myself, remembering that whoever this woman was, she didn't yet know that George Dishey was dead. Or at least was acting as if she didn't. So I said, "Listen, Ray's here to help me with something. He's a policeman." I said it in one of those light, cheery tones that are supposed to convey the thought that everything will, therefore, be okay.

Nina recoiled in horror. Turned. Headed for the back door like a dart.

Now it was my turn to grab a handful of *her* clothing, and I did so with authority. I wasn't going to let this little act dance in here, turn everything on its ear, and dance out again, at least not without some further explanation. As she continued to pull toward the door, I said, loudly and with as much drama as I could stomach, "You can't leave! Not after all this time we've been kept apart!"

Nina whirled around in terror, grabbing my blouse again with both of her tiny hands. "But George would never let police in this house! Never! You must make him leave!" It was not an act. She was shaking.

I wrapped my arms around her, as much to keep her from escaping as to comfort her, and thought to myself, *Okay, smart-aleck, now what do you do? Your host has turned up dead, you've sliced your thumb halfway off, you've made the cops' ten*

*most wanted list, you're a nonperson at a conference you thought
you were supposed to make a big splashy speech at which, you've
been shot at, and now you find yourself featured in a bad movie
about polygamous marriage. Pretty good for a day's work. So what
do you do for an encore?* I squeezed Nina tightly and mumbled
something tender, like "There, there, dear," then added a few
non sequiturs, like "We have so much in common" and "We
just need to get to know each other a little better."

Then it began to dawn on me that this woman and I did,
in fact, have something in common. We had George Dishey.
A conniving little shit who had clearly lied to me, telling me
I was coming to this conference to give an important talk at
a symposium that didn't exist. When had he been planning to
tell me his invitation had been a sham? Sometime after he
trotted me into the conference as his girlie du jour? Was that
the game?

I wrapped my arms more tightly around this woman who
called herself Nina and who said she was George Dishey's
number-two wife. If I could believe that, then it was a good
bet that George had lied to her, too. *If.* "Was George expecting you this evening?" I asked.

Her voice came faintly, but she answered as if it was perfectly natural to be asked such a question. "Well . . . yes . . .
not exactly . . . but this was special."

Perhaps George had expected I'd be gone by now. *Yes,* I
decided, *that was his plan. I would be furious when I discovered
his lie. I would have left by now in a huff. Bring on the next
fatted calf.*

Nina whispered urgently, "Heddie, there's something
wrong, isn't there? Where is George? Why's this policeman
here?"

I was running out of time, and I knew it. In the next few
minutes, I'd have to tell her what was happening, and she'd
know I wasn't Heddie, and she'd most likely tell me nothing

more. I had to frame my questions carefully, neither adding gratuitously to the lie nor tipping her off that I was not the person she thought I was. That was a problem, considering that I had no idea what this Heddie was like, nor where she spent her time, and just then it seemed damned important to know. *What if this is her house, and she was just away visiting her mother? No, that can't be. George told me he was single, or that he was not Mormon, or that—besides, there's no sign of a woman's touch in this house! Okay, so maybe George was a polygamist, and his boasting to me was just a charade to cover it, and Heddie lives somewhere else. Then if so, where?* My thoughts spun in circles as I tried to sort out the lie from the truth. Dropping into this maze of falsehood myself, I blustered, "Well, um, yes, of course you know I'm not usually here on Sundays. I'm here because, um, George didn't call me either, see, and he said he would, and I was worried, and so this policeman is a friend, see. He's a member of my church."

I clenched my teeth into a rictus smile, ruing the ease with which my own lies spilled out. I was no more a member of a church than the Easter bunny was a member of Congress. But my mind was in fast-forward gear, trying to jiggle the next move, trying to sound like a Mormon. I tried to remember what Mormons called their jurisdictions. Stakes and wards, that was it. And they called themselves Saints, not Mormons." I said, "He's in my same ward. Listen, I'll just call him in here, and we'll—"

"George is *missing?*" Nina squealed.

"Well, not exactly. He's—Ray, can you come in here, please?"

I had loosened my grasp. Nina sprang from me, yanked open the back door, and was through it as fast as lightning. I scrambled to follow her, but she slammed the door after her, smashing my wounded thumb as oak crashed against oak. I gasped, sucked for air, screamed at the top of my lungs. Ray caught me as I began to fall, holding me up by my shoulders, bracing his feet to take my weight, gathering me into his arms. My back arched as pain shot through my thumb. "Not me!" I gasped. "Get Nina! Out the back!"

Ray swung me around against the refrigerator, yanked open the door, and dashed into the backyard. As I slid down that hard, cool surface to the floor, I could hear him accelerate through the darkness. The sound of his footfalls faded.

The pain in my thumb was astonishing. It radiated up my arm, fanned out underneath my armpit, and shot through my back and chest. I arched my back against the refrigerator, eyes closed, forcing myself to think of something nice. A softly flowing creek tumbling over granite boulders in the high Rockies, a flawlessly cast dry fly landing in the broadest pool, the perfect trout rising, the soft caress of the afternoon breeze rising from the meadow. Far away, my thumb throbbed, fell off into a hole, and was swallowed.

Minutes passed. Distantly, I heard Ray come back to the phone and call for a search. Then he was near me again, his warm breath as sweet as that breeze. . . . "That's hurting you," he said, studying the fresh stain of blood that now drenched the bandage. No dumb questions from my Officer Raymond. Just straight to the point, a statement of the facts.

"The pain is subsiding. I'm just tired."

"I lost her," he said sadly.

"I'm not surprised. She probably knows a hundred ways of getting in and out of this house unseen. She's like a mouse down the hole."

Ray sighed. "Right. I didn't hear a car start up, so perhaps she's still in the area."

"She would have parked several blocks away. That is, if she drives. With that getup, she may walk everywhere. Or ride a unicorn."

"You talk like you know her."

Did I? Why did that sound true? Was it just that I understood not wanting to be seen? "She's a type. You didn't know George. I didn't either, really, but he was a taker, you know? He took things from people, and the little mice like Nina would be more than glad to share their cheese. The costume was a little unusual, but only in the present tense."

"What do you mean?"

Fatigue filled my head. "I'm not sure what I mean. But I need some sleep. What time is it, Eleven? Twelve? I'm usually in the sack by ten. And hey, it's been a day, hasn't it?" I opened my eyes.

Ray was hunkered down right next to me, his muscular legs doubled easily into a squat. He was loose; not just strong and athletic but also limber. How I loved men with long, muscular bodies. And just then that body was close to me, very close, and he was looking at me, into me, studying me with an abstraction that made me want to jump in through his blue eyes and fall.

Fall where? It wasn't fair. I was just going to have to get laid more often. A little body contact and I was a goner. I was falling for this guy, falling *into* this guy, and we had met under the very worst of circumstances, just the kind of stressful nonsense that would make me lose my composure like this and give myself away for a dime.

I studied him in return. He had his hands up to his lips, covering the lower half of his face, giving me nothing to look into but those clear blue eyes as dark as denim. I wanted to lift my hand and touch his cheek, run a finger down the strong bones of his nose. I had to be out of my mind. He probably had a wife and half a dozen kids at home, wondering where he was. *Yes, of course. He's Mormon, isn't he? He knew* The Refiner's Fire, *not your everyday reading matter, and he lives in Salt Lake City, the Mormon stronghold. And if cigarettes or al-*

cohol have ever passed those incredibly healthy lips, I'll eat his badge.

The Saints, the Church of Jesus Christ of Latter-Day Saints. I had heard enough of their proselytizing over the years, seen their missionaries, young men in pairs riding bicycles from house to house in their Sunday best, with little name badges saying, "Elder This," and, "Elder That." They often seemed sad or lonely, like lost puppies, but they were good soldiers, true to their training. They had an answer for every question, a neat set of beliefs that covered every occasion, a key for every ecclesiastical lock, a hammer to sink every philosophical nail. Like a religion designed by engineers. No ambiguities; in fact, no recognition that ambiguities might exist. Just connect the dots and salvation is thine for the asking. My high school friends had laughed into their sleeves over the LDS articles of faith, howling with mirth at the thought that each "worthy male" would become a "god" in his own "kingdom." I had suspended judgment as best I could, figuring that the missionaries were meekly presenting canned lines. They had sounded like trained parrots to me, but they were young and I figured that there had to be more to the game somewhere if all those hundreds of thousands of people went along with it. But organized religion wasn't for me either way you sliced the baloney; when I'd wanted to think deep thoughts I'd always walked a mile from the house and sat on a nice rock.

Ray as a Mormon missionary. I could see him dressed crisply in that white shirt, those dark slacks and skinny tie, hair buzzed short straight from the barbershop. He'd be hard to resist. Bored housewives would ask him in just for his company, and try to evangelize him in their own ways right back. I looked at his left hand. On the third finger was a plain gold band. I had not thought to look before.

"I'm tired," I repeated. "Time for this Cinderella to turn

into a pumpkin. Or cupcake. Or whatever she turned into."

"Not a mouse," said Ray, still gazing at me levelly.

Now, that wasn't fair, I decided, staring angrily back into his eyes. "No. Certainly not a mouse. You name a good motel, and I'll find my way there. And I'll be there in the morning. Ole Emmy won't mess up your deal with your promotion."

"I'll take you," he said, tensing.

"No, you won't. You have squad cars rolling all around this neighborhood. One of them's pulling up outside right now. Hear it? You've got a job to do. And don't worry, I'll go straight to bed and sleep like a log. I'm exhausted. I'll see you at the conference tomorrow. You'll know me; I'll be the one with the big bloody gauze bandage on her left thumb."

9

BUT I DIDN'T SLEEP. OR ONLY FITFULLY. I HAD FOUGHT to stay alert as I had followed Officer Raymond back toward the center of town, taking turns around side streets and through alleys to make certain we weren't followed. I had ached with fatigue as I leaned on the counter at the Deseret Motel and then staggered up the steps to my second-story room with its lonesome bed, mute TV, and back view over an abandoned lot. I had leaned out that window, making certain there was nothing underneath it that might serve as a ladder, then had double- and triple-checked the lock on my door. My head had buzzed with exhaustion as I peeled off my grass-stained clothes, laid them out on the second bed, slung a T-shirt over my stiffening torso, and lowered myself between the sheets. But as I tried to relax into their plain, virginal whiteness, I had stiffened with fear.

I hate motels. They are never my friends, and in no way do I ever feel safe in them. Now, add to that the fact that I was in real danger, and the mix spelled wide awake and forget about sleeping. Visions of gunshots blossomed in the darkness, growing ever larger, and nearer, aimed right at me, people running, chasing me, following me in cars.

I flicked on the bedside lamp and tried reading for a while.

I had swiped the copy of *The Refiner's Fire* from George's house with this thought in mind: If I found I couldn't sleep, it would surely knock me out again. But it didn't. This time, it drew me in, because I wanted to know what Ray believed, wanted to know *how* he could believe it. My life until then had been predicated around discarding beliefs, pulling out the opportunistic weeds that seemed to grow up wherever human longing for meaning and answers met the inadequacies of human experience and reasoning, hoping that a glimmering of truth might thrive in the space left. That was why geology had drawn me. Science was based on the search for truths, or at least for the facts from which a hypothesis might be built, and hypotheses were built for one thing only: to be tested and discarded if proven wrong, eliminating possibilities, illuminating probabilities.

I read for close to three hours, and discovered two things, both of which I found disturbing: First, the author presented evidence that suggested the founder of the Mormon Church (Joseph Smith) had been a conjurer, a money digger, and a "bogus maker"—in modern terms, a con artist. Nowhere in the text did the author presume to state whether or not Smith was conscious of his purported capacity for fabrication, or whether or not he believed everything he said. In unpleasant ways, Smith began to remind me of George Dishey in his rather charismatic ability to draw people to places he wanted them to go, leading his faithful from New York to Illinois, and attempting to lead some other men's wives to bed, with lines like "I have been looking upon you with favor for some time" and "Please be my spiritual wife." What had George said to me? "Your speech will be one of the jewels of the conference, a source of new angles, new inspiration for a hidebound profession." And I'd bought it. *Geeyak.* But George was also a Ph.D., and widely published, a huge presence within the profession of paleontology. Which was he, saint or sinner?

Second (and this was tougher for me), I had to conclude that whatever else Joseph Smith had been, he had also been inspired, and adept at matters of the psyche and perhaps the soul that I preferred not to contemplate. I prized my own ability to embrace ambiguities, but the idea of a flawed human with godly powers of transcendence left me scared and angry, and stoked my insomnia worse than a strong cup of coffee. Was this corruption of power, or a case of evolution from the profane to the profound? Part of me wanted to believe that George had used occult powers to lure me into his web of deception; that way, I could look upon myself as a victim and wouldn't have to admit my half of the mistake. Disgusted with myself, I threw down the book and turned on the TV and watched infomercials until I was at last exhausted enough to sleep, however fitfully.

At 7:00 A.M., I awoke to the sound of footsteps on the balcony outside my window. I threw off my covers and phoned Sergeant Ortega, reporting on the previous evening's fun and games. He was suitably and sympathetically horrified, but obnoxiously surprised to hear that I had actually left the scene and not tried to spend the night in George Dishey's house. When we were done chatting, I showered and wrestled my hair into some semblance of order, then picked out a knit blouse that didn't need ironing. For the lower half of my body, I chose blue jeans. To hell with trying to look upwardly mobile I decided; no one at the conference cared anyway. A geologist is still a geologist, even if you scrub her and drape her in silk. For my feet, I pulled out my old roping boots—lipstick red but comfortably faded with years of use—and slid on a belt with a Navajo silver buckle just for panache. *Big bad world, here I come.* I checked to make certain that this time I had my keys, opened the door, stepped out onto the balcony walkway, and nearly tripped over Officer Raymond.

He was sitting in a chair about a foot to the left of my

doorway, with his feet up on the railing. "Good morning," he said. "Sleep well?"

I had to grab my chin up off the walkway before I could even begin to think about answering his question. After just staring stupidly at him for a while, I said, "You been here all night?"

He shook his head and smiled smugly. "No, just got here a few minutes ago. An officer named Minton was here, though."

I could feel my face flushing. I wanted to say, *And here I had thought you were beginning to trust me,* but I kept my mouth shut. *Damned fool Em,* I told myself, *here you go again having fantasies about a man. You think he's sitting here because he can't get enough of your perfume? He's bucking for a promotion!* "Breakfast," I growled, and stomped ahead of him down the stairs.

◈

I HAVEN'T MUCH to report in the way of findings from that day at the conference. I spent a lot of time getting my bearings, a thing I would have been doing even if my agenda hadn't shifted from "make professional contacts" to the more urgent "remove self from list of murder suspects." Professional conferences are like that. They're overwhelming, an overload of incoming information, and one must first figure out how to crack into them before one can truly be involved.

So after perusing a bunch of books, maps, and T-shirts that the Utah Friends of Paleontology were selling by the registration desk, then checking out a plenary session on the cladistical analysis of tetrapodal amniotes that was being held in the ballroom, I found my way down the hill to a huge rubber tent like the ones they use to winterize tennis courts. I decided that this must be the events tent the weaselly Vance had spoken of the day before. The program listed it as the place where the poster sessions were being held. Poster sessions are minimeetings where scientists put up elaborate displays showing the results of their current research on big wide easels and then wait nervously to discuss their investigations with anyone who comes milling by. Officer Raymond followed along nonchalantly about forty feet behind me, trying to look like a paleontologist. The jeans and cowboy boots were a nice touch, but he should have lost the SALT LAKE 2002 OLYMPICS T-shirt in favor of something featuring bones and multisyllabic Latin names; he would have done better yet if he'd skipped shaving that morning, had stayed up all night doing something unhealthy, and had perfected the art of looking distracted by intellectual obsessions. When he entered the tent, he melted off into the crowd elsewhere, presumably making himself popular by asking participants if they had a motive for murder.

The thick clouds that had been sliding in between the peaks that towered over Snowbird chose that moment to shed rain. It started as a gentle tattoo on the vinyl dome of the tent, then rose quickly to the drumming of hail. I glanced overhead at the big translucent panels that let in light, to see if they were going to hold the load. Great trains of tiny hailstones gathered, warmed against the fabric, and began to slide groundward. I relaxed and moved on into the catacombs of posters.

I was just glazing over from looking at a display discussing the Eocene vole taxonomy of Montana when I spotted the sharp-faced woman I had noticed the day before. She was noticeable because she was anomalous: Geoscientists are, on the whole, an inelegant bunch, more partial to a "fresh air" look than anything one might see on Fifth Avenue. This woman was strictly Fifth, from her short, dark, classy coiffure to the au courant cut of her tiny pumps. Moreover, she wore makeup, and lots of it, mascara and eyeliner by the bucketload, laid on with artistry and flair. Her eyes were as prominent as her long, arcing nose to begin with, and the cosmetics brought them to within an inch of being overwhelming. I couldn't guess her age closer than a range—somewhere between thirty and forty. She passed a thin pink tongue between her dark red lips. "So, ya int'r'sted in tracks?" she asked in a heavy Long Island accent.

"Sure," I said, "tell me about tracks."

She made an adenoidal throat-clearing sound, very demure, and began her spiel. "What we got hea' is multiple trackways in the Blackhawk Formation. Cretaceous, y'know."

I nodded.

She gestured toward a blowup of an oblique view down the ceiling of one long corridor inside a coal mine, with an investigator wearing a hard hat with a miner's lamp for scale. The coal—the remnant of an ancient swamp—had been removed, revealing above it the sandstone formed when an ancient river levee had ruptured and spewed sand into the swamp. The sand had filled in footprints left by dinosaurs that had grazed through the swamp, dining on the canopies of the trees that grew there. Here and there, the carbonized remnants of the trees themselves were present in the form of fallen logs and even the spreading roots of a tree still standing. The footsteps were broad and round, each individual impression an almost nondescript knob of sand, but in aggregate, they were so consistently shaped and spaced that they could only have been formed by a striding animal of titanic proportions.

"Okay," the track specialist said, "we got adult ornithopods here. See the basically round print with the li'l bump on the front, like it's giving ya the finger?" She pointed at a close-up. Yep, old dinny'd had a middle toe that stuck out farther than the rest.

"Ornithopod. That's like a dinosaur?"

She gave me a sharp look that said, Amateur, huh? and said, "Yep-per. Ovah here, I got the probable species." She pointed at an artist's reconstruction of a very docile-looking creature with legs like pillars, a body like an immense rugby ball, and a neck and tail like snakes.

"You give the tracks a separate Latin name from the track maker."

"Of course. With fossil tracks, you don't know who made 'em unless you got the body fossil right there with its feet stuck right in the sand, right? So we don't have that. So we got to reconstruct it, like, from the bones and from probable tonnage and so forth. So the tracks get a separate Latin name. Here, see? Real nice. Catchy, huh? Yeah." She sniffed, working those adenoids in the dry mountain air. She seemed bored, like I was at least the fortieth person to walk up and peer ignorantly at her maps and photographs.

She was irreverent. I liked that in a woman. I smiled. "Okay, so tell me about this picture." I pointed to a photograph that on first inspection appeared to be of any old pile of sandstone boulders. Wildflowers and rabbitbrush leaned in from the edges, but within the area of interest, all rubble underneath a projecting slab had been removed, revealing one huge footprint knob made by a three-toed animal. The photographer had waited for the perfect sun angle, a low glancing brush of light that would pick up every irregularity.

"That's uppermost Morrison Formation, or lowermost Cedar Mountain, depending on where you call your boundary. That was taken at the Cleveland-Lloyd Quarry. People been digging up bones for half a century before we noticed them."

"Interesting. So what's the latest on the paleoenvironment of the Morrison?" I asked. "Isn't that the domain of Pete Peterson and Christine Turner?"

Ms. Bored sat up a little straighter. "You a stratigrapher?" she asked, checking out my name tag. She was referring to those geologists who specialize in the interpretation of layers of rock laid down by wind, water, and other natural processes.

"Sort of. I work in oil and gas. When I'm not doing forensic work."

"Oh, yeah, you're the one." She sniffed distractedly and looked away, as if she talked to murder suspects every day and so what else is new, like?

"Yeah. I got lucky. So I'm just vacationing here in bone land," I said, being equally blasé. "Em Hansen." I glanced at the lead panel of her poster layout. It informed me that she was from one of the prestigious universities back east.

She twisted her head to one side in a gesture of casualness. "Allison Lee. Yeah, Christine and Pete and that gang from the Geological Survey have been working on this formation since I was in high school. They're just synthesizing the new big picture now."

"So you been working dinosaurs long?" I asked, kind of girl-to-girl, now that we'd established how cool we both were.

"Yeah. Bones, the bigger and older the better. Tracks and traces, eggs, nests, all that stuff. Kind of different for a girl from Lawn Guyland, but what you gonna do? My grampa took me into the city to the Museum of Natchul History when I was eight, and I was hooked. After that, it was every Saturday I could get him to take me back there, or up to Yale to the Peabody Museum, or please, Grampa, please let's go to Wyoming, or out here to Utah, or Denver, or any of them places. He was a nice guy. He had bucks. He took me to every major dinosaur museum in America by the time I was in college, and then he was nice enough to pay for that."

"Girls didn't go to college in your family?"

"Not so's you'd notice it." She gazed at me languidly, settling on my left hand. "But what's marriage when you can study one-hundred-fifty-million-year-old tracks? So what did you do to your finguh there?"

"Slammed it in the kitchen door."

"See? Kitchens are dangerous places."

"Don't I know it. Give me sandstone and the open spaces any day," I said wryly, completing our discreet bit of girl bonding. And I stared at my thumb a moment, turning my hand palm up and then down again, still amazed at the fresh gauze Ray had put on it when we'd reached his car.

"So you were staying at George's house when he got killed," she said bluntly. "Was that ugly or what?"

"It wasn't anything," I replied, happy to have someone to confide my great big nothing in. "He just took off early yesterday morning, and the next thing I know, the police are at the door asking what's up." I shrugged. "I hardly knew the guy. He just called me out of the blue one day and told me about this conference and invited me to attend. I'd heard of him, so I thought, Well, I like fossils as much as the next person, so why not? So then he offered me a place to stay. What can I say? I'm a cheapskate. I said yes. How was I supposed to know he was going to, er, end up dead? So. You know him well?"

Now Allison shrugged. "Everybody knew George. It's a small fraternity," she drawled, building onto our woman-to-woman understanding.

"He was a dinosaur type, right?"

"Yeah."

"What was he working on?" I asked.

"Oh, him? Carnivores. All them boys with the really big egos got to do something with sharp teeth. It's a tick with them."

"Oh? Where was he working?" I continued. "Did he have a dig going somewhere?"

"Do I know? George di'n't take people out to his sites."

I cocked my head to one side. "I thought it took a lot of

people to work a dinosaur site. I mean, like I watched one on TV, you know? Lots of rock to move, and the bones themselves weigh a lot, right?"

A veil seemed to drop over Allison Lee's intelligent eyes. She shrugged her narrow shoulders. "So he liked to work alone, not show anyone anything until he had it in the bag or something." Her eyes glowed a little more brightly again as her lips curved slightly and she said, "You got to put a guy like that out of your head. Yeah, so he got you with the old 'star speaker at the big symposium' line. Hey, he does that every year. Poor ugly George always had to have a babe on his arm. Poor you, you got snookered. Get over it; you got some pretty classy company."

"You mean—"

"Me?" she said, placing a delicate hand across her breast. "Sure, I'm a sucker, but he didn't like city girls. He goes for au naturel types like you."

"He ever married?"

"Him? Who'd marry him? He had a love affair with himself!"

"You didn't like him much."

"Who did? Okay, so he screwed my college roommate."

"So you mean he was a Don Juan?"

"Huh? No, not that kind of screwed. I mean like screwed her over. Promised her he could get her all sorts of prestige and assistance if she got into this particular program at a particular school. She applied. She got in. Turned out he wasn't even affiliated with the department, let alone the university. She'd already packed up and moved there, at some expense, and, like, who was going to fund her research? Nobody, once she was dumb enough to open her yap to the department and say, 'Where's George?' They *already* hated the bastard over some other gag he'd pulled."

"But why do that? What did it gain him?"

"You got me. Maybe it was his way of jerking off, or he just lost track of who he'd told what. Or maybe he saw her as some kind of threat and thought he'd mess with her. Either way, it really hurt her feelings and got her off on the wrong foot professionally. So I like the idea of him down there hoppin' on hot coals." She pointed toward hell.

"Was he any kind of a scientist?"

"Who knew? We never got to see his sites, remember?"

"But he worked carnivores, you said."

"Yeah, but we never saw his evidence."

"You mean he was maybe inventing things?"

"No . . . he had photographs of prepared stuff, but that's all he'd show anybody. Most other people at least keep their bones in a known collection somewhere, like at a museum, so everybody can see them and draw their own conclusions. But not George."

"Where do you think he put them, then, if he was digging them up?"

She shrugged again, beginning to look a little bit nervous maybe to be giving up so much information. "Try his basement." She looked down the long aisle formed by the nearest two rows of poster easels, as if willing someone else to come by and interrupt our conversation.

George's basement. A big empty nothing. "But he published his findings. Right?"

"Oh, come on. You call that publishing? Sure, he published; he spread it all through the newspapers and magazines. If you asked him, he'd tell you he only published in popular magazines because they got his results out faster, but he knew better than to present his data where it could be scrutinized."

I knew this kind of talk. It was how scientists badmouthed each other without going on record as having done so. It was a dicey business for a scientist to call a colleague a slob: a sort of "she who has not analyzed evidence wrong may cast the first stone" proposition. "But no one drummed him out of the corps?" I asked.

Allison began to squirm a little, as if her blouse had started to make her itch. Evading eye contact, she said, "So who was he working for? No one."

Playing devil's advocate, I said, "But he had a doctorate."

Allison sighed disgustedly. "Yeah, he had his doc all right. He had a job for a while, too, but he didn't get tenured. Like I say, he did some quickie science."

"But wait, isn't he teaching at the university here?"

"That, he would like you to think. Lissen, this sort of thing happens sometimes; he had a nice dissertation, but then, well . . ."

I didn't let it go. "So what are we saying here? Was he with a museum? Maybe he was working independently on a grant?"

"Nope. Nada. *Bubkes*. Nothing."

"Huh. So how'd he make a living?"

Allison leaned pointedly away from me, willing someone else to walk up to her easel and drive me away. "Got me."

"Funny, he had a house and all. I mean, it wasn't like he was renting a studio apartment or something. And aren't houses getting expensive here in Salt Lake?"

She cocked her head to one side distractedly, a Who knows? gesture.

"So George was in Vietnam," I said.

"Was he?" she said, yawning.

"Yeah. There was a photograph of him with some helicopter buddies. He still see them?" I was thinking, of course, of the man with the high cheekbones and the frightening eyes. Frightening to me now as much because he bore a resemblance to the man who had followed me the night before, and shot at me.

"Who knows what kind of people George hung out with?

He liked the limelight, all right, but then you didn't hear from him for months. He was a carny act."

"What do you mean by that?"

"I mean, guys like that, you don't see the real guy. You see what they want to show you."

"Tell me more."

Allison now looked anywhere but at me. I had pushed the line of questioning entirely too far.

I steered quickly onto other ground, hoping to get just an ounce more information from her. "So what about your roommate. Did she—"

"Lissen, you want to know what you need to know about George Dishey, you should go on Sherbrooke's field trip tomorrow."

"There's a field trip tomorrow? I didn't see it in the program."

"Nah, it's his big surprise. But the jungle telegraph has been busy, and everyone knows something's up. Like I say, it's a small fraternity."

I thought for a moment. "So why is it I want to go on this field trip?"

"A picture is worth a thousand words."

"Okay, fine, I'll see about signing up. So are you telling me Dishey and Sherbrooke worked together on stuff?"

Allison laughed—a quick, humorless grunt. "Not those two. Not hardly."

"So then—"

We were interrupted as Allison leaned forward to offer her fingertips to be shaken by a passing colleague. "Howie, nice to see ya. My love to Gwen. Ya wanna see my latest tracks?"

The man smiled pleasantly, made a vague hand gesture, but moved on by.

I began again. "So Dishey and Sherbrooke—"

"Okay, you want to know about Dishey and Sherbrooke?

They roomed together at Yale. It was a little before my time. Go ask someone who was there. Better yet, ask Dan to explain it to you." Allison made a swatting gesture, as if flies were buzzing in front of her face. "Go on the field trip. You can't ride that bus without hearing all the dirt you could hope to dig in a month of poster sessions."

"Your roommate," I said. "Did she—"

Allison stood up and turned away from me. "Lost track of her."

"Oh." My heart sagged in my chest. I had succeeded in making this woman uncomfortable. And I had begun to descend into a dim, fusty world, a land of resentments and petty bitternesses, a circle lower into hell than I had meant to travel. I tried to focus my mind on the faces of other people who stood here and there among the easels, bending their highly trained minds toward their favorite topics of intellectual pursuit. As I observed them, I realized that I also was being observed: About forty feet away, standing near a display I'd passed earlier on the adaptive morphology of the pachycephalosaurids, stood Earthworm Magritte, the stump-shaped man who had declared it high time that George Dishey left the planet. He was watching me closely, stone-faced, and with concentrated interest, as if I were a movie.

I turned back to Allison Lee. "Do you know, ah, Dr. Magritte at all?"

"Worm? Everybody knows him."

"A bit outspoken, is he?"

Allison shifted nervously in her seat. "Listen, the Worm's just another drug-related tragedy from the seventies. I mean, he's a good guy, right? And so he's a bit rough around the edges. Who cares? Everyone gets so worked up. It just makes me sick."

"But I mean, he—"

"Listen, Magritte's *okay*. Look, here's his business card."

She fished a card out of her pocket, sorting it from a collection of twenty or thirty she must have garnered that morning from friends visiting her booth. It read:

EARTHWORM MAGRITTE, PH.D.
PROFESSIONAL
SHIT STIRRER

Egos trimmed	*Paradigms shifted*
Dirt dumped	*Errors illuminated*
Banality noticed	*Astral planes torqued*

"See?" she said. "You can't take anything he says too seriously."

"Oh. But—"

Allison had had enough of me. She narrowed her eyes and went on the offensive. "So who was the beefcake you were here with yesterday?" she began. "Please tell me he's your brother. I mean, what a looker!"

I was saved from having to volley her question when she turned to a skinny man with a drooping mustache who was just walking up. "Hi, Fred. How's tricks? You wanna hear my spiel about trackways?"

I drifted away from Allison's poster session, hoping to put a nice, big easel between myself and the unrelenting stare of Earthworm Magritte under whose gaze I was beginning to feel naked. I moved a couple of aisles down and pretended to peruse a display entitled "The Histological Quantification of Growth Rates in Plated Dinosaurs," but I soon found that Earthworm Magritte had trended that direction as well, and that he still appeared to find me more interesting than the posters. I didn't like being observed, not one bit. There was something anomalous about the man, something too far out of the ordinary to be quite sane. Professional shit stirrer, indeed. Was he the stuff of murder?

"You into thyreophorans?" someone asked. I turned. A tall, dark-eyed man with short salt-and-pepper hair was standing quite near me, lounging with his hands in his pockets. Though easily in his fifties, he had the trim, sinewy build of a man who has systematically kept himself in shape. "Enjoying the sessions?" he asked. It was the first time at this conference that somebody had taken the trouble to speak to me before I had first spoken.

"Sure. Great," I said as I quickly scanned his face, then dropped my gaze to read his name badge. Tom Latimer, it said. No university affiliation, just the town, somewhere in Illinois. I had noticed quite a few people with no affiliations, so that wasn't strange in itself, but there was something odd about this guy. What?

"Are armored dinosaurs your specialty?" he asked.

"No."

"Oh? What is?"

"Stratigraphy. I'm just visiting from the oil patch." I was immediately sorry I'd said so much about myself. This man made me uncomfortable. Why was that?

"I see. Meeting some interesting people?" he asked casually. A little too casually.

"Sure."

The man continued to look at me. I looked at him. Neither of us said anything for a moment. Out of nervousness, I asked, "So what's your specialty?"

"I'm an illustrator. I do dinosaur illustrations for kids' books."

"Oh." I let the volley of questions drop on my side of the net, hoping he'd just walk away, but he didn't. He seemed to be waiting, and I wasn't sure for what. I'd been to conferences and conventions before, and had been hit on more than once; yeah, even a plain Jane like me. There are a lot more men than women in the geosciences, and youngish unattached females are considered premium game for convention funsies. But much as this man's opening lines were typical of that kind of hit, there was something in his eyes that didn't seem quite amorous. Or friendly. Not unfriendly, exactly, but let's just say I didn't get the buzz that he was trying to get sociable for sociability's sake. My stomach began to tighten. I smiled coolly, said, "Excuse me," turned, and headed straight for the exit of the tent.

I marched through the rain to the next building, which I knew housed the exhibits portion of the conference. Ray fell in thirty feet behind me as I searched out the exhibits room and found it. Inside, there were rows of tables with bored-looking vendors sitting behind them. The tables were stacked with flyers, pictures, technical widgets of interest to paleontologists, scientific texts, antique monographs, lavishly painted illustrations of dinosaurs, even sculptures. I wondered if this was the kind of work Tom Latimer did, but I couldn't feature him sitting at an easel. I studied the men who sat behind the tables selling dinosaur art. They didn't look much different from Latimer—same ordinary dress, same close haircut, but Latimer had seemed more . . . more what? More attuned to something other than dinosaurs.

I wandered down the line of tables, taking in the wealth and variation of materials for sale. A cast of the skeleton of *Utahraptor* strode the carpet, horrifying claws poised for the kill, long balance-beam tail curving to accommodate her stride. A life-size reconstructed head of *T. rex* yawned at me from a wall like a trophy head from hell, its eight-inch teeth luring me in for dinner, its tiny eyes glassy with lust. Not for the first time, I wondered at man's fascination with the terrible, the horrifying, and the immense.

I came across one table that featured stacks of books by two paleontologists who were famous partly for the depth of their disagreement on each other's interpretations of dinosaur behavior—Horner and Bakker, stacked right next to each other. I was wondering idly if the vendor was trying to start a friction fire when I found myself needing to scoot in closer to the table to let a man pass with his preschool-age son. They were a pleasant change from the overserious faces of the paleontologists, so I tracked the pair as they moved down the line of tables. When they reached an exhibit of special pastes used in preparing fossils for exhibits, the exhibitor grinned and leaned over his table to offer the kid a chunk of what looked like rock. "Here!" he said. "Want your own piece of dinosaur bone?"

"Sure!" said the kid. He reached out and took it, eyes alight.

The child's father asked, "Is that real bone?"

"Certainly," said the exhibitor. "I have a bag full of bits like that." He popped his eyes at the child. "It's part of the neck frill from a *Triceratops*, sonny."

The father was as delighted as the child. "This is great," he said. "The wife's giving a paper here at the conference, and we just tagged along. I had no idea there'd be fun stuff like this for kids! What do you say to the nice man, Nate?"

"Thank you!" the child sang.

The father had one more question, the kind a man knows to ask if his wife is in the profession: "What locality did this fossil come from?"

The exhibitor pointed down the room toward a man wearing an Australian-style hat with one side of the brim folded up. "You can ask him. That's the guy who gave them to me."

The man with the hat had been strolling along the line of tables toward us with his hands in his pockets, looking at books. Just looking, not buying or even picking them up, as if he didn't want to leave fingerprints. But when he heard himself mentioned, he stopped abruptly, turned, and ever so smoothly walked away and out the back door of the room.

I turned to see if Ray had noticed the man, too. He had. I headed out the same door. The man was nowhere in sight. I moved quickly through the maze of hallways that wound through the building and found myself back outside.

The man with the hat was talking to someone near the walkway that led uphill toward the Cliff Lodge. For the moment, it had stopped raining. I took a moment to gauge the man, trying to understand what his purpose might be in attending the conference. Was he some kind of vendor? He seemed better dressed than many of the other conferees, less intellectually distracted, and almost theatrical in his choice of western-style vest and Australian hat. He wore no name badge. The instant he saw me watching him, he broke off his conversation and headed up the path toward the Cliff Lodge, his stride quickly lengthening.

I hurried to fall in beside him. "Enjoying the sessions?" I asked brightly, wishing I could think up a more sincere conversation starter than the illustrator with salt-and-pepper hair had unsuccessfully used on me.

The man with the hat nodded noncommittally and further lengthened his stride. It was a steep path, his legs were considerably longer than mine, and he was clearly in shape and used to walking. When he was well ahead, I heard someone speak behind me. "*He* sure as hell isn't going to talk to *you*," the voice said.

I turned, to find Vance, the weaselly little guy with the drooping blond mustache and broiled skin who had reported the problem with the poster tent to Sherbrooke the day before. "Why not?" I asked.

"Commercial collector," he sneered.

I opened my mouth to ask him what a commercial collector was and why Vance thought one wouldn't talk to me, but I was interrupted by a heavyset guy with a wiry beard who was converging on us from uphill. He was wearing a T-shirt that read ORNITHISCHIANS DID NOT HAVE CHEEKS. "Vance, you old ectotherm!" he boomed. "Haven't seen you since undergrad. Whose fire you toasting marshmallows on these days?"

I moved quickly out of range of Vance's hissing reply. I wanted to stay well ahead of Officer Raymond, whose athletic grace was making the steep grade into flat ground, and I didn't want to hear a piss-and-moan session about academic life. My brain was beginning to bog down from strain, lack of sleep, and a deepening sense of alienation. I had hoped in going there to feel like a colleague, or to at least feel like an accepted member of the geological scene, but I did not. People were avoiding me, and now even taking shots at me. What had I done to deserve such ostracism? Did they, like Officer Raymond, think I might have murdered one of their brethren? Or worse, did they lump me with George Dishey and presume I was a sloppy scientist? I wondered how long it would take to atone for my sin of foolishness and rid myself of that taint.

I pushed those worries out of my mind, telling myself that there were more important things to concentrate on at the moment. I told myself also that there would be time enough to probe the tough little minds of Vance what's-his-name and Allison Lee a little later on, after I had poured a cup of hot black coffee from the urns in the lobby outside the symposia under way at the Cliff Lodge. I was wrong.

10

I WAS JUST RAISING THAT CUP OF COFFEE TO MY LIPS WHEN Ray materialized at my elbow. *Bam*, like out of nowhere. I hadn't seen him coming. Just like the night before, when the gun went off. I jumped, spilling coffee on one of the magnificent Persian carpets that were so lavishly strewn about the floor. I almost swore, then wanted to swear again when I realized that I had suppressed that curse out of the embarrassment of thinking Ray was somehow better than I was just because he went to church and didn't cuss. Or I presumed he was a churchgoer. I sure as hell wasn't.

I turned toward him and fixed him with a glare I hoped would put him in his place, wherever that was, took a noisy suck at the coffee his religion forbade him to drink, and waited. The gesture was meant to say, How dare you presume to trot up to me whenever you wish?

But the look on Ray's face cut right through my bluster. His taut body muscles said *alert*, his face said *urgent*, and his eyes said *now*. He took the coffee cup out of my hand, set it down, clamped a hand on my arm, and turned me toward the escalators that led down to the main entrance. "We have to go," he said.

"Why?" I demanded.

"I'll tell you on the way."

"You'll tell me *now*."

Ray glanced left and right to make certain he would not be overheard. "Someone's already tried to get into your room at the motel," he said. "If I'm going to keep you safe, this is not the place." He had me moving now, in a beeline for the front doors. Suddenly, he jerked to a stop, his eyes wide.

I looked where he was looking, out through the glass wall at the exquisitely manicured ski slopes, which now glowed with the soft richness that only thick clouds and rainwater can bring out of autumn foliage.

"Below," Ray said tersely.

I lowered my gaze.

Three tour buses had pulled up by the front entrance. Their doors were opening. People were climbing off, filling the driveway, now churning about, now opening the cargo doors, now raising placards that said GOD LOVES US! and DON'T INSULT OUR LORD! They swung the placards into position, turned with ominous quiet toward a hand raised by their leader.

I said, "What the hell—"

"Protesters," said Ray. "We heard they might show up." He changed course and steered me the opposite way, toward a flight of stairs that led to a side entrance.

I jerked to a stop in a protest of my own. "Protesters? What in hell's name would anyone want to protest about a paleontology convention? And *wait!*" I tugged my arm loose. "Damn it, Ray! Who are those people and who exactly is this 'we' who heard they might show up?"

Ray tensed further as the sounds of chanting reverberated through the glass wall. " 'We' is the police department. *They* are creationists. Now—"

"Fundamentalist protesters? *Really?*" I gaped toward the windows, fascinated. "You mean . . . Oh, I get it. They think paleontologists are out to get them because they believe in evolution. What a crock!" Then it occurred to me that, as a Mormon, Ray might also be a creationist. Had I offended him? "So does 'they' also mean 'not Mormon'?"

Ray raised an eyebrow sardonically and tried again to steer me away from the window.

I said, "Go? Just when things are getting interesting?"

Ray replied by dropping my arm and putting a hand over his face.

I was beginning to enjoy the way he said more with his body than with words; it was eloquent as well as extraordinarily sexy. I smiled at him, enjoying watching him just stand there looking exasperated. But then he took his hand away from his face and I could see that he had moved beyond annoyance to fear, and that fear shot straight into me. I had not wanted to hear what he had said about people trying to find their way into my motel room—I had wanted to think that that hadn't made sense, that no one could know where to find me. But now my emotions cracked through the protective wall my intellect had built, and sheer terror roared in. It roared to the beat of the angry chanting that now flooded up the escalator well from the entrance below, and I whispered, "Why would anyone come looking for me? What do I know that could hurt anyone?"

Ray reached his hand toward me, palm up, in supplication. "Why would anyone shoot at you last night? We can get out this side door," he said, and added, now raising his voice to be heard over the chanting, "*Please.*"

We hustled down a short flight of stairs toward the side exit, only to find that way jammed with protesters, too. We shot across the lobby, and fetched up against the doors that led into the ballrooms where the learned talks were being presented. As we ran, I saw Dan Sherbrooke striding toward the main entrance, a look of mystified outrage pasted across his face. He seemed querulous, as if thinking, *How could anyone presume to assault this extension of my personal being in this way?*

Once again, I threw on the brakes. "Wait! Sherbrooke looks like he's going to stir some shit here, and it might tell us something."

The protesters now packed the opposite end of the lobby, barring all other exits. They had ceased their advance, content to intimidate with their chanting and the sheer numbers of their presence.

Ray opened the ballroom door and stared through to the far side. Satisfied that this provided us an exit through the kitchen doors, he held up an index finger and looked me in the eye. "One minute," he said. "One."

The protesters now began to sing, borrowing their tune from an old children's hymn and cramming in words that didn't scan: "God created us, how do we know? Because the *Bible* tells us so!"

Sherbrooke allowed them three verses and then raised one large pudgy hand. "Please!" he roared, "Ladies! Gentlemen! How may I help you?" His words were cordial, but his chin was raised in indignation.

A television reporter squeezed past the head of the phalanx and popped in next to Sherbrooke, pulling her cameraman with her. Sherbrooke drew her deftly to one side, helping her set up her camera angle. There was a ponderousness and a courtesy in his motions that suggested that he might just possibly have already been acquainted with her, might, in fact, have known that she was coming. As she finished adjusting her jacket and got her microphone lined up, a man in a pale green suit strode inward from the head of the crowd, approaching the camera. "Brethren!" he boomed, raising a hand in saintly greeting. He turned dramatically, slowly, regarding the room from one far corner to the other, then finally turned back toward the camera and swung his hand over his heart. "Brethren, let us pray!"

Sherbrooke drew his lips up so tightly that I could all but hear his anus pucker at the other end of his alimentary canal. He did not appear to like being upstaged.

"Almighty God," intoned the preacher, "lend Your light to us today that we might bring the grace and majesty of Your truth to those gathered in this palace of earthly delights. Lead them in Your wisdom and teaching, that they might find the true knowledge of Your Word and discover the joy of knowing that You created them. Help them find Jesus, that they might enter Thy kingdom. Amen."

"Amen," murmured the protestors.

As he suffered the affront of being prayed over, Sherbrooke drew himself up even taller. His large soft eyes glared out through his glasses like dark goldfish perceiving a horrifying world. I could almost hear the gears in his braincase hiss into smoother running as the heat of his anger thinned the viscosity of their oil.

The preacher sucked in his breath to address him, but the reporter had already swung the microphone toward Sherbrooke.

"Gentlemen, ladies," Sherbrooke said unguently, "thank you for your interest in our work. If you have any questions regarding our proceedings here, I am certain that this kind agent of the local media can arrange a *proper* forum from which we *all* might grow more, ah, enlightened. However, we do ask, if you wish to attend our conference, that you register at the front desk as the rest of us have done. The men and women who have assembled here have come from all across our fair continent—indeed, from continents all across the planet—to present their findings to one another in a *civilized* and scientific manner, and I do not wish for them to be harassed or interrupted in any way."

Ray gave a tug at my arm. "He has them quiet. Good time to go," he said.

"Just when the party's finally getting interesting?" I said, laughing nervously. "Golly gosh, Ray, it looks like Brother Sherbrooke's worked hard for this moment. The least we can do is give him the courtesy of watching."

Ray turned his quick gaze from the crowd to me.

"This is *theater*," I said. "Look at Sherbrooke—he's all but laying Shakespeare on them. And that preacher, who wrote his lines? Come on, I'll bet they met at a bar in Cincinnati and cooked this up for the publicity it would generate for both sides."

Ray squinted at me in disgust.

"Well, *look*, Ray, I mean *really* look at them. They each need the other or there's nothing to be dramatic about. Poor stiffs like you and me, we're here to do our jobs—you know, try to figure out whether birds are really descended from dinosaurs, or find out who killed George Dishey. Those boys have a much more complicated agenda."

Ray summarily put a hand against my back and shoved me through the door and out through the kitchens beyond, flashing his badge at each surprised face. Outside the service entrance, I caught sight of the man with the Australian hat. He was just pulling open the sliding side door of a van that was parked about fifty feet away, almost out of sight behind a big disposal bin. It struck me as odd that he would park there instead of in the main parking lot with the rest of the conferees, so I watched the man over my shoulder as Ray steered me forward. As the sliding door reached its fully open position, enough light filled the van that I could see that there was another man sitting in the backseat. He had a dilapidated appearance, all faded plaid flannel and patched jeans. His fingers were thickened from hard labor and his wrists thin and sinewed. Most spectacularly, he wore his beard almost a foot long, in a curtain of pale brown whiskers that fell straight from beneath his jutting cheekbones, hiding his mouth. As his head swung my way, his eyes opened wide in surprise, narrowed, locked on mine, and then seemed to catch fire as a smile slowly split his beard from his drooping, feathery mustache.

My mouth fell open. It was the helicopter pilot from the photograph in George's living room. I'd have known him anywhere. Not just because of his startling looks—now half-covered by the whiskers, a beard as long and straight as the one on the man who had shadowed me—but because of the light that seemed to burn from his eyes. Through those glowing eyes, he shot a toxic slug of emotions to me, an invitation mixed with seductive menace. I felt pierced, like a hot dagger had just been shoved through my heart. It was a helpless feeling, as if he knew something I didn't and the only way I could be free of him was to kneel down and let him flow through me. "Ray!" I gasped.

Ray pulled me even harder, mercifully snapping my attention from the man in the van to himself. I swung my head to look into his eyes. He was concentrating, a look of irritation clamped on his face. I could tell he wasn't listening, that he wouldn't listen, that he was sick of my interference, that—

"That's the man!" I whispered. I glanced back again. The door to the van was rolling shut.

"What man?" he muttered, still pulling me toward the main parking lot.

"Ray, listen!" I said, louder now. "There's a man there in that van! I saw him in a picture in George's house! And he looks like the guy who shot at us!"

Ray stopped and swung his attention to the van, but it was already rolling, disappearing down the service lane around the back of the building.

"He's getting away!" I said stupidly, stating the obvious.

Ray dropped my arm and yanked a small spiral-bound notebook and a pen out of his breast pocket and began to write.

"Ray!"

"I got the plate number. I'll call it in."

"He was with a commercial collector," I gasped, uncertain what that meant.

Now Ray grabbed my arm again and kept me moving until we had rounded the building and fetched up next to his prowl car, where he flashed his badge one more time to get the buses moving out of his way. His face was set in blank concentration, and he was no longer looking at me. As he opened the door on my side of the car with one hand, I saw the other begin to rise, as if he was going to apply pressure to the top of my head to push me into the car, a move I'd seen police use with drunks in downtown Denver.

"I'll give!" I said. "I'll come along quietly."

And I did give. As I sank into the seat, something inside of me began to collapse. Ray closed my door and hurried around to the other side, got in, picked up his radio microphone, and called in the number of the van's license plate. "Detain occupants for questioning," he said, and gave the case number. Then he replaced the microphone in its cradle and leaned toward me, his near arm curled protectively around my headrest. He waited for me to speak.

I let out a shaky sigh. "Okay, I'm scared. What am I supposed to do? This guy who looks like the guy who shot at us last night—it isn't him, but it could be his brother—was right here at this conference, and if his brother doesn't mind shooting at us, maybe he doesn't, either. I could have been killed, damn it! And all my gear is back at that motel. How am I supposed to walk in there and get my stuff, knowing that whoever fired that rifle last night is probably watching again? And how the *hell* did they know where to find me?"

Ray raised his free hand to scratch his forehead. "Um, Bert already had your bags picked up. An officer turned your car in for you. You don't have to go back there."

I flopped my hands about in exasperation. "Great. So what am I supposed to do for transportation?"

Ray straightened up, buckled his seat belt, and said, "I told them you could ride with me."

◈

I KEPT MY eyes closed all the way down Little Cottonwood Canyon to the wide turn where the road swung out of the sharp fault-carved face of the Wasatch Range. I didn't want to talk, didn't want to open my eyes and look at Ray and wonder what in hell I was doing riding around in somebody else's puzzle. I wanted to say, Let me go home. Leave me alone. Let me sleep. I know nothing.

But I knew that the time for leaving had been long before I arrived. I was stuck, I was implicated, I had no alibi, and God only knew what had really happened. If I had been in Ray's shoes and had found a corpse at 9:30 A.M. and had seen some woman breaking into the dead man's house at 10:30—a woman who just happened to have arrived the night before, no less—I'd be watching her myself. The police could not let me leave just yet, and even if they did, there was now this little matter of my personal safety. I had made the mistake of thinking that both men involved in the break-in and shadowing the night before had been clumsy, but clearly the man inside had been much smarter, had had a vehicle hidden nearby, had managed to follow us to the motel without attracting Ray's notice. And if he had managed to track me that far, then he could just as easily track me home to Colorado, a place where there was no Officer Raymond, no nice guy do-gooder with an inexplicable urge toward keeping my skin intact. So I had to face facts: It was in my best interest to stay, help Ray crack the case as quickly as possible, get the trigger-happy nutcase who had shot at us behind bars, and then go home and sleep.

When I finally opened my eyes, I rocked my head back and

forth to pop a couple of kinks out of my neck and sighed. Ray glanced at me out of the corners of his eyes as he negotiated another turn. I took time to examine him at leisure, taking in the muscular forearm that extended to the steering wheel, the firm abdomen, the astonishingly perfect profile with its full lips and strong brow. He sat in the relaxed but alert posture that only people with fine muscle tone can approach. For the fifth or sixth time, I decided that he was not real, that I was dreaming, and that I might soon awake.

Feeling my eyes on him, he glanced at me again, then fixed his gaze rigidly on the road. I smiled wistfully, thinking, *If I have to wake up in someone else's nightmare, it might as well have its attendant daydreams.*

As if reading my thoughts, Ray stiffened ever so slightly. His free hand rose to his face and made a self-conscious exploration of his nose.

I looked away. "You come across that van on the way down the canyon?"

"No."

"And no one else has seen it, either," I said, knowing I would have heard it on the radio, which had been burbling away with its flow of police business.

"No."

"What's up-canyon from Snowbird?"

"Not much."

I let my line of questioning drop. Ray was the homeboy, the one who knew all the local routes like the back of his hand. He had certainly followed me through the streets of Salt Lake City without being noticed, so he'd know every route in and out of Little Cottonwood Canyon. And I didn't ever want to see the man in that van again. Instead, I asked quietly, "Where are we headed?"

"Police headquarters."

"Hmpf. Is that an invitation or a requirement?"

Ray's near shoulder rose a fraction of an inch, as if warding me off.

"Sorry," I said. "I'm feeling pretty . . . well, you name it. This situation is . . . All right I'm defensive as hell, and I wish for your sake you weren't stuck baby-sitting me, and I wish like anything that right now I was knee-deep in a trout stream in the high Rockies instead of eyebrow-deep in this mess. No offense, you've been great, but . . ."

Ray nodded but kept his eyes on the road.

❖

DETECTIVE BERT LOOKED up as we walked into his office. His insane grin slopped from one side of his face to the other in greeting. "Ah, the little lovebirds," he gushed. "Been out gathering twigs for your nest?"

I stopped short, my stomach tightening. Pressuring me was one thing, but this was harassment of a different kind. Bert was accusing a married man of . . . well, taking an interest in another woman, and that was . . . well, it was sexual harassment, wasn't it? Just because it was between two men didn't make it something else. Or did it? Did men harass each other in the workplace in the same obscene ways they harassed women? I looked toward Ray for some clue as to what Bert's jab was all about.

Ray had stopped, too, and had snapped to like a soldier standing at attention, hands tucked behind his back. "Reporting," he said tersely. I was just far enough behind him that I could see that his hands had tightened into fists.

Bert lurched up from his desk. "Re-por-ting," he sang. "How charming. Here, let's get the little lady a chair." He whipped his side chair around for me to sit on. He made a burlesque of brushing it off, even opened his palm toward it in offering.

I remained standing.

"You don't want it?" he asked mockingly, eyes popping. "My, my, my, my. I thought anyone who could rivet *Officer* Thomas *Brigham* Raymond, *Junior's* attentions must deserve a chair. Oh, ho, ho, ho . . ." He yanked his own chair into a better position for a casual interrogation, dumped his behind into it, and leaned back. The springs in the seat squealed sickeningly under the strain. He shifted his butt this way and that, searching out what appeared to be just the perfect angle, then hoisted his long legs up onto his desk and stared at Ray blankly. "I'm going to have your ass," he informed him bluntly.

Ray did not flinch.

I blinked. The "Junior" explained why he was nicknamed off his last name rather than his first, but Thomas *Brigham* Raymond? I reeled at the recognition that I might have been traveling with a local blue blood, one of the legion of great-grandsons of Brigham Young, the Mormon leader who had brought the faithful to Utah, among them his fifty-three wives. I swung my attention quickly back to Bert. Was he *not* a Mormon, and therefore bitter about the limitations on his career an outsider could find within a sectarian society?

"I'm going to have your ass," Bert repeated, "for personal involvement with a suspect. I'm going to have your ass filleted. I'm going to have your ass marinated. I'm going to have your ass—"

"What do you mean, 'personal involvement'?" I butted in. "And are you calling me a suspect? You say that to my face!"

Bert grinned his ghoulish grin at me. "I just did," he said. I had succeeded only in shifting his wild eyes from Ray to myself, and I immediately felt so chilled that I wasn't certain I owed Ray that much, even if he *had* saved my life.

Ray continued to stand at attention.

"You were talking about me, right?" I said idiotically.

"Was I?" Bert cooed.

I gave him a look like stink. "You got a question for me, or can I leave?" I said disgustedly.

"Do I?"

"Oh, cut it out," I said. "Are you running a murder investigation here, or are you just in the business of making people uncomfortable? I am too tired and too sure of my rights and too fed up from too long a history of being hazed by men on the job site to take any more of your crap."

Ray shifted slightly. His lips took on a tinge of a smile.

Detective Bert stuck out his lower lip in a parody of petulance. "Well, I—"

"That was a rhetorical question," I snapped. "Officer Raymond here has been doing a nice job of keeping me alive. I appreciate that in a policeman. And I mean, really, if you haven't anything more for us than a few more degrees of heat, then let me make you a present of what I learned this morning at the convention so I can get on with my life." I wanted to add, Because you're so full of shit that if I gave you a big-enough dose of Ex-Lax and waited five minutes, I could fit you in a shoe box, but I thought better of it.

Bert's smile sweetened. He sat up straight, pulled up to his desk, and picked up a pencil. "It's your party, Sherlock."

I shook the stiffness out of my shoulders. Cleared my throat. "George Dishey was not well respected by his colleagues. He apparently cut corners and practiced what's considered questionable science. This would rile a lot of people who feel compelled to do it by the book. Anyway, he had to be making some sort of living—but how? He had no connection with the university here or with any other respected scientific institution. He reputedly liked to work alone, which is unusual, because big-bone guys often have to heft considerable tonnage."

"Do what?" Bert asked. He was scribbling studiously and did not look up. For the first time, he had forgotten to be obnoxious to me, and I felt almost comfortable with him. I watched him write. The shallow muscles about his forehead worked as he concentrated. With his guard down, I could momentarily see past the bluster into a lonely, intelligent man who probably found no place of repose except his work.

I looked away, unprepared to feel sympathy. "The fossils they work with weigh a huge amount. If you're lucky enough to find the skull of a big carnivorous dinosaur, for instance, or, say, the pelvis of a big leaf-eater, you're talking about several cubic feet to a cubic yard or more of solid rock, because you leave the bones in the surrounding matrix—that's the sediment that filled in around the dead animal's bones and lithified . . . ah, turned to rock—when they pull the fossil out of the outcrop. The bones are usually shattered into pieces and quite fragile, and by leaving them in the matrix, they protect them as far as possible. They cut away as much extraneous rock as possible, and protect exposed surfaces of bones by wrapping them in burlap soaked in plaster. Then they hack out as much underlying rock as possible, leaving just a few pillars. Then they come in with a crane and break it loose and hoist it onto a flatbed truck. Sometimes, like if the site is really remote or halfway up a cliff, they bust the budget and hire a helicopter—you know, a Huey—to come with a sling. The point is, it's not a one-person job."

Bert looked up. "How do you know all this?" he asked.

I shrugged. "I read. Like Dave Gillette's book on *Seismosaurus*. Great descriptions of the art of fossil hunting. And I watch TV. PBS, the Discovery Channel, that kind of stuff. I'm a scientist, remember. Watching someone else do the work is how I relax."

Bert's shoulders lurched with a silent chuckle, and he chanced an unarmored look my way. "Okay, so your guy maybe hired some day labor when he had something heavy."

"Well, fine, except that usually you're out there with a team of grad students and informed citizens chipping away at the rock like rats at a wheel of cheese, because even a well-funded dig can't afford to pay for labor. And what's stranger yet is that he could even afford to dig himself. You're out there digging instead of working at some other job, for starters, and then there's all the equipment, and food and lodging—okay, some kind of tent—and flatbeds and Hueys don't come cheap. George Dishey couldn't afford to be a dilettante. He had at least one extra mouth to support, maybe more—did you find Nina?—and a house—did he own it?—and his colleagues didn't like his methods. A mite tough to get an NSF grant when you're considered a sloppy dude. So where's he getting his money?"

"NSF?"

"National Science Foundation."

Bert scribbled another note. "Anything else?"

"No. Or yeah. Dishey roomed with Dan Sherbrooke at Yale. Sherbrooke's the conference chair, and my registration packet says he's with the university here in Salt Lake. So Sherbrooke would be in a position to help Dishey, but if I read between the lines correctly, there was no love lost between the two of them. And Dishey was in the habit of letting on to people that he was with the university, which he was not."

"Such as to yourself?"

"Yeah, such as to suckers like myself. Go ahead, rub it in."

Bert scratched another note, tipped his head back, and offered the ceiling a ruminant grin. "Liars. I love liars."

"Yeah, they're a laugh a minute."

"Anything else?"

"There's something going on with the commercial collectors, what or whoever they are." I told him about the man who wouldn't talk to me, and the frightening man I had seen in his van.

He wrote another note. "Anything else?"

"Yeah. What happened to George Dishey that you guys are so jumpy?"

Bert's face went momentarily blank, then hardened slightly, as if he were slipping in and out of focus.

I said, "It was something gruesome, right?"

As Bert continued to stare at me, I felt a wave of nausea wash over me. He stared right into me, and I saw in his eyes the quick concentration of a man grabbing for an oar as he is washed overboard. In a flat tone, he said, "It was indeed gruesome," then looked back at his notes as if concealing a sense of personal insult and said again, "Anything else?"

"No. Uh. Well, I was thinking of heading up to the university here and seeing what I can see, but I've been given to understand that you turned in my car."

Bert kept writing. "That is a fact. If you want another car, you are free to hire one, but the one you had has gotten a little too well known around here. And you may go wherever you want around this fair city, little missy, but you might as well ride down West Temple on an elephant, for all the hope you have of blending in with the crowd. For my part, I am not in the business of assigning round-the-clock protection to murder suspects. Now, if Romeo here wants to take personal leave and drive you around in a private car, that's one thing, but as of right now, you are no longer getting free cab service from Salt Lake City's finest."

I stared at the top of Detective Bert's round head as he continued to concentrate on his notes. I would have risen to his last bit of bait if the lecturing patriarch act hadn't been so much easier to take than the grinning ghoul. "Fine," I said. "You got my luggage around here somewhere? I can find my own way out."

"Lover boy here will show you where your gear is. And remember, you are not yet free to leave the state of Utah.

Enjoy your visit and be sure to stay in touch," he said, giving me one last weird, toothy grin.

I headed down the hallway. Ray fell into step behind me. I noticed that he did not pull abreast. However garden-variety obnoxious Detective Bert's message had been to me, his message to Ray had been seething with threat. "Just show me where my bags are," I said flatly. "I'll get myself covered. Don't get me wrong—I really appreciate what you've done for me, but I'm not interested in getting you fired."

Ray said nothing. He led the way down a flight of stairs and up to the glassed-in watch station, where my bag waited forlornly. Before I could get to them, he picked them up.

"No," I said. "Let me carry them. I mean it. I don't want you getting shit on my behalf."

Ray stared into my eyes until I met his gaze. "Detective Bert may be a lot of things, but the arbiter of good manners, he is not," he said.

I sighed and said, "Lead the way."

Instead of heading for the main entrance, Ray headed back through the building, out a back door, and into the employee parking area. He marched up behind a late-model four-wheel-drive sport vehicle and unlocked the back. He put my bags in it. Then he turned back to me and handed me the keys. "Be back here at four-thirty," he said. "Please."

"This is your truck," I told him, too surprised to think of anything more intelligent to say.

He didn't even nod.

"I can't take your truck," I said.

"Well, I can't see you taking cabs all afternoon."

I sagged up against the truck. "Look, I'm grateful, really, but—" I stared at my feet. Fatigue had now culminated in a headache, a real corker. My thumb throbbed. I wanted to go home, I hurt, I needed to lie down, and I could make no sense of what was happening to me. Mr. Beautiful had just offered me the use of his personal vehicle, at probable risk of his job. People didn't do that sort of thing for me. Or at least not people I'd met only the day before, and certainly not men as handsome as Ray was.

"Just try to be careful," he said, and walked away. At the door back into the building, he paused for a moment, and, just as the evening before when he'd been about to climb into his car at the curb outside George Dishey's house, I saw his lips move silently for a moment. Then he slipped a key into the door and passed through it, snapping it shut behind him.

I snapped out of my stasis and chased after him. Tugged at the door. It was locked. I looked at the key chain in my hand. There was only one key on it, just the one for the vehicle. No house key I could match to the address on the registration papers that no doubt rested in the glove compartment, no key into the inner sanctum of the police station or into any other building to which he was privy. He was being generous, but not foolish.

I sighed again and walked back to the vehicle. It was a nice color and had the kind of metallic paint that shows dirt, but of course it was spotlessly clean. I sighted down along one side. Not a scratch or a ding, and perfectly waxed. If it had ever been off the pavement, I'd eat my hat.

I got in and thought about napping in the front seat and just waiting until he came off duty, but then I reconsidered, fired the ignition, and drove away. I was four blocks away, dialing in a nice distracting radio station, and making my first evasive turn to find out if I was being followed, when I realized another thing about Officer Thomas B. Raymond: he was not only generous and unfoolish but also unnervingly good at getting what he wanted from this little woman geologist.

11

FINDING A PARKING PLACE AT THE UNIVERSITY OF UTAH is an exercise in stealth. Parking is at such a premium that you must spot a pedestrian with car keys in his or her hands, follow her into a parking lot (sneering threateningly all the while at anyone else who appears to be thinking of challenging you for the spot about to be vacated), and then hover menacingly until the moment is ripe to roar triumphantly into the space. When I'd finally enjoyed my fifteen nanoseconds of parking fame, I jammed a handful of coins into the meter and headed for the building where the Department of Geology and Geophysics lurked.

The walk to the department was not as sanguine as the job of finding a parking space. In Ray's vehicle, I had been a hunter of parking spaces rather than the hunted, a coyote rather than a mouse. Inside that metal shell, I had felt a perhaps overestimated measure of safety, almost as if Ray had lent me his personal bulletproof vest, and the job of finding a parking space had been a welcome distraction from thinking about getting shot. But outside, I felt naked, and I had hundreds of yards to travel before I met the cover of the building. I stayed off the sidewalks, walked between tall trucks as much as possible, and tried to think about the scenery.

The University of Utah covers a huge, sprawling, incredibly tidy campus high up on a relict bench cut by—no kidding—the lapping waves of that ancient inland sea. Or at least that's what we geologists believe. We refer to the lake that cut those benches as Lake Bonneville, to distinguish it from the incredibly salty and shallow remnant that still lingers, known as Great Salt Lake.

Along with every other beginning geology student, I had been taught about Lake Bonneville in freshman geology. Imagine a body of water covering the whole northwestern third of the state, a closed drainage called the Great Basin. Imagine the water level eight hundred feet higher than it is today, an inundation that would cover Salt Lake City right up to the foothills of the Wasatch Range. Imagine waves lapping along the shoreline, slowly cutting a shallow beach ramp into everything they touch. The wave-cut benches of Lake Bonneville can be traced for miles along the foothills, now increasingly obscured by the encroachment of housing.

I gazed out across the desert basin alongside which the Mormon faithful had raised their earthly haven. Lake Bonneville's waves had last lapped its uppermost shoreline some fifteen thousand years ago, back in the last Ice Age, when glaciers were still grinding a formerly hilly Wisconsin into a flat plain. Fifteen thousand years. Fundamentalist Christian theology owned that the earth itself was only six thousand years old, the sum of the ages described in the Bible. To what biblical catastrophe would they ascribe the appearance and near disappearance of this titanic lake? Noah's Flood? A punitive act of a wrathful God, rather than the dazzling integrated process-and-response systematics of a God who had set in motion a set of physical laws that lavished the universe with spellbinding beauty? I smiled to myself, privately enjoying the range and variability of human beliefs. I believed that the earth was 4.5

billion years old, and the universe at least 12 billion. And what came before that?

Yes, there was the rub. Back then, an instant before that big bang that most scientists think marks the beginning of our universe, lies a question. In the power of that instant lies the awe that inspires most scientists' true religion, because at that nexus between physics and metaphysics, everything crosses back over from scientific measurement into a question so primal and unmeasurable that it is asked not just by scientists but by every religion, culture, and tribe that has ever existed: How did the universe come into being?

I stopped, hiding for a moment between two large trucks, and watched a jet rise from the airport over Great Salt Lake. The irony of man's imitation of a bird rising over an environment all but forbidden to man rubbed oddly at my mind. The world seemed to float on a thin layer of insensitivity. Cars rolled by, airplanes flew, and birds sang, oblivious to events that were driving me with such fear. I wanted to cry.

I recalled what some Hindus believe—that the great god Shiva is slowly blinking his eyes, and that each time He opens them, a universe is created, and that each time He closes them, it is destroyed. I had always liked that image, and indeed, in this day and place, when in any instant a man might again aim a rifle at my spine, pan to follow my strides across this parking lot, and squeeze its trigger, I found comfort in the thought that there might be something as magnificently much larger than myself as Shiva.

I forced myself to let my belly relax into a deeper breath. I closed my eyes and felt the solidity of the pavement beneath my feet and the rock beneath that, felt the density of the earth hugging me to it, felt it spinning on its axis, felt it hurtling through space in its trip around the sun, felt the solar system whirling through space as part of our galaxy, felt the flight of galaxies escaping from the site of that primal explosion we call the big bang. Always in times of greatest stress, if I contemplated the vastness of the universe, I did in some measure relax, comforted by the knowledge that I was but a small speck in creation after all, a mote in the enormity of God's eye, a fleeting arrangement of atoms that would in due time cycle back into the earth from which I had come and be reshuffled into something else, blended back into the grace of the natural world. In my very insignificance did I find my immortality.

This day, that sense of comfort would not come. Death was too near, throwing everything out of that precious sense of proportion. *I'm not afraid of being dead*, I told myself, *but I want to go naturally, and not in the fear of the moment.* Pushing myself to start walking toward the building again, I wondered if perhaps that is why our species prefers to live to a ripe old age; we instinctively seek to exit life through the process of entropy, at peace with our universe.

I stepped back out into the open, a scared rabbit coming out of the sage. With every step I took, horrid images of what George Dishey's corpse might look like flooded my head. George had not enjoyed the luck of his instincts. George now lay cold and empty in a morgue, grotesquely murdered. *His body must have been mutilated; otherwise, someone as cool-headed as Officer Raymond would not have been so jumpy. . . .*

I hurried across the rest of the lot and sprinted across the last street, wondering if George had once walked this pathway himself. What had he thought about death, if he thought about it at all? Certainly, Mormons believe in an afterlife, and a pretty rich one at that. Milk and honey on the other side, not to mention nine yards of goodies no one else has even thought of. What had Nina said? We'd all be together in the Celestial Kingdom? If I could believe the waifish Nina—and my gut told me I could—George had at least told her he was a Mormon. If I could believe George, he was not. At best, that reeked of poorly closeted existentialism, and at worst, of a Rasputin-like contempt for his fellow humans. So which was it?

I pushed open the door to the geology building, hoping I might just find a few answers there.

◇

THE SECRETARY IN the Geology Department regarded me from behind forearms raised and twisted together like a pair of caduceus snakes. "May I help you?" she asked.

"I hope so," I began carefully.

She inhaled noisily, exhaled, let her arms float to her side, and sat a moment with her eyes closed. After perhaps another five or six seconds, she opened them again and smiled perkily. "Desktop yoga," she said. "Really clears the blockages I get from typing and holding the phone against my ear."

"I see."

"Were you looking for someone?"

"Yes. You."

"Oh. How nice. And what might I do for you, then?" She had big clear blue eyes and short blond hair cut in a bob. She was a tall woman, about forty, and she had an extraordinary collection of farcically colored plastic dinosaurs and trolls, jauntily displayed all about her desk and on the bookshelves behind it.

"My name is Em Hansen. I'm a geologist, I'm from out of town, and I'm here for the paleontology conference up in—"

"Oh, yes, you're the one who was staying at George Dishey's house when he got killed."

"Ah, yes."

"You're kind of a celebrity," she said brightly.

"Wonderful."

"Wow. You were right there just before he left his body. Lots of flux. I'll bet that clogged your stomach meridian."

I decided to let that one pass, moving on instead to matters that had a vocabulary a hick from Wyoming could negotiate. "Okay, you know who I am. This is good. See, I'm kind of in a jam here, trying to find out what I can about the whole situation, because the police haven't a clue who did it, and I'm right there looking anomalous."

"You stick out like a sore thumb," she observed, staring pointedly at my bandaged hand.

"Ah, yes."

"I read a lot of detective novels." She picked up a paperback from her desk. "I read them in off times, like when there's nothing for me to do here. Like today. Everybody's up at the conference, you know. I mean Dan Sherbrooke, our paleontology guy. Margie Chan's here, but she's teaching a class, and she's not a paleontologist anyway. And there's—"

"Actually, I was hoping you could tell me something about George Dishey."

The secretary blinked her big blue eyes. "Like what?"

"Oh, anything. Like what the beef was between him and Dan Sherbrooke."

"Oh! Oh, you mean fun stuff like that. That's easy. Dan and George used to be roommates, you know, only they didn't wind up friends. Rivals, more like." The secretary popped the cap off a plastic water bottle shaped like a polar bear and took a swig. "Gotta stay hydrated. So yeah, they were rivals big-time. They're famous for it. I mean, if it was a private fight I'd stay out of it, because it's really not my business to talk about department people to total strangers like yourself—bad karma, you know, and a good way to get fired—but this fight is, like, *legendary*. I mean, they could make a *movie* about it."

I made myself at home, leaning one hip up against a counter laden with university catalogs and special program brochures. "What form did this rivalry take?"

"Oh, they were like always trying to top each other with their big dinosaur finds, stuff like that."

"They hated each other bad as Cope and Marsh," said someone behind me.

Now, there was an image. In the early years of paleontology, in an age when wealthy gentleman paleontologists had lounged in the laboratory and sent assistants out into the desert's heat to dynamite fossils out of the rock for them, Cope—a man of overweening ego—had made the mistake of bragging over his finds to his rival Marsh—a man of overweening competitiveness. Cope had been a Quaker, a man who believed in the truth so slavishly that he had been incapable of lying or of perceiving a liar. But Marsh's conscience had been built on different lines. He was a crafty old shit who bought off Cope's field operatives, stealing Cope's finds right out from under him. Cope took the competition past the grave, willing his skull to science, so that the volume of his brain could be posthumously measured against Marsh's. Marsh had laughed at him even there, eschewing this final challenge, but Cope's skull has remained in a museum collection as a type specimen of the human species.

I spun around to see who had spoken. A little man with a badly trimmed mustache stood behind me. He wore army-surplus lace-up boots and had a sagging gut that pushed a plain polyester shirt out over a cheap metal belt buckle that read TRUCKER.

The phone on the secretary's desk rang and she said, "Oh! Gotta go!" and answered it, leaving me to talk to the man with the mustache.

"I'm Lew," he said.

"Em Hansen."

"I know. I been listening." He cocked his head to one side, appraising me. "You want to know what the dirt was between

Sherbrooke and Dishey? Come with me. All it'll cost you is whatever dirt you can tell me."

I scurried after him down the hallway, casting a quick wave to the department secretary, who was now cheerfully informing the caller that she was sure he could retake the course he'd bombed the previous semester if he really insisted, but that of course he'd have to pay for it again. Lew led me on a merry trot along a hallway, down two flights of stairs, out across a parking lot, and down across a broad tree-lined green toward a large building that announced itself as the Utah Museum of Natural History.

As I hurried along behind Lew, I tried to figure out who he was. He had the look and smell of a department fixture, one of those guys who's been around so long that he's ossified in place and no one can figure out how to fire him. His posture was both arrogant and sunken, giving him that air of absolute security cut crosswise with a hangdog sense of fatalistic depression, but the huge wad of keys swinging from the metal clip on his belt argued against professorship.

"Do you teach here?" I asked, diplomatically shooting high.

"Me? No, they don't pay me well enough for that kind of stuff."

"Department tech?"

"You got it. I'm the guy that keeps the big dogs in line."

I smiled, certain I had found the perfect informant. There is nothing like a long-suffering underling to call it like he sees it. Information is power, and all that. I had only to watch for gratuitous fabrications, divide the dirt left over by two, and adjust a little for redeeming qualities he would fail to perceive in others.

Lew led me into the museum, signed me in at the desk— "Security," he said importantly—then took me down a flight of stairs and through a heavy door into the basement. He shuffled a ways down a hallway and approached a door, whiffled through his access-is-power array of keys, and chose one. Applied it to the lock. Swore underneath his breath. Chose another key. Succeeded in opening the door. Waved me into the room.

I found myself in a tight, no-frills laboratory littered with workbenches, peculiar tools, and wide metal storage shelves. Specimen storage was instantly recognizable even in the dim light that filtered down from the basement window high on the far wall. I could see the dark hulks of very old bones peeking out at me, big bones, bones that could only have belonged to something as large as a major dinosaur. I qualify that because not all dinosaurs were large. Some were as small as chickens. But Dan Sherbrooke was definitely a big-bone kind of guy.

Lew flipped on the banks of fluorescent lights, bathing the room in cold illumination. It was a homey, disarrayed room, coated with pale dust, sort of like having the backyard in your basement. The dust clearly stemmed from the process of picking plaster jackets and rock matrix off of fossils. And matrix picking there was, all up and down the heavy tables that commanded the center of the room, an astounding array of huge femurs and colossal vertebrae, each in a state of unearthing. The delicate tools of the operation lay all about, as did the crumbling wreckage of excavated rock. "There," Lew said, sweeping a hand across the scene. "That's what the fight's about."

The door to the lab opened behind us and I heard someone come in. A slight young man hurried past us, hunched painfully at the chest. I recognized him from the conference: he was Vance, the small weaselly fellow I had first seen nattering at Dan Sherbrooke about a problem with the poster tent and had last seen hissing to me about commercial collectors. Without making eye contact with either of us, he sat down at the table, switched on an exhaust fan, bent over a bone, and set furiously to work cleaning matrix off of it with a dental drill.

"What am I looking at here?" I asked, awed by the size of the bones before me.

"*Allosaurus fragilis,*" Vance said without looking up. "About the biggest, fastest predatory dinosaur on record."

"Bigger than *Tyrannosaurus rex?*" I asked.

Vance grunted disdainfully. "*T. rex* was bigger, sure, but he was a wanna-be. A scavenger. Or are you one of those Bakker fans?"

I tried to figure out how old Vance was, to sort him into *S,* for Dan's student, or *C,* for colleague. His skin was already creased, but it looked to me like sun damage and there was no sag under the chin or fold around the mouth. I guessed that he was somewhere in his twenties. He had wispy mustaches the color of butter and thin, unkempt hair pulled back into a ponytail. He wore the same wire-rimmed glasses, white T-shirt, and sagging pants I'd first seen him in at the conference—or another set just like them—like he hadn't changed clothes in two days, but the brand names and style were au courant. *I,* for impecunious, not *E,* for eccentric. That and the youth argued for *S,* for student.

As I watched him scratch away at the fossil in front of him, I contemplated the fierceness of his concentration. He went at his work with a fervor that held the twitchy overtones of barely contained anger. I had seen the type before. As a student, he was newly converted to the manias of the profession, hell-bent on advancing the science, and certain everyone but himself was a fool. I had seen him now three times, and had begun to feel a certain antagonistic affection for him. He was, after all, the only person at the conference who had spoken to me without seeming as if there was something he was either wanting from me or trying to keep from me.

"I've heard about the controversy surrounding *T. rex,*" I said. In dinosaur land, *T. rex* had the biggest of the two-legged meat-eating big. The leaf-eating sauropods—those big long-necked dinos that walked on all fours like *Brontosaurus* and *Seismosaurus*—were infinitely larger yet, but at six tons and the height of a two-story building, *Tyrannosaurus* was no slouch. But it was the interpretation of the dinosaur's feeding strategy that was in question. Was he really a king, or just an opportunist?

Vance paused to proselytize. He turned toward me but stared at the floor while he made short chopping gestures designed to convey the intensity of his message: "They named it *T. rex* because its six-inch-long fangs were so fucking big: *Tyrannosaurus rex,* the tyrant lizard king. Everybody's hung up on *big*. That's bullshit!"

I smiled at this petite man who was worried about size. He was right: we are a culture devoted to such images—to biggests, longests, tallests, firsts, and fiercests. "But once that name was dealt out, it stuck," I said. "I love watching those debates on PBS specials. In this corner, we have Bob Bakker, the guy with all the hair and the funny straw hat, and he thinks *T. rex* was the mighty hunter who chased his prey at high speed, grasped it by the spine, and throttled it—like a Russian wolfhound or something. In the other corner, we have Jack Horner speaking to us phlegmatically from some dig site in Montana, and *he* thinks *T. rex* was just a scavenger who kind of lumbered onto the scene after dinner had begun to grow ripe, days after it had died of natural causes. What's the latest evidence?" I asked.

"The bones tell the story," Vance answered without looking up. "You do a cast of the inside of the skull and what do you get? A big optical lobe, like you'd need for a visual hunter like a hawk or an eagle? No. You get a big olfactory lobe, just like a vulture." He emphasized his statement with a decisive slash with his dental tool.

"But dinosaurs weren't birds," I said.

Lew snorted contemptuously.

Vance said, "Nope, they weren't birds, just bird great-granddaddies."

"And great-grandmommies?" I asked.

Lew snorted again, stuck his thumbs into his belt loops, and slouched.

Vance flinched each time Lew snorted. Studiously ignoring the lounging department tech, Vance flipped his glasses up onto his forehead and stared at a flaw in his fossil from only millimeters away. "*What*ever," he muttered, "but also, the legs aren't for running. The length and cross-sectional area of the femur is all wrong. And I know, I *know* what Bakker says about the size of the Achilles tendon and the cnemial crests on the tibia, but that's all *qualitative* analysis, without a shred of *quantitative*."

"Oh." He was beginning to lose me. "You've compared their proportions to those of modern animals."

Vance sighed with exasperation. "He'd be *unstable* at high speeds, even if he could reach them instantaneously, and he'd fall over and break something under the weight of his own fall!"

"You mean an animal can exist that could crush itself by its own weight? That seems against nature."

"*Elephants*," Vance said, brushing fiercely at a bit of plaster dust with a whisk broom. "You sit an *elephant* down with a dart so you can tag him, you've got to get him up fast, before he suffocates."

"Oh. But dinosaurs weren't mammals. They were reptiles. You can't compare them straight across."

"*Avian*," he corrected.

Avian, similar to birds. Interesting, but I needed to redirect the conversation to the fight between Dan Sherbrooke and George Dishey, not Cope and Marsh or Horner and Bakker. "So Dan has an *Allosaurus* here."

"This is *one* of Dan's allosaurids. *One* of them. *Dan* at least has the wit to compare *individuals* before he draws conclusions about a whole *species*."

Here I could follow him. Paleontologists like to compare as many examples of a species as they can before publishing on it. That way, they are better able to discuss the range of characteristics within the group, rather than getting caught describing a genetic freak or a malformity as the norm. "What did George Dishey go after?"

"About anything he could find lying around."

"Kind of like a vulture?"

Vance made a horizontal slicing motion with one hand. "*Exactly*. That's our George. Fucking roadkill pimp."

"Roadkill?"

Lew muttered, "It's what you call a poorly preserved fossil."

I thought for a while. Surely there was no way for paleontologists to dictate what they were going to find. They were the ultimate scavengers, opportunistic hunter-gatherers who just went after whatever the gods of erosion happened to leave at the surface. That was the big gag about bone hunting: A perfect skeleton could lie a millimeter beneath the surface and a paleontologist could walk right over it and never know it was there. So it was not really paleontologists who found fossils; it was rain and wind and ice, those busy little forces of weather that dig constantly at the landscape all around us. "So, Vance," I said, "you don't think much of Dr. Dishey's work."

"What's there to like? He published gray literature, fucking puff pieces in *Ladies' Home Journal*. I'd have liked to have seen him go up against a jury of his so-called peers just *once!*"

I considered asking Vance what George Dishey had done to him to get him so pissed. But just then, Vance slammed down his dental pick. "I mean, I don't get why you're sounding so supportive of him. You were his last conquest! Doesn't that sting just a little?"

I thought long and hard before answering. I was embarrassed, yes, but not as much by the appearance that I was George's last bimbo as by the fact that I'd bought one of his lies. I cared about trusting myself, and being taken in by George's lies had shaken my self-security. Tit for tat, I presented about the nastiest comeback I could think of, as much to see what would happen as to get my licks in: "Why, are you jealous?"

Vance's eyes shrank into slits. "*I* am not a *groupie,*" he sneered. "I do real work. I collect real data. I form hypotheses and have the balls to present them to my colleagues, laying my ideas open to scrutiny, asking that they be supported or disproven. *That* is science. *George* wrote popular jerk-off articles that the boys and girls *swooned* over. I mean, shit; *you* saw him!"

"Saw him what?"

"At the conventions. He'd walk around in his paleontologist suit—we wear T-shirts, he's got to wear a baggier one; we wear our hair long, he's got to wear his longer, a mockery of the rest of us—waving that fucking brass jaw of his! Like he was *trolling* for *groupies!*"

Vance's venom was so caustic that it took me a moment to recall that he was talking about a man two decades or more his elder. I smiled. George Dishey had probably been growing long hair and whiskers while Vance was still in diapers.

I indulged myself in an urge to touch the wide end of the four-foot-long femur at which Vance was picking. It was rough and cold. "I can't for a moment believe that personal style has anything to do with this. So it's really something else, isn't it? Spell it out to me, Vance. What was George up to that pissed everybody off so much?"

The young man spun around in his chair and faced me, his hands balled up into fists. His face had turned so red that I was afraid it might explode. Through his tiny yellow teeth, he hissed, "He sold bones!"

"He what?"

"*Sold* 'em. Went out and dug them up just to *sell* 'em. Regular *whore!*"

"Is that what you meant by a 'commercial collector'?"

Vance's face darkened to almost purple. "That's too kind a term for George Dishey." Vance's hands began to tremble. "Oh, sure, there are amateurs out there who'll sell a find to a rock shop, and there are even pros who have a regular business doing that kind of supply. But they aren't *Ph.D.'s.* George *was.* That's *prostitution!*" Having said this, Vance jumped up from his chair and raced out of the laboratory just as abruptly as he had entered it.

"Oh," I said. But I didn't understand, not really.

◆

I WAS QUIET for a moment, waiting for the proverbial dust to settle on the scene. Then I asked Lew, "Is there something I'm missing?"

Lew turned his hands outward. "Hey, I'm just a tech."

"Oh, come on, Lew, you brought me over here to show me something."

Lew stared at the floor, deciding how much more he was going to tell me. "Let's just say that grad students get a little . . . unbalanced after a while. Me, I go home at night and have a beer, watch a little TV, and life doesn't get so serious. But these students," he said, his voice taking on a heavy note of insinuation, "they bust their humps for wonderful old Dan or some other blowhard like him, living in some lousy tent eating beans, trying to dig up something good enough to write their dissertation on. And you know there's no job waiting for them. Kind of makes you wonder if they're quite right in the head, don't it?"

"You're saying Vance is a little overwrought."

"Now you're talking." Lew started switching off lights.

"Gotta save energy," he mumbled, as we left the room.

I thought, *So you think Vance killed George. Or you'd like me to think he did. Why?*

"Now it's your turn," he said.

"What do you mean?"

"You want anything else from me, you tell me what you got on Dishey first." He observed me through narrowed eyes, a parody of the smart guy extracting information from the stooge, or was he hiding a deeper intelligence than he let on?

I thought for a while. Should I tell him about the man who had ransacked George's house, or just give him the bare essentials about the sequence of the phone call and George's abrupt early-morning departure? "I don't know much," I said.

Lew grew truculent. "Sure you do." He looked insulted.

"Well, like I told the police, George left early yesterday morning, before it was light out. Someone phoned. He went. Next I know, the police have found his body."

"Where?"

"They won't tell me."

"How'd they kill him?"

"They won't tell me that, either." Shifting the interrogation back to him, I said, "How well did you know George?"

He lifted his shoulders a half inch and dropped them again. "Not well. He was around."

"Who'd he hang out with? He have any friends?"

Another shoulder twitch. "Some of his old army buddies. Okay bunch."

"Like maybe a helicopter pilot or two."

"Maybe." Lew's eyes narrowed and opened again, as if he was thinking, or trying to cover his thoughts.

"You know a guy he hung out with who maybe had high cheekbones and a long beard like the pictures of Moses?"

Lew's lower jaw shifted forward a fraction of an inch. After a moment, he said, "No."

He's covering something. "He have a wife?"

Lew considered. "Don't think so."

"So you didn't know him that well."

He shrugged again. I was treading on thin ice: It would not do to push a knowledge broker too far off the edge of what he knew. He might start making things up just to sound important.

I said, "He like little girls, maybe?"

Lew smirked. This was clearly a new idea to him, and he liked it.

With disgust, I said, "Well then, that's all I know. Show me more about collecting, would you?"

One more shrug. "Okay. I'll take you to the collections room." He led me down a short hallway and up a ramp to another room. This one was much larger, both wider and longer, and it appeared to turn a corner at the far end. The underground guts of the building showed—supports and large pipes and conduits running this way and that—but fitted in around these necessities, packed floor to ceiling, were specimen storage cabinets, hundreds of them. Specimens of classic fossils winked out at me from every corner: mastodon skulls from the Pleistocene, turtle shells from the Cretaceous, dinosaur bones by the bucketload. The sight was overwhelming.

As we entered the space, a slender woman stood up from a table and met us. She fixed dark, richly luminous eyes on me and smiled. "Hi, are you here from the conference?"

"Yes," I said. "I'm Em Hansen." I pulled my name badge out of my pocket to show her.

She extended a delicate hand. "Jane Whitney. I'm the museum's paleontology collection manager. Sign in here. What would you like to see?"

I looked around the immediate area. A man sat at a wide table, scrutinizing a fossil turtle. Catacombs led off deeper into the basement, all lined with more drawers of specimens.

Lew spoke. "Em here's just trying to get a feeling for things. She's trying to figure out what all the shouting's about."

"Um, yes," I said. "I'm a stratigrapher, not a paleontologist. But I'm trying to learn more about fossil collections and collecting. I've been in a lot of museums, but I'd never dreamed that there was so much in storage beyond what the public sees."

"Oh, yes," Jane replied. "In fact, there are some museums that have no public displays."

"Why?"

"They're purely working collections."

"But why not share them with the public?"

"No money. Not enough money or manpower to prepare the specimens for display. Look here," she said, pointing at a large block of rock still swathed in its protective plaster jacket. "This shouldn't even be in here. The dust off the plaster is a problem. But we had no place else to put it. This is the pelvis and partial spine of *Allosaurus*. It's an important find because it was partially articulated. It will tell us lots about how the bones set together in life. That is, when we find time to train a volunteer to prepare it. There's no way we could afford paid preparators for all of these."

"But once you've prepared it, will it go on display?"

"Probably not. The public doesn't want to see just the pelvis and spine. Now if it was just the skull, that would be a different matter."

"Oh."

"Most just don't know enough biology to be interested in only the pelvis and spine, unless it's really huge, or the only part of that particular creature on record."

I thought of what Vance had said about size and smiled ruefully. "I understand that much of your field collecting is done with volunteers, too. I'm wondering how that works."

Jane's warm eyes grew even warmer. "To tell you the truth,

I sometimes wonder myself how we get them interested. After all, you're out there in the blazing sun with gnats crawling into your ears and warm beer and bad spaghetti for dinner, dry camping, with no place to wash, but you rue the day you've got to go back to town." She shook her head, smiling at the memory.

"Why?"

"Because when you find something, it's better than any feeling you can imagine."

The joy of discovery. Every geologist, no matter what stripe, understood that. "You just want to know a little bit more," I said.

"Always. We scratch away for every little clue we can get that tells us something about how these animals lived. Not just how big they were, or how they stood or swam or crawled, but how they *lived*." She laughed, leading us down an aisle into the catacombs, where she turned her palm up toward a case filled with huge teeth and jaws. "Take the dinosaurs, for instance. Everybody gets so het up about what killed them, what made them go extinct." She pulled out a drawer. "An asteroid, some people say. Climate change. Mammals eating their eggs. You know what grabs me? Not how they died, but how long they *lived*." She selected a jawbone twice the length of my hand and laid it tenderly across my palm. "Feel the serrations along the edge? *Allosaurus*. Each tooth is curved back toward the throat. She bites you, you're caught. Notice how it's actually two bones, hinged in the middle. Most carnivorous dinosaurs had that. It gave the jaw flexibility, so it could hold on to an animal that was thrashing."

I held the jawbone with care. "It looks like the bronze one George Dishey had, only smaller."

"Yes. This one's from a juvenile."

As I goggled at the ferocious biting equipment that rested on my hand, marveling that it had belonged to a child, Jane pulled out other drawers, zeroing in on favorite specimens. "The dinosaurs were around for a hundred and eighty million years, lived on every continent on the earth. They were more diverse and advanced than you'd imagine, and I'll bet we haven't even found examples of whole groups."

"Why not?"

"Some of their ecological niches would not have been preserved, and if the sediments they died in weren't preserved, then *they* weren't preserved. Like any alpine species."

I had never thought about the possibility of alpine dinosaurs, but it was true—mountain habitats were not preserved in the rock record. It was the plains that were preserved, the areas where sediments eroded from the mountains were deposited by the action of wind and water. The bones of any animal that died in the mountains would be ground to dust as they were borne downhill. "But alpine dinosaurs? Really?"

"There are alpine birds. Ptarmigans. They grow white feathers in the winter, so they can hide in the snow. But remember also that the global climate was much warmer during the Mesozoic, so we aren't necessarily talking about snow. And they could have migrated up and down the mountains, like many modern mammals, such as sheep and deer. We know they lived in the Arctic regions, because we find their bones there. So they must have migrated long distances, just to follow the vegetation. Like elk."

"Elk," I echoed. I imagined Jackson Hole, Wyoming, with hadrosaurs grazing by the lakes instead of elk. "Herds."

"Yes. And they cared for their young, some of them. Adapted like crazy." She stopped by a drawer, pulled it out, and handed me two short black bones. "Metatarsal bones— the foot. The same bone from two different allosaurids. See how this one is smooth on the end and this one rough? Disease."

"Arthritis?" I asked, amazed. It had never occurred to me that dinosaurs might ache like humans do.

"Not that, but something like it. Here's a rib that broke and healed crookedly. See the extra bone that built up around the injury? There are people who study just the diseases evident in museum collections. Dinosaurs were wonderful," she continued, replacing each bone and drawing out others for me to examine. "They evolved to fill every major niche of the terrestrial ecosystem, even flight. And you and I, our kind have been lucky to walk upright for three million." She shook her head slowly. "And it doesn't look like it's going to take an asteroid to kill *us*."

"Yeah," said Lew. "We'll just kill each other."

My shoulders tensed. For a moment, I had relaxed into the pleasures of learning. Suddenly, I was back on a murder case, watching my back.

Jane said, "Yes, we do have our problems, don't we?" She considered the rough-ended bone in her hand. "Disease." She placed it back in its place in the drawer. "Pollution. Ignorance. Greed."

Taking care to keep my voice calm, I said, "Tell me about the greed."

Lew spoke. "Yeah, that's where George Dishey comes in. Him and Sherbrooke always had to one-up each other."

Jane said, "Heavens, I heard that George died! Isn't that terrible? Dan must be beside himself. They were roommates at Yale, weren't they?"

Lew said, "Yeah. But Sherbrooke came from money; Dishey came from a blue-collar background, like myself." He looked at me through narrowed eyes.

Jane said, "Oh, you hear a lot of gossip about those two, but you shouldn't take it seriously."

"Try me," I urged.

Jane unlocked a metal case, and I was immediately engulfed in the reek of crude oil. She pulled out a skull that looked new, save for a thin coating of tar. "Know what this is?"

"Wolf?"

"Exactly. Dire wolf, La Brea tar pits, Pleistocene. Looks like new, huh? That's because it is, geologically speaking. It isn't even mineralogically altered."

"Neat. But what about Dan and George?"

"Oh, Dan got a grant; George had to get a better grant. George found a fossil; Dan had to find a better one. Dan got a girl; George had to . . . well, you get the picture. Dan published on some little anatomical thing he'd figured out, George went into print just to say Dan was full of it. Or he'd find out what Dan had discovered and publish something about it in the popular press before Dan would dare to. It's not a nice story. They really both ought to be embarrassed. Well, at least Dan might still be."

"But Dan won. He got the jobs, the status within the society. How'd that happen?"

Jane closed the tar pit case and leaned against it. "I shouldn't be talking about this."

"Why? It seems a lot of people don't want to talk about this."

"It's a small community. You don't badmouth people."

Lew snorted.

I said, "We're talking about a murder case."

Lew snorted again. He was beginning to remind me of a pet pig a high school friend of mine once kept.

"Vance said George sold bones," I said. "That sounded like a big deal. Why?"

"Look at it this way," Jane said. "You can't get the information you need from a bone you buy at a shop; it's too far removed from its context. You need the bone in place, lying relative to other fossils." She gestured with her hands, staring down into a dig site she saw laid out before her in her mind's eye. "You need the reference of the surrounding rock outcrop, and all those other little clues that tell you how it lived, how it died, how it got buried, all that. And you need all that information with the stratigraphic sequence above and below, so you can know how old it is relative to other similar specimens and what environmental pressures it was encountering, so we can make interpretations regarding evolutionary pathways. Without all that, it's just a bone."

"So you're saying you need the evidence from the rock around the fossil to fully understand it."

"Yes. How old is it? What else was living at the time? Was it buried in a lake? A river? What kind of river? A perennial stream that flowed through a desert?" Jane's hands began to move with the pictures that were emerging in her head, her right hand fluttering like wind on the water, her left hand describing the river's bend. "Did that mean the animals were crowding together at a water hole, fighting for resources? Was the herd on the decline?"

I was ranch born and bred. Herds I understood. Herds crowding together at the watering hole in a semiarid climate, with coyotes on the hunt. That was the life I had lived as a kid in Wyoming. Cows miring in quicksand, falling over into the water, drowning, making a nice feast for the coyotes. "But dinosaurs aren't cows," I said, forgetting to fill in the leap that connected my thoughts.

Jane said, "No, they weren't. The cows came later, much later."

"I have a hard time imagining them moving in herds."

"Some species did; you find them in mass burial. Others, no; you only find them alone. Just like us mammals. Or modern birds. Some flocked; some hunted or browsed alone. Some ate seeds and leaves; others went for meat. Some apparently laid their eggs in rookeries and cared for their young. They were a great bunch of animals."

"I still have a hard time featuring them. I mean, giant reptiles filling the world?"

Jane led onward to another case, obviously relieved to be back on the subject of something dead a little longer than twenty-four hours. "Like I told you, they weren't just a bunch of big dumb reptiles. Think of them as more like birds. You compare them to lizards, like their name suggests, and it doesn't work as well. That was the mistake everybody made the first couple hundred years we looked at these bones: We thought they were lizards. Terrible lizards. Dinosaurs. That's what the name means. Think of them as lizards and it's hard to imagine a herd of them gathering by a water hole to drink, but think of them as birds and all of a sudden we can see them moving in flocks, gathering for the protection of numbers, feeding together, nesting together."

"Like flamingos, or pelicans."

"Sure. Lovely, elegant things, moving as gracefully as birds. The early paleontologists mounted *T. rex* standing upright, dragging his tail, but they had to break its tail to do that, mount it dislocated—no kidding—and also dislocate its back, and neck. All because they looked at those big bones and thought heavy and thought lizard and assumed it'd have to drag its tail even to walk. But think of their spines as balance beams. Think bird. Think light for their size. The bones weren't always made of rock."

"So now they mount them head forward and tail out in back," I said.

"Yeah," said Lew. "Or go like Bakker and have them rearing up and dancing."

"You don't think they did that?" Jane asked, shooting him an impudent smile.

"What do I know?" Lew joked. "I'm only a tech."

Jane curled up a delicate hand and gave Lew a playful punch on the shoulder. "Yes, you're a tech, but you have a feeling for them, Lew. You're good. You've worked with Dan for years. You've been in the field with him half a dozen times."

Lew's face clouded. "Yeah. I've worked out there alongside Dan for years, carrying his damned equipment, busting my back in those pits, getting heatstroke. Vance thinks he's just invented suffering for science, but I've been at it since before he was born."

I looked at Lew more closely, reappraising him. Had he been jealous of Vance's closeness with his professor? Had he brought me here so I'd suspect Vance of murder? Or did he feel sorriest for himself, and want to nurse a grudge against Dan?

Lew hung his head. "Then Dishey has to go and make it all a contest. He yanked the damned things out of the ground as fast as he could, just to make his name big, just to make a buck, just to beat Dan."

I watched the emotions that flickered across Lew's face. Much as his tone and gestures spoke of an almost morose dedication to Sherbrooke's interests, the glint in his eyes suggested a crafty consciousness of the theatrical effect he thought he was projecting.

12

As I followed Lew back up across the university campus, I peppered him with more questions, and he alternately shrugged his shoulders and made grunting noises. As we reached a fork in our paths, I said, "Oh, come on, Lew, you have something else you want to tell me, so why don't you just spill it?"

Lew looked almost miffed. Then he said, "You want to know more about Dan and George, you come on Dan's field trip tomorrow."

It was the second time that day I'd heard that line. I'm slow, but I do catch on. "Okay, sign me up."

He nodded. "The buses leave Snowbird at seven A.M.," he said.

Snowbird. I had a feeling that I wasn't going back to Snowbird, not if Officer Raymond and the Salt Lake City police force had their way. I figured that they were right to be concerned. If I embarked at the conference, who knew who might be watching me get on that bus? And I didn't like what this Lew was selling, either, but I'd have to take the chance that he was greedy enough about his infernal information mongering that he'd keep quiet that I was going along on the trip, if indeed he had anyone dangerous to tell. "Any way I can catch up with the game at the destination?" I asked.

"No way. The location's a big secret."

"Why?"

"Poachers."

"Oh." I let that go for the time being. "Anywhere else I can get on?"

Lew scratched his head. "I guess you could slip on at the Salt Palace. We're making a detour past there to pick up some journalists about seven-thirty. Our Dan's got to have the camera on him."

"I noticed that about him," I said. "Like today at the conference. A bunch of fundamentalists started picketing, and I'd swear Dan was more worried about upstaging them than disputing their ideas."

Lew smirked. "Ol' Dan scored big this time. They're going to do a press conference on the evening news. That's like hitting the jackpot for our Dan."

"A press conference? For a protest rally?"

"Sort of. That way he can show off Vance's work like it's his own." He snorted.

"Oh. Is that why Vance was so wound up?"

"Nah, Vance is always that wound up. He's been working all summer on this location we're going to tomorrow. You'll see. His doctoral stuff is riding on it, but Dan wouldn't let him remove anything from the site before the conference guys got a look at it."

"What's the problem with waiting?" I asked.

"Poachers," Lew said again, as we parted near the walkway back to the Geology Department. "Always we got to watch out for them damned poachers."

"You mean like people stealing game? Why? Do they get trigger-happy or something?"

Lew shook his head. "Naw, I'm talking about the guys who like to remove your fossils for you after you've gone to the trouble to find them and dig them out and get them ready to pop."

"People do that?" I asked, appalled. It didn't seem quite sporting to swipe someone else's find.

Lew shook his head contemptuously, like I was hopelessly naïve.

"That's disgusting!"

"Welcome to the big bad world."

I couldn't keep up with his venom. "So has Vance found something that's going to rock the scientific world?" *That would have complicated things,* I thought. *If George kept stealing his thunder, Dan might have felt moved to go to extreme lengths to stop him from doing it again. . . .*

"I'm sworn to secrecy. You don't get on Dan's digs unless you toe that line."

"I hear that no one knew where George was digging, either."

"Ha," said Lew. "At least Dan eventually lets the world know where the fossils came from. Dishey probably *dreamed* the bones he wrote about." He turned his back and began to shamble away up the walk toward the geology building.

"Wait!" I called after him. "Who are these poachers you keep talking about?"

Lew turned around, walking backward, still moving. He shrugged his shoulders. "Ask the commercial guys."

I had about had my fill of people baiting me toward asking a question, then referring me to somebody else when I asked it. "Explain this to me, damn it! Who are these people?"

Lew turned his back to me again and kept on walking up the hill. "Who knows? Maybe it's somebody local, maybe it's not."

He was waffling, and waffling meant he knew nothing more. At his level of the professional food chain, knowledge is power, and he didn't want the world to see his powerlessness. For the time being, I gave up.

◇

BACK AT THE police station, I was in for a surprise.

"We found Nina," Ray said as he turned down a hallway. He presumed I would follow him. He was right.

"Where?" I asked, dumbfounded. "When?"

Ray led me into a dark room. I'd been in rooms like this before, in the Denver police station. It was full of electronic recording equipment and had a window made of one-way glass, so that interviews in the next room could be watched and recorded without the subject's awareness. When we had arranged ourselves in front of the glass, Ray finally answered my questions. Sort of. I mean, decency dictated that Ray had to say something. Nina looked like hell. Her appearance hit me like a blow.

"She was in the crawl space underneath a neighbor's porch," he said.

She was filthy from head to toe, her pale blond hair dingy with dirt and cobwebs. Her clothes were gray. I couldn't see her face, because she had pulled herself up into a tight ball, hugging her slender knees to her chest as she scrupulously held the hem of her skirt down to her ankles with one hand. Her knuckles were white. A female detective sat in the room with her, going over her notes, reading them aloud in a drab monotone. "Suspect was asked her name. Suspect did not answer. Suspect was asked to state her residence. Suspect did not answer. Suspect—"

"Get her out of there!" I said.

"Want to help?" asked a voice behind me.

I turned. It was Detective Bert. Two other men stood beside him. I had been so shocked by Nina's appearance that I hadn't heard them enter the room. One was a kind of nondescript middle-aged white guy and the other I had seen before. He was Tom Latimer, the dark-eyed guy with the salt-and-pepper crew cut who had tried to strike up a conversation with me at the conference.—the guy who had told me he was an illustrator of children's books. Just as I had thought, the police had positioned plainclothes cops up in Snowbird to work the crowd.

I fought to control my anger—anger at the police for not believing my innocence, anger at these detectives for incarcerating pathetic little Nina, anger at Bert for being the shithead he was, and anger at Ray for reasons I didn't care to name. To Bert, I said, "Yeah. Sure. You got some other damn thing you want out of me, you just name it. Just get that girl out of that room!"

"We can't hold her much longer anyway," the nondescript man said calmly. "We were just wondering if you'd like to talk to her. Maybe she'd tell you something. What you see in there is all we've got. She has no ID Her clothes are even handmade. No labels."

I was ready to explode. The bland tone of this man's voice somehow made me even madder than Bert's usual insinuating, snide notes. "How long has she been in there?" I demanded.

No one said anything, which meant she'd been in there for quite a while. "What are the rules for retaining citizens without a warrant?"

No one answered.

I spoke again. "Okay, so you want me to go in there and get her to talk, have a real girl-to-girl tête-à-tête and get her to spill her guts. Lovely."

The nondescript man nodded. "Yes, we do. We were hoping you'd like to help us with this; get this whole George Dishey situation buttoned down." Bland, bland, bland—like let's get this done so we can all go home a bit early.

I fantasized that if I'd had a bat in my hands just then, I would have started swinging. I wanted to hit someone real bad, and not just out of righteousness. I wanted to get even with them for dropping me into this hall of mirrors just as surely as they had dropped in Nina Dishey. We were just two bugs being examined under glass.

But the true horror was that I wanted to know what Nina had to tell just as much as they did. Between my teeth, I said, "Let me in."

◆

NINA DID NOT look up when I entered the room. She just sat there, unmoving, as if she were made of stone.

I turned to the woman detective and said, "Could you leave us, please?"

She did.

I pulled a chair away from the table and sat down.

Nina was so still that she did not appear to be breathing. I began to think she was some sort of three-dimensional photograph.

I sat and thought for a while about what I was going to say, and what I was going to ask. Finally, I said, "Nina, my name is Em Hansen. You mistook me the other day for someone named Heddie. I'm sorry I didn't straighten out that misunderstanding then. I'm just going to talk for a while, and maybe you'll have something you'll want to say and maybe you won't. Be assured that whatever you say or do is being observed, and not just by me. I've sent the woman out of the room, but at least four men are standing on the other side of that mirror, watching, and they can hear everything we say in here. We're also being filmed and our voices are being recorded. It's what police do."

Nina's hands clenched her leg and hem, pulling the skirt even more tightly across her. I saw that the side seam had been hand-stitched with tiny, if somewhat irregular, stitches.

I took a breath and continued. "I am not with the police. I

am a geologist, like George. I had just arrived in Salt Lake City the night I met him. I am here for a conference he was going to attend. I guess they've told you by now that George is dead."

As I said this last, Nina took one long, shaky breath.

I cleared my throat and spoke again. "So they've asked me to talk to you and they hope you'll say something to me. You surely don't have to say a word. I'm going to tell you something I don't like about myself, and it's this: I don't necessarily have your best interest at heart. I'm in here because they don't know who killed George and so they may as well think I did it. Until we find out who killed him, I'm on the hook, just because it looks suspicious that I was at his house the night before he died. And so you don't have the anxiety of worrying about what I was doing with your husband alone in that house; I was there as a guest of the conference and nothing more. I had never met George before. Our acquaintance was strictly professional.

"Now about you," I continued. "You told me you're his wife, and I believe you. They've been bugging you to tell how that can be when you didn't live in his house, haven't they?"

Nina did not respond to my question.

"Yeah," I said, "so they've had you in here awhile, and that's just awful. Have they given you anything to eat?"

Nina still did not answer me. I was beginning to wonder if she was in an ordinary state of consciousness.

I buried my face in my hands. I said, "I bet I'm beginning to sound like them. First they try food and then they try veiled threats. Who knows what other little intimidations they put to you. Bah. Dear God in heaven, help us both."

I felt a movement in the room and looked up. Nina had turned her dirt-grimed face toward me, laying her cheek gently on her knees. Her face was swollen from crying. She moved her lips, just one word with no sound, but I could make it out: *Amen.*

Tears slid out of Nina's pale eyes as she continued to look into mine. I began to cry, too. It was the only sane thing to do.

Nina ungrasped and regrasped her knee. I saw fingerprinting ink on her fingertips.

So they ran a check on her and found nothing, I thought. *She's absolutely clean. No ID, no labels in her clothes. She came out of nowhere. It's like she doesn't really exist.* "You're like a missing part of George," I whispered.

Nina shifted her head slightly, so that her face was not fully visible to those who stood behind the mirror. Her lips moved again. *I loved him,* they said.

I considered taking one of her hands in mine, then thought better of it. "Have they let you see him?" I asked.

She shook her head, just a tiny wobble.

I stood up and rapped on the glass with my knuckle. "Hey! You want to let a widow lady see her husband?" I asked angrily. "No more sideshow until Nina gets to see George!"

A moment later, the door opened and the unnamed, nondescript detective showed his head. "This way," he said.

I said, "Where are your glasses, Nina?"

She looked up at the detective.

"Give the lady her glasses," I demanded, once again on the edge of hollering.

The detective produced a large envelope, which held Nina's thick, ugly glasses.

"Sign for this, please," said the detective.

"The hell you say," I seethed, snatching the envelope from his hands. "That's child abuse, keeping her glasses from her," I added, wondering how old Nina truly was. "You should be ashamed, mister."

Hands trembling, I opened the envelope and put the enormous glasses on her tiny face. Her eyes appeared to pop larger behind their magnification.

I helped Nina to her feet and guided her through the door and down the hall after him. Officer Raymond fell into step behind us and the two men took us down elevators, outside, and into a car, and through the gathering evening traffic to another public building. There, they took us downstairs into an atmosphere thick with the scent of disinfectant. The medical examiner, a woman in her fifties, presented us with forms to sign and asked for identification. "Here's mine," I said, presenting my driver's license. Just to hear what she'd say, I said, "Nina, you don't have anything, do you?"

Nina shook her head.

"It is irregular to show the remains to anyone who can't identify themselves as next of kin," said the medical examiner.

The detective spoke. "I'll vouch for them," he said. He turned to Nina. "A signature will do it," he said casually. I heard a note of seduction in his voice; he was luring her, leading her along the path to giving up just this one little clue about herself. I could see him running to a handwriting expert with the results.

Hands trembling, Nina picked up the pen and wrote her name, Nina Dishey, in minuscule schoolgirl cursive. I signed my name, too, and we were taken through to a room with a television monitor. On it appeared George Dishey's face, profile view, reclining, eyes closed. His nose was banged up and his skin was mottled with lividity. It was a dead face, a dull face. George, for all his unpleasant quirks, had been a man of considerable charm, charisma, even; a man whose face had been alert and engaging when he was alive. My stomach tightened.

"Can you identify this man?" asked the medical examiner.

I turned and looked at Nina, stifling an urge to retch. Her

eyes had grown enormous with alarm. She approached the monitor and touched it, then quickly withdrew her hand, which then flew to her lips, to her throat. She darted around to one side of the monitor, trying to find another way into it. To me, she whimpered, "Do they have George's head in there?"

My God, I thought. *She doesn't know*— "It's just a picture, Nina, don't worry. George is in another room." As her agitation continued to grow, I said, "Ray, we have to take her to the real thing or she's going to blow."

Ray stared at Nina incredulously.

"She doesn't know what a television is," I said, enunciating the words sharply to cut through Ray's confusion. "She's from Mars, Ray. Get these people to take her into the room where the body is!"

Ray's eyes widened but he snapped to and made things happen. The medical examiner groused for a few moments but then led us through into a very cold room in which there was a gurney holding an opaque long plastic bag. Inside the bag rested the form of a man. The first half foot of the bag had been carefully laid back, exposing George Dishey's inanimate face. I had to push a video camera out of the way so that Nina could approach the corpse.

As she neared the body, Nina's hands rose up like tiny wings, fluttering, hovering now to either side of George's uninhabited cheeks. Silent tears flowed down her face and dropped like pearls into the sunken spaces that held his lidded eyes. "Darling," she whispered. "I'll be with you soon. Tell Heavenly Father I'm coming."

I told myself I was watching the onset of madness. It frightened me to hear another human speak of death as just a doorway to be walked through. But another part of me knew that Nina was entirely sane. Sane, but naïve. Sane, but . . . more than sane; the Nina who stood before me was joyously sane, vibrantly alive, and in a state of grace, a thing that I could recognize but about which I knew pathetically little. I felt scared and confused. My ignorance, I could accept, but I did not share the corner of the reality from which she spoke. To me, alive was alive and dead was dead; I was in this life and wanted to stay here as long as I could, and above all, I did not want to be dispatched from it even a minute ahead of schedule, especially by violence.

Nina's hands came gently to rest on George's silent cheeks. She stroked his hair, which still lay stretched across his temples, pulled back no doubt into the ponytail he had habitually drawn it into. She flicked a bit of broken leaf from his beard and reached to unzip the bag.

"Stop there," the detective said, lunging toward her.

Nina ignored him and gave the zipper a mighty tug. As the cover came back from the corpse's chest, I felt my stomach sink past my knees.

13

"OH, GOD!" I HEARD SOMEONE GASPING. "OH GOD, OH God, oh—" As I bent over from the hip, my head cleared, the ringing in my ears lessened, and I realized that I had been the one who had been making all the noise. Nina had simply fainted.

The corpse was naked, undressed for postmortem examination. George had been neatly sliced in places by the medical examiner, but that was not the problem. No, the problem was that his torso had been mutilated. Slashed hideously from side to side, peppered with lines of puncture wounds and ripped hideously by some coarse-toothed sawlike instrument. Bone was visible where the blows had crossed his ribs, but his abdomen was the worst. His abdomen was a mess of spewed guts.

Waves of nausea swept over me. Nina moaned at my feet as the medical examiner cracked a tiny vial beneath her nostrils. The reek of ammonium carbonate reached my nose as well and I snapped further back to my senses. I felt Ray's strong hands grasping my shoulders. I leaned back and felt his warmth. "Sorry," he said softly. "You weren't supposed to see that."

Having finished with Nina, the medical examiner calmly stood up and closed the bag.

"Who—or what—in *hell's* name did that?" I wailed.

"That's what we all want to know," said the detective as he helped the medical examiner zip the bag back over the corpse's head.

"Now I understand why you guys have been so upset," I said. "I haven't seen a mauling like that since a mountain lion got one of our calves."

No one answered.

Nina had rolled onto her side and was moaning.

I bent and held her in my arms. "I'm so sorry," I said. "Oh, Nina, if I'd had any idea how bad that could be, I would never have suggested we come."

Nina trembled. "Dear Heavenly Father, help me," she whimpered. "Help me, Father. Take away my thoughts. Take me home with You *now!*"

"What thoughts, Nina?" the detective asked.

Nina's shaking increased to the level of near convulsions.

"Let's get her out of here," the medical examiner said congenially. "She'll feel better upstairs where it's warmer."

◈

NINA HAD NO more words to give the police. Grace had given way to raw fear, and she couldn't have gotten words out from between her clenched teeth if she'd tried. A discussion ensued among the detective, the medical examiner, Officer Raymond, and myself regarding what to do with and for her next. Finally, I said, "Ray, why don't you and I take her down to Temple Square so she can pray, or whatever Mormons do. I mean, the woman's lost her husband and had a nasty shock; don't you think she might like to seek a little comfort from the Almighty?" I almost corrected myself by amending that to Heavenly Father, but something about patriarchal imagery was sticking in my craw just then.

The detective spoke. "We have a little problem here. None of us knows where Mrs. Dishey resides. She clearly does not live at the deceased's. She was carrying no identification when we found her, and . . ."

I turned to her. "Where do you live, Nina?"

Nina squeezed her eyes tightly shut and shook harder.

"Okay, no joy there," I said. "Back to the Temple. Want to go to Temple Square with me, Nina?"

She nodded uncertainly, thought, then nodded again with vigor. "I've heard about the Salt Lake Temple. Can I really see it?"

The detective took us all back to the station, where Ray led us to his vehicle, which still held my bags. When shown the car, Nina moved automatically toward the backdoor and climbed into the backseat, where she sat bolt upright like a schoolgirl waiting to be asked to recite. I reassessed her age. Eighteen going on twelve.

Ray drove and I sat in the backseat with Nina, holding her hands. As we turned north on Main Street and the Salt Lake Temple of Jesus Christ of the Latter-Day Saints came into view, Nina at last relaxed just a hair. I greeted the sight more doubtfully.

The Temple is six stories of massive gray granite capped by another fifty feet or so of tall triangular spires, a wedding cake of big ones, medium ones, and little ones, the tallest one to the east surmounted by a gilded statue of a man blowing a horn. It's hard for me to quantify what there was about it that unnerved me. It was something in its architectural style, something I couldn't quite characterize, something that failed, to my prejudiced eyes, to say *church*. I was not raised as a churchgoer, but I'd been to a few and seen pictures of hundreds of others, large and small, in art history books and such, and this one somehow did not fit with the rest. It was too heavy, too forbidding, more like a mausoleum than a place of worship. I looked away.

"You . . . ah, we can't get into the Temple," Ray said.

"That's okay," Nina said. "I just want to sit in the Temple grounds awhile and take a little comfort. Prayer is a private thing. 'Ye must pour out your souls in your closets, and your secret places, and in your wilderness. . . .' " Her voice trailed off, her recitation complete.

I looked questioningly at Ray.

"Alma thirty-four: twenty-six," he said, and when I still looked mystified, he added, "Book of Mormon. Or, if you prefer, Matthew six:six, 'But when you pray, go into your room and shut the door and pray to your Father who is in secret.' "

"Oh."

Ray parked the vehicle and led us into the Temple grounds. Nina moved quickly to a bench beside a tall statue of Christ, sat down, and lifted her face toward her God.

Ray took up a position behind her, feet apart, eyes scanning Temple Square. Every inch of him said *protection*. I wondered if it bothered him to find himself worrying about such things in his holy place.

A woman wearing sensible shoes and a dark blazer moved toward us. A badge on her left breast read SISTER HARGROVE. She said, "Would you like to take a tour today?"

"No, thank you, Sister," said Officer Raymond.

Sister Hargrove's eyes brightened and her spine straightened prettily. "Oh, Brother Raymond, I didn't see it was you."

Ray nodded and kept his eyes moving.

Sister Hargrove persisted, looking my way. "Who are your friends?" As her examination dropped to my legs and feet, her expression went blank. I was clearly not dressed for the occasion, and neither was Sister Dishey, but at least my face was clean. I gave Sister Hargrove a winning smile and said nothing.

Ray said, "We've just come for a moment of silent contemplation."

"Certainly," said Sister Hargrove, turning and moving away toward the next stray visitor.

When she was out of earshot, I whispered, so as not to disturb Nina, "So, Ray, where do we go from here?"

Ray said, "You got me."

"We got a murder investigation that's two days old with no real suspects. Certainly by now, you know it was neither of us. Even if you still think either of us capable of such a crime—emotionally capable, because certainly neither one of us had the strength or the stomach to do anything like that to a human body—the forensic evidence will by now have eliminated us from your list. He can't have had a drop of blood left in him. Those wounds were dealt from close range, and with great force. George was not a little guy. Neither Nina nor I could have pulled that off physically, let alone mentally. Besides, whoever did that would have stepped in the blood that butchering job shed and left a trail of footprints. Even if the footprints are my size, you've been all through my gear and found nothing, so please cut the nonsense and tell me you know I'm clean!"

Ray stared painfully into space.

"So we got young George's second wife here," I continued, "and if you think she's a fake, you're out of your mind. She made her own clothes, she gets her hair cut by someone with dull scissors, she rides in the backseat, and she's never seen a television set. Add all that together with the kid you see sitting inside that getup and you know damned well this is no act. You got some pretty rural parts of Utah here, so I'm guessing Nina lives way out in the back of nowhere, where they don't ask questions of big families with a surplus of adult females."

A deep blush rose up from Ray's collar. When I moved

around in front of him so he could no longer evade eye contact, he stepped around me, and, leaning over so he could speak into Nina's ear without touching her, and said, "Are you about ready? It's time for us to go."

◇
◇
◇

14

◇
◇
◇

RAY TOOK US TO HIS MOTHER'S HOUSE.

That sounds like a happy and convivial event, except that you'll remember that Nina and I were the subjects of a murder investigation, and he had been told to quit getting involved with the subjects or he'd be sent home with his ass in a sling.

I could have argued, but I didn't. I was done trying to save Ray from himself. He wasn't giving me the courtesy of trusting me, and I wouldn't have been surprised to hear that the dressing-down he had gotten from Detective Bert was an act staged for my benefit. I thought it unorthodox that Ray would take us to his mother's house, but nothing I had experienced in my forty-eight hours in Salt Lake City had made much more sense than that, so I just smiled when I saw the lady and said, "Hi. I'm Em Hansen. It's nice of you to have us here."

"Call me Ava," she said. She was beautiful. Stunning. A monument to expensive cosmetics, healthy eating, comfortable living, and extraordinary genetics. It was clear where Ray had gotten his looks. She had the same high coloring, the same cheekbones, the same tilt to the corners of her eyes. I would have felt intimidated if the circumstances of our meeting hadn't been so far past normal experience as to seem absurd. She examined me carefully. "Welcome to our home," she continued. "I'll put you girls in the guest room at the end of the upstairs hall."

Girls? What the hell.

Nina and I followed her up a short flight of carpeted stairs. "I have a change of clothes you can put on, Nina," Ava was saying. "You're a little bit smaller than any of my daughters, but I've saved some of their clothes from when they were younger. Are you about a size four?"

Nina had been bearing up pretty well since we had left the morgue, silently crying now and then but mostly just being silent, and had made her entry into Ava's deluxe spick-and-span home with only a modicum of cowering astonishment. But now she turned her head toward Ava, her eyes growing wide with something that looked pretty close to terror.

I said, "I don't think she knows her dress size, Ava. She's very clever, makes her own clothes." What I didn't say was, *And I'll bet there is no pattern available for this dowdy, high-collared style.*

"Well, we'll just see what we can find, then," Ava said kindly.

By the time we reached the room, Nina's expression had shifted from uncertainty to awe. "Pretty," she said, taking in with widening eyes the stately glamour of the six-bedroom house.

It was a handsome, spacious house, elegantly and expensively decorated, and the guest room had the diaphanous atmosphere of a butterfly's garden. The curtains, bedding, and table skirts were done in tasteful floral prints, the walls were painted a gentle shade of pink, and the carpeting sank deliciously beneath my feet. Two windows stood open to the west, taking in the late-afternoon air and a spectacular view of the sun dipping low over the Oquirrh Mountains. Great Salt Lake shone golden with the light to the northwest. In the near ground, a small but well-kept garden encircled a swimming pool, and birds twittered as they grouped for the coming night. The whole setting worked on me like a balm. I wanted to sit down in the comfortable overstuffed chair by the windows and maybe stay there a year or two.

Ava got Nina set up with towels and soap for a good scrub in the tub in the private bathroom connected to the guest room. "You just turn these handles," Ava said. "This one's hot water and this one's cold. Use as much as you like, dear." I had to hand it to Ava; she was getting Nina's measure pretty quickly. And when Nina began to look agitated, Ava beat a hasty retreat so she could disrobe in private. She grabbed a box of gauze out of a drawer on her way, and without comment, she redressed my thumb, which had begun to get grubby.

Thus reconstituted, I followed Ava downstairs to the living room, which enjoyed a cathedral ceiling and views west toward the Oquirrhs, north toward Salt Lake City, and east onto the steep rampart of the Wasatch Range. The sun had just kissed the crests of the Oquirrhs, shedding a deep rosy glow onto the Wasatch front. I decided that the couch would do as nicely as the overstuffed chair upstairs and so I sat there.

"Can I get you some refreshment?" Ava inquired.

"This view is refreshment enough. Thank you," I answered, and as she began to leave the room, I added, "And thank you, really, for having us here. Ray must have told you there is some danger involved. He took all precautions to make sure we weren't followed here, and he is good at what he does, but still . . ."

Ava turned and looked at me, drawing her already splendid body up into a near parody of good posture. "He's a good boy," she said. "He wouldn't bring danger here, however slight, unless he had a very good reason."

Boys. Girls. "Do you have other children?" I asked.

"Four girls. Three of them will be here for dinner." She smiled fleetingly, a quick, polite crimp of her lower face muscles. "Now, if you'll excuse me . . ." She faded through an archway into the kitchen beyond.

"I'd be glad to help you," I called after her.

"No need to, my dear. It's all but ready and the table is set."

I dully realized that if the table was already set, this meant she had known Nina and I were coming. I tried to remember if Ray had stopped at a phone to tell her. I leaned back, resting my neck on the soft back of the couch. I could not recall a moment after our visit to Temple Square when he could have done that.

As the red glow of the evening sun faded from the Wasatch, I drifted into sleep.

◆

NINA WOKE ME a half hour later. "Dinner's ready," she whispered excitedly.

Dinner was going to be exciting? I fought to reorient myself in this room, in this house, in this city, in this life. "Who . . . what's going on?" I mumbled. I had been sleeping hard.

"Ray," Nina whispered. Same excitement.

"Excuse me, Nina," I said, "but Ray what?" I looked around the room. He wasn't there.

"I understand now," she said cryptically.

"Understand what?"

"I thought you *knew* each other already."

"Huh?"

"There's such . . . interest between you. I thought you'd been together for a while, that it was all decided. Now I *understand*."

I sat forward in the couch, instantly grouchy. "Good. That's one of us. Understand *what*, Nina?"

"You just *met*. It *isn't* all decided. But it *will* be."

"Nina, you lost me. What on earth are you talking about?"

"What in *heaven*."

"Nina!"

"You were *meant* for each other. Heavenly Father—"

"Nina," I said impatiently, "I think you need to understand that I'm not a Mormon."

"Then you'll *become* a Mormon, and then he can help you know what to think afterward."

I sighed. Ray might have the authority in this town to tell me what to do, but there was no way *anyone* was going to tell me what to think. "I am not a Mormon, and . . . and I'm pretty sure I could never be one."

Nina giggled. "Oh, silly, why not?"

"With respect, Nina, because I don't believe what Mormons believe."

Nina smiled and shook her head at me, as if I were a recalcitrant child. "You never know till you try!"

Try believing? "Well, thanks, but I'm used to a different way of life." My words doubled back on me: I hadn't tried much else, had I? An argumentative sliver of my mind added, *So what are you saying? You're stuck on being lonely and tense the rest of your life?* I felt for a moment as if I'd been trout fishing and had stepped on an unseen rock beneath the waters and it had rolled. Snapping away from these fatigue-charged thoughts, I said, "Ray's married, Nina, and that's really all that matters. I . . . where I come from, men only have one wife." I said it like that should end the conversation. It did not. As Nina continued to smile smugly, I insisted, "The man's wearing a wedding ring, Nina. In my book, that means, Hands off."

"Well, yes, Ray's married, and he wears that ring in honor of his *first* wife, but even if you only want him to have *one* wife in *this* life, *that* shouldn't stop you."

"Nina, you're not making any kind of sense I can follow."

Nina smiled beatifically. "Ray's first wife died."

My pulse quickened. I felt an odd mix of panic and hope. "Dead? How do you know?"

"I know because I asked Kirsten. I *knew* you'd want to know but wouldn't *ask*. You're so polite about *asking* things."

My mind was racing. *He's single!* my heart said. *He scares me!* my stomach screamed. "But . . . then why the ring?"

"Well, because Ray married in the Temple, sealed for all time and eternity to his first wife. She's waiting for him in the Celestial Kingdom."

I closed my eyes. "Let me get this straight," I said slowly. "Ray's wife died, but they're still married, because they vowed 'forever' and not just till death us do part.' Did I get that right?"

"Yes!" Nina was pleased. Her student was catching her lessons well.

"Well then, if he marries again, is the new wife also forever?"

"If he's sealed to her, yes!" *You're getting it!* her tone said.

I opened my eyes and stared into hers, incredulous. "So then, even if he didn't seal to the second wife, in the eyes of the church, he'd be practicing polygamy?"

"Mm-hm."

I opened my eyes and looked at Nina. "And if he didn't seal to wife two, then when he dies, he leaves her and goes back to wife one, in a sense." Part of me was immediately thinking, *So who cares what he believes? Enjoy what's here and now and let the chips fall when he dies,* while another part of me was screaming, *Oh sure, just hook up with a guy who believes A while I think B. What a recipe for success. Hell, the whole reason I feel so attracted to him is that he detests untruth as much as I do.*

As I realized what I was realizing, that in this one fundamental way Ray and I were like twins born to separate families, both wary even of our own reflections in the mirror, Nina cocked her head to one side. "But why wouldn't you want to be sealed to him?" she asked. "He's going to be a god in the next life."

15

DINNER BEGAN AS DISCONCERTINGLY EASY AND PLEASANT as the house was serene and lovely. I say disconcerting because I'm not good at being . . . well, at ease. My social confidence is not titanic on the best of occasions, and here I was, walking into a brand-new context with a man I found entirely too attractive, and meeting his family, all at once, just after finding out that he was, er, available, and therefore, based on his recent behavior, possibly . . . interested in me.

There were eleven people present. Ava explained that it was Mormon tradition to gather on Monday evenings, something called "family home evening." The sisters and their miscellaneous families had filed in full of hugs and kisses for Ava. Only one son-in-law out of a possible two appeared, and Ray's father was also absent. The call of business must have taken priority, I decided.

Ray sat at one end of the long blond maple table and Ava sat at the other. Down one side sat sister number one, a gorgeous brunette named Chloe, with her two older children in booster seat and high chair (her third child lay sleeping in a playpen behind her, sucking peacefully on a pacifier, and she was visibly pregnant with a fourth); and sister number two, another gorgeous brunette named Katie. Katie's year-old child slept next to Chloe's in the playpen. On my side of the table sat Nina (scrubbed pink, her fine, straight hair flying about with static), looking awkward and slightly uncertain in a spiffy lavender frock with a ruffled collar; Katie's husband, a stiff-looking young man named Enos; and sister number four, a teenager just blooming into the family good looks. This was Kirsten, whom Nina had grilled for details of her brother's love life. Sister number three, Annette, I was proudly informed, was away on mission.

Dinner began with grace said by Ray, all holding hands, heads bowed. I clenched my teeth. Even if I hadn't been experiencing the feelings I had for Ray, this would have been a dichotomous moment for me, as I both enjoyed being included and wished I wasn't being subjected to someone else's ecclesiastical language. The "Dear Heavenly Father" stuff was beginning to wear thin.

In my parents' house, God was a name taken in vain just before "damn it," Father was what I called my dad when I was in trouble, and church was a place you went to watch the neighbors get married or eulogized. On the other hand, I felt giddily grateful to sit with a family who got along together, as dinner at our house was a time of great tension, during which my father and I stared into our plates or out the window, avoiding my mother's gibes. My mother, who had a tongue as sharp as a filleting knife, would sear us with her eyes, saving the full heat of her discontent for times when, if things didn't go her way, she could stalk out of the room without forsaking nourishment.

Ray's family seemed to enjoy its own company. There were smiles and looks of contentment all around, and while corrections were offered to children who shrieked or ate messily, these admonishments were matter-of-fact, not shaming or charged with negative emotion. I cynically searched each face for signs of strain but found none. Enos seemed a bit absent, and one of Chloe's kids was having a hard time of it, but, I was assured, the poor thing was coming down with a cold. In my mother's house, a cold was greeted as a character flaw. I began to feel so soothed by this family's harmony that it gave me the jitters.

Each time I looked up from my plate, I caught someone looking at me. *I'll bet you find me interesting,* I thought. *Here I am, the murder suspect your darling Ray brought home. I'm ill-dressed, bandaged, and plain as mud. You're wondering just like I am, What can he possibly see in her?*

I tried to think positively, to give this family the benefit of the doubt, but my none-too-sturdy self-esteem was making heavy work of trying to keep its spirits up. As dinner hummed along, I grew so unsettled that I tried to distract myself with thoughts about the George Dishey case. "Did anyone catch the news this evening?" I asked.

Nobody had. "Why?" asked Katie. "Did something important happen today?"

I glanced at Ray, who did not lift his eyes from his plate. That meant he had not told them what had happened at Snowbird. That was work; this was family. Had he told them anything about the murder, or about my involvement in it? *Yes, Ava seemed to know what I was talking about when I mentioned danger. . . .*

"Well," I said, choosing polite phrasing, "I'd been hoping to catch coverage of a press conference up in Snowbird. The Society of Vertebrate Paleontologists is having a meeting there. Paleontologists are almost by definition evolutionists, and I understand they were going to debate a group of creationists. It was supposed to be on the news."

Katie said, "Enos doesn't believe that Heavenly Father wants us to waste time on such thoughts. Isn't that right, Enos?"

Enos took a bite of casserole and nodded sagely.

Katie's rote answer chafed me, like a grass seed working its way inside a sock. I studied her for a moment. Her splendid looks seemed to mask a slightly acid disposition, hidden behind a lovely smile but given away by a subtle droop to the corners of her eyes. How old was she? Not more than early twenties, and she had a child already. Had she gone to college? She glanced at me over her chewing for a moment. There was a glint of challenge beneath those heavy eyelids.

"Where does the Mormon church stand on evolution?" I asked. I told myself that I just wanted to know. Brigham Young University had a thriving geology department, so that meant the Mormon church was okay with evolution, right? I was annoyed too quickly to admit to myself that Katie had hit a sore spot I had been too preoccupied to remember to cover.

Everyone was quiet for a moment. Ray squeezed his eyes shut for an instant, opened them, stared wide-eyed into his plate, and chewed.

Katie cleared her throat. "What's evolution got to do with dinosaurs?" she asked.

"Everything," I answered. "That's the whole game with paleontology—to try to understand how all the different species evolved, and how some of them went extinct. Isn't that so, Nina?" I smiled at her, sure she would chime in with something George had taught her. "What did George tell you about that?"

Nina swallowed a noodle, smiled wistfully, and said, "They drowned in the Flood."

That did not compute, so I ignored it for the moment. There was something more than a bit apples and oranges about Nina, this naïve young thing in rags who claimed to be the widow of one of the best-known paleontologists of his day. Did she mean Noah's Flood? Would he have told her that as a joke? Was she being funny? "Does the Mormon church teach creationism?" I asked no one in particular.

"What *is* the teaching on that, Ray?" Ava asked evenly.

I was beginning to wonder where Mr. Ava was, or, more specifically, how long he'd been gone. Ray was sitting in what I presumed to be his father's chair, and being asked likewise to embody his authority. He cleared his throat uncomfortably. "There is no policy on that," he said simply.

"The church has better things to think about," Enos added.

"Oh," I said. I said "Oh," instead of the response that crowded into my head about five seconds later, which was, *Isn't the church even half as fascinated as I am with the question of how we all got here?* But by the time that thought had entered my mind, I had decided it was time to keep my mouth shut before I got any more than my foot caught in it.

Someone asked someone else to please pass the butter, and I got to looking around the walls of the room, kind of abstracting myself from the group to give myself a chance to calm down, and I noticed a portrait over the sideboard of a very plain man with eyeglasses and a gentle, patriarchal smile. Beneath the portrait, on a special shelf beside a lit candle, lay leather-bound copies of The Book of Mormon and a volume entitled *Doctrine and Covenants,* all carefully arranged and lovingly displayed. Resting on bows that had been artfully tipped up onto the books was the pair of eyeglasses depicted in the portrait, cocked and ready, as if their owner might at any moment return and lift them to his eyes. The tableau had the flavor of a private altar. I concluded that Ray's father was dead.

Katie spoke again, her tone a bit too studiedly light just to be joking. "So Em, you believe we're descended from monkeys?"

"No," I answered evenly, "but I do believe that monkeys and humans are descended from a common ancestor."

Katie laughed. Her mother shot her a warning look that said, Be polite to our guest, but Katie said, "Then you think Adam and Eve were the parents of monkeys."

I stopped with a forkful of carrots halfway to my mouth. I had heard that some people believe the Adam and Eve story literally, but until that moment, I had not met that belief in direct conversation. I put down my fork and folded my hands on the edge of the table. "Let me tell you what I believe, Katie, and you can tell me what you believe, or not, whatever you please. I believe in evolution, but let me define my terms: evolution is change through time."

Katie rotated her head slightly to one side in an expression of doubt.

I said, "I believe what I can observe directly, and as a scientist, I hold this empiricism to an even higher standard, requiring that the phenomena I observe be repeatable. Only then can I be sure to observe objectively, and consider all possible variables so I can hope to sort out cause and effect."

"What do you observe about this family?" Katie asked.

She may not have gone to college and learned to stretch her mind around alternative beliefs, but she wasn't stupid. I smelled a trap, but I was beginning to get riled and ran right into it. "Well, I look around this table and I see Ava's striking good looks repeated in all of her children—the wonderful angles of the bone structure, the beautiful coloring, the tilt to the corners of the eyes—and yet I also see other traits she doesn't have. For one thing, Chloe has her father's nose—that is Mr. Raymond in that portrait there, isn't it?—or should I say, a nose very much like her father's, and I can see ears shaped like his in his grandson."

"And?"

I raised my hands and interwove the fingers, taking care not to alternate them evenly. "I know from the work of other scientists—men and women whose work I trust—that each time an egg and a sperm unite, DNA reshuffles their coding information like a deck of cards, taking some traits from each parent to form a new individual. That's change, through time.

With each generation, with each new *individual,* there is change from its parents. That's all evolution is. I can observe the results, and so can every person alive. We all say, 'He has Grampa's ears,' and 'She has Papa's nose,' so in a sense, there's a scientist in every one of us, an observer. Perhaps this shuffling, this process of evolution, is entirely random. Perhaps it is driven by divine plan. That, I don't know. That, I haven't personally observed, one way or the other. I would suggest that a divine plan, if it doesn't follow the system of physical laws that have always been present, is subjective, and therefore not repeatable or without unobservable variables."

Katie smiled, raised an eyebrow, and said, "Of course it's by divine plan. Heavenly Father rewards us for living a worthy life by giving us beautiful children."

Here, Ray shot her a look. Perhaps there was a Mormon teaching against arrogance. Whatever was behind that look, Ray, as usual, was communicating more with his body than with words.

"Listen, I didn't mean to start a big debate," I said, feeling like shit because I certainly had. "I'm a scientist. I practice the scientific method, which is designed to test ideas scientists have regarding observations we have made. That's all it does. And these observations are made with our five senses, or with instrumented extensions of them. If you have a sixth sense that tells you why you've inherited this trait or that, I can't argue."

Katie smiled sweetly and nodded.

I stared across the table at her, thinking, *You'd damned well better be glad there's a scientific method, sister, because if you value your children's capacity to transmit your good looks to another generation, you'll be glad to know that there are scientists hard at work on your behalf. They're studying such interesting phenomena as the drop by half, in our lifetime, of the concentration of sperm in the average human male's semen. That's half his firepower gone; how far do you think that trend can run before you wind up with no grandchildren? And you grew up here in Utah, where there have been aboveground nuclear tests just upwind, and scientists are out there with Geiger counters.* Here I dropped my mental tirade, because, of course, scientists were the ones who had made those bomb tests possible in the first place. Sometimes it's best to keep one's mouth shut. I counted to ten and then tried to shift the conversation away from my beliefs to hers by asking, "What exactly does the Mormon church teach about the origin of life?"

Nina answered in a singsong voice, "We believe that Heavenly Father created the heavens, the earth, and all living things in six days. It's just over six thousand years old." Then, with great enthusiasm, she concluded, "We're in the final millennium!"

A chunk of carrot lodged in my throat. All eyes turned toward Nina. Her face had brightened and a gentle smile had found its way to her lips. She was looking heavenward, her hands clutched ecstatically to her breast.

"Yes," I said slowly, "according to the calculations of Bishop Ussher, the earth celebrated its six thousandth birthday in October 1997."

"But you believe differently?" Katie asked.

I tried to count to ten again but got lost by four. "Yes, I do. Modern scientific thought and analysis suggests it's more like four point six *billion* years old."

"Give or take a few thousand," said Katie.

"Katie, that's enough," said her mother.

Katie's eyes went blank. "Sorry, Mother. I meant no unkindness."

"Apologize to Em, dear; she's the one you've been baiting."

Katie turned toward me, opening her mouth to speak, but I held up a hand, the one that happened to have the big wad of gauze on it. "I'm the one who should apologize. Sorry." Uncomfortable showing my physical wound as well as my psychic ones, I dropped my hand, wincing as I hit my band-aged thumb on the edge of the table. I felt confused and agitated. The fights at my parents' house never ended with apologies.

Nina said, "George says that Heavenly Father made the earth just *look* old to test our faith."

As my mouth sagged open, Katie turned toward Nina. "Nina, what church do you attend?"

Nina blinked. "Well, I'm Mormon. . . ." she said, letting her voice trail off oddly.

Ray, who had scrupulously worked to train his five senses on his dinner throughout my skirmish with his sister, kept his head bowed toward his plate, but his eyes were now alert and on Nina.

Katie said, "But I don't recall that teaching. Which ward do you attend?"

Nina's mouth opened and closed again. "We . . . I attend . . . I'm not . . ."

"Not supposed to say?" I asked.

Nina closed her eyes and nodded. The color had drained from her face.

With exasperation heavy in her voice, Ava said, "Katie, you are my most inquisitive daughter. But can you please set your curiosity aside for now? I am concerned that you should save your questions for your hours of prayer, so that your curiosity might better sustain your faith."

"Certainly, Mother," Katie replied. "Kirsten, could you please pass the rolls?"

◆

RAY LED ME out onto the patio above the swimming pool while the other women cleared away the dinner. "I'd prefer to be helping them clear the table," I told him. Little that I liked adhering to presumed roles of male and female behavior, I wasn't ready to be alone with him. Not now, and maybe not ever. My brain was wired to examine everything, to consider every idea and bit of evidence it was presented, and I just couldn't stand to consider that his world might be right and mine wrong. That would be too shattering.

"I need to talk to you before I go home," he said.

And be alone with the memory of your wife, I thought. "Okay," I said with a sigh. "But shoot low, Sheriff, I'm riding a Shetland."

Ray stared out into the dance of lights that was Salt Lake City. "I'm sorry if things got uncomfortable in there for you," he said. "My sister—"

"No, I'm the one who's sorry," I said, pulling myself toward my moral center. "Through bitter experience, I have learned that it's better to apologize as I go along than to store up a load of guilt and idiocy for worse humiliation later on. I bought into a fight in there, and when it went bad on me, I was more defensive than the situation warranted. I've just been sucked into so many debates with creationists that I've gotten to the point where I've started throwing the first punch." Even though this sounded like an apology, it was, in fact, a challenge. I wanted to know what Ray believed. I wanted to know if there was any hope for a relationship with him, any hope that I hadn't been dreaming when I imagined that a life of questioning might be truly welcome with him. I wanted him to speak, to string words together, to tell me what he was *thinking* for a change.

Ray said, "It's true that the church has no policy on all that."

"Oh," I said. It was beginning to be my reply to everything.

"Brigham Young admired the work of Charles Darwin."

"Huh?"

"He said, 'The glory of God is intelligence.' "

"Mmm."

"It's carved in the walls at BYU."

"That's nice."

Now Ray said, "Mmm."

"Well," I said, "I guess I don't really *care* what other people believe as long as they're not saying that all people who don't agree with the power elite must suffer in silence or be exterminated."

The corners of Ray's lips curled. His eyes danced. "That's harsh."

I looked away. I couldn't look into those dark blue eyes and see that spark and not feel ignited by it. "Well, yeah, but the thing is, I do feel exterminated, or just a little part of me does, every time some proselytizing zealot sticks a foot in my door and chants a pat system of beliefs at me."

"Ouch," he said.

Embarrassed, I said, "I was thinking of the Jehovah's Witness missionaries, not yours. The closest contact I've had with Mormon missionaries was when a couple of your guys got lost and stopped to ask directions to the highway from a back road near my folks' ranch. You go on a mission?" I asked, immediately wishing I hadn't. Part of me preferred to leave my knowledge of Ray as generic as possible, lest my fantasies collapse under the harsh weight of reality.

"Yes."

"Oh."

"In New York City."

For once, Ray had offered a piece of information about himself unasked. It felt oddly intimate, and in spite of my best instincts, I began to lower my guard, and my mind slipped unconsciously into absorbing this bit of data, analyzing it, seeing where it fit. It made sense that he had done his mission in a city, rather than in the country. I could not see Ray in some Third World country, slogging along a dirt trail from hut to hut in a narrow black tie, black pants, white shirt, and ELDER RAYMOND badge.

He said, "I'm hoping you won't mind staying here a day or two to kind of keep an eye on Nina."

I snapped back to present time and space, furious. "And see what else I can get out of her? Maybe get her to say something self-incriminating?"

Ray bowed his head. He'd jammed his hands into his pockets and now he hunched his shoulders to his ears. Between his teeth, he said, "She seems to trust you."

"She's a grown woman. Why not just let her go home?"

Ray said, "We don't know she isn't a minor."

"Right," I said, "and she may or may not have been George's wife, but she didn't live with him. So where is home? Maybe she's eighteen or even twenty now, but how long has she been married?"

"And why's she dressed in rags?" Ray continued. "What kind of care is anyone taking of her? Think about it, Em; she doesn't come from the same kind of life you and I have known."

His words cut to my heart. I thought, *I have not known a life like yours*, but I said, "Maybe she's a reincarnated hippie."

Ray sighed in exasperation.

"No sale, Ray; you're going to have to spell it out for me. What is it you're trying to get out of her?"

He said nothing for a while; then, evasively, and with great discomfort, he said, "There are groups that don't conform to central church teachings."

"So?"

"Polygamy is no longer, ah, sanctioned by the church."

"And?"

Ray struggled, but got the story out. "And there have been cases of very remote . . . very isolated groups that have split off from the church. But they still call themselves Mormon. They get pretty far out there in their beliefs and teachings. Like marrying off fourteen-year-olds. Like . . . Em, Nina seems frightened. She didn't go home when she ran away from George Dishey's house. Have you thought about that?"

"Yes, but—"

"What if she fears a beating? The matron who frisked her down at the station found bruises that looked like they'd been systematically applied. She also found burn scars and in her fingers bones that had been broken and poorly set."

"Jesus Christ!"

"Maybe she knows who killed George, and—"

I groaned. "She told George's corpse she'd be with him soon . . ."

Seeing that he'd made his point, Ray said no more.

I said, "But I can't stay here tomorrow. Can't your mother look after her or something?"

Ray looked a question.

Mentally shaking myself free of the irons he was putting on me, I said, "I haven't had a chance to tell you what I learned this afternoon at the university." I cut to the chase, explaining why I couldn't babysit Nina. "I'm going on Dan Sherbrooke's field trip. Don't worry, I've made arrangements to get on the bus down by the Salt Palace Convention Center, not up in Snowbird. It'll get me out of shooting range all day and I'll learn stuff that might have a bearing on the case. If it has no bearing, then I'm in no danger going on the trip. I can ask people on the bus all kinds of things. You see, Dan and George had this competition going, and—"

"No."

"You've got no way to hold me!" I stared straight into Ray's eyes, and he stared back at me, furious and frightened.

Katie spoke from the doorway. "Momma's waiting for you to lead the prayer," she said.

Ray gave me two more counts of heat, spun around, and stalked into the house.

I watched through the doorway as he stormed about the living room, marching this way and that past his astonished family, now picking up a book, now marching out to the entryway and returning with a small vial, now putting both down on an end table and rubbing his face with his hands. All waited patiently as he collected himself. No one spoke as he stared for a while out a far window, then turned, bowed his head, raked one hand through his hair, and mouthed silent words. At last, he lifted a calmed, tired face to his sisters, mother, brother-in-law, nieces, and nephew, smiled to Nina, and began to speak audibly. "Dear Heavenly Father, we thank you for the bounty of health and happiness Thou hast bestowed upon us. We ask a blessing upon this family and upon our guests. May each" He looked up at me. "and *every* one of us know Your love and guidance in the days ahead and travel always in Your light and protection. In Christ's name, amen."

"Amen," answered the gathering in the living room. All sat with arms folded across their chests, heads bowed.

"Amen," I whispered, my eyes brimming with tears.

"We'll have no lesson tonight," he said. "It's late already, and Timmy needs extra sleep."

Several heads bobbed up in surprise.

"Um, but until we meet again, we shall all contemplate the miracle of continued revelation. We shall all pray that more of God's plan for each and every one of us will be revealed."

Ray nodded to Enos, who rose and followed him over to the miniature rocking chair in which Timothy sat sniffling. Enos put his hands on the child's near shoulder.

"Dear Heavenly Father," Ray said, "I ask that you bring the bounty of renewed health to Your son Timothy." Ray opened the vial and poured a drop of oil on the crown of his sniffling nephew's head. He closed and pocketed the vial, placed both hands atop the child's head, and closed his eyes for a while. "In Christ's name, amen."

"Amen," said his family.

Ray and Enos then moved to Nina. "Dear Heavenly Father—" Ray was interrupted as Nina slid off the couch and knelt in front of him, eyes closed, arms folded in prayer. The women's eyes widened at what was apparently an unusual posture for receiving a blessing. Ray said, "Dear Heavenly Father, we ask that You shine Your special light upon Your daughter Nina, that she may grow in Your love and kindness. Help her to know Your plan for her. Enfold her in Your comfort in this, her hour of need." He anointed her head and placed his hands upon her flaxen hair. Enos put his hands on her shoulder. "In Christ's name, amen."

"Amen."

Then Ray turned toward me. He stared out through the open doorway at me, a silent invitation to come and be blessed. A few heads turned, watching me in curiosity.

My feet were frozen to the ground.

Ray bowed his head again, and said, "Dear Heavenly Father, we ask a special blessing also for Your daughter Emily Hansen, that she may also know Your deepest love and guidance in the days to come. In Christ's name, amen."

"Amen," said his family.

I could not respond. My lips had frozen, too.

16

I AWOKE FROM A TERRIBLE DREAM IN WHICH SHINING bronze teeth were flying toward my face. I sat bolt upright in bed, gasping, the image of those teeth, four inches long, curved, serrated, continued to sink into my now-waking consciousness, biting, twisting. . . . I switched on the bedside lamp, fighting to clear the image from my mind.

Nina was gone. I felt it in the center of my brain before I fully understood the scene that was in front of me. I swiveled my legs out from under the bedclothes and stood up.

Nina's bed was empty, the sumptuous comforter neatly replaced over the pillow and the flannel nightgown Ava had lent her laid tenderly across the bed.

Still reeling from the strength and horror of the dream, I ran across the room and checked the bathroom. Nina was not there. I grabbed my jacket on the way out into the hall and ran for the stairs, flicking on lights as I went, unconcerned about how much noise I made or whom I awoke. I searched the kitchen, the living room, the study, and the dining room, and as I doubled back through the kitchen, I almost ran smack into Ava. "What's happened?" she demanded, pulling her robe more tightly around her throat.

"Nina's gone. Made her bed. Gone." I felt a chill run

through me, a sensation like getting wet. It set off a series of associations." I said, "We need to check the pool."

Ava threw the sliding door wide and flicked on the patio light.

I broke into a run and charged toward the pool. A little voice in my head said, *You're not a swim*mer. *What do you think you're doing?*

I hit the water feetfirst. The chill jabbed every inch of my body like needles, but I groped about in the water, feeling for flesh that I feared would be as cold. As my lungs began to scream for air, I came roaring to the surface, thrashing, clawing for the side. "I—I can't find her!" I screamed.

Ava broke through the surface ten feet from me and spluttered, "Kirsten! The light!"

Suddenly, light flooded the waters, and I saw Nina's silent form beneath the surface, a flower with petals formed of wafting hair and dress, an improbable angel hovering in the waters. A haze of blood bloomed from one side of her head. "There!" I yelled.

Ava bent and dove, her strong athletic arms driving her quickly to the sunken girl. I watched her grasp Nina and kick, lifting her from the bottom. The water's surface shattered again as Ava reached for air, reeled Nina into an armlock, and pulled toward the steps at the shallow end of the pool with strong, certain strokes. "Phone nine one one!" she yelled. "I don't think she's breathing."

"Already got them on the line, Mumma," Kirsten called from the edge of the pool. "Send an ambulance. Hurry!" In the soft illumination from the underwater floodlights, I saw Kirsten's slender hands set down a cordless phone and reach to help draw Nina out of the pool. She grunted as she fell backward onto the decking, hauling Nina's limp form with her.

Ava hurried up the steps and the two rolled Nina onto her back, checked her pulse, and listened for breath. Mother and daughter glanced quickly at each other, shook their heads, and set to work initiating CPR. Kirsten straightened her arms, placed both hands on Nina's chest, and threw her weight toward it. Ava bent, pinched Nina's nose, closed her lips around Nina's pale mouth, and breathed.

Kirsten fell in rhythmic lurches onto Nina's rib cage. Ava listened. Breathed. Listened.

Suddenly, Nina coughed, sputtered, and belched pool water onto the decking.

Ava said, "Good, you foolish girl, breathe the breath God gave you!"

Kirsten asked, "She okay, Mumma?"

Nina's eyes fluttered open. She coughed again, moaned, and raised a hand to the wound on her head.

"She'll be fine," Ava told Kirsten. "Phone Ray, will you?"

"I already did."

Ava gave her daughter a kiss on the forehead. "When did you do that, you clever girl?"

"Just before I dialled nine one one. Speed dialer, Mumma. He answered on the first ring, and all I said was, 'Nina's in the pool. Come,' and hung up. Do you think I ought to give him another call?"

"No, that will do it. But unlock the front door so the medics can get in. Nina's bleeding."

Nothing bleeds like a head wound. Blood now coated the decking underneath her head, eerily dark in the light from the pool and porch light. Nina began to shiver, as much from shock as from the cold. "Th-th-thank You," she said. "D-dear Heavenly F-father, th-thank You."

Ava folded a fresh expanse of her nightgown, pressed it against Nina's face and said softly, "What are you talking about, girl? You're not making sense. You try to kill yourself, and now you're thanking God for saving you."

"N-no!" Nina said. "I didn't! I . . . I tripped."

"You what?" I said.

"I . . . I was just out here to pray," Nina said in a tiny lost voice. "I can't swim . . . I . . . I heard a noise . . . I'm not used to the city . . . I stepped backwards and tripped over something in the dark. I *know* better. Brother Neph—"

"You were out here praying? You'll catch your death of cold!" Ava scolded.

"Th-thank You, F-Father!" Nina bawled. "You sent Your angel into the waters to draw me out! Dear Heavenly Father, th-thank Thee for Thy m-mercy! I am reborn!"

"Thank Em, dear." Ava looked up at me and gave me a look I could not quite decipher. "What woke you, Em?" she asked. "Which one of your five senses told you Nina was in trouble?"

I couldn't answer. In the moment that Nina had given herself up to her prayer of thanksgiving, her face had stretched long and her eyes had focused into pinpoints of light. With the softness of her youth thus erased, I noticed for the first time how high her cheekbones were, and recognized the antic glow of charismatic zealotry I had seen that morning up at Snowbird in the face of the bearded man.

❖

AVA BRUSHED AND dried Nina's hair as if she were a little girl, delicately arranging it around the butterfly sutures the paramedics had applied to her forehead. "There, now," she said soothingly, "that's lovely. You have lovely hair, Nina; so soft and shiny. George is surely smiling on you from heaven."

Nina tugged the high-necked flannel gown closer to her throat and leaned up against Ava, heightening the effect of childishness. "Do you really think so?" she asked. "I do so want him to be proud of me."

"Oh, Nina, he *is*. What more could a man ask than that his wife love him as you do?"

Nina snuffled. "I did my best."

"And your best was *excellent*."

I watched from the comfort of my own bed, wishing someone would care for me like that. But Ava was intent on Nina, who had suffered more than just a dousing. And, I was sure, Ava saw no need to comfort me. I was, after all, still good old poker-faced Em, the one who needs nothing, asks nothing. The one who manages at all times to shy away from such things as intimacy.

"Ava," Nina asked tentatively, "your husband has passed on, too, right?"

"Yes. . . ."

"Well, I was wondering . . . how do you . . . know for sure that he loved you, too?"

Ava turned off the dryer but continued to comb Nina's now glossy hair, running the brush with one hand and smoothing it with the other. "Look into your heart, Nina; you know the answer to that question. When you fall in love, all the world seems to smile at you, but that's not love. Loving is an active verb, a thing you do, not just some feeling that overwhelms you today and fades tomorrow." She glanced sidelong at me, just a split second, but I noticed. "Look at how he treated you, not what he said. When you love someone, you do for that love what you would do for yourself, or for God; you care for it, nurture it, do right by it, follow its dictates, no matter what it costs you. Love is rewarded for its own sake, with a deeper satisfaction than the flesh can know." She glanced at me again, and this time I was certain she was sending me a message. Was she warning me away from her boy or instructing me on how to love him?

Nina said, "But what do I do now, Ava? George is gone!"

Ava drew the crown of the girl's head to her lips. "That will come to you, Nina. You continue to love him, that's all."

Nina contracted, and the tears began to flow again. "He . . .

he looked so *awful!* His chest was ripped open. And . . . and he was *gray* and *purple!*"

Ava put her arms around the girl and rocked her. "Nina, my husband died slowly. In great pain. He had cancer. By the time he died, he was shrunken up like a lizard. His cheekbones stuck out like a skull's. His eyes were yellow with jaundice. His breath was . . . indescribable. He shook. He moaned. There were big red scars from the surgeon's incisions all over him. But I told myself that deep inside he was still the boy I'd married. I let him see that in my eyes. I held my love up to him instead of a mirror, so he could see his true self and not despair. Now you do that, too, Nina; look into your heart to the man you love there, and know that he is strong and whole again, and waiting for you in the Celestial Kingdom, loving you just the same."

Nina sniffled. "I want to. . . ."

Ava smiled into Nina's eyes. "Think of him as the god he is becoming. It's easy. It erases that other image. That fades, and you get back George as you knew him at all ages, and all times. Now get some sleep. Everything will seem easier in the morning." She laid her fragile houseguest back against the sheets, pulled the covers up to her chin, and kissed her cheek just as if she'd been her own daughter.

◈

TWO HOURS LATER, Nina spoke to me from the darkness, her voice hushed by the soft pillows and comforter that surrounded her head. "Em?"

"Yes, Nina?" I tried not to sound as exhausted as I felt.

"Thank you."

"It was nothing, Nina."

"How can I ever repay you?"

"I'll think of something," I said flippantly. I rolled over and looked for the fifth or sixth time at the bedside clock. It was half past three. Ava had left at two, and each time I had nearly drifted off since then, Nina had let out a quavering sob. I despaired of getting further sleep.

"Em?"

"Yes, Nina?"

"How did you know I was d-drowning?"

"I—" How *had* I known? "I woke up from a dream is all. You weren't there, so I went looking for you."

"What was the dream?"

"It was—" No, I couldn't tell her about those teeth. Not if I ever hoped to have her get back to sleep and leave me hope of doing so also. "Oh, I don't know. I don't remember."

Nina was quiet for a moment, and then she said, "Em?"

"Yes, Nina?"

"What *are* you?"

I tensed further, fearful that the poor chick thought I was an angel. "What do you mean?"

"I mean, you're a Gentile, but George said there were different kinds."

I recalled the Mormon definition of *Gentile*—anyone who is not Mormon—and said, "I'm a freethinker, I guess."

"What's that mean?"

"It means I follow what makes sense and seems truest."

"But isn't that *dangerous?*"

This idea startled me. "No, I don't think so. Don't you think everyone should have the freedom of their own beliefs?"

"But Brother Nephi says that freedom of belief is the handmaiden of the Devil. He says—"

"Brother who?"

"Oh!" I could hear the swish of crisp bedclothes rubbing together as Nina pulled herself up into a ball.

"Who is Brother Nephi, Nina?"

Breathlessly she answered, "I'm not supposed to talk about him to the outside!"

"Why not?"

"Because he's God's annointed, and we have to protect him from the evil of small minds." The words came out like a recitation.

I thought about asking how small she thought my mind was, but I let it go. So she was part of a cult led by a paranoiac, or perhaps some escapee from the law who was hiding under the cloak of religious propriety. So what. As long as he didn't know where to find us, I wanted desperately to sleep. "I'm sure he knows what he's doing," I said, trying to keep the note of irony out of my voice.

"If he even knew I was staying in this house, he'd be angry."

At a loss for anything more intelligent to say in comfort, I mumbled, "Don't worry, Nina. Brother Raymond gave you Heavenly Father's blessing tonight, and I'm sure *he* knew what he was doing, too."

But what had Ray been doing? That entire scene had been alien to me, a glimpse into another world. I was still trying to figure out what channel my mental television had been tuned to.

I heard sobbing. Nina had the waterworks running again. I lay in the dark, listening, wondering when I could hope to greet the oblivion of sleep again. I folded my hands on the counterpane, resigning myself to the likelihood that my brief snooze on the couch before dinner and the two or three hours of sleep I'd gotten before Nina went swimming might be it for the night. I stared balefully at the illuminated dial of the bedside clock. It was almost four. After Ava had left, I'd listened to Nina sob for two hours, and now this. Girl talk, panic, and more sobs. Ray was right: Nina didn't come from a background anything like mine. "What about George?" I asked. "How would George have liked you to handle this time of stress?"

Nina sucked in her breath. "George was *wonderful*." She snuffed. "He was like a *dream*."

I stretched my arms up and put them underneath my head, giving up the hope of sleep in favor of more information about George. "Tell me about him, Nina. Please. I get so many conflicting stories about him."

Nina slipped out of her bed and came to sit on the edge of mine, her tiny form barely jostling the springs. "He was always so *kind* to me," she said. "I knew he'd be kind the first time I met him."

"When was that?" I asked softly, making my voice easy, soothing, in hopes that it would move her over the invisible threshold that was keeping her from telling what she felt tightly constrained against telling.

"Eight years ago," she said dreamily.

"How old were you?" I whispered.

"Ten. . . ." She sighed, lost in the cushion of memory.

"How did you meet him?" I asked, trying to make my voice a warm draft for her to follow. I felt like I was keeping a soap bubble aloft, afraid to touch it with anything but my breath, hoping it wouldn't burst.

"I was out driving the goats and I found him digging in a hole. I ran to get Brother Nephi, of course, and he got his rifle and said he was going to go work some magic to make him go away, but then hours later, he brought George home and we killed one of the chickens and had a feast of thanksgiving. It was very exciting. Mummy told me later that George and Nephi had known each other in the Before Times, so it was okay, and that George would help bring us manna, and that was why I was given to George, you see, to seal his life to ours."

"Manna? Before times? Wait—"

"Before the Anointment."

"Oh. So Brother Nephi was not anointed at first."

"Oh, no. He lay in the Valley of the Shadow of Death and he took a Magic Potion and an angel came to him and anointed him and told him that he would rise up and sow his seed plentifully and bring his tribe through the Years of Hardship to the Promised Land." As she recited these words, her voice tightened from proud to anxious, and she quickly added, "But I shouldn't be telling you that."

"Oh," I said, not sure what else one says when confronted by such a story. "And so George brought you manna?" I was trying to remember what manna was. Some sort of food or sustenance lying free for the taking in the desert . . .

"I shouldn't talk about it."

"Oh. Well, that's fine, Nina." And, as if I were making conversation just to keep her company, I said, "Tell me more about George, then. What was he like when you met him?"

"He had more hair on his head." She giggled. "But still that lovely beard, so soft. He sat me on his knee and told me stories."

I knew I could not ask certain questions, like Where was that? "How nice," I sighed. "What stories did he tell you?"

Nina was warming to her narrative. "He told me about the different animals that lived on the earth before the Flood came. He told me about *Allosaurus,* and *Camarasaurus,* and *Stegosaurus,* and about how they lived by the rivers that flowed across the earth then, and about how they ate plants that were different from the ones that grow here now."

"How wonderful."

"Oh, yes. . . ."

"And did he ever take you to see these animals?" I asked, letting my voice communicate the wonder all children feel around the marvelous, no matter how old those children may now be.

Nina paused, and I knew she was considering what she could

and could not say. Clearly, there were imponderably strong threads of secrecy stitched everywhere through her life. I imagined a polygamist subcult living far out from town, scratching out a living on its wits and slim resources, keeping itself hidden, keeping its secrets from the world. It would have to be a group that had something to hide, or at least felt an unusual need of privacy. Into this, George Dishey had stepped. Someone Brother Nephi knew. George had held Nephi's trust; or, if my gut feelings about evangelists who swore their minions to secrecy were correct, the two found they had a lot in common and had simply struck an agreeable deal. Manna, indeed. What kind of business had George done with them, that he was willing to take a child in marriage to seal the deal? George, a master liar, a charmer who sat a little girl on his knee and told her stories of gigantic beasts that God had seen fit to punish by erasing them from the earth with a gigantic flood. . . . I had to fight not to shudder, for fear it would shake Nina from her reverie.

In a little voice, Nina said, "I really shouldn't tell you about the animals."

I tried another tack. "When did George marry you, Nina? Tell me about it, please. Was it wonderful? I've never been married." We were back to girl talk, the evergreen stuff of bonding among females of all ages.

"Four years ago today," she said wistfully. "He told Brother Nephi that he must wait until I was of *age*."

Fourteen . . . "A real gentleman." I winced over what the wise men of Utah considered the age of consent among females.

"Yes. Brother Nephi said that was okay as long as he took me out to his camp with him right away."

My stomach lurched. George had waited until she was fourteen to marry her, following not the letter of the law but its spirit, but had taken her to his bed at ten? The image horrified me. This didn't make sense. "I'm not sure I understand. You, uh . . ."

Nina suddenly giggled. "Well, yes, he took me to his camp and gave me hot chocolate to drink and told me stories and taught me the names of the stars. I always liked those visits. It was like I was *special*." Her voice fell into a whisper. "And he was so *gentle*. He said he wanted to wait until I was grown before he . . . you know . . ."

I took a wild guess. "Consummated the marriage?"

The bed jiggled up and down. Nina was nodding her head, tittering with excitement, and then suddenly she was crying again.

I sat up and scooped her into my arms. "Oh my God, Nina, you don't mean he had never made love to you, and you thought that now he was going to, and—and now he's *dead?*"

Nina's head bobbed up and down underneath my chin. Her sobbing ripped into outright howls. I was now holding Nina the woman.

"Oh no . . . Nina, is it your birthday?"

"Y-y-yesterday!"

"Holy shit!" I expostulated, then caught myself, apologized for my blasphemy, and said, "But wait, that's why you showed up Sunday night? You were coming to be with George on your birthday?"

In a tiny voice, she said, "Yes."

My mind started to implode. Struggling to fit the puzzle together, I said, "Did George know you were coming?"

A pause. "No."

"No clue? Did he know it was your birthday?"

"Well . . . well, he *should* have. I mean, I *told* him, last time I saw him, and . . ."

"When was that, exactly?"

"Well . . . a month ago, maybe?" Her voice sounded tight with impending humiliation.

"But he didn't say, 'Come on up to my house' then, or anything like that." In consideration for her feelings, I quickly added, "Not like that *exactly*."

"No—because, well, you'd have to understand that it was just after the Punishment, and—"

"The what?"

"Well, I had sinned again, and I had been given my beating, and—"

"Someone was *beating* you?" My mind ran wild. I thought, *We'll just see what Brother Raymond and the police department have to say to someone who's beating you; that is, if I don't get to the son of a bitch first!* "Who's beating you? Was it *George*, Nina?"

"Oh no!" she hastened to assure me. "George would *never* do that! George was *gentle* with me, just like I never made mistakes."

"What kind of mistakes?"

"Well, this time it was because I put the wrong flavor of preserves in Brother Nephi's sandwich."

"Someone *beat* you for—"

"Well, yes, of course. Brother Nephi is a Living Prophet, and he had to cleanse me of my errors so I could be worthy. But George was astonished at the bruises, you see, and he gave me a key to his house, and drew me the map of how to find his house, and said if they did it again, I should go there, and he's my husband and—"

"You mean you'd never been to his house before?"

"No. Never," Nina said, as in Scout's honor.

"But you came across that yard as if—"

"Oh, I know!" she said proudly. "And me never in a city before and everything! But that's because George drew such a good map. And because he taught me so well. And oh, Em, finding the city was strange and marvelous, just like George said it would be. I always thought there'd be plagues and monsters past where the road gets hard, but no. I just stood by the road and prayed, and angels stopped their trucks and cars and brought me here. George always said, 'Nina, you are a good map reader, the best. You can find anywhere just by reading a map. You're my very best finder.' "

"And what did he have you finding, Nina?"

"Well . . . bones. You know, like *Allosaurus*, and *Stegosaurus* . . ."

My jaw went slack. I almost flopped back against the pillows, but fought to keep my body and voice under control. "Did you dig for bones with him, too, Nina?"

"Oh, yes," she said proudly. "We *all* did. That's what we traded for the manna! You know, like the dried fruit that will survive the millennium, and the canned meats. And the thing is, Brother Nephi said that picking up the bones rids our lands of all those creatures Heavenly Father wanted to punish, and the Gentiles paid George *money* for it! Can you imagine? But of course, I needed to be punished, too, so—"

"But Nina," I gasped, trying to grab a rein on this conversation, "who was beating you?"

"Brother Nephi, but of course, I'm supposed to take my punishment and accept God's revelations through them. You see, it was for my own good, but George said it was nearly time that *he* should be giving me my revelations, and, well . . ." Her voice trailed off, losing its way in a blur of soft syllables.

"Is Brother Nephi your pastor?"

"Oh, no. He's my prophet. And my father."

As she said "father," Nina went oddly limp, and as I felt her slackening posture, I thought dully that I had heard about this response, that a child accustomed to abuse would sometimes flop like a doll when it began to happen again, for the fifteenth or the hundredth time, and might do it even when only remembering the trauma. It was a protective thing, I had been told, as if the soul took flight from the body for just a little while, until the torture again ended. I was talking to a survivor of scenes I could not imagine, of people beating her tiny body without remorse, working out horrors of their own at her expense, telling her all the while that it was for her own good.

I began to sway slightly in the bed, rocking Nina with me, holding her in my arms like the child she was. My heart grew outward to envelop her, wishing protection and love upon her. I wanted to say something comforting, like Oh, Nina, I'm so sorry, but feared that naming the abuse just then might be too shattering, feared she'd have to run from me to keep it locked up in the box it had come packaged in, a box labeled "Punishment," a huge dark compartment of the weird, drama-spiced world in which she had somehow managed to grow up.

17

MORNING CAME SOFT AND WARM TO SALT LAKE CITY. AVA
knocked on my door at 5:30, but I was already up, still awake
from my conversation with Nina, although she now snored
softly in her own bed. Having already more or less bathed
during the night, I had only to dress and find my way downstairs. I pulled on a pair of jeans, a T-shirt, and my beat-up
running shoes, drew a rather disreputable old jacket with polar
fleece lining out of one of my bags, and checked its pocket for
the little equipment kit I always keep there. Today was a field
day. Geologists like to be comfortable when they are outdoors,
and prepared. The kit held several things I'd found useful over
the years: a tiny first-aid kit containing iodine, Band-Aids, a
pair of fingernail clippers, a sheet of moleskin to treat blisters,
and a bulb to suck out snake venom; a Mylar space blanket in
case I ever had to bivouac in the cold or rain; a waterproof
vial full of strike-anywhere matches; and a small metal signal
mirror.

Ray appeared in the kitchen when I was about halfway
through munching down a bowl of cereal. For the past few
hours, he had been asleep in one of the vacant bedrooms upstairs, having apparently decided, after being called out for the
swimming pool fracas, that he would get more sleep there than

by going home again. He was barefoot, and I marked down one more check on the positive side of his list: His feet were beautiful. Some folks may find it strange that I should even notice a man's feet, but I do. Most people's feet are utilitarian sorts of things, rather homely in their proportions, often flat or somehow awkward-looking. Ray's were like something out of Greek sculpture. He was blessed with perfectly formed feet, his arches high, his toes graded from large to small along a graceful curve. I could imagine them flexing as he ran and jumped and caught balls in all the sports he must have played, a symphony of motion. Above these marvels of human engineering, he wore another pair of his pristine blue jeans and a gray sweatshirt that read simply BYU. The curve of its collar exposed perhaps a millimeter more of his neck than I'd seen before. I sighed.

"Sleep okay?" he asked, striding soundlessly across the kitchen to the refrigerator.

"Sure. You?"

"Fine." He poured himself a glass of orange juice and drank it, standing there with the refrigerator door still open, the glass in one hand and the carton in the other, one long draft. He refilled the glass, stowed the carton, and closed the door, then came to the kitchen table and sat across from me, his eyes on the glass. "I don't suppose you'd not go today if I asked you?" It was a question, a plea.

"No. I see no reason not to go." I shrugged. "With luck, Nina will be asleep all day. What else is there for me to do around here?"

Ray took in a breath and let it out. "Stay safe."

"I'll be with fifty or more paleontologists on a big lazy bus. How much trouble can I get into there?"

Ray rubbed his face with his hands. "One of them might have killed George."

"Maybe. Let's say that's one hypothesis. I've been collecting data that says Dan Sherbrooke had it in for him, or perhaps Vance the grad student. But at the same time, their worst provocation was professional jealousy, which is seldom enough to move one man to kill another. Scientists aren't as passionless as they look in the movies, but then again, we pride ourselves on being logical, and murder is not that."

Ray shook his head in agreement.

"So who else do we have?" I said. "Who's on the list of suspects?"

Ray turned his face away.

"You can't tell me," I said. "Fine. So I'm still on the list. But let's also say this about scientists: We are trained observers, and we are intelligent. Putting those two things together, and also considering the obvious fact that no witnesses observed the murder of George Dishey—"

Ray looked at me sharply.

"Oh, come on," I said. "That's simple deduction. If you had a witness, you'd be looking for whomever *that* person saw, instead of harassing me and Nina. So we can say that whoever killed George had the intelligence and good sense to kill him without being observed. Correct so far?"

Ray stretched and sighed.

"Fine. So far, so good. Next, if you were willing or able to talk to me about these things, you would point out to me that whoever made those wounds across George's chest was not feeling calm or rational when he did so. But we'll set that aside for a moment. Now, also setting aside the fact that George was a very provocative man who was generally disliked and distrusted among his paleontological colleagues, do you have evidence that leads you to suspect anyone else in particular? I mean anyone who might be on this well-populated bus full of highly trained observers, none of whom would be so stupid as to kill anyone in front of any of the others?"

"No."

"Then what's your problem?"

Ray stared a long while into his juice. At last, he said, "I've had a . . . what you'd probably call a premonition."

"Oh. You mean, like a message from God that says I should stay home."

For the first time that morning, Ray made eye contact. He smiled, one of those lopsided deals that bespeaks an irony. "Precisely."

I rocked my head back and stared at the ceiling. "Hoo boy. Here we go." I wanted to say something insulting, like *Did you get the winning lottery numbers while you were at it?* but stopped myself in time. My church, I was quickly coming to see, was the faith I had in the physical world, the world of rational events that could be analyzed and comprehended. Because I did not believe in metaphysics, purported messages from God—a phenomenon I sure as hell had never experienced and could not observe in others—therefore had to come under an area I defensively labeled "irrational." But getting angry about the irrational is more irrational yet, and I found myself once again counting to ten.

Ray said, "Mother told me about you waking up just when Nina went into the pool. Think about it, Em: You didn't wake up all the time she was moving about the room getting dressed and making the bed, but you must have come awake the instant she fell in, or she'd be dead now."

"Oh, so now you think *I'm* psychic. I woke up then because I'd had a nightmare; that was all—just dumb luck." And then? Well, then I'd made a series of analyses, the kind geologists make, quick leaps of intuition. And intuition, I had come to know, was a talent for matching observation with previously observed circumstances. I had seen that a distraught girl had tidied her few effects and left the room, and had thought of suicide. That meant the pool. No, I had felt cold and thought pool, but the result was the same. So what if I had been right for the wrong reason.

Ray's eyes flashed. "Not psychic—connected."

"What are you talking about?"

He set down his glass and reached his hands across the table, palms up, a beckoning, an invitation. "You read *The Refiner's Fire*. This is the alchemy he writes about. This is the magic!"

Something in his look set off a nervous tension, a sort of vibration, just below my navel. I leaned back and put my spoon into my now-empty cereal bowl. For half a minute or so as my stomach danced its nervous jig, I indulged myself in looking into this man's eyes, mapping them. I was transfixed by the light that seemed to shine from their bright mosaics of indigo blue specks. It was a frightening moment but also deeply gratifying, just the two of us meeting with our minds over the breakfast table, exchanging something of our hearts and souls. I wanted the moment to last, but knew it couldn't. At any moment, Ava might find her way back into the room and come to hover, enforcing her marvelous son's chastity. But for this moment, he was mine. My friend, however odd the circumstances of our meeting. My companion. What could I say to him that was not already communicated through our eyes? I knew that the moment I spoke, we would return to rational space, that place where my unbelieving mind must assert itself and burst this bubble of rapport, of understanding, of hope that he was right, that he spoke with God, and that God had known of my existence and taken time to pass along a warning of what was to come. I did not want to speak. I wanted life to exist continuously within a moment shared with this perfect man in this quiet kitchen.

Ava bustled in, all practicality and perfunctory early-morning smiles, dressed in a light teal green workout suit and white athletic shoes and socks. With the efficiency and high energy of a person who does not consider options, she had taken exercise while the morning was still fresh, keeping her splendid body functioning at maximum output for her age, gender, and genetic makeup for yet one more day. "Ah, Em," she said brightly, "I see you've found the breakfast makings. Good. Did you get some juice? You'll need it today, wherever you're going. The air is very dry here in Utah."

"I'll be sure to get some."

"I have a water bottle for you if you want it."

"Thanks, that would be great."

"When do you need to leave for the bus?"

"About ten minutes."

"Ah. It's time for our prayer, then."

Ray said, "Wait until we're leaving, please, Mother. Em and I were just discussing if, in fact, she's even going."

Our fleeting chunk of infinity completed, I said, "I am."

❖

ON THE WAY to the Salt Palace, where I would meet the bus, Ray turned down Second Street South. The Salt Lake City police station loomed into view.

"Why are we stopping here?" I asked uneasily.

"Someone here wants to talk to you," Ray said.

"Who? You aren't taking me in for more questioning, are you?" Ghosts of the horrid treatment I had witnessed there the day before flashed before my eyes. Was he going to keep me there all day, to keep me out of trouble? And worse yet, had they found new evidence that suggested that I had killed George Dishey? What did they have on me? I did not have Nina's capacity to curl up in a ball and ignore them, and for a moment even the threat of interrogation had me thinking I must somehow have killed George; in my sleep, perhaps. The bronze teeth made me do it. God only knew.

As the memory of my awful nightmare about teeth rose

again in my mind, the method of George's dispatch from among the living finally struck me. "Oh no!" I gasped.

Ray pulled his vehicle quickly to the curb and put a hand on my shoulder. "What is it?" he asked.

I looked at him in horror. "Oh, Ray, I know how George got those wounds."

"How?" He didn't want me to know; I could see that in his eyes.

I narrowed my eyes in fury. "Ray, I don't want to tell you, because then you're going to get it jammed even further into that brain of yours that I could have done it. So what will it be, Ray? You going to trust me, or what?"

He exhaled slowly. In an instant, he seemed to age ten years. "How?" he asked sadly.

I closed my eyes in resignation, certain I could not tell him. But then it dawned on me why Ray could not trust me. He couldn't trust me because he was in love with the truth more than anything else, and people in love with the truth scrutinize everything, even their mother's love for them. So that meant there was only one way to deal with Ray, and that was to tell him the truth and withhold nothing.

I said, "Whoever killed George did it with the Golden Jawbone." I told him about the *Allosaurus* jaw, with its long, curving teeth and their sharp serrations, so lovingly reproduced in bronze.

Ray winced.

"Yeah," I said, "that's why there were all those puncture wounds, and all in rows, and that's how all those deeper gouges were cut. He was disemboweled, just like a Jurassic lunch. He almost always had the thing on him, or at least in his backpack. That's what people say. I've held an original in my hand now, an actual fossil. Only the one I held was smaller than George's, a juvenile. It was a fearsome thing, but it fit my hand. There are protuberances along the anterior end of the thing that would give a person a good grip, and the bronze would have given it momentum. Those teeth were made to cut. In the hands of an angry man, the full-sized bronze would have been a cruel weapon."

Ray's jaw muscles worked. He was thinking.

"And if you think for a minute I could have done that to another human being, let alone any other animal, or even a gunnysack full of oats, you just don't know me very well yet. I'm an angry person, yes; but I'm not violent."

Ray sighed. After a moment, he turned and looked down the street through the windshield, then restarted the vehicle and moved on down the block to the police station. There, he parked his vehicle in the lot and led the way through the check station and up the elevator to the same floor on which Detective Bert had grilled us both the day before. My stomach tightened as I braced myself for another battle of wills. "When we get in there," I told Ray, "I'm going to ask that horse's hind end Bert whom he told about my whereabouts."

Ray ducked his head and knit his eyebrows. I knew Ray's body English so well by now that he may just as well have said I'd guessed right.

I rounded on him. "Who did he tell?"

Ray closed his eyes in resignation. "Sherbrooke."

"Sherbrooke," I muttered. "Mr. Wonderful. Mr. Big Guy. Mr. Get in Bed with Murderers. Mr. . . . So *he* killed George?" I was surprised to realize how much the idea surprised me.

"I don't know," he said firmly.

But Sherbrooke had been at the conference yesterday morning at the time someone was going through my room. *Or was he?* I tried to remember. I couldn't recall actually seeing him. *Did he send Vance? No, Vance was at the conference. Lew? No, I wouldn't trust him with a job like that—too self-interested. Then whom had he sent? The commercial collector with the Australian hat?*

I was going to get some answers, and the time was now. I traversed the last ten yards to that doorway, and, with my head down like a ram about to butt its enemy, I entered the room.

"*¡Hola!*" said a familiar voice, very cheery. "So nice to see you, my friend." It was Sergeant Ortega.

I went stiff with surprise. I said, "Carlos, how'd you—"

My round brown friend held up a hand to quiet me and smiled a parody of his most self-effacing smile. "Me? I got on a plane is all, last evening. It was past midnight, to be exact, because that was about when I could no longer believe that I could sleep. I told myself, Carlos, your friend cares for you, and she would call like she said she would if she was safe. So she is not safe. You must go to Salt Lake City and see if you can help her."

I closed my eyes in shame, wanting at the same time to slug him for delivering his punishing line in front of Detective Bert. "Carlos, I'm . . ."

"Sorry," he said, guiding me out of the room. "Em Hansen is always sorry. She would stay in better touch, but she has better things to do. But right now, your better thing is to find your friend a nice jelly doughnut, don't you think?"

I melted into his warmth and snaked an arm around his ample waist. Halfway down the hall, I said, "I don't know where they keep the doughnuts, Carlos."

"I do," he said merrily. "Hey, I been here three hours already. You think I don't got my priorities? First thing I do is find the doughnuts. Next thing, a good burrito stand. But now is still breakfast-time, so now is more doughnuts."

◈

IN THE EMPLOYEES' snack bar, I watched Sgt. Carlos Ortega of the Denver Police Department Homicide Squad down three jelly doughnuts and spoon three heaping teaspoons of sugar into his coffee as I brought him up to speed on the life and death of George Dishey, Ph.D.

"Nasty," Carlos said as he licked sugar off his thumb and forefinger. "Very nasty. Whoever killed him was very angry."

"The marks they made—"

"I seen the pictures. Regular Bundy. Pass the cream, will you?"

"Since when do you take cream in your coffee?"

"Doctor told me to eat a more balanced diet," Carlos said. "So I'm putting *leche* in my *café*. It's very good."

I took a moment to look over my rounded friend. The doctor was right: He did not look as healthy as I had once known him. He had gained even more weight, there were new lines in his face, and here and there I saw threads of silver in his straight black hair. Carlos was beginning to age, and I had just done my bit to accelerate the process. "I'm sorry about not calling, Carlos."

"I know."

"It must have cost a mint to fly here on such short notice."

"My sister Rosita is a stewardess on United. She got me on free."

"Oh." I felt deflated.

"And I got to take the ten o'clock back. Big meeting this afternoon in Denver. But yes, I was worried, and I phoned here and they didn't know where you were.

"Ray didn't tell them where I was?"

Carlos shook his head. "He must like you. So they asked me a lot about you, so I thought maybe if I came here I could help a little, get you home sooner."

"Thanks. Really." Then it hit me: Bert, or someone else, had showed Carlos the photographs. Carlos had been playing with me. I said, "How much else did they tell you, you . . . how you say 'tease' in Spanish?"

Carlos wiped his soft lips with a paper napkin and said,

"This Bert is an interesting character, full of bluster, but he left the room for a while, and the file was not difficult to find. Professional courtesy. What you want to know?"

"Tell me."

"You got to ask."

"Carlos! Where'd it happen?"

"Where do you think?"

"Well, inside city limits."

"Why do you think that?" he said, his shoulders heaving with merriment. He had lost a night's sleep over me, and he was going to have his fun. Unfortunately for me, cops are into sick jokes.

"Simple. It had to be, or it'd be someone else's jurisdiction. Voilà."

"Oh, now you're French. *Qué bueno*."

"So you tell me how the body was found, and where."

All merriment vanished from Carlos's face. "It was a very nasty scene. The body was found Sunday morning at a self-storage unit by a man who had gone out to get his speedboat. He had the unit next to the deceased's. Deceased had an end unit. The roll-up door was closed and locked, but there was a smear of fresh blood leading out from under the door, across the pavement, and around to the side of the building. He found the body there, facedown in the dirt."

Hence the scraped nose and face-down lividity. But why drag the body out the door? Not only did this not hide the body; it made the murder more obvious by leaving a trail of blood. And if the murderer wanted to give himself time to escape, he should have left the body in the storage unit and just close the door. "So the guy who found it called nine one one, and the rest is history."

"Yeah."

"What else they got to go on? Fingerprints? Footprints?"

"Oh, a few things. Boot prints in the blood, the things that were in the storage unit."

"Right. Anything distinctive about the boot prints?"

"Government-issue boots, the kind of cheap mass-produced stuff you can pick up at any surplus store."

"As opposed to the newer cheap mass-produced stuff that's coming out of China and Korea."

"*Corecto.*"

"What was in the unit?"

Carlos took a long draft of his coffee. "Bones."

A little *ping* went off in my head. Little connections went *click*. "You mean fossil bones."

"Yes.' "

"So who was this unit rented to? George?"

"*Lo mismo.*"

"George alone."

"*Verdad.*"

"So that's why there weren't any fossils to speak of in his house," I said.

Carlos looked questioningly at me.

"A paleontologist needs bones to study," I explained. "You can use the collections at museums, but you also go out and find your own. George worked with very large animals, dinosaurs. Dinosaur bones take up lots of storage space. So where was he storing his collection? He wasn't affiliated with any legitimate institutions. Everyone knew he was digging up fossils, because he was apparently selling them, so, then, where was he storing them? In the self-storage unit. It makes sense. They weren't in his home. Two reasons. Not enough room, and the damned things are messy, kick up a lot of dust and rock matrix. If he's got the bones at the self-storage unit, he can use his home as his academic base, keep all his books and journals there, write his popular papers there, and process the bones through a storage locker. Kind of like separating church and state."

Carlos nodded affably.

I said, "Thing is, though, that his esteemed colleagues said he was *selling* bones. I'm thinking that was how he was making his living, seeing as how he didn't have any other visible means of support. So here's a question. Did whoever killed him have an interest in those bones? Was it perhaps a business partner, or a competitor, or just an outright thief?" *A person interested in the bones, who thinks dead bodies should be left outdoors.*

"It seems there is quite a bit of money in the fossil business," Carlos said quietly.

I shut up and waited for him to elaborate.

He took another sip of coffee. "There was a case up in South Dakota a few years ago. Commercial collectors dug a *T. rex*. They named it Sue, after the woman who actually found it. It was an extragood specimen, nearly complete. Very rare and highly prized. They told the landowner they were going to put it in a local museum, paid him a few thousand bucks. But once they had it in the lab, they put a price tag of a million dollars on it. The landowner wanted it back all of a sudden. The Sioux Indians said it was theirs. When the federal courts finally settled on who owned the thing, it was auctioned at Sotheby's for something like eight million dollars."

I whistled. That was a lot of dinosaur. "You say 'a' case."

Carlos nodded, studied his coffee mug. I knew this kind of quiet in him. It meant he was considering what to tell me. There was history between us, a long, tense history of him telling me to quit cases and me defying him. And digging in deeper.

"How bad is it this time?" I asked.

Carlos stared into his coffee. "That guy over there by the Coke machine? He's FBI."

I didn't look around. It hadn't occurred to me to wonder if we were being watched, but of course we were. *A killer who likes blood and knows the value of bones.* I gave up and stared over my shoulder at the guy. Short, salt-and-pepper hair, and a lean build. It was good old Tom Latimer, the man I had first seen at the conference and then here at the police station the day before. He gazed at me blankly through his flint-dark eyes, as if it were perfectly normal to be sitting there listening to our conversation.

I said, "Why don't you just join us?"

The man picked up his coffee mug and did so. He did not say anything, just sat down at our table and continued to drink his coffee.

"Your name isn't really Tom Latimer, then," I said.

"No. But you can call me that."

"Would you care to tell me your interest in this case?" I asked as calmly as I could.

Not Tom Latimer set down his coffee and dumped in another container of half-and-half. "Oh, customs fraud, wire fraud, mail fraud, things like that."

I about fell across the table into his face. "George Dishey?" I said.

The FBI agent shrugged his shoulders. "Hard to prove. That Sue case led to discoveries that led to prosecution under the RICO Act. Racketeering. Organized crime. You lift a fossil off of federal land and say you got it off of private, so you're doctoring the paperwork right there, but all you've done so far is collect without a permit and lie a little. But then you use the phones and the mails to make a sale, and that's wire fraud and mail fraud, because it's stolen property. Then you transport it through U.S. Customs to, say, Japan, where you've got a collector who wants it for his bank lobby. You tell customs the price tag was a hundred thousand, but the Japanese paid you five. Customs fraud. You got maybe a couple dozen people helping you, and you start paying off a park ranger to tell you when the patrols are so your guys won't get caught poaching. Racketeering. Organized crime. All felonies. All federal."

I said, "So George Dishey was selling fossils, and you

maybe suspect him of some of the above. And maybe Dan Sherbrooke's even involved. And maybe . . ." I let my voice trail off. There were too many possibilities.

Not Tom Latimer nodded. "Like I say, very hard to prove. You got to get the paperwork."

"And now the guy's dead," I observed.

"Yes," he said. "But with George Dishey, there's another interesting little wrinkle. We didn't have enough to get a warrant on him to search his storage unit until he turned up dead, but then it's evidence for a capital crime, and we had it top to bottom."

"So you found the paperwork?"

"No. Other evidence. We looked for fingerprints."

"Right."

"And whoever did the murder was smart enough to wear gloves. No discernible marks in the blood, and you know we tried. But there were other fingerprints. Some of them may have been old, but they were readable. And one of them was quite interesting to us."

"Who?" I asked. *Vance? Lew? Dan Sherbrooke?*

"It was a guy named Willis Teague. The name won't mean anything to you, but it does to us. We were following his activities with great interest, right after he went AWOL from the service while being investigated for bootlegging military weapons off-base."

" 'Were' following him. Not 'are' following him?"

"His predilection for illegal weaponry would have interested us enough, but then we got word he had joined a paramilitary extremist group. Then he got crosswise with its leaders and went even further underground from there. Lost track of him twenty years ago."

I did some mental math. "So he was in Vietnam. Was he a helicopter pilot?"

"Funny you should ask." Not Tom Latimer smiled at me, a nice, slow, conspiratorial smile.

"He was the guy in the picture at George's house," I said.

"Smart woman. The police missed that one, but I caught it when I went through the house yesterday. I called up George's service record, and there was our man Teague. George was part of an intelligence unit, and Teague was part of his crew. But things didn't go well for them. They got into trouble for trading army rations to starving villagers for their family heirlooms. Antique altars, artifacts like that. Not that such peccadilloes were all that unusual, but George forgot to polish the right brass, and the two did a little time in the brig."

"George, George," I said, shaking my head. "And this Teague. Missing for twenty years, you say. Which means he's not dead, but you've been looking for him?"

"Yes."

"Why?"

"It seemed he used his helicopter to drop napalm on the villagers' crops, just to make sure they were hungry enough to part with the goods. And he had certain other rather antisocial proclivities."

"Such as?"

"Such as 'liberating' land mines from the army base they rotated him to back home, that sort of stuff. Oh, and aggravated assault, but that's more a matter for the police."

"And good old George had a picture of this guy in his house."

The FBI agent leaned back and smiled pleasantly. "Kinda makes you wonder."

"And this phantom's fingerprints were in the storage unit. Where?"

"On tools. Digging equipment. But there were no fresh fingerprints in the house except George's and yours, and there were none on the stolen car. We lifted a partial of another man's thumb print off one of the shell casings we found in it, though, which suggests the shooter loaded it a while before and wasn't thinking about covering his tracks when he did that."

I said, "Then it was probably a hunting rifle."

"Yes, or something you'd carry in your pickup if you wanted to be armed but blend in with the crowd. We had reports of a beat-up green pickup with gun racks in the neighborhood earlier that evening, but no guns, and by the time we got that report, it was nowhere to be found."

I said, "I saw him yesterday."

"Who?"

"Teague."

Not Tom Latimer's eyes went wide. "Where?"

"At the conference. Hiding in a van out behind the Cliff Lodge. Officer Raymond called in the license plate numbers. What ever became of that?"

Carlos said, "Detective Bert just wrote a note on that. Clean. They found the van farther up the canyon, parked at a private home—no one in it, no one around. It was registered to a Frank Smeely."

The FBI agent sat up and grinned. "Gotcha, you dirty low-life!"

"Who?" I asked.

He said, "Smeely is another commercial collector. Into the high-stakes stuff like the guys we prosecuted for the Sue case. I got fingerprints and prints from military boot in Dishey's storage unit and I got my military escapee in Smeely's van. Connect the dots."

"The guy with the Australian hat."

"That's his style, yes."

I said, "But that doesn't prove who killed George."

"No."

I saw again in my mind's eye the piercing look the man in the van had given me—an outrageous, soul-consuming come-hither stare—and felt a tour through a witness protection program looming in my future. I began to fidget with the salt shaker on the table, focusing my eyes on it, wishing it contained the whole universe within its simplicity. I said, "I had a glimpse of the guy who was following me. The shooter. He was wearing gloves—that's what made his fingers seem so thick—but he wasn't the man in that photograph. Well, I mean, not exactly. They looked kind of alike, maybe."

"Kind of like they were brothers, maybe?"

"Yeah."

"Yes, I saw your Identikit make. Our disappearing man had a kid brother. Also of the disappearing variety."

The memory of Nina's face in full reverie filled my mind. The high cheek bones, the riveting stare. Were these men her kin? "What do you know about him?"

"Dropped out of school at fourteen. Not a mental giant."

I sighed, remembering how easily I had spotted him, and how quickly he had panicked and fired on me and Ray. "That fits." What had the man in the house been looking for when I came back more quickly than expected and interrupted him? "So you looked for George's paperwork in the storage unit, but it wasn't there. Were there any file cabinets at all?"

"Yes, a small two-drawer. But both drawers had been emptied. Except for one sheet of paper that had slipped down underneath the bottom drawer."

I opened a palm upward. "Which said . . ."

"It was an order form for Perma-Pak. That's nitrogen-packed food."

I squinted. "Explain."

"If you want food with a nice long shelf life, you get it dried and packed in cans in nitrogen. Number-ten cans, in this case. Imagine what you'd do with a number-ten can of egg mix, for instance. It'll keep up to five years until you open the can, but then you have to use it pretty fast. So it would help to have a big family, right? That's about fifteen dozen eggs, as it turns out."

"How do you know that?"

"I phoned the contact on the order blank. It's a place out in California. Nice woman answered the phone. She said she was surprised that I actually had an order blank, because their sort of customers usually phone her up from a pay booth and order it by the truckload—they get fifteen percent off that way—but they want to pay by cashier's check and arrange a dead drop. You getting the picture? No paper trail."

"Militiamen?"

"Militias, yes; she said Perma-Pak was number one on the gun-show circuit. She said someone had put her name and number down on some Web site as the woman to call for the dried foods. She calls them the 'YTwoK crazies.' They're all certain that Armageddon's going to hit in the year 2000. So you pack your basement full of canned foods."

Manna, I thought. *Dried food . . .* "But wait," I said. "George lived alone. And I looked in his basement, and his refrigerator, for that matter. All he has is a week's supply of frozen burritos."

"Then that means he's either stockpiling somewhere else or acting as the go-between for somebody else."

"Beans for bones," I said.

"It's a possibility," the agent replied. "And George made notes on the bottom of the sheet: he'd evidently divided his allotment."

"With whom?"

"With a guy named Lew."

I spun the salt shaker in the center of the table. "The geology department tech at the university here. He went on digs with Dan Sherbrooke."

The FBI agent whistled. When I looked up, he was smiling blissfully. "So Dan's in this after all."

I said, "Could be. Running a dig's expensive. And there's all that prep work, and you got to pay for storage, and—but wait. Two drawers of filing is next to nothing. Anyone with a Ph.D. makes notes. It's ground into you. A love of data. Information is power. Even if George didn't like being pinned down on *his* facts, he had a roomful of books at his house, so he'd have records somewhere. So where were the rest of his files?"

"Right," said the agent. "There weren't any marks on the floor to suggest that any other file cabinets had been removed, either. So where were his sales records? He had to have something to show the IRS, even if they were cooked records, because we've got his income-tax returns, and he lists sales to Smeely's delightful little enterprise, among others. George didn't have sales papers at home, either, and there were nothing but magazine articles, profession-related E-mails, and video games on his computer. Which all suggests he had another storage unit somewhere else. Where? If you were a person who liked your privacy and you'd just committed murder, you'd want those records, wouldn't you?"

"Yeah," I said. "And if you were in the business of selling fossils but you'd lost your middleman, you'd want to find out whom to contact. And then the mysterious Mr. X tosses the house. And then Bert tells Sherbrooke where I'm staying. And then someone tries to get into my motel room. And then I see your disappearing man at the conference in Smeely's van."

The FBI agent grinned. "Interesting, huh?"

I hung my head in misery. "Ver-r-r-y interesting."

❖

AT THE SALT Palace, I waited inside the six-story-tall cylindrical glass entrance foyer, which was in fact a sounding chamber. Eight glass doors opened inward to the convention hall, and sixteen opened outward onto West Temple. Over each pair of doors was mounted a tall wooden acoustic sound box, like an organ pipe. Outside, along the sidewalk, stood a row of windmills, cocked at differing angles turning at differing rates in the morning breeze. As each blade completed a full rotation, an electronic pulse was transmitted to a corresponding sounding box, and a soft, ethereal tone reverberated through the chamber. I had never experienced anything like it before, and I was transfixed, soothed, in love. My stomach had been in a knot since speaking with the FBI agent, and I wanted to hang on to this fragile bit of tranquillity. Just as with the moment of looking into Ray's eyes, I did not want to leave and face the outside world again, the world of professional jealousy and scientific scrutiny and child beating and renegade helicopter pilots with gun fetishes, but neither did I want to go farther inside. Just then, inside scared me even more. How much sweeter to remain in this place between in and out, in the comfort of man-made shelter, but soothed by this acoustic reminder of nature's power and presence.

Ray waited with me. We were both silent, savoring our moment of safety.

At 7:30, the bus arrived—the first of two, in fact—and I nodded good-bye to Ray. "I see old what's-his-name getting on the second bus," I whispered, carefully not looking toward Not Tom Latimer.

Ray continued to stare up into the sound chamber, his lips moving silently.

I said, "If he's along, you don't have to worry about me, right?"

Ray's eyes tightened with worry. "That's not the message I get." He lowered his gaze to me. "You have the phone number?"

"Yes," I said, patting the pocket that held a slip of paper

with his mother's phone number on it. If anything went wrong, I had promised I would call him there. He would be spending the day there baby-sitting Nina.

"Go if you must," he said.

❖

AT THE TOP step of the bus, I was greeted by that usual moment of social stress in which I, as newcomer, must make eye contact with a miscellany of strangers and decide which of the open seats I shall occupy. Two seats on each side of the center aisle, four columns of faces, eleven rows, all regarding me blankly, or staring out the windows, or falling back asleep, or focused in conversation with the persons nearest them. Dan Sherbrooke looked up briefly from where he sat up near the driver, his eyes magnified into his usual look of doelike surprise by his jury-rigged glasses. They held no special spark of recognition, let alone guilt. His face hung with apparent uninterest. I hurried past him.

I found a roost about four rows from the front, next to a tall man of about sixty who had a full head of gray hair and a kind, thoughtful face. We introduced ourselves. His name was John, and he was curator of the vertebrate fossil collections at a large midwestern natural history museum. "So you're into dinosaurs," I said.

John smiled. "Dinosaurs. You want to know what I think of dinosaurs?"

"Yeah."

John pantomimed spitting on the floor. "I think *that* of dinosaurs. Now, fish to amphibian, early tetrapods, *that's* where the interest is."

"Oh, really? Why?" I asked as the bus pulled out into the stream of southbound traffic and began its turns toward the highway.

John regaled me for a space of fifteen or twenty minutes

with a string of multisyllabic Latinate words I could only tan-
gentially understand, and that much only because he spoke as
often with his hands as with words, and larded his descriptions
with more familiar words, such as *jaw* and *leg*. But his enthusiasm for his topic was infectious, and it was a pleasure to
indulge, for the time being, in the safe, orderly life of the
intellect. As he chatted away, I watched out the window for
indications of where the bus was going. It turned south onto
Interstate 15, whizzing past the rush-hour traffic flowing north
from Provo.

As John wound up his dissertation on the marvels of early
land-dwelling four-limbed creatures, I said, "Thanks, I enjoyed
that. But let me ask you: What do you say to people who ask
you to justify your work?"

"What do you mean?"

"I'm talking about the people who don't believe in science,
or in the work for its own sake."

"You mean the bureaucrats who want me to justify the work
in dollars and cents. Like the folks who value the space program only because it brought us Velcro and Tang."

"Yeah."

"I ask them how they expect to do conservation if they don't
understand evolution."

I sighed with pleasure and relief at his simple pragmatism.
"Thanks. I needed to hear that. I got into a wrangle with a
creationist last evening, and it's a pleasure to be reminded of
how passionately a scientist cares about his work."

"Why, of course we feel passionately about it," John replied. "If we weren't passionate, how could we devote our
lives to trying to understand just a little bit more about creation? And there's the irony. We are studying creation, after
all."

"Right," said a bearded man across the aisle. "We just aren't
studying *special* creation. Although I've never seen that theory

scrutinized. I wonder how it would stand up?"

John said equitably, "I like to think I keep that theory out on the table while I work. This is science, after all. We are supposed to keep an open mind."

The bearded man shook his head ruefully. "Doesn't it just burn your ass, John? Those assholes from the religious right had the gall to picket us! I mean, what's their problem? Do they feel confident in their beliefs only if everybody agrees with them? They'd never make it in a scientific arena, where the whole job is to present ideas and evidence with the hope that someone will shoot it down if you're not right."

John nodded his head thoughtfully.

"I had to leave just as that was heating up yesterday," I said. "And I missed the TV coverage of the press conference. What happened?"

"You missed nothing," said another voice.

I looked up over my shoulder. Earthworm Magritte had moved up the aisle and was perched on the arm of a seat a row behind me. Today he was wearing a clean, if threadbare T-shirt with CALIFORNIA MUSEUM OF PALEOBIOLOGY, NOT OPEN TO THE PUBLIC, across it, but the pants looked like the same pair he'd had on the day before and the day before that. From this close-up, he was no less imposing a figure than I had encountered the two previous days, but certainly more human. He had rather sad eyes and, as I had noticed before, smelled pleasantly of mint. "It was the usual sound-bite crap," he continued blunt as ever, "all this shit about 'Scientists are out to disprove the existence of God.' That's an argument that starts out with the presumption that all scientists are atheists."

The bearded man said, "Aw, hell, I don't believe in that God stuff, but that doesn't mean I'm out to disprove it. I got better things to do with my time."

I smiled ironically. He sounded like Enos.

"Well, and so what if you *are* an atheist?" said Magritte.

"Although I'll bet a year's pay you're a closet pantheist. A spirit in every rock."

"I take my spirits *on* the rocks," said the bearded man.

"But think about it," said Magritte, "like John says, here we are devoting our professional lives to trying to understand just a little bit more about what we see around us." He gestured out the window toward the steep rampart of the Wasatch Range, which rose imposingly behind the city of Provo. "What am I supposed to call all this? This is *creation*, a perfectly good noun from a standard dictionary. We're all so fascinated by it that we spend our lives studying it. You want devotional activities, try a life's work on for size. Creation's designs and systems are nothing but exquisite, inspired. And some half-wit with a Bible steps up and accuses us of not feeling moved by it, of not being so damned impressed that we just want to spend our lives sitting humbly at its feet."

We sat quietly for a moment, contemplating our lives.

The bearded man broke the reverie with a defiant laugh. "I'm still an atheist," he insisted. "You're trying to say there's no difference between science and religion. I beg to differ."

"I agree," Magritte hastened to say. "But there's also an overlap. I looked the word *religion* up in my dictionary. The first definition is 'Concern over the unseen,' and things like that. The second definition is 'A specific fundamental system of beliefs and practices agreed upon by a group of people.' You've got to agree that both of those apply also to science."

John said reasonably, "But there's a difference in intent."

"Perhaps," Magritte answered. "But you get my drift. My vote is we redefine our terms, and agree to apply the term *science* to study of matters physical, and apply *religion* to the articles of faith and practice. Then we can save *spiritual* for matters of the soul."

John said, "The picketers would have a field day with you. That's being way too rational."

I heard the familiar sound of Allison Lee clearing her adenoids. Her perfectly groomed face jutted into the aisle three rows back. "Yeah, face it, Worm, there are plenty of phenomena that are not rational, and science and the scientific method cannot address them, but they still occur. Like, your Aunt Mildred won't get on a flight to Los Angeles because she has a premonition. The plane crashes. She even had a sense of the terrain in which it would crash. You can't explain that scientifically, and yet it happens. Or little Freddy has cancer and all of modern medicine can't heal him. The Sisters of Perpetual Prayer get together and lay their hands over him and he's healed. Explain that. And it's time the word *irrational* lost its pejorative connotation."

"Just so," said Magritte. "But now, like I say, you're speaking of spirituality and metaphysics."

The bearded man said, "That can all be explained by coincidence."

"Now I would argue with the fundamentalists that you are refusing to observe that which is right in front of you," Magritte replied.

The bearded man asked, "You having visions again, Magritte? Maybe you had a few drinks with the departed spirit of George Dishey last night or something?"

Magritte grinned, a kind of stretching of his lips over peg-shaped teeth. "Yeah, good old George. He liked to play with reality a bit, didn't he?"

No one replied.

Magritte said, "Now, there's something no one wants to talk about, our dear departed heretic, George. He bent the truth a bit, and we were all too chickenshit to say so in so many words. Too bad George isn't with us today; Dan could maybe rub his nose in the facts once and for all. But then, he wouldn't have showed, and that would have *really* frosted us."

John said reasonably, "We asked him to debate Dan in public, but he wouldn't."

"Yeah," said Magritte, "he played with our minds by accepting date after date and then never showed up. No 'Sorry,' no 'I got a hangnail,' just no George. For that and a thousand other dodges, we all despised him. But we wouldn't say so, wouldn't publicly rip the buttons off his uniform and drum him out of the corps."

"So what?" asked the bearded man irritably.

"So what? So what is we did something a whole lot worse. We just closed ranks on him. Squeezed him out of every job. Shot him down behind his back every time he proposed a symposium. Left him out in the cold."

"But he never showed us his data," said Allison. "No one ever even saw anything he collected until it was in final mount and delivered to a museum—sign here, and here's your bill for some astronomical sum. And God only knows where it really came from."

As Allison spoke, I saw another familiar face peeking from behind the back of a seat several rows behind her. It was Lew, the department tech. He smiled smugly, gorging on this new gossip.

I turned my gaze away from him and focused back on Earthworm Magritte. Playing devil's advocate again, I said, "So why didn't you all just consider him a commercial collector? Don't some of them have Ph.D.'s?"

Magritte said, "Because when you make money the issue, the system is corrupted. Because he started out as one of us, and we all feel betrayed."

"Aren't you being a little dramatic?" asked the bearded man. For him, the conversation had gone beyond intellectual sport, and he looked nervously toward the front of the bus, to see if Dan was listening.

Magritte said, "But it *was* betrayal. Like all the times he published something fanciful or preposterous, just to disagree with Dan. Or like the time he rushed Dan's ideas about that prosauropod into print, shoving it into the newspapers before Dan could get it through the rigors of colleague review. It took Dan two and a half years to get that one out, and by that time, it looked like Dan was stealing from George. And what do we have as a result? We have Dan running a field trip like this one, dragging the press out to the site quick before some- one scoops him. Dan wasn't always like this. George goaded him into it; we all know that. Like I say, the system was corrupted."

I tried to imagine how Dan might have felt about a stunt like that. It must have eaten at him, plagued him like a yowling cat who stands six inches beyond the reach of a chained dog.

"So why *didn't* anyone say anything?" I asked.

Magritte shoved his glasses up his nose. "Because it wouldn't have been very scientific of us to drum him out of the corps; it would smack too much of the Salem witch trials. Science is an open debate. The burden of proof is on the presenter. Salem was a closed debate, where the burden of disproof was on the accused. In science, we don't practice blood atonement."

"What's that?" I asked.

"That's where the blasphemer's blood is spilled into the earth to atone for his sins. We aren't as direct about things. Instead, we just bury our sinners alive. You don't agree with the status quo, you better damn well bow and scrape and kiss butt until you've mollified your elders and they can retire gracefully and maybe claim you as a brilliant protégé. You see, that's how it really all got started. Dan kissed ass and George kicked butt, and guess who got the grants?"

The bearded man said, "Magritte, you took too much acid back in college."

"You didn't take enough."

The bearded man laughed.

Magritte's eyes brightened behind his Coke-bottle glasses. He grabbed the bearded man in a half nelson and proceeded to give him a Dutch rub. The bus broke into roars of laughter. Bits of wadded paper flew through the air from a group of young wags in the back of the bus.

Someone from a few rows away hollered, "What you selling, Worm? You working undercover for the New Age dickheads out there in California?"

Magritte grinned, showing a row of his short, narrow teeth. "Yeah, I'm pushing Amway. I was just working up to that."

"You'd do better with Mary Kay cosmetics," someone suggested.

"Leave the cosmetics to Allison," Magritte replied. "The Church of the Dinosaur Footprint and Baptismal Cologne."

Allison gave him a Bronx cheer. "Cologne? I use only perfume, Worm. But it's all toilet water to you!"

"Wait!" roared another. "The Worm was just getting warmed up. I want to hear his gospel."

Magritte turned and spread his short, thick fingers across his chest. "I think whoever made this place signed Her name on every rock and flower."

"So you're a Goddess worshiper?" asked the bearded man.

"I give equal time to every paradigm," said Magritte.

"That even rhymes," the bearded man rejoindered. "But you couldn't convince me for an instant that someone just stepped up here and built this ball of rock and tissue in just six days. That's fatuous. You know it and I know it."

Magritte looked thoughtful. "I don't go for the literalist translation of the Book of Genesis any more than you do, but there isn't a man or woman on this bus who isn't completely knocked out by the perfection of natural systems, the way they all dovetail and work together. We look out through the windows of our five senses and see such marvelous systems, design, and order, such themes and variations, from the basic structure of matter up to the paths of the celestial bodies, that we can never get enough. The evidence within the laws of nature are god enough, even without the beliefs and liturgy that comes packaged with most religions."

Conversations sprang up in surrounding rows, returning the bus to its earlier state of hubbub. Then Allison's voice cut through the chatter again: "So, Worm, you got God's numbuh; what does Huh business card say?"

Magritte thought a split second and replied, "GOD: No Job Too Large or Small."

Appreciative laughter erupted, and the bus bubbled into intellectual chaos again.

"Nah!" cried a voice, "It's 'GOD ASSOCIATES: A Rhyme, Reason, and Spirit in Every Rock, Tree, and Squirrel.' "

"No! Try 'GOD, INC.: Arcane Knowledge on a Need-to-Know Basis,' " suggested a third.

Yet another voice offered, "GOD, INC.: Sacrifice That Fatted Calf or You're Toast!"

"Nah, too Old Testament!" yelled a heckler farther back in the bus.

"Equal time for Buddhists!" squealed another woman.

"Just phone 1-eight hundred-four-A-DJINN!"

"Or 1-eight hundred-ENLIGHTENMENT!"

"That's too many letters!"

"Then I'm damned for all eternity!"

There were peals of laughter. Paper wads started flying again.

"How about an E-mail address," someone hollered.

"Perfect!" said Magritte. "E-mail is pure energy! The metaphysical utmost."

"God at universe dot com," began another voice.

"Dot net!"

"Dot E D U!"

The busload of happy intellects roared with academic frivolity, spitting out one ticklish idea after another.

My mind wandered quickly from their rowdiness. I was too overtired to stay with it, and too troubled by everything that had been said about the war between George Dishey and Dan Sherbrooke. I fiddled with these new pieces of information in my mind, trying to fit them together with what I had learned from the FBI agent that morning. From what he had said, Dan Sherbrooke was only peripherally involved. Or was he? Was I a coyote chasing the wrong rabbit?

Settling back in my seat, I watched out the window for a while. We had turned off the interstate at a town called Spanish Fork and were heading southeast through a deep canyon that wound up through the mountains. The slopes blushed with the turning leaves of a thousand oaks, punctuated here and there by the gilding of groves of aspens. "Where do you think we're going?" I asked John.

"The San Rafael Swell," he replied.

"How do you know?"

John smiled and ticked his evidence off on his fingers. "Simple deduction. Point one: We are off to see a dinosaur specialist present his current field location, so that means we are going to dinosaur-bearing strata. Point two: We are traveling southeast from Salt Lake City. That means we are heading toward the Morrison Formation. The Morrison is famous as Utah's 'Dinosaur Diamond,' which refers to the localities within the three corners described by Dinosaur National Park, Colorado National Monument, Moab, and the Cleveland-Lloyd Quarry, which last is in the San Rafael Swell. Point three: This is a one-day field trip—in, out—so we can't be going very far. The San Rafael Swell is really the only place close enough."

"That's terrific," I said, impressed. "You ought to be a detective."

"I am," John replied. "But I spell that word *paleontologist*."

I smiled. "What do you think about what our friend Magritte was saying about George Dishey?"

John's face softened, and he thought a while before replying. "Let me answer by telling you one of the things I like best about working in the sciences: We can presume everyone to be telling the truth, at least as he or she knows it. In the realm of pure science, what would be the point in lying?"

I looked down the aisle of the bus toward the long, narrow strip of blacktop over which the bus was rolling, eating up the miles between civilization and the wilderness to which we were heading. John had put his finger on something. He had put his finger on exactly what made it inspiring to work in the sciences. It was first and foremost an exercise in reaching toward the truth.

But George Dishey was a liar. Aside from the deceits his colleagues were telling me about, he had lied to me about speaking in a symposium—of that, I was certain—and if what he'd told Nina about the natural history of the earth wasn't made up out of whole cloth, then he had been lying to everyone on this bus, making a mockery of their rules, or, as Magritte might say, blaspheming their beliefs.

So, then, why and about what else had George Dishey lied? And which lie had gotten him killed?

18

JOHN WAS RIGHT. THE BUSES CAME OUT OF THE CANYON at Price and turned south toward the beautiful, bald, "castle" country of the western San Rafael Swell. It was warming into a splendid day, all deep blue sky and long views down along the Book Cliffs to the east and south into the center of the swell itself. Only a thin haze from a distant coal-fired power plant muddied the air between the swell and the tan cliffs of Cretaceous-aged sandstone and shales that stair-stepped down from the west, but I saw the beginnings of thunderheads building far beyond them over the mountains. I hoped they would stay where they were, at least until we had completed our visit; I didn't savor the idea of pushing a bus up a dirt road soaked by a sudden rain. The Morrison Formation and several of the strata we would cross to access it were largely composed of swelling clays, and roads characteristically followed the valleys cut into the softest layers.

Excitement mounted as the buses swung off the highway onto local pavement at Castle Dale and then headed deep into the country, dropping onto broad dirt roads. Turning at a sign that had been blown into oblivion by shotgun target practice, we branched onto a lesser road, slowed to a near crawl as the buses wallowed over sections that had been washed and rutted once or twice since the grader had last passed through, eased carefully over cattle guards, and finally stopped by a line of low cliffs. Our driver set the brakes of our bus and opened the door at the bottom of the coach steps.

Dan Sherbrooke, who had been talking boisterously with colleagues throughout the ride, rose from his throne at the front of the bus and faced the other passengers. He had added a much-abused fishing hat with the legend STAN'S BAR AND GRILL to his already unorthodox appearance, and its flat crown and narrow brim did nothing to make his rather chubby cheeks look any sleeker. "Make sure you bring your water bottles and hats," he said. "It shouldn't rise above a pleasant seventy-five degrees this time of year, but it is quite dry, and the sun is strong at this elevation. And we have long a hike ahead of us. Sorry that we can't get the buses any closer, but at the same time thank God for that. If this site were any closer to a graded road, it would have been vandalized. Follow me!" he cried jubilantly, and climbed down onto the road.

As I followed the paleontological multitude down off our bus, I saw Vance run off the second bus and dash along the road to catch up with Dan Sherbrooke. His gait was awkward, as he was struggling to carry a collection of poster boards that had conspired to slither apart. His face was set in hard, angry lines, a jack-o'-lantern scowl, not unlike a three-year-old who is gauging a kick he is about to plant in his older brother's behind. His chest was contracted even farther than the last time I'd seen him, and it struck me that for Vance, anger was an armor that provided incomplete covering over a deep, pervasive fear. I wondered what had him so frightened.

I stepped down onto the road and followed him over to where Dan had everyone gathering. "Esteemed colleagues!" Dan cried. "You are about to see something the quality of which a paleontologist sees only once in a lifetime, and that only if he is lucky! One mile and a half from here lie fossil remains so startling that I wanted you to see them for your-selves, to judge them for yourselves. It is said that a picture is worth a thousand words," he continued, his voice swelling and beginning to sound like a carnival barker's. "But a picture has only two dimensions. How many more words can be gleaned from the original three-dimensional reality of fossil remains! Couple those three dimensions to the fourth dimen-sion of *time*, and the picture tells us even more. We as pale-ontologists comprehend the value of seeing those remains in situ, in the full context of the environmental clues of the rocks and other fossils deposited around them."

I noticed that Lew had planted himself next to Dan and was scanning the crowd, his thumbs hooked contemptuously into his pockets. As I was trying to imagine what had him looking so smug, I felt someone's breath against the back of my neck, and smelled mint. Without even turning, I knew that Earth-worm Magritte had drawn up close behind me and was bending to speak intimately into my ear. "I'll be damned," he whis-pered hoarsely. "He's going after Dishey after all; hammering him for never showing his locations to anyone."

Dan paused, hands clasped a few inches in front of his broad, rounded chest. He appeared to be deep in thought. His hands began to move sensuously in each other's embrace, the palms sliding back and forth in an unconscious parody of greed. At length, he said, "When fossils are removed from their lithic context—removed from the history recorded in the rocks around them—much is lost. Here, we will see pristine specimens *in* their stratigraphic context. Vance, give us the stratigraphy, will you?"

Vance all but tumbled over himself in the act of scrambling up to where Sherbrooke was standing. He elbowed Lew to one side and stood there, dwarfed by his expansive mentor, pa-thetically shuffling a selection of poster boards that were pasted up with charts and illustrations enlarged for the benefit of those of us who were standing at the back of the throng. He awkwardly shuffled his first illustration to the top of the stack and handed it to Dan. There was a moment's arbitration as Vance attempted to get Dan to hold the board in front of his chest, covering Dan's face, but at last Dan accommodated him by standing to one side and holding the poster at shoulder height.

Vance cleared his throat. "What we have here is a geologic map of the San Rafael Swell." He pointed to the center of his map. It showed each rock layer in a different color, broad bands of blues, greens, and yellows indicating the expanses where each layer met the surface of the earth. "As you can see, the swell is a big honking dome structure, with the older Permian-aged rocks heaved up at the center leading outward to the younger Cretaceous-aged stuff forming the cliffs we see to the west and north here. Just your little old three-hundred-million-year slice of the earth sandwich." He pointed to each feature on his map. Some titanic force had buckled the earth's crust skyward across this territory, fracturing the rocks along the axis of the hump. It was as if a huge hippopotamus had risen from the depths, and the rock layers stretched across its back had heaved, cracked, and eroded away. This lifting and erosion had removed the layers from the center outward. On Vance's map, the pattern made by the outcroppings of the different-aged bands of rock made an elliptical bull's-eye, oldest at the center and getting younger toward its edges.

Vance took down the map board and lifted another into its place. "Okay, this is the Mesozoic stratigraphic sequence," he said. He was now pointing to a layer-cake illustration depicting the rocks as the flat layers they were before the hippopotamus humped them into a dome. "I'll make this simple for you press people. Sedimentary rock like this is deposited in layers, and you can interpret how they were deposited by the composition of the rock and so forth. The Mesozoic was the Age of Reptiles. It began two hundred and forty-five million years ago with Triassic time; then you have the Jurassic, and finally the Cretaceous, which ended sixty-five million years ago. A hundred eighty million years of time recorded in the rocks. So here are the rocks that were deposited in the Triassic and the Jurassic. Down here at the bottom, we have the Moenkopi Formation. It was deposited under marine conditions to the west and on dry land to the east. Okay, that ocean receded to the west, because next above that, we have the Chinle Formation, which is entirely terrigenous, river and lake sediments deposited higher up from the coast. Then we move into Jurassic time. As you all know, climates were unusually warm during the Jurassic. No ice ages. Utah, where we are here, was about ten or fifteen degrees of latitude closer to the equator, which puts it in the trade-wind belt. Dry, descending air, lots of wind, and we're above sea level, so that puts us in a desert. Think Sahara Desert, with the sea coast a couple hundred miles west of here."

Vance stopped to look around and make sure his audience was following him. Those paleontologists in the group who were first trained as geologists were tightly focused on his illustration. Those primarily trained in biology were listening with polite interest. The press were beginning to look around at the scenery, except for one science reporter I had seen at the conference the morning before, who was scribbling notes like mad and no doubt thinking up a more eloquent way of restating what Vance was telling him.

"Okay, so in this desert, we had sand dunes." Vance flipped to another poster board, which was pasted up with sexy photographs of modern sand dunes on the left and Utah's fabulous ancient wind-deposited sandstones on the right. "The Wingate Sandstone, the Navajo, the Page, and the Entrada Sandstones. Five million years of blowing sand punctuated by the river sands and overbank muds of the Kayenta Formation and a brief marine incursion represented by the Carmel Formation. In this area, these form a sequence over a thousand feet thick. A half dozen miles east of us, the San Rafael River, that lazy little stream we crossed on the way in here, which may do a flash flood if those thunderheads have their way"—he stared out to the west, keeping a weather eye out—"cuts down into these sandstones, forming a landscape just as pretty as your Grand Canyon, but at half the scale." He turned to the crowd. "I for one think this area ought to be the next national park, quick, before some asshole carves his name on the rest of the petroglyphs and litters the campsites with any more Vienna sausage cans."

Appreciative laughter and applause broke out. Someone cupped hands around mouth and shouted, "You're preaching to the choir!"

Vance went back to his lecture. "Okay. So up above all the sand dunes we get one more shallow marine incursion—the Curtis and Summerville Formations—and then we're in solid continental conditions again. The good old Morrison, the land of the dino and the home of the brave." He handed Dan one more poster board, this one pasted up with an artist's reconstruction of the Jurassic landscape. Volcanoes chuffed in the background as dinosaurs gamboled about a shallow river, grazing here, mating there, running from carnivorous cousins over there. "Christine Turner and Pete Peterson are just finishing their big synthesis of the Morrison, the culmination of decades of work. And what do they have to tell us, folks? More desert. We got broad, arid landscapes with a few shallow lakes that can dry up and streams that seasonally wither into shallow little dribbles during the long, parching droughts."

Magritte breathed in my ear. "Vance waxeth poetical."

I smiled. The Age of Reptiles could use an ode or two.

Vance said, "Imagine big-time environmental stress. You got quite a biological traffic jam here as big herds of dinosaurs vie for lunch along the thin vegetative corridors at water's edge. We got the big herbivores—sauropods, ornithopods, and stegosaurs—munching on thin stands of lakeside ferns, cycads, horsetails, ginkgoes, and conifers, occasionally wandering too far into the mud and getting mired. Then there are the meat eaters—herds of *Allosaurus*—coming in after them, risking getting stuck themselves. Imagine volcanoes erupting to the west and northwest, repeatedly showering the area with ash. Ash, sand, and mud. Freshwater crocodiles and turtles. And the exact spot where we're going, algae and ostracodes are in that mud, giving us an interpretation of freshwater lake bed. Mud bank above the lake, that's where we're going. Dan?"

Dan Sherbrooke summarily dropped the poster boards back into Vance's arms and continued the glorious speech. "What we are going to see living in this desert landscape, by this ancient lake shore, is the state-of-the-art predator of the late Jurassic period. Who am I talking about? *Allosaurus fragilis* . . . a fierce creature, thirty-five feet long or longer in adulthood. This animal lived gregariously, and hunted in packs." He stared into the crowd, locking eyes with one colleague after another. "*Allosaurus* was fast, efficient, and as strictly predatory as a cheetah."

Sherbrooke rolled back his head and closed his eyes, savoring the moment, soaking up the rays of the sun like a devotee none-too-humbly receiving a benediction for his good works. He opened his eyes and again scanned the crowd. "*Allosaurus* was the quintessential hunter. She had flattened teeth, with serrations on leading and trailing edges, and each tooth curved backward to hold the morsel and slice through it at the same time." Sherbrooke gestured ferociously with his hands, holding his curled fingers up near his mouth. "Her jaws were slender and designed for cutting. She was an attractive predator, sleek, quick, and clean." He nodded, agreeing with his own statement, then delicately raised one side of his upper lip in an insouciant sneer. "*T. rex*, the vile scavenger, by contrast reeked with the stench of soupy black flesh. Perhaps that explains why *T. rex* was solitary and *Allosaurus* gregarious. *Allosaurus* was the hawk, *T. rex* the vulture."

Laughter rose from the crowd. "My kinda girl!" called one wag over the heads of his brethren. "What's her *phone* number?"

Sherbrooke smiled and paused for dramatic effect, milking the moment, drawing the crowd even further in with his grasp.

"What do you think he's got?" Magritte whispered. "It has to be fabulous, to take a risk like this. You want to see carnivores going for the kill, just wait until this gang warms to the debate."

When Sherbrooke spoke again, his tone had moderated, shifting to a more conversational tone. "We all know the theories regarding the carnivorous dinosaurs. Were they cold, torpid reptiles, or were they warm-blooded, resourceful, more like the birds that have descended from them? One leg of any argument must stand on the inferred behavior of these animals. We search for evidence of their behavior. Did they, like tortoises, lay their eggs in the sand and then depart, leaving their young to fend for themselves? Or were their young like birds—requiring care and feeding from their parents—altricial rather than precocial?" He paused again, letting his brethren resonate on this essential question that plagued students of dinosaur evolution.

Now Sherbrooke's tone waxed evangelical. "We hunger for good evidence, for any clue that confirms or denies our theories. What you are about to see," he continued, raising one index finger triumphantly, "is not just a fine specimen of *Allosaurus*. That in itself would be worth the drive, yes . . . but what we have here is much, *much* more. What we have here is a very nearly complete skeleton, fully articulated!"

A buzz of conversations broke out through the crowd.

"Nice, but . . ." Magritte whispered into my ear.

"You might say, 'Articulation itself is a surprise, a treat, but we have seen that in museums,'" Sherbrooke said arguing against his own point. "Yes, we are always so happy when we find a skeleton that has not been torn asunder and scattered by predators, rivers, or the ravages of time . . . but this specimen, esteemed colleagues, goes even further. This specimen is posed in life position, caught by the terror of a sudden volcanic eruption. As the choking cloud of a glowing red-hot volcanic ash rose over this animal's head and rained down around her, this valiant animal crouched over her helpless *young*! What we have here is an adult *Allosaurus* in *brooding* position on her *nest*!"

From that moment, Dan Sherbrooke could not have said more to the crowd if he'd wanted to. This was a jury of his peers, a group of individual thinkers, and conversations ripped instantly throughout the crowd. Dan had to roar to be heard over the hubbub. "Come!" he bellowed then turned and marched off through the thin desert scrub.

The group flowed quickly in behind him as he headed up over a low hill capped by buffy gray sandstone and disappeared down the other side, his spine heroically straight, his shoulders square. This was his day, his moment; he was experiencing his pinnacle of professional glory.

Like Earthworm Magritte, I wondered why Dan Sherbrooke was willing to risk bringing this gathering of the best and brightest minds in paleontology to the very spot where his data lay exposed, fresh, unanalyzed, his interpretation preliminary and unchallenged. This was confidence. This was bravado. What if he took this specimen back to the lab and, through whatever continued reduction of encasing sediments that must be left in place for transport, he discovered that the juvenile bones belonged, in fact, to some other species? What if they proved even to be of differing ages? Anything was possible.

And what if he was right? *That* would be something. *That*

would make this field-trip stunt no less spectacular than Moses showing a videotape of the Red Sea actually parting.

Magritte fell into step beside me, jamming a faded red ball cap onto his head as he walked. "This is going to have to be better than sex to justify that P. T. Barnum act," he cackled.

We tramped through a desert thinly studded with yellow-flowered rabbitbrush, knee-high brushes of Mormon tea, and a few thin grasses growing out of soft adobe soil, the kind that fluffs up when the occasional rains make the clays within it swell. Such soil compacts with every footfall. I could make out the intricate treads on the shoes of those in front of us, but up ahead, beyond Dan Sherbrooke, the galumphing Lew, and the glowering Vance, the ground appeared unblemished. Dan and his crew had approached their site through another access, leaving no tracks leading off main roads that would invite the attention of the more unscrupulous kinds of collectors. This was federal land; collecting should happen here only with a permit. But it was also open, unprotected, empty land, vulnerable to unnoticed transit by any number of unscrupulous scavengers.

"So, Em Hansen," Magritte was saying. "state your name, rank, and serial number."

"Excuse me?"

"I'm not much for smooth conversation openers. That's the best hit line I've got."

"I see," I mumbled lamely. "I'm not much for smooth conversation continuers."

"I disagree. I've been watching you."

"I've noticed." Had he been staring at me just to size me up for a convention conquest?

"You look too smart to run afoul of George."

"I try to be," I said equitably, trying to accept Magritte's words as some kind of left-handed compliment. "But I'm afraid I bought his lie hook, line, and sinker," I said firmly. "And don't try to put a positive spin on that, or you'll be loading me with the same brand of flattery George used to convince me to give a talk at his blessed nonexistent symposium. And as long as we're being blunt, exactly why *do* you think it was about time Sherbrooke killed him?"

Magritte pondered for a moment, pushed his glasses up his nose as he stumbled slightly over the uneven ground. "I'm sorry I said that. It was over the top even for me. I don't really think Sherbrooke killed him."

I wasn't going to let him off that easily, especially after the elaborate homily he had presented on the bus. Had that been a cover? "But you must have thought George was worth killing even to say that. Were you mad at him?"

"Me? I wouldn't say that. I thought he was provocative. I ought to know. I specialize in being provocative."

I broke a sweat as we scrambled down through a dry gulch and climbed up over a lip of crumbling sandstone on the other side. I had spent too much time sitting lately, too much time pushing papers across a desk, and had gotten out of shape. *No matter,* I thought grimly, *if I can't get this case settled by tomorrow and get back to Denver, I'll be getting plenty of exercise pounding the sidewalks, looking for another job.*

The landscape called to me. It reminded me of the land around my parents' ranch, except drier. I felt an urge to leave the crowd and walk out into it alone, or perhaps just with Ray, to show that city boy a part of my own heritage.

I tried to pull ahead of Magritte, but my legs were shorter and his stronger. The exertion of trying to outstrip him both physically and mentally gave me a swimmy feeling, a sensation of being lost in a fun house full of warped mirrors. I gave up and stopped for a moment to get my breath, hands on knees, head bowed, thinking, *Ray's right: I shouldn't be here. I'm too tired to keep up with the Earthworm Magrittes of the world today, let alone get ahead of them, and who knows what in hell's name is waiting over the next rise?*

When I straightened and looked up, Magritte was staring at me through his thick glasses, drinking me in with such candor and vulnerability that my heart lurched. I saw myself reflected in his lenses, two little Emilys standing gape-mouthed and sweaty in the middle of the desert. "What do you want from me?" I asked.

Magritte said simply, "I have no social skills, but I'm a nice guy."

In that moment, I saw myself reflected more deeply, on the mirror of his soul. I'd have known myself anywhere. Good old Emily Hansen, awkward as hell, trying to find herself a place in the world, but picking fights at the dinner table instead.

Flies were beginning to swarm around my face. A gnat found one of my earlobes and bit. The sting pushed me back into gear, and I started to walk again. *Back on track, Em. You're here to investigate a murder. . . .*

Magritte said, "You don't have to be obsessive to get a doctorate and beat your way up the ranks in a competitive field like vertebrate paleontology, but it helps. We are sane people, mostly, and smart. And we're shy, you know? You're a geologist, what?"

"Yeah."

"Then you know what I mean. We like to be all alone out in the middle of some desert somewhere. Like here, just picking at the data, digging at a fossil, minding our own business. There's a few like Dan here who like the big limelight thing. Or like Dishey, but even he sneaked back into a crack to hide every chance he got."

"Right." *But what was George hiding, aside from a teenaged wife or two?*

I was busy formulating a question, which was going to be

about George, when Magritte yanked the conversation out from under me again, asking, "So who's the Eagle Scout?"

"Excuse me?"

"Your shadow. The pretty boy who was walking around behind you at Snowbird."

"He's a cop," I said. "A nice sane cop."

Magritte's eyebrows shot up in interest. "Never met one of those," he said. "You involved?"

"*Excuse* me?" Candor was beginning to grate on my nerves.

"Then you are. Or you're thinking about it. But maybe there's still hope for me?"

"Excuse *me*?"

"Yeah, you. Sure, you're as awkward as I am, but like I say, you're smart. So what is he, a Mormon or something?"

"Ex*cuse* me?"

"Your Eagle Scout. Real clean-cut. We're in Utah, so that means Mormon. You know, they aren't exactly original thinkers. Crises of faith are discouraged. You'd get bored with him."

I stopped walking again. Magritte stopped also and, as before, turned to face me. Several people had to swerve to get around us. "Listen," I said, "I'm going to just . . . take my chances. Okay? I mean, Jesus Christ, how'd I get into this conversation?"

Magritte looked into my eyes, waiting.

"What's your real name?" I asked.

Magritte did not answer.

"Fine," I said. "Listen, Magritte, there are a number of ways of being dishonest in this world, and some of them are quite subtle. Pretending a word like *earthworm* is your given name is a kind of lie, for instance, when you think about it. Pretending you have a right to speak to me this intimately is another. Now, *if* you don't mind . . ." I moved past him and hurried down into the next arroyo.

◈

TWENTY MINUTES LATER, Dan Sherbrooke halted the march at the mouth of a small canyon that fed out into a wide basin floored with gray soil. "We are almost there," he said. "I have sent Vance ahead to begin removing the cover we constructed over the site to protect it from the elements and from . . . vandalism. The information recorded in this site is, needless to say, unique. I know I need not even mention to those of you in my profession that this site is fragile and that it is best to stay out of the actual diggings and touch nothing, but for the benefit of those members of the press who are new here, I ask that you act as if these fossils—this fabulous, priceless site—were made of spun glass. Very heavy spun glass, which might, in fact, fall on you if you were to lean on the wrong parts of it. Preparatory to removing them to the lab, we have underexcavated the bones as far as possible, leaving only a few pillars to support them, and they cannot be considered stable. Thank you."

Sherbrooke turned away and then back, his face suddenly heavy with feeling. "I have one more thing to say. As you all know, our friend and colleague George Dishey died just two days ago. It is a . . . tragic loss to our profession. There were times when many of us . . . I . . . *disagreed* with George about many things."

The crowd shifted restlessly, once again a loosely drawn collection of individuals having their separate thoughts and feelings.

Sherbrooke said, "George and I engaged in something of a . . . *rivalry*. I may have accused him of unsound science, of hurrying his work into the popular press instead of taking the years-long arduous route into scientific publication the rest of us must labor through to ensure that our literature stays as clear as possible of unfounded ideas stated as fact. I am sure that at times I may have *criticized* George, perhaps more than was quite fair."

"*May* have?" whispered Magritte, closer to my ear than I was braced for. I jumped. I had been deep in thought, wondering if the man standing here warming up to a eulogy of his nemesis could have inflicted the wounds I'd had the misery of viewing. Was Dan Sherbrooke the naïve monument to vanity that he appeared, or in fact a murderer who had cut down his enemy in a fit of rage? And if in rage, then what event could have ripped the lid off of his capacity to contain his jealousy and frustration?

Sherbrooke placed his right hand over his heart and bowed his head for a moment. I noticed that he had not removed his hat. "But all that is ended now, and I say, let the dead rest." He looked up, his dark eyes magnified to a childlike softness by his inelegant glasses. "In that spirit, I would like to dedicate today's viewing to the memory of George Dishey." He dropped his hand from his heart. It swung listlessly by his side, and his eyes took on a distant stare. "Besides," he said at a lower volume, almost to himself, "Even when George was wrong—when he published those . . . ideas of his in the popular press—it stirred controversy, and controversy can force a man to work harder, to really reach for that elusive thing, a scientific fact, an incontrovertible truth." He shrugged his shoulders. He was talking to himself now, a man caught out in public with his innermost thoughts. "It's not a bad thing to work hard, to reach."

Onlookers shifted their weight from one leg to another, cleared their throats. Some looked sideways at a hawk that now circled lazily over a distant reach of grassland, or found portions of the palms of their hands that suddenly required scrutiny.

Dan inhaled, exhaled, and looked up. "Now . . . follow me!" Smiling like a Hannibal who has just crossed the Alps and spotted the green valleys below, he turned, merrily waved one arm in a "wagons ho" arc over his head, tromped out into the basin, and turned sharply left. The crowd flowed along behind him, conversations rising in anticipation.

As I rounded the corner, I could see where the site was. It was something less than a quarter mile away, tucked into a bed of shale close in against the toe of a steep fan of car-size rocks that had fallen from the cliff above. The quarry itself was small, perhaps only twenty by a hundred feet in area. I could see a hole, and surrounding rubble, and a desert camouflage tarp thrown back, and Vance running, yelling, *screaming* toward us. His arms windmilled with horror. I could not understand what he was saying. It did not sound like words.

"What is it, Vance?" Sherbrooke called, for once remembering his protégé's name.

"*Vandals!*" came the answer. "The thieving bastards got our site, Dan! Oh, Dan, they got it *all!*" Vance tripped on a rabbitbrush, fell, and lay howling in pain that had nothing to do with his body.

Sherbrooke threw his bulk into high gear and ran toward the site, joined by several alarmed colleagues. Allison Lee stopped to lift Vance to his feet, but the young man had no strength and tumbled backward. She knelt and held him in her arms, a windswept Pietà of the desert. I found strength that I did not know I had and kicked into a sprint, desperate to arrive at the site before vital evidence was trampled. "Stop!" I panted. "Don't step on any tracks!"

I need not have worried. As I traversed the last hundred yards of uneven ground, I could easily see the deep ruts made by heavy equipment that had come from the north, something at least the size of a backhoe, something big enough to rip the bones of a dinosaur out of the ground in huge ruthless bites.

19

THE FOSSILS WERE GONE. SHERBROOKE'S GREAT DISCOVERY, Vance's doctorate, all gone. For a moment, the only sounds were labored breathing and the clicks of journalists' camera shutters, the whirr of their autowinders. A gentle breeze pushed a lock of my hair across my forehead. The soft twittering of a flight of horned larks met my ears, reminding me of simpler times in the desert, when life had been just a moment with nature. But those times were just a memory; I was standing by a grave.

But the dead were missing; Tiny flecks of dark maroon bone stuck up here and there from the gray clay in which it had been embedded. Straight dark furrows like the gougings of monstrous fangs marked the site where the backhoe operator had ripped the specimens from the ground, no doubt crushing them, springing their delicate ribs, scattering their finger bones, hauling away the big pieces, reducing the rest to paste.

"Who could have done this?" asked a familiar voice of no one in particular. I looked up. It was Not Tom Latimer, the FBI agent playing dinosaur artist. I had to hand it to him—he looked as aghast as the rest of the people present, but I knew that in asking these words at this moment, he was acting as the information-gathering professional he was, timing his inquiry to strike ears at the moment of greatest vulnerability, when he was most likely to startle an answer from someone who would otherwise not have spoken.

Someone answered, "A professional. You'd have to have worked with this kind of rock to know to wet the ground first and make it soft. See the way it smeared rather than crumbled? Without wetting, this shale is like *iron*."

Dan said nothing. For once, he had everybody's attention and no words to speak. I studied him carefully, from the set of his jaw to the slope of his shoulders and the hang of his hands. He was in shock.

I was in shock, too. I understood now what George had been yelling about Sunday morning when summoned to the phone. "You'll bust the thing to pieces," he had said. He had been talking about this fossil.

I looked past him toward Lew, expecting to see at least a sagging jaw or some other measure of surprise, but he seemed only smug. I tried to decide whether this was just his usual manner, frozen in place from years of affectation, or a reflection of his current feelings. He caught me looking at him and shifted suddenly, his hand rising to cover the lower half of his face defensively.

A journalist began to step down into the excavation, but I grabbed him by the sleeve. "Please stay out of the diggings," I said crisply. "It will be necessary for the FBI and the BLM to see this mess in as pristine condition as possible if they're going to hope to find out who did it." I glanced cautiously at Not Tom Latimer to see if I was saying this correctly. He did not make eye contact. He had melted back into the crowd and was scanning the assembled practitioners of the bone hunter's art for reactions. His face was again quiet, impassive. I could read nothing but intense interest.

Sherbrooke's hands pumped repeatedly into fists as he once again stirred to life. Squeezing his eyes shut, he said, "Yes.

We must report this. Does anyone have a cell phone?"

A reporter answered, "Yeah, but I already tried it. I can't get through. We must be too far from a repeater or out of line of sight. Sorry."

"Very well," Sherbrooke replied, turning back toward the path he had followed to reach his destroyed dream. "Then *we* shall go to *them*."

"You can't *leave*," gasped Vance, his voice cracking like the squeal of a trapped rabbit.

Sherbrooke did not even glance back over his shoulder as he replied, "You want to stay here, fine. But the buses are rolling for Price." Darkly, he concluded, "There is nothing to be gained from staying here. This site is finished." He stormed away, his strides lengthening with determination. He was no longer Dan the jubilant, shoulders back and chest raised, or Dan the whipped, arms and head hanging; he was now Dan the avenger, head forward, fists balled, a dark cloud of fury storming across the desert floor.

◆

AT PRICE, DAN'S fury fizzled to maudlin self-pity when he discovered that the office of the Bureau of Land Management was bereft that day of anyone with the authority to help him. As the buses idled in the parking lot outside, he stood at the broad Formica counter, whining piteously at the secretary, demanding again and again, "Isn't there anyone here today who can help me?"

"I'm sorry," the woman replied, patiently matching each iteration of his plea with another version of her blank governmental ignorance, "but the geologist in charge of that site is not here. I would be glad to take a message. . . ."

"Where's Shirley?" Dan whimpered. "She *knows* me. She'll—"

"Shirley is on maternity leave," said our middle-aged matron. "*I* am replacing her until she returns."

Vance chose a less child-to-mama approach than Dan. "You get on that cell phone and tell that shithead geologist of yours to get his ass down here!" he shrieked. "You may be over-extended and underfunded and *stupid*, but this is an *emergency!* This is fucking *Armageddon!*"

The woman inclined her head forward, staring at Vance over the tops of her glasses. Knowing that a "Listen here, sonny" speech was about to follow, I quickly said, "Ma'am, excuse me, but these men have just seen a huge amount of work go down the drain. I'm hoping you can find someone who can help us. Is there anyone else in the office today with enough authority to call in a law-enforcement agency?"

The woman shifted her gaze, now appraising me. "I will see what I can do. In the meantime, perhaps you *gentlemen*"— she spoke the word slowly, savoring its inappropriateness— "would like to give me a number where you can be reached."

"You aren't getting rid of us!" squealed Vance. "We're *tax-*payers! We're—"

"Enough, Vance," said Sherbrooke, grabbing his graduate student by the front of his shirt and dragging him summarily toward the door. "Madam, we can be reached at the Mecca Club, where we shall be drowning our sorrows."

The woman's eyes narrowed at Sherbrooke's receding back, and I knew he had just said *booze* to a Mormon.

◈

PRICE MAY LIE smack near the center of a state ruled by the long arms of the Mormon church, but it grew up as a mining town, a working-class, give-me-liberty-or-get-outa-my-way sort of place, and the row of bars down the main drag of town prove it. It is an unlovely, unadorned city of outmoded square buildings built for shelter first and grace last, a place to do business, an escape from the boiling heat of summer and the raw chill of winter. The buses moved like lost elephants down the street, lumbering toward the watering hole Dan Sherbrooke had named. Two blocks west of dead center downtown, they pulled to the curb and disgorged their passengers, who followed their host through the 1950s-era doorway into the Mecca Club. Inside, the man behind the bar nodded hello to Dan. He was a tall, stiff man of advancing years. He had the bleached look of one who seldom sees the sun. He had been polishing the top of the bar when we entered, but his hand stopped moving when he saw the swarm of thirsty paleontologists that was following Dan through the door. This was Utah, wherein to order anything stronger than 3.2 beer, one may not just walk into any saloon and ask, but must be a paid member of a club. A member may, however, bring any number of guests.

Dan said, "They're all with me."

The bartender nodded and began to set up glasses.

And at that, Dan seemed to collapse. "The usual, and keep hitting me," he moaned, dropping his body onto a stool. He leaned onto the bar, preparing to fold himself up in the arms of alcohol. As Dan's paleontological brethren crowded in around him, the bartender unceremoniously poured a double shot of Jack Daniel's, which Dan downed in a gulp. The bartender never asked, and Dan never offered, the reason for his sudden appearance with seventy close pals; it was life as usual at the Mecca Club, and what are ya havin'?

When it was my turn, the bartender turned his gray face toward me and hoisted his eyebrows a millimeter in inquiry. "You got a telephone here?" I asked.

"Through the door into the café, turn right," he answered as he rotated his head a fraction of a degree to look at the man next to me. "Next?"

I shouldered my way through the crowd and found the back

door, made a right turn at the back of the adjoining short-order café, headed down a narrow hallway that kinked back toward the bathrooms, and fetched up by a pay telephone. I punched in Ava's number in Salt Lake City and followed it with digits from my credit card. After two rings, Ray answered.

I said, "Where's Nina?"

"Right here. Why?"

"Like right next to the phone?"

"No. In the kitchen with Mother."

"Can she hear you?"

"No."

"Can she pick up an extension and listen in?"

"No. Now, what—"

"We're in Price," I said. "Someone got Sherbrooke's site."

"Got it?"

"Stripped it. Went in with a backhoe, looks like; really did a job."

Ray's voice took on the intensity a bird dog displays when it spots a grouse. "Where are you now?" he asked.

I told him. "It looks like this gang is settling in for a serious drunk. Nobody had much stomach for their box lunches, but they're thirsty for a little forgetfulness. It really hit everybody hard. It's like a wake in there, only nobody's telling funny stories about the deceased." I turned and glanced up the narrow hallway to make certain no one was listening. "Can you get down here? I think we can maybe follow those tracks. They stand out like a sore thumb." I shifted the phone to my right hand, shoving my bandaged hand back out of my line of sight. For the work ahead, I could not dare to contemplate my own vulnerability.

"What are you thinking, Em?"

"Well, it strikes me like this: You've got a murder and the FBI's got grand theft and racketeering. The two crimes meet in George Dishey. The murderer knew where the bones were stored, even called George out to meet him there, because that's where the crime was committed. So far, so good?"

Ray inhaled, exhaled. "Right."

"So the question becomes, who else is stuck between the two crimes? Well, the answer is Nina."

Silence.

I wanted to spit. It was way past time for Ray to quit treating me like a suspect. I said, "Last night, she told me all about being George's best bone finder. So that means she was part of a larger group. *Group* means *family* to that girl, *family* means *polygamy*, and *polygamy* means . . . well, a splinter group, right? We passed a big house on the way in here. It did not look prosperous. So maybe it's the guy George knew in the army and maybe it's not, but whichever way you slice it, they're scraping for a living and at least one of them has a taste for violence. So they've got a scam harvesting fossils off of federal land without a permit, and she's George's best finder. You can damn well bet she's been taught to evade the authorities; she's probably been taught to think they're the devil incarnate."

Ray said dryly, "Thanks."

"You're welcome," I said just as dryly. "But the fact remains that Nina is part of a group George used to find the fossils. So the question then becomes, Where are Nina's people? Might they be out here?"

Ray's breathing became deeper, noisier—an athlete taking on oxygen before a sprint.

I talked even faster. "So I'm down here at Dan Sherbrooke's fossil site. Dan and George worked dinosaurs of the same time period—the Jurassic—so that means the same age of rocks. Everyone tells me that George was secretive about where he went collecting; that's why we don't know where Nina's from. So who's to say Dan didn't stumble onto George's harvesting grounds? I should have put it together earlier—the Morrison is famous for dinosaurs. *This* part of the Morrison—right here along the San Rafael Swell—has them, in abundance, and it's also a nice place for hiding all sorts of activities you don't want the law to know about. Vance was cussing and shrieking about right-wing bigots all the way back to the bus. He says the swell is lousy with everything from shiftless rednecks and out-of-work coal miners to Ku Klux Klanners. Is that *true?*"

With some embarrassment, Ray said, "Klanners, yes."

"Well then, how about a group of gun-toting, renegade Mormon, ultrafundamentalist, polygamist wackos? Tom whatever his name is—because it isn't Latimer—told me you have fingerprints at Dishey's storage unit that belong to a prize survivalist gun junkie who went underground more than twenty years ago. So maybe George began working down here a while ago and stopped at some out-of-the-way homestead to ask directions, and there he was, longer hair and a biblical beard, but George knows it's him. The guy's desperate now. He's completely paranoid, he's got a big family he's controlling with his self-obsessed ideas, and they're trying to make it out here on nothing but buckshot jackrabbits and Mormon tea. You ever been down here?"

I stopped to take a breath and nod to Not Tom Latimer, who had sidled in from the bar and was listening intently.

Ray paused. "No."

That pulled at my heart. "You grew up three hours away and you never even went camping down here?"

Another pause. "Dad had asthma."

"What about the Eagle Scouts?" I prattled.

"No, I played sports, remember?" He was trying to sound jocular. I had hit a nerve.

"Well, okay, it's a big place with lots of little canyons. I've been looking at a map a man on the bus had. It's mostly BLM land, but there are a few inholdings way out in the middle of nowhere." I looked at Not Tom. "Just the kind of place to hide with your tribe while you wait for the year 2000 to blow you into the next kingdom, or whatever you might be expecting."

Ray said, "I suggest you keep your voice down."

He was right: In my excitement, I had let my volume rise. "I'm alone down a back hallway; so no, nobody's listening. Except your pal with the salt-and-pepper crew cut here."

Not Tom Latimer leaned his mouth toward the phone and said, "Hi, Ray," then straightened up and started scanning the hallway, his eyes always moving. Somehow, he managed to look casual, as if he were just awaiting use of the phone or access to one of the bathrooms.

Ray sighed in exasperation. "*Please*, Em."

I was really rolling now, completely immersed in my theory, long past being a good girl for Ray or anyone else. I was beyond the reach of his brooding, devastatingly blue eyes. He was a pleasant abstraction back there in the tameness of the city, where everything—life, the streets—was laid out on a grid, and I was out here smelling the wildland, huddled up against a pay phone in a humble little café in a sad-looking burg built on coal in the back of nowhere, my own emotional and spiritual backyard.

I began to spin my free hand, making wider and wider gestures, willing Ray to understand what I was saying. My hurt thumb began to throb with the motion. "Or, if you *really* think you're the chosen few, maybe you don't *care* if you're squatting on public lands. Maybe you think it makes perfect sense to bilk the heathen public, round up the bones of drowned animals that God has damned and sell them. But you've got a problem, if you don't like dealing with the public. You've got to go through someone like George. George has the connections. George doesn't mind bending the rules a little. And George knows the market for things that excite the public—he's been feeding them science candy for years. Do you follow me? Ray?"

Ray sighed. With sadness I could not understand, he said, "Straight as an arrow."

I had thought he'd be happy, excited as I was to be homing in on the resolution to the case. He wanted to make detective, didn't he? So what was his problem? The chase was on! Uncertainly, I said, "Well, okay, good. Can you get a tap on Ava's phone?"

"Why?"

Not Tom Latimer echoed Ray's question with a tip of his head.

I said, "This is what I'm thinking: You tell Ava within Nina's hearing that you're coming down here to help me. Tell her we're heading into the desert southeast of Castle Dale. You guys will need a search warrant, and you can only get one with an address, am I right? So while you're driving down here, Ava can give Nina plenty of chances to get to a phone and warn her family. The goons listen in and get a fix on where she's calling, and we'll know if we've got the right place." I stood up straight and grinned into the phone. This was brilliance, or so I hoped.

"*If* they have a phone."

"Yes, if."

"And if she's still speaking to them, after that last beating."

"Of course she is. Yes, she's been horribly abused by these Brother So-and-So guys, bartered off at ten to seal a business deal, but she didn't hide under a porch Sunday night because she was afraid of going home to another beating. She's a survivor, and the way she has survived is to think it's her job to take beatings. No, she stayed put because she was there for a purpose and wasn't going to leave without fulfilling it."

I made eye contact with Not Tom Latimer to make sure he was with me. His eyes flashed like distant beacons, and he gave me ten percent of a smile as he made a circling gesture with one hand that said, Keep going.

I said, "She may look like a child, but she's eighteen years old and as red-blooded as the rest of us. She went to George's house that night with high expectations, expecting to get . . . sleep with her husband for the first time. She gets there expecting her long-delayed wedding night bliss, and *wham*, the place is running with cops. But she wouldn't just *leave* again. She was devoted, eighteen, and determined. She hunkered down to wait for George."

The FBI agent rolled his eyes.

I said, "Think about it, Ray. That girl's under incredible stress, and when all else fails, survivors go on autopilot."

Ray said, "Meaning what?"

"Tap the phone, Ray. Get yourself down here. And watch your back."

Ray was silent for a long while then said, "Give me the number where you are. And put Tom, um, Latimer on. It's going to take me a few minutes to get this together."

◇
◇
◇

20

◇
◇
◇

THE FBI AGENT TOLD ME HE NEEDED TO MAKE A FEW CALLS
himself. He'd receive Ray's message when he called back, then
find me in the bar. I headed back through the inside door into
the Mecca Club.

The *Allosaurus* wake was in full swing. Geoscientists are a
lone-wolf lot, given to long periods of professional and personal solitude punctuated by short bursts of intense socializa-
tion. Alcohol is the great antidote for shyness. In circumstances
such as these, in which our basic hesitancy is exacerbated by
both professional anxieties and personal emotions, we can get
drunk on one beer and the power of suggestion; but cram
seventy of us into a small hall belly-to-belly, thereby pressing
our instinctive need for space and privacy up against our secret
longing to belong, and we switch to an overgregarious jollity
and are almost instantaneously plotzed.

The room was concussed with the roar of conversation, each
voice growing louder and louder in order to be heard over all
others that were doing the same. Movement within the room
was all but stalled, so orders for more beer were being volleyed
hand over hand toward the bar, accompanied by folded money,
and glasses of suds were flowing back. People who had studiously not noticed me until that moment were suddenly glad

to see me, wanted to know what I was drinking, wanted to know if they could pass *me* overhead toward the bar, because maybe I could sing for them. I smiled pleasantly as I pressed my way slowly toward the front door, listening for interesting conversations.

As I squeezed past the knot of people who were helping Vance gas his brain, I heard a young woman next to him shout over the din, "Well, there goes another critical piece of data. Bye-bye advancement of the science. Let's just send everyone to the dinosaur theme parks or the movies, issue them their *T. rex* T-shirts, and give up on trying to educate them."

I paused a moment to listen.

"Yeah," a man with a nose like a shark's fin mused at ninety decibels, "imagine learning everything you know about dinosaurs from *Jurassic Park*!"

"Spielberg did okay," shouted another. "At least he had Jack Horner there consulting. But Spielberg needed *T. rex* to be a predator to make the plot ugly, so that's what the public gets." Another said, "And let's gloss over the fact that *T. rex* was Cretaceous, not Jurassic."

Vance screamed, "Fucking assholes!" about nothing in particular and everything in general, and took another guzzle of his beer.

A nerdy-looking fellow raised an authoritative finger and roared, "You can't write Spielberg off that easily, or Crichton, who, you'll recall, wrote the book. Even Shakespeare understood the value of feeding some banal entertainment to the masses while he drove the plot toward a higher truth. It's always the job of the brightest and best educated among us to raise the level of the game. Should we leave it to the least among us? Or the greediest?"

"Sure!" shouted the young woman. "Feed 'em candy for the mind while you steal their lunch money. Just give me a job where I get to do paleontology!"

"Who are you guys?" bellowed another. "The arbiters of who gets to learn what? That's arrogant as hell!"

I pressed onward through the wake.

"This fucks everything. It's fucking hard enough to work in this field without this kind of crap going on," a paunchy man in his fifties was hollering to a confederate as he gesticulated sloppily with a full glass. Droplets of cold ale flew through the air. "Sherbrooke gets media-happy to compete with Dishey and what does it do? Drives the price of bones up even further. Good thing this is public land out here. If it was private, all the ranchers would sell to the highest bidder, and we'd never see another speciman. How the hell are we supposed to compete with this shit?"

"I hear you," his listener answered at the top of his lungs. "It's fatuous, this business of making fossils a business. A fossil's either priceless or worthless, unique in all the world or just another lump of rock. I'm ready to quit and sell insurance."

"Yeah, to hell with my doctorate," shrieked a skinny man next to him. "Let's just round up all the bones that are left and sell them to the Chinese for charms or something."

"Take dino-dust tonic," squalled the paunchy man, imitating a B-movie Chinese accent. "Prease yo' young wife!"

I moved on. I didn't want to know where the bones of the 149,000,000-year-old mother and child that had just been ripped from the naked desert were going to wind up. I wasn't drunk, and couldn't hope to be. I had too much yet to accomplish before the sun set on the San Rafael Swell.

I was almost to the front door when a woman lost her balance as I squirmed by behind her. She took a fast step backward, pressing me facefirst into Earthworm Magritte's broad chest.

When Magritte recognized who had just been planted on him like a bug on a windshield, he smiled, reached his beer around my neck, and took a noisy slurp from beside my opposite ear.

The woman behind me continued to lean on me. The room was so crowded that she had neither enough room to straighten up nor to slide to the floor. I grunted as the last of my oxygen supply was squeezed from my lungs, put my hands against Magritte's chest, and steadied myself.

Magritte brought his other hand up and found the tip of my chin. He lifted it and began to lean his lips down toward me. The mixed scents of man, pine, and beer washed across my face.

I jerked my head back and shouted, "What are you doing?"

"I'm going to kiss you!" he shouted back, his voice almost swallowed by the roar of the crowd even at this incredibly close range.

"Why?" I pleaded.

He smiled warmly. "Because I like you!"

I gasped, "Let me go!" and pushed with everything I had, knocking the woman behind me who knew where. Magritte released me, and I headed for the door, but I was immediately caught in another box canyon of human bodies.

Magritte grasped my arm. "I'm sorry," he shouted, but at arm's length, I was reduced to reading his lips.

It was a long time since anyone had simply said that he liked me, or that he was sorry for an affront. I looked into his shyly inviting eyes. Being this close, this candid, was simultaneously comforting and deeply threatening. "No, *I'm* sorry," I shouted, wondering what exactly I meant by that.

Magritte stuffed his beer glass into a nearby empty hand guided me through the press of bodies and out onto the sidewalk. "What's your hurry?" he asked hopefully.

I could still barely hear him. My ears were ringing from the ruckus in the Mecca Club. "I gotta meet—" I stopped myself before speaking Ray's name. It wouldn't do to let this man, or anyone in this group, for that matter, know where I was headed.

"Your Eagle Scout," Magritte said, completing my sentence.

I said nothing. Ray, *my* Eagle Scout. Yes, I was already thinking of him as mine, even though he was forever wedded not only to another but to a whole way of life I stood outside of.

Magritte tipped his head in query and stared into me, pressing his suit. "Well, he isn't here yet. We can just hang out here and get to know each other a bit," he said, still holding my hand as if we were about to dance.

Why *not* tarry here awhile and get to know Magritte? He was not unattractive, in a stocky sort of way, and the contents of his mind interested me intensely. For all his bluster, he had an innocence to him, a vulnerability that came with candor and openness, rare in a man. I hesitated. If I gave in to him, then what might Ray think? Ray, who had married in the Temple, a big stone edifice that scared me, married for time and eternity to a woman who had gone on into that eternity ahead of him. Was she waiting there, as Mormon beliefs suggested, or had she already been reborn on another continent, as a Tibetan lama, perhaps? And was she the only woman Ray had ever touched in the deepest earthly sense, the only woman who had shared his bed?

Magritte's hand moved gently against mine, massaging it with hope. Feeling a sympathetic body touch mine warmed me like liquor, soothed me, inspired a thousand nerve endings to ask, Why not? Magritte blended with Ray in my mind, in my soul, making one man, a superman, a mixture of traits so powerful that my stomach began to flutter. What if I could have the body and charisma of the one joined to the openness of the other?

Ray in bed. I would have gone there with him, had he asked me; I knew that now. I had known him only two short days, but they held a year's experience and shock, and we had moved together through it. But now I felt drawn to Magritte. Was I running from Ray, just as I now pulled from the limits of Magritte's reach? As I stared into Magritte's hungry, unguarded eyes, I wondered how many women he had had. Ten? One hundred? Where was the specialness in that? There was strength and sanctity in Ray's chastity, and I longed to be as innocent, longed to be his one special mate. "Listen," I said, "I got to take one thing at a time."

Magritte's face softened. "You can't hitch up with a Mormon."

"How do you know that?" I demanded.

"Because you seek your own answers."

"Don't be so dramatic."

"Nah, I've watched you both. You always lead, and he follows. And look at the work you do. Geologists think in probabilities, patterns, and overlapping fields, not in straight lines from A to B. Mormonism is a religion designed by engineers. They've got an answer for every question and a chicken in every pot. It's not just a religion; it's a tribe, a way people live. I've got nothing against that for folks who want that, but even if you could jam yourself into the slot they've got waiting for you, you'd die of boredom being told what to think." He pulled my hand now up against his chest.

I felt his heart beating. "It wouldn't have to be like that," I said wishfully. "Ray has a loving family, and they all seem to pray directly to God. . . ."

Magritte looked sad. "They talk to God and get their own revelations—is that the language? Hey, so do I. If your Eagle Scout went on a mission, then he's a member of the Aaronic priesthood. That's important to him. He has experiences there that reinforce his faith. We all do. I'm on this field trip today to get new revelations and reinforce my faith. The thing is, the human mind seeks a context for these experiences; we all do. Ray probably figured he had things wired, and then he met you, and you've made his wires smoke."

I tugged at my hand, trying to pull away.

"Oh, don't be so damn humble," he said. "You're incredible. Bright, quick, soft, and fierce. Your Eagle Scout wonders if your magic isn't somehow greater than his. He's *got* to pull you in, just to find out if that's true."

I screwed up my face in disbelief. "Me? Magic?"

"Yeah, you have the stuff, Em Hansen; you're just young yet. Ask yourself: would you really have the freedom of thought and motion you're accustomed to, or would they seek to influence you at every turn?"

"I think they believe that's right."

"You *think*. They *believe*. What about what you *know?*" Engulfed in his own, he thumped my hand gently against his massive chest.

My mind pitched and reeled through its impressions of Mormonism, Ray's unnervingly serene family gathering, the grid of city streets that always told me where I was relative to the Temple, the Temple itself, with its architecture. . . . "What is it about the Temple, Magritte?"

"It has no windows," he said softly. "No windows. It's a crypt, like they don't want you seeing in. They're keeping secrets."

A lack of windows. All other churches opened their eyes to the sky, drinking in God's light, but the Salt Lake Temple looked inward. Shaken, I focused on Magritte, staring in through his impossibly thick glasses to the telescopically small eyes he trained back on me. "Why does that scare me?" I asked.

Magritte smiled wistfully. "Because you're a Middle American Protestant, like the rest of us poor schmucks, taught to believe that it's all been written, that all has been created, that all you have to do is read the book. We don't mess with anything we can't see, or something dark and dirty will happen. Then along come the Mormons. They take your deck of cards, reshuffle it right in front of you, and slip a joker into it. They talk to God, have revelations, do faith healings, tell you they have the answer and you don't. To a Puritan, that's conjury; that's fingernails on the chalkboard: If you went around talking about visions and the power to heal, your church elders would call you a witch and burn you at the stake."

I leaned into Magritte's grip. He was right, I was hopelessly a Puritan. Virtue is its own reward, but we're all getting punished anyway, our motto. Woe betide me, I was just as stuck in my beliefs as a creationist.

He tipped his head closer to me. "Think it through," he whispered into my ringing ears. "He may have a hot line to God, but he's probably never had an original thought in his life. How long would you last with that?"

I patted him on the chest and pushed myself away again. "Fine," I said. "You may be right, but *I* don't know that. I got to go."

"Why?"

I could have answered diplomatically, offering some time-worn excuse, but a serving of bullshit was not what Magritte had asked for. So instead, I told him the truth: "Because I need someone more stable than I am."

Magritte looked deep into my eyes. "So do I," he whispered sadly back. "So do I."

◈

THE DRIVER OF the second bus was standing on the sidewalk, eyes shut, her hands slowly caressing an unseen form in front of her. Allison Lee stood beside her, arms folded across her chest, watching.

"What's going on?" I asked, looking over my shoulder to

make sure Magritte had made it back into the club. He had.

"Artemis here is clearing the bladder meridians of a *Camarasaurus*," she answered.

"Come again?" A bus driver named Artemis? In Utah? She didn't look Greek.

"Its aura," Allison explained. "She's rolled it onto its back so she can work with it."

"It's so sweet," said the bus driver. "Like a golden retriever!"

I wondered if the din inside the Mecca Club had done something to my ears. "We don't have this sort of stuff in Wyoming. What's a meridian, and why's she stroking it?"

Allison explained, in her Lawn Guyland glottal drawl, "It's Chinese medicine. The subtle energy pathways of the auric body get clogged."

"In whose aura?" I asked. I was beyond subtlety myself. I was reeling. Having just had my emotions hit by a truck wearing MAGRITTE license plates, I wasn't sure I could handle a dinosaur aura in the middle of Main Street.

"This dinosaur here," Allison said, pointing into the empty space in front of the driver.

"But there's nothing there," I said doggedly. "Come on, Allison; the last dinosaurs died sixty-four million years ago. *Camarasaurus* almost a one hundred and fifty million years ago."

"Time means nothing in metaphysics," said the bus driver. She giggled. "I'm stroking a dinosaur tummy, so I should know."

"No, you're—"

"Sure, the animal's body died a long time ago. I'm hip," said the driver. "But it got stuck thinking its soul was dead, too. But the soul never dies. This one needs to go on to the astral plane, where it can get what it needs." To the invisible dinosaur soul, she said, "There now, sweetie, can you find some friends to help you through? Here, I'll open a passage-way for you." She rotated her hand clockwise, waited, then rotated it counterclockwise. Then she turned to Allison. "Okay, the big long-neck is on its way; now let's go after that pack of carnivores."

"What are you *talking* about?" I persisted.

Allison said, "Aw, I went on one of the preconference field trips, and we visited the Cleveland-Lloyd Quarry. This camarasaur died there, and at least forty-four allosaurs. The big leaf-eater was being hunted by the fang guys when they all got trapped in the mud at the bottom of a lake. Nasty way to die."

"They all died in terrible fear," said the driver soberly, "and couldn't let go of the earth energy."

Allison said, "So I been feeling kinda tired ever since. Artemis here did a bioenergy scan on me and found out I kinda sucked their auras up or something."

"She felt sorry for them," the driver explained.

"So she's clearing them out of me and sending them on their ways. So they got stuck in the mud, but what *killed* them, Artemis?"

The bus driver squealed, "Ooo! Earthquake!"

"Oh, you mean the mud went thixotropic?"

Artemis's eyes opened and closed again. "They don't know that word."

Allison said, "It turned to soup. Sucked 'em down. They're drowning."

The driver nodded. "Some of the females are pregnant."

This was too much for me. "They were egg layers!" I argued.

The driver smiled sweetly. "Carrying fertilized eggs, same thing," she said patiently. "Mmm, the energy of the carnivores feels different from the little leaf-eater."

"Camarasaurs weren't so little," I prattled on. "They were

as long as a football field and probably weighed twenty tons."

"You wouldn't know it from its aura," Artemis replied serenely.

I rocked my head back and stared up into the sky, wondering what parallel universe I had just fallen into. First Mormons with loaded decks and now New Age bus drivers with midget dinosaur auras. I watched darkening clouds drift across the infinite heavens and admitted, deep down inside and only to myself, that I was scared.

❖

TOWARD LATE AFTERNOON, the FBI agent slipped away down the street to acquire a car, and the party at the Mecca Club began to cycle their beer-distended bladders through the rest rooms preparatory to loading onto the buses and heading back to Snowbird. My stomach churned with hunger and the urgency of my plan. I needed salt and water against dehydration and food energy for desert travel. I headed into the café and ordered a hamburger and a packet of potato chips, the perfect foods, swilled some black coffee, and settled in to wait.

There was a small commotion as Lew and Vance all but dragged Dan Sherbrooke in from the bar and poured him into a booth. A waitress hustled over to them with a pot of coffee and they began to pour it into him cup by cup. Just as the FBI agent reappeared through the front door of the café, Dan bawled dramatically, "Thank you, Lew. You're always there for me. My friend."

"Some friend," Vance seethed, his own liquor loosening his tongue. "You *knew* that site had been hit, and did you tell us? No!"

"What are you talking about?" Lew whined.

"I saw your boot prints on top of the backhoe tracks when I first got to the site. Maybe you even drove that backhoe in there yourself!"

Lew lunged toward the wiry little man and yanked him up by his shirtfront.

Vance dangled from Lew's fists, screaming, "Go ahead and hit me, you thieving shit!"

Lew dropped Vance and staggered backward until he fetched up against the counter. "Okay, so maybe I was there before the field trip. But I didn't trash it! It was already like that when I got there."

Dan had turned and begun to rise from his seat, swaying. "Lew? Lew, you *knew*?"

Lew jammed his hands into his pockets and shrugged, a boy caught playing with matches. "Yeah. Okay, so I was coming back from fishing on Sunday and thought I'd check on the site. But fossils was already gone!"

"Just *thought* you'd take a look," Vance sassed. "Just *happened* to drive by!"

Lew pursed his lips and made his appeal to Dan. "I come out here for years with you, and what do I get? You finally find something good and take *this* little shit down there to lift it instead of me! I wanted to *see* it was all. So yeah, I was here, but it was already gone! Just tracks, like today!" He flailed his arms wildly, trying too late to express nonexistent horror and loss. "What was I supposed to do?"

I turned and glanced at the FBI agent to make sure he was getting all of this. He was.

"What were you supposed to do?" Dan drawled, lumbering to his feet. "I'll tell you what you were supposed to do. You were supposed to tell me, for starts! I would have canceled the trip!" He leaned forward and bellowed, "What were you dreaming of, letting me come ahead on down here? You sniveling bottom-feeder! You whore's offal!" With sudden ferocity, Dan swung a huge pudgy fist into Lew's jaw.

Lew staggered and fell. His head hit the floor like a ripe melon. He lay still a moment, stunned, then drew his hands over his face and howled, "It was *George* 'at stole the thing, Dan! You *know* that! *George* did it!"

"Do you think me cretinous?" Dan bellowed. "George had not clue *one* where that site was!"

"Did too!" Lew squealed from the floor. A practiced sniveler, he knew better than to rise while his opponent was still riled. "His stoolie told him! That beard-o freak with the rifle!"

Everyone looked at Dan expectantly. He looked back at each of us, his eyes alert with something he was not saying.

The FBI agent moved swiftly into position, deftly placing his hands under the fallen man's shoulders, as if Lew's safety and comfort were all he cared about. "This sounds important, gentlemen," he said, mollifying all parties present in the time-honored way a sober man handles drunks. "*Tell* us about this, Lew. Tell us about George's stoolie."

Lew said, "Aw shit, George always had his little informants. Losers. Geeks. These ones were no different. Shit, Dan, it was that beardo guy led you to this *Allosaurus* site in the first place. You remember him!"

Dan popped his eyes in assumed outrage.

Vance stared at his professor in shock. "But you told me *you* found that site!"

"Well, I . . ."

Lew sat up, wobbled, and touched a hand gingerly to his lip, which was beginning to bleed. "Since when does Dan move an inch when he can con someone else into walking a mile for him? Your *hero* here paid him in food, Vance. Beardo led him to that site and Dan paid him in *food*." He laughed, a high, tittering schoolgirl giggle, and winced when it made his lip hurt.

I said, "Canned food?"

Lew looked at me, his mouth sagging in hurt surprise that I had information he hadn't given me yet. "Yeah. Number-ten cans of dried fruit, egg mix. Beef jerky. Those bones were worth hundreds of thousands—millions!—and he pays them in *dried fruit*! I couldn't believe it. Best deal since Sir Francis Drake bought New York from the Indians for twenty-two bucks."

"That was Peter Minuit and Manhattan Island," Sherbrooke corrected haughtily. "And it was trinkets, not cash. Twenty-*four* dollars' worth."

Not Tom and I exchanged looks. The glint in his eyes seemed to say, Questioning drunks is fun, huh?

I said, "So Dan, you bought the canned food from George. Did he maybe introduce you to this finder, too?" About then, nothing that had ever occurred between George Dishey and Dan Sherbrooke would have surprised me.

Dan said nothing.

Lew said, "I saw them sitting with George right here in this café!"

"Never!" Dan protested.

Vance screwed up his face and said, "George was *here*?"

Lew looked from face to face, recovering his sense of self-importance swiftly. "Sure." He looked both ways, artlessly covering his complicity. "He said he was just driving through, but *I* knew better. The waitress here knew him by name."

Dan's face reddened. To Lew he roared, "You told me you'd just stumbled across this guy in the café. And all the time, you were in bed with George?"

Lew stuck out his lower lip petulantly.

"Which waitress was here?" I asked.

"That one," Lew answered.

The FBI agent turned toward the woman behind the counter, who had lit a cigarette, the better to enjoy the show. "Yeah, that was me," she said. "But they wasn't all together. That TV guy with the bushy beard was here with this guy and that other with the long beard first." She pointed at Lew with her cigarette. "Then George goes out the back door and this one comes in the front." She pointed at Dan.

So George had engineered the whole thing. What better way to know what Dan was up to than to set up his digs?

Dan stared at Lew, his mouth agape. Lew shrugged.

"What did the other two man look like?" asked the agent.

She flicked at the cigarette and said, "Oh, he was a skinny fellow with a long beard like Moses. Kinda creepy. Didn't want no coffee or beer—that type. He set down there by the back booth, real nervous like, with George. Didn't seem to like it when he kept him waiting there. But I liked that George. He always tipped *good*." She sniffed at Dan, as if to say, Unlike *you*, fella.

The agent stepped toward the counter. I had to move quickly to get a look at the picture he slipped out of his breast pocket to show to the waitress. It was an enlargement of the helicopter pilot from the picture in George's study, computer-enhanced to show the man aged and bearded. I was amazed by how much it looked like the man I had glimpsed in the van.

"Yep. That's the one," said the waitress.

I grabbed the picture from the FBI agent as he attempted to palm it back into his shirt pocket and maintain his cover as Tom Latimer the dinosaur illustrator. I stuffed the picture under Dan Sherbrooke's nose. "Know him?" I asked furiously. "Ever maybe tell him where I was staying?"

Dan looked stupidly at the picture. "No."

"Then who *did* you tell, Dan?"

"Tell what?"

"Where I was staying. What motel. The police told you Monday morning, and unless you hit my room yourself, you sent someone else in your place. Now, who was it?" I demanded.

"What are you—" Sherbrooke stopped in midsentence. "Oh. Oh, I see what you're saying. Yes, the police mentioned that to me, but it only stayed in my mind because I couldn't for the life of me understand why he thought I'd want to know.

And yes, come to think of it, I did pass the information along."

I stared at him, appalled. He was either a fantastic actor or had no idea that I'd been shot at and that, therefore, giving out my room location might endanger me. "Who'd you tell?" I asked doggedly.

Dan said, "What's-his-name Smeely, the commercial guy. Did he find you?"

Disgusted, I thrust the picture back toward the FBI agent. As he retrieved it, he asked the waitress, "You ever see them in here at any other time?"

She shook her head. "Nope."

The questioning was interrupted as Artemis, the bus driver, stuck her head in the door from the sidewalk. "You guys ready?" she asked. "Everybody else is on board."

Vance staggered to his feet, took Dan's arm, and began to lead him toward the door. Dan draped his long, rubbery arm around the slighter man and blubbered, "Oh, Verne. What would I do without you?"

"Remember my name, for starts," the young man said bitterly. "Come on, Dan, let's hit the road."

Lew stumbled to his feet and headed after them like a dog who's used to getting the smallest, driest bone to chew on, hates knowing it, but has no inspiration to find himself another master.

I looked at the FBI agent, who shook his head. "They have alibis," he said softly, so that only I could hear him. "Dan and Vance, each other. Lew, his wife."

I opened my mouth to say something but couldn't think what to say. I had asked them every question I could think of but still couldn't blame them—at least not directly—for George's death. Yet somehow I felt that they deserved at least part of the blame. They had been half the war of vanities that had put George at risk; I was sure of that. Yet what, precisely, was the connection between bone theft and murder? Had George threatened to expose the complicity of one or more players? Or had the pissing match between George and Dan simply fomented to the point where somebody, somehow, had to get hurt? And had George meant for Dan's *Allosaurus* to be stolen?

There was another piece to the puzzle that still lay hidden; I could feel it. Something twisted. Something strange about the relationship between George and Nina, and all the other women, including myself, that he had used or misused. Something sad and somehow poignant, because he had been kind to Nina, after all, and not taken advantage of her slight little body for anything but finding fossils.

The shuffling trio were halfway out the door when I suddenly thought to ask, "Hey, Dan! Do you know Heddie?"

Dan turned. "Heddie . . ."

"A friend of George's?"

"You mean Pat Hedlund?" he asked.

"I don't know," I replied. "Was she his wife?"

Dan looked confused. "He," he answered. "He was some high school friend; used to come up to Yale to visit him. The two of them were very close. . . . 'Heddie' was George's pet name for him . . . wouldn't let anyone else call him that . . . wouldn't let anyone else *near* him, for that matter." He shrugged his rounded shoulders.

My brain made a sort of pinging noise. *George, you clever old liar, you. You had a wry sense of humor under all that deceit.*

"You know where Heddie's living?" asked Not Tom Latimer conversationally.

Dan let out a muted belch and adjusted his mangled glasses. "He was killed in Vietnam. George never really got over it. Took two years off between undergrad and his doctorate and let the draft get him. Said he had to go 'kill a gook for Heddie.'

Set him back behind the rest of us professionally, right from the start." Dan shook his head judgmentally. "The graduate schools didn't take him as seriously when he didn't apply right out of his undergraduate program. Put him too far back in the line when the funding was being handed out. Why?"

◇
◇
◇

21

◇
◇
◇

NOT TOM LATIMER DROVE ME EAST OF PRICE TO THE AIR-
port under darkening skies. The thunderheads that had played
above the western cliffs through the past hours had spread
north and eastward, licking cold fingers out over Price and
engulfing the canyon that led back to Salt Lake City.

"You'll be in a Bell Jet Ranger," he told me. "They won't
take off from Salt Lake until they know they can get straight
through this squall line, so it may be awhile. Fully fueled, they
have a cruising range of only two hours, with a safety margin
of twenty minutes. Once they get here, they'll refuel. You'll
be able to get down to that site again easy, get your evidence,
and, daylight permitting, maybe scout the immediate neighborhood. What did you say Dishey's site should look like?"

"Nina said it was up close to some cliffs, kind of a lean-to
thing. I imagine it was camouflaged, and the Swell is a big
area. And that's all assuming I'm right. Maybe she isn't even
from these parts."

"And maybe they won't get through from Salt Lake. And
even then you might not be able to proceed. I don't like the
way those anvil clouds are leaning out over the desert."

I looked balefully out across the bluffs that led away toward
the open lands, no longer certain whether my plan made sense.

The FBI agent handed me some folded paper. "Look, I rounded up the BLM maps for the area and this other one, which shows a kind of shaded relief of the mesas and canyons out there. And here's a USGS two-degree sheet. Take a look at them. Memorize them."

"I've got a geological map here," I said. I unfolded it.

"Is that the one Vance was showing this morning?" he asked, giving me a look that said, You little scamp.

"I *borrowed* it from Vance. Took me a while to peel it off that board. He won't be missing it for a day or two, not until the headache he's going to wake up with clears away. See? It shows the different geological formations—different colors for each one—where they outcrop at the surface. This purple one is the Morrison Formation." I traced the band where it curved along the western ramp of the San Rafael Swell.

The FBI agent glanced at the map and then back at his driving.

I said, "The color band gets real wide here and here because the formation is lying almost flat and the rise of the land is gradual, so the surface exposure is like a shallow slice through it, opening it across a wide area." I made a shallow slicing motion with one hand. "Like if you're looking down on top of a three-layer cake and you chop it vertically, you hardly see any of the middle layer, but if you slash it at a shallow angle, it shows up several inches wide."

"I get it. Neat."

"How long a flight is it from Salt Lake?"

The agent looked up at the sky. "An hour or so. It's a fast ship."

"Ship?"

"I rode a lot of choppers in Nam. I don't envy you this ride."

"No?" I grinned. I had recently won my wings, finally, after running out of funds repeatedly while completing the flight hours necessary for my pilot's license. But that was for fixed-wing craft. A helicopter was a rotorcraft, a bird that could fly straight up. I was thrilled that Ray was bringing a bird, even if it meant that my dear pal Detective Bert was also coming along. Leave it to Ray to do it by the book and tell his superiors my entire analysis and plan.

Not Tom Latimer's smile faded. "No. I've been in a crash. Not fun."

"Were you hurt?" I asked gingerly. I didn't like to think about the downside of flying.

"Just a compressed disk or two." He shifted uncomfortably in his seat.

"What happened?"

"We hit some wires. They'll flip you right onto your nose. It's ugly. Even if you pancake straight down, the rotors bend, you know, and hit the ground a split second after the craft does, and they shear off and take off like a knife-thrower's in town, take out the tail boom and so forth. The skids crumple and the cockpit cracks like an egg, but that engine's still moving. You don't go straight down unless you're in a stationary hover, which pilots hate to do unless they're quite a ways up, because you need either airspeed or altitude to effect an autorotation to cushion a dead landing."

"You know a lot about this for someone who doesn't like flying."

He smiled. "Amazing what you learn when the pilot's in the next bed in the hospital.

"So you're moving forward when you start to go down, maybe sliding through the air at an angle, say, of forty-five degrees." He held a hand over his head, then brought it slap down toward his knees. "Think on it, the heaviest block in the whole ship's up over your head—the turbines—and it's spinning and still has momentum, so it yanks the roof forward. The wall behind the pilot's seat folds up on him and squeezes the air out of him. You die of asphyxiation if the impact doesn't get you first."

My smile had turned to concrete. "Thanks. I needed that, I'm sure."

Not Tom smiled again. "Think nothing of it. Still sure you want to do this?"

"Sure. There aren't any wires out there. We're talking about the back side of nowhere."

"I don't care who's backside you're flying around. Power lines are the least of it. Don't forget—don't you *ever* forget—that this time you're going out there because you think the boys who got George Dishey might be waiting for you."

He was right. In my chase for the truth—in my haste to be *right*—I was leaving myself open.

◈

NOT TOM TURNED the car in through a gate onto the tarmac of the rural airport. The facility consisted of several low buildings and a gas pump, a few planes tied down, and, on the far side of the runway, a row of hangars. He parked the car and we got out and stared up into the sky, to the rising bluffs to the south, and down the long straight face of the Book Cliffs to the east. "Almost five," he said, fidgeting with his car keys. "You're running out of daylight."

"They could have gotten here faster by road," I said, smiling. "But then I wouldn't get to go flying. I don't care what you say, I'm excited about that."

"Great." Not Tom pocketed his keys and turned up the collar of his jacket. His face had gone wide-eyed and stiff, like a cowboy readying himself in the chute for a ride on a Brahma bull. He suddenly winked at me. "Let's hope Ray ain't the airsick type," he said, a teasing smile finding its way onto his lips. As he continued to look at me, I stopped smiling, and he dropped his smile, too.

"You know anything about the Mormons?" I asked.

"A little. I'm not a Mo myself, but I've been out here a bunch of years. You pick it up after a while."

"You sound like we're discussing a foreign language."

"May as well be. The church is, in fact, a subculture, anthropologically speaking. Its members have their own way of looking at things, their own way of talking, even."

"So now you're an anthropologist? What are you going to be next week, a rocket physicist?"

He gave me an acerbic look. "I haven't always been an FBI agent," he said. "But even in the Bureau, we study things. The more you understand people, the better we can do what we do."

"May I know what you think of the Mormon church?" I asked.

Not Tom considered my question. "They have strong families. They don't drink, don't smoke. They cooperate toward building a strong society, humble themselves before something bigger than they are. They look after their own. Those are all good things."

I wished I could look at things that simply. I'd built a life for myself in Denver. It was a small life, work-harried and solitary, but satisfying enough of the time to get me past the days when I felt inclined to question what I was doing. Then I'd come out here and gotten shot at and found myself close enough to Ray to feel his heart beat, and the genie was back out of the bottle. The previous evening sitting at the Raymond family table had put me up against the fact that I felt alone and afraid in a universe in which others found contact and security, and today I'd met people who were relaxed enough to delight in the doglike auras of herbivorous dinosaurs. My cosmos was in an uproar, all previous sense of order disordered. So I gave Not Tom my most piercing look and said, "What aren't you saying?"

Not Tom stared at his feet and kicked idly at a pebble that had found its way onto the blacktop. "I try not to judge people for their beliefs, as long as they don't infringe on my liberty. I've done my best to make peace with these things, and I leave them to make theirs."

I stared at the agent, this matter-of-fact man in his middle years. He was the kind of guy you might not notice, unless you look at who's left after you subtract all the people around you who are doing something nutsy, or trying to get your attention for some neurotic reason or other. He seemed to be just hanging out, thinking deep thoughts, and watching the ball game of life. I said, "You've made peace, huh? How'd you pull off that little bit of mental jujitsu?"

He shrugged his shoulders. "Well, I used to make myself crazy trying to decide what was true and what wasn't, that kind of stuff. Then one day I figured out that there were more than two categories in this life; not just true and untrue but also a third category. Call it 'I don't know.' In science, do you make yourself nuts over the questions you haven't even thought to ask yet?"

"Sometimes. It's a possibility I have to consider."

"Well, I bet you don't lose sleep over it. You tell yourself you'll never get it all figured out anyway, so why get so uptight? And just because you can touch and smell and taste and see and hear the physical world doesn't mean that a metaphysical world doesn't exist right next to it, or on top of it, or in the same place. And if it does, that makes room for all sorts of possibilities."

"You mean like astrology, or auras."

A gust of wind whipped down the runway, trailing the wind sock out straight across it, a sure sign of a coming storm. A flash of lightning blanched the clouds behind us.

The agent saw this, too, and looked reflexively toward the pass, from which he hoped to see the arriving helicopter. Nothing. He said, "I don't make any sense out of star charts, and I sure don't see glowing coronas around people's heads, but that doesn't mean someone else doesn't. Huge portions of the world rely on astrologers, and when it comes to auras, why else would the medieval artists paint golden halos around the heads of saints?"

"There's a connection I've never made."

"Precisely. In my business, you learn to look at evidence from new angles, or you're going to miss something that's staring you in the face. Such as the possibility of being wrong about everything. But like I say, as long as no one's getting all het up about things and assaulting my liberty to think as I please, and as long as I'm behaving myself, too, no one's getting hurt."

"And so maybe if someone believes the earth is six thousand years old—which sounds like hooey to me—and they can't perceive what I see—a divine, systematic beauty in a much older, evolving earth—maybe that's okay."

Not Tom smiled another tease. "What the hell," he said. "Everybody's got to have a gimmick."

"So do you think the Mormons might be right?"

"About what?"

"About anything."

Not Tom's smile broadened. "Boy, something's sure got your fire lit. Or some*body*."

"Yeah," I said simply. I had learned something from Magritte after all: that being direct and dropping the defensive bullshit had a certain charm, and got business done a whole lot faster.

The agent raised his eyebrows appreciatively. "I heard it said once that the maturity of a civilization can be measured by its ability to laugh at itself. Maybe the Mormon culture can't do that yet." He shrugged again. "But what the hell, maybe mainstream America hasn't arrived at the belly-laugh stage yet, either. And like I said, Mormonism is a subculture. Or call it a 'tribe.' Different from your tribe, I'll wager, different in big ways. It's hard to change tribes, real hard."

We heard the sound of an aircraft engine and both immediately turned around, the wait beginning to press on our nerves.

A small plane that had taxied to the end of the runway had started its takeoff roll. I watched it accelerate, rotate its nose upward, dip a wing into the cross-wind, and rise into the late-afternoon air. Five hundred feet into the sky, it turned eastward and darted away from the storm. I looked westward. The clouds over the pass seemed to be thinning.

I kept talking to distract myself from the tension that was consuming my bowels. "Okay," I said, "you're talking about laughing at yourself, as in the ability to see ironies. But what about lies? You got a place for them in your pantheon?"

"Lies?"

"It seems to me this whole case—for that matter, everything that's happened to me since I arrived in Utah—has revolved around lies. George Dishey was a gold-plated liar. He lied to get me here. He lied to his colleagues, it seems, pumped out lies and fiction and plain old wild-assed ideas just to keep the joint jumping. He lived a lie with Nina. I'm betting a lie got him killed. But how did he get away with telling lies for as long as he did? His colleagues tried to throw him out long ago, but they couldn't, could they? No, because he just popped up somewhere else, dishing up his exciting stories to the popular press. They couldn't blow the whistle then. Why not? Because they didn't want to look priggish, or, worse yet, they didn't know for certain which part of George's palaver was truth and which was fiction. It's the uncertainty we all deal with in the sciences, and if you don't stay humble, you wind up just as buffoonishly vain as old Dan Sherbrooke, setting yourself up for one kind of a fall or another." Nervousness was making me garrulous again.

Not Tom said, "Ah, so that's why we heard Sherbrooke credit Dishey's ideas as having stimulated research. His ounce of humility."

"Yeah. And the irony is, he's probably right about that. Science is done by human beings, after all, and, as you say, we have a way of collecting into tribes. The Flat Earth tribe, the Expanding Universe tribe, the Survival of the Fittest tribe. It's something of a stunt to think original thoughts when you know you're going to get a whole lot better funding for your project if you agree with the status quo. Sometimes it takes a gadfly like George to annoy people into new ways of thinking."

"So you're saying that scientists are not always impartial."

"Hah. We get wedded to prevailing beliefs just like the next person. The difference with most of us is that we take pains not to lie. Like John told me on the bus today, we trust each other's honesty. If we misinterpret data, we've made a mistake. If we get hooked on a belief beyond the point of reason, we're lying to ourselves. But it astonishes us when someone blatantly, consciously lies."

"Then I can see why George Dishey had such an easy time of lying."

A small falcon plummeted out of the sky and nabbed a rodent that had unwarily ventured too far from its burrow. "Right. So where are lies on your 'Yes, No, I Don't Know' scale of reality? How far can lies coexist with the truth?"

Not Tom ran a hand through his short, graying hair. "I wish I knew the answer to that," he said. "I could take early retirement and go fishing."

"You must deal with liars all day long. Aren't most criminals liars of one sort or another?"

Not Tom nodded and glanced at his watch. "Some are prize liars like George Dishey—pathological liars, regular sociopaths." He scanned the western sky for the arrival of the helicopter.

I knew I was beginning to lean on the man, but there was something elusive I had not yet grasped about the whole George Dishey conundrum, and as the sun began to slide toward the western horizon, I felt I had to grasp it quick before I got on that helicopter and flew out into who knew what. I needed to understand who was out there, what was waiting for me. "I couldn't lie to save my life. At least not to anyone but myself. I gave it up in adolescence. It was just too difficult to keep track of what I'd said to whom. If I told the truth, I could keep track of it, because the truth makes sense to me. So how do criminals get away with it? Don't they teach you something about that in FBI school?"

Not Tom rocked from heel to toe, still watching the sky. "Sure they do. You see, the best way to tell a lie is to attach it to the truth."

"What do you mean?"

"Well, if you're going to lie, you wrap it around something that's true, so if you get caught, then you just say, 'I made a mistake about that part, but this other part is true,' and that makes you look like you meant well. If you can keep people misled, or confused, you've got 'em."

"Like George attaching a 'special symposium' lie to an 'SVP Conference' truth to get me to come to Salt Lake."

"You got it."

"But what did that buy him?"

Not Tom turned his head to look at me, examining me in a new way. "An honest face to stand next to him. A little truth by association. You're a nice kid. You wouldn't have made a stink, and if you had, he'd have fed you some other line of bullshit, like that the symposium was canceled for some reason or another."

I fell quiet for a moment, letting "nice" and "honest" be compliments, drawing a tiny sip of nourishment from them.

Not Tom changed the subject. "So if you're right about Nina, George has been digging down here for quite a while."

"Hadn't you been watching him?"

"I only started looking into his activities a few months ago. I had to clear some other caseload and then start setting up my cover." He shrugged his shoulders, hands in pockets. "This murder just kind of ripped the case open."

"Is that a good thing?"

"No, that's a bad thing. The police were able to get to his hard drive at his house before the guys with the rifles got there, and that's good, but maybe it'll be enough to lead us to the rest of the ring, and maybe not. George was not at the center of the network. I may be able to clean up his corner, apprehend his underlings, but in doing so, I may lose any chance of following them back to the linchpin, and it's the connections to the central brains we're trying to get."

"Then you know who that is?" I was appalled. All this, when they knew who was behind it?

"Sure. These guys work right out in the open. They attach the lie of theft to the truth of doing business with the public. But George was too high-profile to run the shop. And too compromised by his ego."

"What do you mean?"

"The Sherbrooke thing. Petty competition. That's a waste of energy if you're a crook. George was supporting his habit, staying in the game, but a shit-stirrer like him couldn't really run the show." He made a gesture of dismissal, a flicking gesture with one hand.

"Or maybe he was driving Sherbrooke to find bigger and

better things, so Dan would do his excavation work for him."

Not Tom considered this. "I don't think so. Didn't you say he sounded angry or upset when he was called out Sunday morning?"

"Yes. Oh, I see what you mean. So you think whoever ripped off Sherbrooke's site with the backhoe phoned George and told him about it, and that was how they got him to go to the storage unit so they could kill him. So they didn't actually have the bones with them. It was just a ruse to get him there."

"Mm-hm. Yeah, that's what I've been thinking, ever since we saw Sherbrooke's site. And because of the way George was killed."

"What do you mean?"

"You go to the trouble of draining the blood out of somebody's body like that, dragging it around so the blood can soak into the soil, it has to mean something."

"What?"

"Someone didn't like George's brand of bullshit so much that they decided it was time for him to pay. Spilling blood onto the ground is the big payment."

"Explain."

"It's what the Mormons call blood atonement. Grisly little custom."

I didn't fully understand what the man was saying to me. We were scanning the skies now, hands in pockets, watching for that helicopter like it had our lives riding on it. "So you had the same ideas I had. Why didn't *you* call the Salt Lake police this afternoon instead of me?"

"You got to the phone ahead of me. And I have to say, your idea about using Nina as a decoy is inspired."

"Should I take that as a compliment?"

He looked at me again, out of the corners of his eyes. "I don't think so. You see, now you've involved an uncontrollable variable. And perhaps an innocent bystander, not to mention a possible minor."

"The police liked the idea," I said defensively.

"Bert bought it. Ray was against it. Me? I just wouldn't have had the balls."

I tried to take this criticism like a soldier, but I felt my heart sink. I was finding that I liked this man, liked working with him, and wanted him to approve of me, or at least admire my methods. "You're right," I said simply.

He nodded, recording my contrition. "The thing is, you understood Nina perfectly, and that's why they're going with your plan. Understanding character and motivation is half the game. And if you're right, if Nina comes to ground out here in the swell and leads us to the people we think she's going to lead us to, we'll have a nice tight case. But we have to keep you alive, because you're the only one who saw Willis Teague with our friend Smeely."

"So what is the game? What are these people up to, and why is the FBI involved?"

He leaned back, trying to release the tension in his spine. "They collect fossils on federal lands without permits. They fake the location records, make a specimen from another county, or even another state, sometimes even another geologic time. Then they pretty it up—take a bit of earth history and make it into a bauble—big dino in scary posture, which maybe it never struck in life—and then they sell it to the highest bidder. They create the market, jacking up prices by playing one bidder off against another, working people's greed and vanity just like the worst of the antiques dealers. You see, fossils used to be history. Now, they're decorations. You should see their inventory—I've attended the big fossil show in Denver. Made me sick—huge hall full of any kind of dead animal or plant you might want to collect. Everything from shark's teeth mounted on refrigerator magnets to a big *Ed-*

montosaurus—full mount, three hundred and thirty thousand dollars, delivered anywhere in the world, make your corporate offices so much more attractive. And that's just the unsexy dinosaur. That *T. rex* they called Sue went for eight million at Sotheby's."

"What kind of people are these?" I asked, recalling the slick, conservative look of the commercial collector who had eluded me at the conference.

"Most of the pros work within the law. They work only on private lands or Indian reservations, giving the owners a cut. It's still baubles instead of history, but it's legit. But then there are the guys who love to bend the law. They'd do it no matter what business they were in. They like to think they're smarter, somehow above the law. Or they they think the law should be changed to suit their business interests, so why not just behave as if they've already been changed?"

"The permitting laws?"

"That and the Antiquities Act. They want the whole works repealed. They lobby hard, and when they can't get what they want by playing fair, they go the other way. You'd be amazed. We've got paper trails that lead into every Federal agency involved, even the Forest Service and the U.S. National Park Service. They have little stoolies letting them know when the patrols are going out, so they can nip in and get the bones when nobody's watching."

"But those guys *have* a job. What do they want to get involved with organized crime for?"

"It's a lifestyle thing, usually. They get into a habit like gambling, or driving fancy cars, things their salaries can't support."

"So they're lying, too," I said.

He looked at me sharply. "What do you mean?"

"They're compulsive. When you're compulsive, you're lying to yourself, not admitting that the gambling rush or some damned object you buy with your blood money isn't going to make you happy, isn't going to fill the hole in your soul."

Not Tom favored me with another smile. "You're good," he said. "Want a job?"

"What, with you?" I smiled back. "But you're a liar, too."

He put a hand mockingly across his chest. "I?"

"Yes, you. Your name ain't Tom Latimer, and you ain't no artist. Unless your artistic medium is bullshit."

Not Tom shrugged equitably. "You're right, of course. Lying for the truth is like killing for peace. But . . ." His voice trailed off. He glanced at his watch again.

"So what are you going to get the bad-guy commercial collectors for, collecting without a permit?"

"Nah. Some local magistrate will let them off with a wrist slap—a hundred-dollar fine for plundering a hundred-fifty-million-year-old site. Some nice local joy boy who's known the collector all his life and thinks I should go back to Washington and let the locals make a living. That's a kind of lie right there: It's okay to steal if we do it to put food on the table. You see? The 'we need food' part is true, but the method of getting it is not."

"Because it's against the law?"

Not Tom rammed his fists farther into his pockets, shoving his shoulders up nearer his ears, finally showing some emotion. "What's a law? A law's a reflection of the will of the people, or a good one is. But laws are slippery, easy to disavow, depending on whose 'side' you're on, just like our local magistrate who thinks I should go back to Washington. Don't ask me how many times I've fudged my taxes. No, a law is not enough to get you on the flying bucket of bolts you call a helicopter, not enough to send you out into the desert to look for people you've never met who disemboweled a man you didn't like. What makes you go is the lie. You go because you want your truth to gain the upper hand. Am I right?"

We both stood quietly for a while, watching the western sky. In a small voice, I asked, "What's *your* truth?"

"My truth? My truth is leaving the campsite better than I found it." He laughed, a quick snort. "Doesn't sound like much, does it? You can say, Who gives a shit about dinosaur bones anyway? Don't we have enough of them? But I say no, life is precious, every minute of it, and every detail of every creature that lived before me, and every creature that hopes to live after me."

"We're all on one earth," I said.

"That sure is how I see it. Those bones are part of our history and our heritage, and at least on these federal lands, we've been able to claim them for the people. That's democracy in action. You wouldn't let someone walk into your classroom and start tearing pages out of your history books, so why let them steal any part of what those books are written about? It's time to value *natural* history just like any other part of ourselves."

I stared at the tarmac for a while while the man next to me stared up into the sky. The day was almost gone. The hours in which we could still find that site had ticked down to minutes. "Thanks, whatever your name is," I said, wondering if the FBI had sent him out to the far wastes of Utah because he was too human.

"Theft is undemocratic," he told the sky, and to me he said, "Here comes your ride."

22

THE HELICOPTER SLID TOWARD US THROUGH THE YELLOW-ing sky, the mighty thudding of its blades growing to a deafening drumming as it moved overhead. My hair kicked up around my face and my shirt buffeted against my chest as it descended, slowly, touching both skids gently onto the ground. The rotors slowed infinitesimally as the whine of the turbines began to descend, and then, bit by bit, the blur of whirling metal resolved itself into two sweeping blades. The pilot, a surprisingly slight person, stepped down out of the cockpit and walked briskly off to find a fueler. My jaw dropped as what I thought should be a man turned slightly and I saw the silhouette of her breasts and the rounding of her hips. A bolt of unease shot through me. This had not been in the plan. My breath shortened as I tried to understand why it bothered me that she was a she. Was I sexist? Had I rigged this whole adventure in my mind as one more dramatic moment to be alone with Ray, or at least the only woman around him? *No,* I realized. *I'm afraid for her. She makes this real.*

As I thought this sobering thought, two more doors popped open, and first Bert and then Ray appeared from opposite sides of the passenger compartment in back. They met by the front of the helicopter and walked toward me in close communication, discussing a sheet of notes Bert held on a clipboard.

I waited for Ray to look up and see me. I couldn't help wondering how he was feeling about me, whether he still found me interesting, or if, with these latest developments, he had decided I was too much of a troublemaker.

Ray took the clipboard from Bert and continued to stare scrupulously into his notes.

Lightning flashed overhead. The rumble of thunder came too quickly afterward. The storm was moving over Price now.

Bert gave me his gallows grin. "Hey, so it's the junior detective," he bellowed across the tarmac. "You get a signet ring in that box of Cracker Jacks, too?" He strode toward me, closing the final distance quickly on his long legs.

I fixed a noncommittal gaze into his pale green eyes and tried to remember that there was a human being beneath his nastiness.

Bert ignored me and turned to Not Tom Latimer. "What's the buzz from ground patrol?"

Not Tom said, "My latest contact says Nina went over the backyard fence at Ray's mother's house forty-five minutes ago and thumbed a ride south. One of our unmarked cars picked her up. Fast little rabbit, she is. Made the interstate in ten minutes flat. We almost lost her. We have a listen-only channel open, but she isn't saying much."

I spun around toward him to say, You didn't tell me that, but I stopped myself. I made a mental note: *They still aren't telling me everything.*

"Good," said Bert. "My dispatcher said no calls out from Miz Raymond's house, so our bogeys have no phone, like you supposed. Real bunch of millennium survivalists, looks like. Off the grid and into the country. Wonder what kind of firepower they have hidden in their bunker?"

"Let's not find out," said the FBI agent, "or at least, let's leave that to Alcohol, Tobacco and Firearms. They're on their way."

Bert's already glowing eyes flared even brighter. He was pumped up, almost salivating. "Great! Gonna be quite a party." He looked to the west and south. "This storm's gonna blow over quick. We still have enough light to see. In, out with this chopper quick, so we don't arouse their interest; wait till our rabbit gives us an address, then send in the hounds. Now, you—" He turned his crazy peepers my way. "Your job is to take us to this site soon as my pilot gets fueled. Out, back, real simple; all you got to do is show us your location and any other little geological goodies you want to lay on us so we can tie this up to that warehouse in Salt Lake. You understand?"

"Like the fact that the bones might be radioactive?" I asked.

"Really!" said Bert, his eyebrows shooting up appreciatively. "Now, what does that mean?"

"That's another thing I picked up on the bus. Uranium likes to attach itself to organic matter. Imagine it in the groundwater, flowing along in solution, and then it hits organic matter like a fossil log, maybe, or a bone. *Bam,* it come out of solution and into the bone, where the accumulation slowly concentrates. A lot of the dinosaur sites in this area were originally found by uranium prospectors. There's so much uranium in the bones that the paleontologists use scintilometers to prospect for fossils sometimes. You might be able to match concentrations in bone chips left over in the site to the contraband in storage. Or you could use it as a way of looking for hot debris in whatever truck they used to move stuff. It's also probably part of why George Dishey stored his stuff in a locker. You know, keep the heat away from his house. It can cause cancer if you keep it close for too long."

"Nice, nice, nice," said Bert. "We'll keep you around to

lecture to the kiddies. Now, when we're done with you today, if you want to wait for us by the airport here until we're done with the collar, fine—or you can find your own way back to Salt Lake City." He put a hand mockingly over his heart. "But I am a law-enforcement professional, sworn to protect tender little innocents like yourself, and when the fun begins, you're back here where you can't get hurt. You hear me?"

"Yes." My nerves were screwed to an intensity that had me almost shaking.

The pilot walked up to us and introduced herself to Not Tom and me. "Joan Howe," she said. She was cheerful, enthusiastic. My stomach turned.

I waited for Not Tom to give her his true name, but he just smiled and shook her hand. I said nothing, too unsure of my feelings to engage in social niceties.

I decided to phone Carlos while I was still alive. I said, "I'll be right back," and headed toward the flight service station in the building behind us.

"Where you going?" Bert called after me.

"The bathroom," I replied. *Try following me there, wise guy.*

Carlos wasn't at work or at home, but I left a message on his machine. As I was heading back around the corner of the building to rejoin the crew by the helicopter, I ran smack into Ray.

"Hi," he said, catching me by the shoulder while I regained my balance.

"Hello," I said.

He was making eye contact now, staring straight into me, reaching for something I've seldom shared with anyone. "You don't have to go," he said.

"I know."

He had both hands on my shoulders now. "I . . . don't want to lose you."

I reached up and touched his cheek very gently. "You won't."

❖

THE HELICOPTER BROKE out of the clouds and moved smoothly through the air, chasing the fading rays of the setting sun across the desert. I looked over to where Joan Howe sat beside me, her expert, slender hands working the controls. Her blond hair stuck out in wisps around the edge of her helmet. I noticed that she wore an engagement ring, and a snapshot of a rakish-looking boyfriend showing off a prize trout grinned at me from the place where it was taped between the avionics and the radios. I could hear her voice inside my helmet, like twin spirits that had found their way inside my ears. "We didn't have payload room for the FBI guy," she was explaining to me. "We got a big spotlight hanging from our belly. It weighs almost fifty pounds. We would have had to leave fuel off to carry him, shortening our range."

I was still sorting out my surprise at her gender. *I'm a pilot myself, and I work in male-dominated professions all day long, and always love it when I find a fellow female to work with. So why is this bothering me?* I wondered. "I don't think he particularly wanted to come, anyway," I said. Not wanting to jinx our flight, I didn't tell her that he'd already been in a crash. "Are you a police officer?" I asked.

"No, pilot only. It works better that way. If I was an officer, too, I might get my priorities mixed, get caught up in a chase that wasn't safe. This way, my number-one priority is to operate this craft safely."

"I'm glad to know that," I said as I stared down through the Plexiglas floor panel that started just in front of my toes and swept up to meet the windshield. The ground was flying away beneath my feet—an uncanny, slightly sickening sensation. The whole front of the craft was Plexiglas, a big clear bubble that jutted to a rounded nose shaped not unlike the visor of a medieval helmet. "I understand overhead wires are a problem," I said.

"Right. You can't see them. But we have wire cutters mounted above and below the fuselage." She pointed down below us and up over our heads at forty-five-degree angles. "About ninety percent coverage. If a wire hits us in the face, it'll be deflected up or down into the catchers, which would grasp it into the cutters. Above the upper cutter, there's a small gap and then the rotors. If it hits the top of the rotors, it's like hitting a Frisbee that's flying through the air—kinda whips it away. This ship's just plain loaded with safety equipment."

"I'm glad to know that, too," I said, both excited and uncertain. From the moment I had felt the vibration of the turbines firing up, felt the secondary wobble set off by the accelerating rotors, smelled the wash of jet fuel before she snapped shut her door, watched the RPM gauges—T for turbines, R for rotors—run up into their narrow green operating zone, I had been both hooked and terrified. No carnival ride enjoyed the bite of reality this bird had. "I fly fixed-wing craft," I said. "Most of them have a control wheel. I see you use a joystick."

"It's called a cyclic," she said, patting the control between her knees. "Don't ever call it a joystick, or a helicopter pilot will laugh." With her left hand, she patted another lever that lay between the two front seats like a gearshift. "This is the collective. Feathers the rotors, controls lift. Cyclic controls the pitch of the Frisbee, gives us pitch and roll. Pedals control the yaw." She moved each one to demonstrate. As she moved the cyclic, I could see the disk-shaped blur of the rotors tilt this way and that. It did look rather like a Frisbee. The odd thing was how smooth the ride was, but I realized that unlike a fixed-wing airplane, which flies through the wind, a helicopter creates its own. And controls it, or at least up to a point. I crossed my fingers that the storm would stay out of our track.

Through a brief break in the western clouds, I could see that a fingernail moon was setting. If the storm dissipated, we would have a dark, starry night. We were on our way into the dry lands, unpolluted by the lights of cities or security lamps. The stars would be especially brilliant. *If* the storm dissipated, which looked unlikely; the tops of the anvils reached almost overhead.

I straightened the map across my knees. I had chosen the shaded relief map rather than the air chart, as it had the best detail for drainages and rock outcroppings. "Follow that draw on the other side of that hogback," I said.

I could not see Ray and Bert where they sat behind the partition between the forward and aft sections of the cabin, but I could hear Bert's voice in my ears through the rear intercom hookup. It was a bit like having him inside my head, an uncomfortable sensation. "Take us lower," he said. "I don't want our bogey seeing us coming."

"Okay, but I got limits," answered the pilot. "As long as I'm moving fast, I can fly fairly low, but if you want me to hover, I want altitude, in case I've got to effect an autorotation."

Autorotation. There was that word again. It was a word that field geologists using helicopters had learned to fear. Autorotation was what a helicopter did when its engine went out. Lacking true wings, it could not glide down; it could only drop helplessly like a raw egg until the pilot lifted the collective and flared the rotors at the last moment, essentially cushioning the landing with air.

"This isn't the best craft for sneaking up on someone," Joan said.

"I'll risk that," Bert answered. "You just fly sweet and nice and try not to look like police, so we can get in there and see if we can get the lay of the land and follow these tracks little Emmy found. I'm feeling lucky tonight, sweetheart. I'm feeling these tracks are going to take us right to Mr. Bad!" He cackled, a sound relentlessly unpleasant through the earphones of my helmet, like having a rude bug loose inside my head.

I turned my mind away toward the ground that was sliding quickly past below me. I could see why, even with fear of autorotation, geologists loved to work via helicopter. One could claim an infinitely adjustable overview not possible from the ground. Vast quantities of time could be saved as one sprinted from point to point, setting down quickly to gather data, springing up again, hovering to take a better look here, pivoting in place to glance quickly there. I could see the broad layers of rock spread out before me, trace them quickly with my eye. I could see the Morrison Formation now, see it open out its soft, easily erodible belly in a valley or a ravine here, watch it disappear underneath another layer of younger, harder rock there. The Morrison's soft mudstones had been deposited in ancient lake beds and flood plains. It had lain buried, its fabulous fossil treasure hidden, for over 100 million years, a vast cemetery quietly holding its secrets. Now the region had been uplifted, and the deposition and burial of rock layers were being reversed by erosion. The sparse desert rains and arid winds now plucked at the shaley surface of the formation, carving the rocks slowly, inexorably into a broad badlands carpet broken by the occasional limestone or sandstone ledge. It occurred to me suddenly how little of its enormous expanse actually kissed the surface; just a thin interface between the volume that had already been eroded and all the billions of cubic miles of rock that still lay buried, and which would stay buried long beyond my lifetime, or perhaps all the remaining lifetimes of the human race. On this interface lay the few bones that nature had contrived to reveal to us, a mother lode of tissue turned to stone that drew the love and lust of the bone hunters. That which had been eroded before the advent of human curiosity was already lost, carried downstream, ground to dust. That which lay underneath the countless tonnage of overlying mountains and mesas would for the time being stay hidden, a task of excavation too costly in time and equipment even for the most committed. Bone hunting was a game of luck and perseverance, of walking the same ground again and again, hoping that this year the winter runoff had removed that critical millimeter of veiling mudstone that obscured a natural treasure; the enthralling magic of history disclosed for some, the love of strangeness and beauty requited for many, the ecstasy of treasure lust fulfilled for others.

We deflected now down the last valley the buses had driven, flitting over the rounded badlands hills and broken sandstone ledges that formed the strata that time and process had laid down over the Morrison. I directed the pilot to retrace our steps, to pass known landmarks to more quickly find the site. Now we reached the place where the buses had stopped. I pointed to the left, and we rose up over the ramp and east-facing cliffs formed by the Dakota Sandstone, a cliff-former above the Morrison. I could see the trail we had beaten into the ground with our footsteps, a dark scar of disturbed soil snaking over the varying terrain, barely visible in the dying light. Joan swung the helicopter smoothly over the trail, slowing slightly, still covering in minutes what had taken fast-hiking paleontologists half an hour to transit. Now we were hard over the site, in the shadow of the Dakota cliffs, deep in that broad, dark basin—hovering now, our pilot still leery of power lines, even with no poles in sight. She turned the ship slowly this way and that, choosing her spot, staring through the Plexiglas floor underneath her feet as she at last bled off her lift and settled the craft onto the ground. "Shall I shut it off?" she asked through the headphones.

"Leave it running," Bert answered. "I'm not here for a natural-history lesson; I'm here to scope for tracks."

Joan looked at me. "Just pop the door and keep your head down," she said, "and remember, don't you even think about taking a stroll aft of the passenger compartment. There's a second rotor spinning back there." She smiled, her rosy lips and well-scrubbed cheeks a picture of healthy youth framed by her helmet and boom microphone. I realized that she was younger than I, and felt uncomfortably responsible for her. In that moment, the full gravity of my decision regarding Nina came home to me as well. Had I lured her into harm's way, too?

"Thanks," I said, and unlatched my door. It popped open on a pneumatic strut, like the back door of a hatchback car. I took off my helmet, ducked my head, stepped down over the skids, and scuttled out toward the dig site. Bert and Ray met me there. "This is the spot," I shouted. "You can see where the teeth of the bucket bit in, like here, here, and here. Dan and his crew had taken their tents so it wouldn't be as conspicuous. You can see where the camouflage tarps were attached, and here is some of their digging equipment. They always drove in from the south, there . . . but it looks like the backhoe came from the north." I pulled out the BLM map Not Tom had given me. "I don't know how that trail hooks up to the roads. We've got the BLM maps, which would show all their bladed roads, but little double-track jobs like that are ranch trails and wouldn't be on it. But look here; they can't go too far in that direction without running into the San Rafael River."

"Ranch trails?" Ray asked incredulously. He looked out of place, as if his pristine white running shoes repelled the sticky clay soil on which he stood.

"Yeah, the BLM manages rangelands, and a lot of them are under long-term leases to the ranches. It's thin forage through here, but you can see the occasional cow pie." I pointed to an old one, grayed with dryness. "Looks like someone used this area for spring pasture but then moved the herds on. There's a little regrowth. The grass is probably waiting for winter moisture to come back. The ranchers generally own very little of the land they use. They prove out a few hundred or a thousand acres at best, or their grandparents did—just the good bottomland, land with water, where they can raise their winter hay—and they rely on government rangelands to rent for summer grazing. It's the ranchers who find most of the bones. While they're out searching for lost calves." *Or send their child brides to search for them*, I thought to myself. I could see George leading Nina over this ground, making a game of spotting bones.

Bert had drawn a bead on the receding backhoe tracks. "Let's get cracking, kiddies," he said. "I can hardly see my hand in front of my face."

✧

WE LIFTED BACK out of Vance's valley, as I had come to think of it, and glided over the fading tracks. It was not long before they led over a thin outcropping of limestone and faded out.

"Bring us into a low hover!" said Bert.

"You know I don't do low hovers," Joan said irritably. "They call that 'going under Dead Man's Curve.' "

"Aw, screw your curves, Joany, honey, scuh-*rew* your curves!" Bert's cackling again filled my ears.

I thought of saying something protective of this fresh-faced pilot I had drawn out into this situation, but Bert was still yakking through the earphones. "Hey, Emmy, what you make of those dark cruds there?"

I saw what he was seeing. "What you're seeing is clods of mud that dropped off his treads onto limestone."

We moved forward but quickly lost them.

"I can't see anything in the dark here," said the pilot. "You want me to put her down again? Or maybe switch on the light?"

"No!" said Bert. "No lights! At this altitude, they could see us for miles!"

"And you don't think whopping around out here with old thunder blades isn't drawing their notice?" she quipped irritably.

"Ya gotta strike a balance, sister. Risk over reward, risk over reward. Nah, shit, just rise up and make an arc off there toward the center of the swell, like you're heading back to Price, but sort of taking your time turning."

"You got it, cowboy."

Joan raised the collective again, lifting the craft higher over the desert floor as she pushed the cyclic forward. We gradually gathered speed, moving through the night air at thirty, now forty miles per hour. The western sky had reached the ultramarine blue of late sunset, and the shadows among the draws and gullies beneath our feet had grown black as pitch. We slowly traversed the mile or so width of the Morrison outcrop, glancing to the east in search of houses, but spotted none. I looked at the map, scanning for the tint that indicated private lands.

Seeing what I was doing, Joan reached over and touched the boom microphone that jutted from my helmet. A miniature flashlight came on, casting a tiny red glow that reached just to my lap. "Lip light," she said. "Hit that switch if you prefer green light, or white." She grinned. She clearly loved her equipment.

As I stared down past the map, I saw something odd pass beneath the Plexiglas panel by my feet. "Wait!" I said. "Did you see that?" We were crossing over the western edge of the Morrison outcrop again, right where it fetched up underneath its westward-tilting cap of the Dakota Sandstone. Deep in a small, narrow canyon cut into that sandstone, I thought I'd seen a machine.

Joan slowed the forward motion of the craft and pivoted, swinging the fuselage underneath the rotors like a pendulum. I wondered how Ray was taking this, hoped his stomach was as athletic as the rest of his body.

We neared the canyon. "I think I see the backhoe," I said. "There's something parked in that slot canyon, right where you'd only see it if you flew over low or rode past on horseback!" Excitement rose in my heart. "Wow, this is great! You can turn this bucket anywhere you want, can't you!"

I heard Bert's low chuckle through the headphones. "Take us on in there low and easy, sister, and switch on the light."

I saw Joan's hand twitch on the cyclic. The ship slowed its forward motion. "It's dark and it's narrow," she said. "I don't like it. It can't be more than a hundred feet top to bottom."

"I don't give a damn," Bert replied. "That's an order. You take us in there and switch on your damned light!"

"The ground rises. I won't have my altitude, and I'll have to bleed off my airspeed. You know what the height-velocity diagram looks like, Detective!"

"Fuck your diagram. I want to see that backhoe!"

The pilot hesitated. "Okay, I can give you a hover just at the rim, flick on the lights, but I'm not going below that rim, and I'm not going to land in there."

"That will do, darling."

Joan set the helicopter in a dead hover and looked at me. "I'm giving you the controls on the light. The manufacturer calls it the Night Sun, and they aren't just a-woofing. It packs thirty million candlepower. Up to now, we could have passed for sightseers, but only cops are nuts enough to carry spotlights. If I raise it much above the rim here, we're gonna light up like Rudolf's nose on Christmas Eve—you get it? The idea is to light up the canyon—on, off—get your glimpse, and get out. I could control it from the cyclic here, but I'm going to be concentrating on keeping us away from the sides of those cliffs." She handed me a control box and threw a switch on the cyclic. "Take a good look. That toggle gives you left, right, forward, back. That one's focus; wide area or fry your guy. That's on, off. Try the toggles, but don't turn that on until I tell you to. I don't like setting my belly up for target practice."

I figured out how to hold it in my bandaged hand, then fiddled with the toggles while she maneuvered the helicopter slowly over the canyon. I could just make out the looming shapes of boulders tossed about a water-scoured floor, and, hulking in the deepening shadows of night, a shape that could only be man-made. I thought about saying it was a backhoe for sure, that I didn't need the light.

"Now," she said.

I flicked the switch, and was momentarily blinded as the light flooded the canyon and my retinas. I hit the focus, swiveling the Night Sun toward my target. A backhoe, sure enough. But to my surprise, as I swiftly swiveled the light around the remainder of the tight canyon, I spotted also a crude lean-to, a pickup truck, and . . . a man. He looked familiar, an eerie copy of the distantly glimpsed bearded man who had followed me two nights earlier through the downtown streets of Salt Lake City. I opened my mouth to tell Bert, but the man in the canyon had a gun, was raising it—

"Get out of here!" I shouted, fumbling to extinguish the light.

Joan yanked up the collective and back on the cyclic, but it was too late. In the darkness that once again cloaked the canyon, I saw the bright flare of muzzle flash. I blinked to clear my retinas. A dark blue blotch tracked in my vision.

Red lights had erupted all across the top line of the instrument panel. A horn yelped mercilessly in my ears. I heard the high whine of the turbines wind down, watched helplessly as the turbine needle plummeted toward zero, saw the rotor needle whip sickeningly after it. Joan jammed down on the collective, counted, "One, two," yanked it back up, said, "Oh shit," and we hit, *slam*. My head jammed down on top of my spine as the rotors followed us to the ground, still spinning. They snapped downward and bashed into the canyon floor, snapped us into a spin as the aft rotor collided with the tail boom, threw us lurching into a sickening tilt against a rock.

Everything had gone ghost-quiet. I tried to orient myself. The lights of the radio console still glowed red around a wide blue patch of blindness left by the flash of the gun. I saw Joan's hand jerk down toward it, spin one dial to 121.5, the international distress frequency, heard her gasp, "This is—"

The Plexiglas beside her shattered with the impact of the next bullet, silencing her last call.

I wrenched my way free of my harness and crumpled onto the floor, then reached for her wrist to take her pulse. Dead. A scream rose in my throat and jammed as I thought, *I killed her. This was all my idea. I*— I glanced about the tight corner I had wedged myself into, trying to make my blotched eyes work in the dim light from my microphone boom, trying to make sense of the explosions I was hearing. Gunshots.

The door popped open behind me. For one terrible instant, I feared that I was alone with the gunman. Hands grasped me by the hips and yanked me backward, jerking my head as I rolled onto the ground and my helmet reached the end of its wire tether. Something popped it off. A hand took mine and tugged me hard toward the nearest boulder. In the last instant before I tripped, rolled, and helplessly followed the hand, I looked into the backseat of the helicopter and saw Bert's staring eyes, glassy with death, an image that burned itself into my memory in the split second I beheld it. His eyes seemed to stare through me, almost apologetic in their softness, as if to say, You were right—my brusqueness was all an act. I was just as lost as you are. Good luck where you're going.

I fell backward and fetched up against a heaving chest, a warm, firm body. Ray.

"Bert's dead," he whispered. "The pilot?"

"Dead."

A chunk of sandstone exploded inches from my face, spraying me with shards of cutting quartz. One eye filled with grit. I blinked, filling my face with pain. Tears welled up around the hostile object, blinding me in one eye.

"Can you run?" Ray whispered.

"I think so."

"Come."

He lifted me backward up onto my feet, wrapped an arm tightly around my back and tugged me into a run. We scrambled upslope toward a jumble of truck-size boulders. I wondered how I could suddenly see them, then realized that we were running down a beam from a flashlight, escaping its source.

Crack! Another shot from the rifle. We dived in behind another boulder, squeezing into a hole that deepened, giving down into cold earthy air. I scrambled downward into a maze of passageways between the rocks, squeezing like a blind spelunker into the narrowing openings, badgered by the patch of brightness that confounded my blindness.

"In here," I urged. "I can smell a cavern."

We squeezed down into the rocks, feeling our way toward the dampening air. The tight embrace of the stone opened suddenly into a low room, barely big enough for a fox to stand, but enough for us to sprawl, gasping for breath.

"We can't stay here," Ray whispered. "He's coming."

"Follow me," I whispered back.

"It's so narrow. . . ." I heard the fear in his voice, a rising pitch.

"Ray, *follow* me! Hold on to my ankle." I groped onward, following the ground upward, sniffing like a badger for musty air. It freshened in a place where outside sounds grew louder, less muffled. I squeezed away from the unseen opening, continued to climb. I reached a place where the space between the boulders was narrower than the length of my thighs. I could no longer go on hands and knees, instead had to push myself along with my toes. Instinct screamed in my ears, telling me not to go into a space that confining, but I had no choice. I was pushing along blindly, going by scent and touch alone, and there was no larger opening through the tumble of rocks. I had to pray that the sheer weight of the stones would hold them in place, and that the shifting and pressing of my own tiny weight would not send them tumbling farther down the slope.

As I pressed and pulled my way through the narrow passage, Ray let go of my ankle. Fear shooting through me like an arrow, I scuttled up into a larger space, where I could turn around and reach back for him, groping in the darkness. I felt his hand. It was stiff and wet with nerves. "I can't do it," he said so softly that I had to strain to make certain I had not imagined hearing him. My ears still rang from the gunshots, and now they pounded with the closeness of my own pulse.

"It's the only way," I whispered back.

Above my head, slivers of light played through gaps in the boulder pile through which we were climbing. The man who hunted us was scanning, playing his flashlight through the rocks that carpeted the slope, searching for his prey. I braced my feet, grabbed Ray by the wrist with both of my hands, and pulled with all my might. I heard a scuffle as he pulled with his other hand. Emerging into the space beside me as helpless as a newborn child, he lay a moment, curled up, his head lolling onto my thigh. I touched his face. His eyes were closed and his lips were moving in silent prayer.

The flashlight beam played through the gaps in the rocks over our heads again and we moved onward through the rock catacombs. I tried to reckon how far we had come up the canyon wall. Twenty-five feet? Forty? We had had to make so many turns that I was uncertain. A moment later, we hit a dead end, turned, moved to our right, stopped as the light found my hand. For the first time since the helicopter had fallen to earth, I saw my own flesh. It was not tan, but red, red with blood, drenched by the spray from Joan's ruptured body, a stain made as death blew past me in a cordite wraith.

I dared not move. I stopped breathing and prayed deep inside my mind. *Heavenly Father, or whatever Your name is, hear me now. I don't want to die. Not yet, not like this. . . .*

The light moved on, and I heard the man outside stumble farther away over the surface of the rocks. I inhaled slowly, thankfully, and felt the earth embrace me, a solidity of ground supporting my body and soul. Ray's hand found the crown of my head and cradled it, protective even in his fear. I could hear his pulse meld with mine where the curve of his wrist arched over my ear. I let myself breathe.

The man returned, stumbling over the tumbled surface of the rockfall. And now we heard his voice, a fearful, gasping voice, still frighteningly close, no more than ten feet away above our rock tomb: "I shot a helicopter!" it whispered.

We heard static, a garbled answer, the sounds of a handheld two-way radio.

"It had me cornered! Had to!" the man whimpered.

Now the voice on the hunter's handset came through clearly: "Manti, you stupid shit! You done it this time." The voice was angry and lethal, yet curiously close and intimate, like the voice of a gnat in my ear; a miniaturized voice on a radio turned down low in an attempt that we not hear it.

"What was I supposed to do?" the gunman whispered urgently to the radio. "Let 'em *see* me? I was right by the backhoe, Nephi!"

"You *had* to," drawled the voice over the radio. "Just like you *had* to kill George. Then I got to clear up your mess and make us another contact to get our manna. You God-cursed moron. Now we got another mess to clean up. You ain't even explained yourself for the first. You think you can get away with murder? God and all His angels will punish you, boy!"

In terror, the man above us shrieked, "It wasn't murder! George *blas*phemed! He had to *atone*!"

"Blasphemed, *hah!* You miserable tick on my hide! I saw what was left. You ripped him to shit. You call that blood atonement? I call it pissed off, man! Our contact to the *manna!* What he ever do to you?"

The reply from above our heads was a whine, as pathetic as a child who'd dropped his ice cream in the dirt. "All that time, and he'd never bred her *once!*"

"Who?"

"Nina!"

The voice on the radio growled, "So she's barren. How's that *blasphemy*, you idiot?"

"No, he *lied* to us! Took God's chosen and . . . and didn't *touch* her!"

Nephi paused before his reply. "How you know that?"

Manti whimpered, "That man told me. The one from the university."

"That fool with all the keys?"

In the darkness of my hiding place, I thought, *Lew?*

"No! The big one with the fish line on his glasses."

Sherbrooke! So they had met out there in the desert, the Yale-educated paleontologist in search of the answers to riddles and the half-wit cult follower looking for the bones of the damned to trade for manna. What could they have talked about?

"I *told* you you shouldn't talk to him! Outsiders is only good for business, and you leave that to me!"

Manti's voice wailed on: "He said George only messed with people's heads, that he never did breed with no one, not women, not men, not no one. He said it was all a big joke to George. And I *asked* Nina. I had to beat it out of her, but she *told* me. . . ."

Nephi's voice came back over the radio, crackling with rage. "That scheming, conniving . . . faggoty . . ." His voice trailed off into a froth of venom, but then suddenly the radio rasped with laughter. "Nina?" Nephi roared. "Wait, you mean you killed him over *Nina?* She was *nothing*. The *least* of my spawn."

I squeezed my eyes shut. George had been killed out of jealousy? *No*, I realized. *Blasphemy runs deeper than jealousy. Blasphemy is that name you have for something that brings humiliation to the depths of your soul—that deep, visceral sense of betrayal that comes when someone tells you that you sacrificed yourself for a sham.*

I could see the picture in its entirety now. This Manti had followed his brother into the desert and toiled for him, humbled himself before his brother's charisma, stood by, blinding himself to his loss of dignity and reality, all the time telling himself it would be worth it because there would be a prize. And then he'd stood by as that prize, his precious, coveted niece, was bartered away. Brother Nephi had fashioned himself to be a god in his own kingdom, but he knew that a kingdom needed to be fed. I could see it now: desperation and malnutrition, and then along came George, looking for the bones of dinosaurs, and an alliance was rekindled. He could control Manti and the others with food, but how to control George? He had a plan for him, too: If he lured George to indulge in that ultimate in control games, the sexual corruption of a child, it would forge a guilty, titillated addiction to his covert clan.

But George had been more clever yet, and had not indulged. Was he just being shrewd? Or had George kept hidden within his twisted soul a heart that no one but Nina knew.

Whimpering, the man who stood above us said, "She . . . she was s'posed to be *mine!*"

"We needed new blood. I *told* you."

Manti sobbed piteously. "But she didn't have no babies, and it wasn't *her*, like you *said*; it was *him*. He was—" He broke off with the effort of thinking. "*You* were lying to me!"

"Never mind that now!" snapped the voice on the radio. "You kill everyone on board?"

I stopped breathing. My mind swam with the horror of the stunted, medieval people who so automatically wished for my death.

Pause. "No. Got two of 'em. The other two are in the rocks."

The radio answer was garbled.

"But Neph, you—"

The voice over the radio cleared. "God sent you a tough challenge this time, didn't he? All right, let's see what we can salvage of your pathetic little ass! What's it say on the helicopter?"

"P-O-L-I—"

"Police? You hit a *police* helicopter? You don't know Satan's wrath till one of them comes down on you! You say two of 'em got away?"

"Yeah."

Ray drew breath and held it.

"They make any calls before they leave?"

"What do you mean, calls?"

"Over the helicopter's radios, shithead!" The voice over the radio was rising, soaring into a panicky anger.

"I—no. One of 'em had a mike to his face, but I shot him."

I wondered grimly whether it would have made a difference

had he known he was shooting a woman. I began to shake, the reality of death sticking to me like the blood that covered my hands. *It was my idea, my vanity, that led us to this trap, that killed this woman. And Bert, another fool for the truth, just like me.*

"I'll be right there," came the voice over the radio. "Where did you say they are?"

The man above the rocks was beyond panic. That could only mean that he feared Nephi even more than he feared us. "They're in the rockfall on the south side of the canyon, down in those cracks where Nina always goes. I got 'em pinned. They can't get in there too far, and there ain't no way out of there 'cept I can see 'em."

"Right."

My heart sank into the ground. Were they right? Was there no way out?

Manti said hopefully, "Should I burn that helicopter?"

"No! That would be like setting a flare. Leave it! But wait— there's a little box on board that'll be transmitting a distress signal. Should be in the left-front corner of the cockpit. If you can find that, put a bullet through it."

"Okay. . . ." The gunman sounded doubtful, edgy. But, like a bull cornered in a corral, he was all horns and brute force, ready to do what he had to. I heard him shift as he prepared himself to climb down off the rocks above us and move toward the helicopter.

As the voice on the radio faded away with increasing distance, it took on an oily, soothing tone. "Now, don't worry, boy; this is just another test of your faith. Reload that rifle and stop your whining; Heavenly Father's on your side."

◇

THE SHOT THAT silenced the emergency location transmitter in the helicopter rang out moments after the second man arrived, grinding up the canyon in a truck with a slipping fan belt. At the sharp report, I jerked back from the aerie I had at last found my way to near the top of the rockfall, then eased back to a position from which *I* could keep watch while Ray faced the other way and searched for a route out of the canyon. Manti had been wrong. We had found a route through the rocks. Nina had only ever looked for cover beneath the tumble of rocks, not passage through it. Coming out another exit would have only put her right back where she'd started, in the hands of this strange tribe with its contorted set of beliefs.

Ray had managed to make it through the labyrinth with his teeth gritted against fears I could only guess at. The densest part of the tumble had thinned, until we had emerged onto a cladding of scattered boulders lying directly on the shaley slope. We had inched sideways and upward, until we now crouched three-quarters of the way up the slope, perhaps seventy feet above and one hundred feet laterally from the helicopter. Above us jutted the source of the boulders, an overhanging lip of sandstone perhaps fifteen feet thick. We huddled behind a stone not much larger than a hay bale, kinked and aching, gingerly rubbing camouflage dirt onto our faces as we scanned the cliff face for a route up past this last pitch of the climb.

"Manti, you imbecile!" Brother Nephi called. "The guy in the backseat is still alive!"

Ray's face swung from looking up to looking down. I fought to control a gasp. With terror, I realized that there was nothing we could do to help Bert. The thin starlight barely illuminated the whites of his eyes.

I turned and peered back down the slope. I could make out the silhouette of each boulder, could see the faint glow of the instrument panel lights on the face of Brother Nephi as he reached around inside the cockpit of the downed helicopter. I had found him striking—even riveting—when I had seen him in the van, but now, moving about the wreckage, he was a gaunt assemblage of swaggering hips and tumbling beard, an eerie mutation of sensuosity. His deep-set eyes glared as if set in a naked skull—quick bullets of intelligence reflecting the instruments' glow. He scanned the cockpit systematically, scavenging for useful equipment with the hands of one who had known this machinery before. He knew we were there, knew he'd have to find us, but he seemed unconcerned, unhurried in his movements. This more than anything inspired me to fear him: he clearly knew something I didn't.

"Take ye to the devil!" he roared, and fired again, dispatching what was left of the dying detective. Nephi threw back his head and howled like a wolf, his triumph filling the canyon. Then, almost abstractly, he added, "Now we got to bury this mess."

Ray's hands squeezed my shoulders, catching me before I fell forward with the urge to vomit. We huddled together, stifling the sound of our breath.

When I next looked, Brother Nephi was half inside the cockpit and cabin. He extracted two pistols from the passenger area, and from the front cockpit he took a flashlight, some pens, and the elastic straps off the pilot's knee board. As he jostled the pilot to remove it, her head lolled with a disturbing semblance of life, and her face swung into view.

"Nice move, Manti," Nephi muttered bitterly, the intimacy of his voice carried to us by the crisp, close acoustics of the rocks, the desert air, the night. "You ruined a perfectly good helicopter. And you shot a woman." To himself, he said, "We could have *used* a woman."

"A woman? How was I to—"

"Shut up and keep searching."

"I *been* searching. I—"

"*Patience*, Manti. Use your *head*. Shut up and *listen* for them. They're in there somewhere; I *feel* it. Now, don't you worry.

Ma will be here any moment with the dogs. Remember, they found Nina that time she tried to hide."

Dogs? *So that's why he's so confident. Even if we get free of the rock pile, he can track us faster than we can run. A home-court advantage.* I felt Ray tense beside me. I put my lips to his ear and whispered, "Are you armed?"

His return whisper was bitterly angry. "No."

Brother Nephi asked Manti, "You get a good look at 'em?"

"The female was that one I followed in the car."

Nephi's teeth flashed with a grin. "Ah . . . Little Emily! Come on *out*, sweet thing!" He threw his head back and howled with laughter, the sound echoing off the canyon walls. "Brother Nephi's got a *surprise* for you!"

I pressed my lips together, hoping I would not vomit.

Suddenly, the lights went off in the cockpit, returning Brother Nephi to a moving bit of darkness. Satisfied in his urge to scavenge, he had thrown the master switch and now was returning to the greater task of dealing with us. He stretched, surveyed the canyon walls, and said, "Fire up that backhoe, Manti."

"But I got to watch the rocks, like you said."

"No, *I'll* do that. You get that bucket raised and start crushing that cockpit. Come *on*, man. Use your *head*. All our hard work to build this kingdom, and you think I'm going to give it up over a little screwup like this?" He laughed, a big high-pitched howl of mirth. "That big guy from the university dug us up those bones. Dug 'em up all pretty, just like George said he would. Saved us the trouble." Suddenly, his voice was hard with rage. "Of course you had to bust them all to hell with the backhoe getting them out!" His voice calmed again with disturbing swiftness as he continued, talking to himself now, soothing himself: "But we got enough. We got enough. Smeely's gonna do us. Don't need that George anymore no-how, no sir; ol' Nephi's gonna be fine. . . ."

The last piece of the puzzle snapped into place. Brother Nephi had ransacked George's house to find the name of his sales contact, not me. But by then, I knew enough to be dangerous. I had left my motel room before they could find me there, and then had seen Nephi and Smeely together. I had to be eliminated. And now I had delivered Ray to the same fate.

Nephi's voice snapped again with anger. "So what you waiting for, Manti? You think we can just leave this hulk out here for the cops to find? We got to get this thing buried!"

"But what if they bring another helicopter? They'll see my spoils pile," Manti replied, advancing his first quick thought of the evening.

Nephi moved over to the truck. "You ain't making no pile of dirt, brother. You're gonna crush that chopper and push it up against the rocks. Then I'm gonna have me a little fun with some of this fine C-four."

Explosives! Brother Nephi was going to tumble the pile of rocks onto the helicopter. We had to move, and move quickly. *As soon as he starts that backhoe, we'll have the cover of noise. . . .*

Nephi hoisted a box out of the pickup bed and moved up onto the rocks toward us, as if he somehow knew where we were perched. It was time to move, but where?

He set down the box. I heard a match strike, saw a flare. His bony face was again visible, eyes aimed straight our way, glowing like embers as he cupped his tiny fire in his hand to stifle the gentle breeze that still rose up the canyon. With the cooling of the desert night and the coming storm, the air would soon condense and flow downward, and with it, our scent; but for now, the sweet smell of marijuana curled past my nostrils. For all his bravado, Brother Nephi was calming his nerves.

"Nephi!" came a new voice, low and urgent. "This ain't no time for visions!"

I glanced down the canyon. A scrawny woman was arriving,

leading two small hounds. Their approach had been unnervingly quiet.

"Hush, woman!" Nephi replied, and then, in the most reasonable of tones, he informed her, "Heavenly Father revealed the need for me to smoke. Wouldst thou question His word?"

"No. . . ."

He laughed unkindly. "Besides, this joint is laced with the power of angels."

Angel dust. Quiet dogs, high-powered rifles, and people who move like specters through the dark. They lived off the grid, just as Not Tom had said, without the decadent support of electricity. They knew the dark intimately, were at ease in it. The light of a single match was brilliant to them. They knew this terrain as if by braille—knew its every rock and hollow without seeing—and were used to moving through it in the darkest night.

Ray squeezed my hand, gave it a tiny tug. I swiveled around and pointed toward a notch in the cliff above us. We could brace ourselves in there while we searched for a route up over the canyon rim, and pray that the explosives did not knock us loose.

We eased our ways up over the rocks, slithering like snakes, hesitant to breathe for fear of being heard. Beneath us, the dogs started sniffing. One yelped. I glanced down over a boulder as we slid past it. The dog was sniffing inside my abandoned helmet, had caught my scent, pulled toward the rock pile.

Ray swung into the notch. There was a tumble of rocks leading to within six feet of the top. We could get out! He climbed onto the top and lifted himself up onto the capstone of the canyon and motioned for me to follow, but I knew that his move had taken more strength than I could hope to muster. I ran my earth-chilled hands up over the rough surface of the rock in search of hand- and foot-holds. I found none. The dogs barked and scratched, their sharp claws skidding as they climbed the rocks. I reached, praying to the gods of the rocks and the sky to lift me.

Ray's hands closed around my wrists. He gave three small tugs, a deft message that said, Jump on the count of three. I looked up. He crouched above me with his chin almost down to the rock, his arms making up the distance I could not reach. I eased my feet to the highest clefts I could find, tugged once, twice, and, on three, jumped. He lifted with amazing force, fell backward, and rolled silently deeper onto the top of the cliff.

He did gymnastics, too, I thought numbly as I tumbled after him.

As I rolled my head this way and that to get my bearings, Ray whispered, "Which way?" his voice barely louder than the sigh of the wind.

"West," I whispered.

"Which way is that?"

"Which—" At that instant, it hit me that Ray was lost. Away from his city, away from the orderly grid of streets and the mental map of his known universe, he was not oriented to the earth I knew so intimately. "But how did you shadow me through the city?" I asked.

"I could *sense* you," he replied, painfully aware of what I was asking. "You're a strong signal."

I didn't have time to consider what he meant by that. I had gotten him into this mess and it was up to me to get us back out of it. "Pay attention to the storm," I breathed. "It's coming from the west." I could feel the wind now strongly in my face, the cold rip of wind that comes before the downpour. I read the clouds, gauging the time before it would be upon us. Lightning flashed. I counted one, two, three . . . fourteen seconds before I heard the rumble of thunder. Two miles.

A horrible rending of steel against Plexiglas and more steel told us that the bucket of the backhoe had found the helicopter.

The crushing continued rhythmically. I prayed that they had removed the bodies first.

I tugged Ray's hand and we began to rise, ready to scuttle over the uneven surface. I could see the far lights of civilization to one side of the nearest storm cell, distant pinpoints of hope.

Lightning flashed again, momentarily bleaching the landscape.

Ray jerked me downward. We dropped flat onto the rock, balling ourselves behind a ledge of stone. I squeezed my eyes shut again, willing my retinas to reset and read the darkness. Opened them, saw what he had seen: the sharp, unnatural silhouette of a rifle flicking across the skyline. The eerie shapes of one, two more hunters were closing on us from perhaps one hundred yards away. They moved closer. Two more rifles, in the hands of a slender boy and a woman with billowing skirts. And, like their kin in the canyon below, they were horrifyingly silent, unheard even with the wind behind them. I wondered how many more were out there, and from what direction they would come.

More of Nephi's insurance, I thought bitterly. They had circled around to the west of the cliffs, taking up positions where the ground opened up. A third one appeared, another woman, or perhaps yet a girl.

I tugged Ray's hand to the north, toward the cover of more rocks, and we moved like crabs, barely lifting our faces from the stone, praying that we would not be betrayed by another flash of lightning. I found a crack that ran across the cliff top and I dropped down into it. Ray followed. Grit blew into my eyes. The crack widened, sinking to a merciful three feet deep, but it was full of sharp stones and the stinging spines of cacti. I clamped my teeth and moved along on my hands and knees, stifling the desire to gasp, to weep, to howl at my misery and fear.

The crack led down into deeper and deeper cover, until we

were able to crouch, pitting our shod feet instead of tender flesh against the desert's cruelties, but the spines of cacti continued to find their ways through my thin athletic shoes. Something moved under my hand. A snake? A lizard? A rock tilted under one foot, wrenching my ankle to the left. I froze until it stabilized, listened above for sounds of our pursuers, moved onward.

I rechecked my bearings. The crack was guiding us toward the east-facing rim, back toward the wide basin of the Morrison, but north of the canyon where our helicopter lay broken like the fragile bird it was. I willed the crack to swing farther northward, farther from the mouth of the canyon, but I knew in my heart that it would not, that it would instead follow the forces of the earth that had formed it, straight as an arrow. It at last met the cliff face in a chimney of rock three or four feet wide, through which rose the scent of the shale below. I turned, waited until I felt Ray's breath against my cheek. "We can get down here," I whispered.

"How?" Ray whispered back. We could both see the drop. Too far to jump without being heard, and no certainty of the softness of our landing.

"Put your back against one wall, feet against the other. Like this." I jammed myself into the chimney, pushing hard against the opposite side with my feet, and began to walk downward. My shirt quickly rode up, exposing my back to the teeth of the thousand sharp grains that jutted from the stone.

As I reached the bottom, thirty feet below, I arched my head skyward and searched for Ray's shape. In the next flash of distant lightning, I saw the silhouette of his head and shoulders as he leaned out over the top of the chimney. It occurred to me only then that he might be afraid of heights.

I willed him to descend. Urged him with all my heart.

I saw him twist his head backward, listening, a shape of darkness picked out against the stars that were now being eaten by the overreaching clouds. He tensed, looked downward, hesitated. One leg swung out, and then the other. He began to ease downward.

By the time he reached me, Ray was bathed in sweat. It was thick and acrid, laden with the scent of fear moved close to terror, but he said nothing. I ran a hand up across his forehead and he took it, reflexively moving it from his head to his heart. His chest heaved with the effort to catch his breath. He lifted my hand to his lips and kissed it. "Lead on," he said shakily.

"This way," I told him, pointing north along the cliff. "A half mile up, there's a river. Turn left. Another half mile, there'll be a confluence. Take the middle fork. It will lead us straight to Castle Dale."

"And if we find more kids with rifles?"

"Turn right. Follow the river. But either way, you go ahead of me. You can run faster. The dogs will follow my scent, not yours. If they catch up with me, you'll still have a chance."

Ray squeezed my had. "No. We stay together."

I squeezed his hand in return.

We found our way quickly down the rock-strewn slope back onto the Morrison clays and picked up speed on the flat, staying close to the line of cliffs, seeking what slim cover of shadow we could find against the moody starlight that was so quickly being eaten by the storm. Up on the cliff, I heard a dog bark, one quick yelp. It would be only minutes before the dogs led their masters down off the cliff. I prayed that the slot would delay them. Perhaps those on the cliff top could see us even now, two shadows in the crosshairs of their rifle sights. I longed for the cover of the San Rafael River, where the waters might shroud our scent and the shrubs might grow thick enough to hide us.

All along the cliffs, I felt eyes of children on my naked neck, the eyes of children who knew the crazed face of hatred, feared it until it had squeezed their breath, knew it intimately, lived each day with the specter of its glowing stare and jutting cheekbones, its sorties into the strength of angels. The punishments of Brother Nephi would be swift and ruthless, and chased quickly by the blundering panics of Manti, his witless second hand. The children who pursued us would fear that wrath until it tore them, twisted them, compelled them to eject their torment and call it Satan. And Nephi knew how to dress the devil in my clothes.

I pushed fear from my mind and tried to play the images of the agent's maps in its place. I conjured the placement of cliffs and the river. It flowed southeast from Castle Dale, winding tortuously down through a shallow canyon of its own. We would follow it upstream, and where it cut through the Dakota cliffs, choose the middle fork of three, toward those distant lights, a telephone, a sheriff. My mind spun with contingencies, frothing with worry. We would pass houses before we reached the town—I had seen them from the bus that afternoon—but what kind of soul dwelt inside each one? Was the nearest a nest of rifles? Would a door open to a mainline Mormon who would receive Ray like a lost son, or find another recluse from the law?

My feet were heavy with the dampness that had seeped into them in the rockfall, but my lungs were filled with the sweetness of life-giving breath, propelling me along at a smooth lope. Ray ran easily beside me, his fingers loose, conserving energy. "Leave me," I said, "Run till you reach the river. Turn left. Middle fork."

He stayed right by me, eyes ahead.

A muted *whumpf* signalled the detonation of the C-4 explosive. I reached inside for my last ounce of speed and sprinted.

I heard the hounds bark eagerly behind and above us, heard Nephi's truck emerge from the canyon and grow nearer. The last hundred yards toward the river flew by beneath my feet.

I could hear the water now. The sound was muffled, telling me that it flowed below us, below a cut bank, in a channel. I imagined the drop, bracing my muscles for the descent. The bank would be steep, but the clay would crumble into a slope nonetheless. I reached the brink of the bank and slid on the soft clay, my heels finding the angle that would carry me safely down to the floodplain where the river rushed.

I heard Ray stumble behind me, then accelerate, his feet uncertain in the darkness. The ground leveled out onto gravel. I kept running, heard the sound of rippling water close now, wheeled left, upstream, toward life as I had known it. Heard the crack of another rifle shot—

Something heavy splashed into the water to my right. I dived instinctively away from the rifle shot. Downstream. Away from town, from help, from hope. Rolled, fetching up in low brush by the river's edge.

I listened for Ray.

Something large floated quickly away from me, a dark mass breaking the soft, dappled reflections of the starlight on the rippling water. Losing precious time disentangling myself from the scrub, I waded shin-deep into the water, reaching, searching for Ray's body in the water, lost my footing in the rush of current, and fell. The river was swift and deeper than I had imagined for an autumn stream in the desert. It had swelled from a shallow stream into a rushing river, gorging itself on the storm that had played along the hills all afternoon. I thrashed, groped for the bottom with my feet, hit it, lost it, let the waters carry me onward. I reached for Ray in my mind. Tried to sense him. East. Cold. My mind filled with a panic fantasy of Ray lifeless, his blood billowing out around him like a halo—

I was chilled to the bone. Knew I had to get out of the water or die. The river curved right, sweeping me behind the cover of the tamarisks. I reached for their branches, caught a broken twig sharp into the pad of my damaged left thumb, released.

I kicked, rolled onto my back, following helplessly along the current, the stars high above me, the dark wall of the tamarisks crowding the channel. I saw the high, distant light of a jetliner following a westbound route through the night sky, thought of its passengers, tired businessmen homeward bound, mothers with restless children, stewardesses rolling carts with drinks and peanuts down the aisle. I dreamed a signal of my distress, wondered if my tiny voice might whisper in the pilots' ears. Wait, they'd say; I hear a person in the darkness, a human lost in the desert; let's find her, warm her, raise her to our wings and feed her peanuts, wrap her in blankets. The fantasy held such sweetness that warm tears ran from my eyes into the roiling waters of the San Rafael.

Slowly, I realized that the waters were ebbing, carrying me from the channel to the shallows. I rolled. One foot hit, and then the other, and I was aground. I climbed out on the sandbar and watched for Ray, tracing the bouncing starlight down the riffles, hoping for a glimpse of the interruption his dark form would make.

He was not there.

I could sense you. You're a strong signal. . . .

I reached with all my senses. Nothing.

I wiggled up into the cover of the tamarisks, squeezing between their myriad whiplike branches, now catching a spider-web across my face, now flushing a sleeping bird. The tamarisks danced in the wind, sighing, rubbing their branches together like a madwoman wringing her hands. I found a small clearing and sieved my thoughts from the burble of the rushing waters. I was cold, dangerously cold. I worked quickly to shuck off my blue jeans and wring them dry, and then my socks. Poured water from my shoes, rechecked my pockets to see what resources they might hold, wishing for the pocket-knife Ray had taken from me two days ago, so long ago, a lifetime past in a place far away called Innocence, in the time before Salt Lake City.

I found two quarters and a dime, and my little packet was still there. I knew that the matches would be dry, their heads were coated with paraffin. I briefly considered building a fire. Abandoned the idea. *The matches won't light wet tinder, and they'd find me in an instant. I considered wrapping up in the Mylar blanket. But I'd reflect lightning like a beacon.*

I wrestled off my jacket, wrung out its burden of wetness, skinned off my shirt. The jacket I put back on; it was synthetic fleece and would warm me even with its dampness. The jeans were a greater problem. They were sodden, and wet denim, I knew, would leach the strength from my muscles. I pulled my knees up underneath my jacket, wrung the heavy fabric again, and waited. Listening. I did not have long, I knew. I must decide either to leave the jeans behind or reclothe myself in them. Thinking of the thousand scratches the tamarisks could lend me, I struggled back into them, staggering with the effort. I wrung my socks again, worked my stiffening fingers over the laces of my shoes, got up, looked and listened for Ray one more time, heard shouting along the banks behind me, and moved.

I played the maps across my mind again: To the east, if I were above the banks, I faced two, three miles of badlands and cliffs, then a two-mile climb up a long, gradual slope to a BLM campsite named the Wedge. It might hold campers and, with them, radios, or with luck a cell phone angled high enough to send my voice to Price. I needed help desperately, and not just for my sake but for Ray's. Was he alive? I peered again through the branches, searching for him, longing for him. He had felt the danger, but I had lured him down here anyway. His blood would coat my hands just as surely as those now buried in the canyon.

A cold stab shot through me as I realized that the Wedge was on the north side of the river and I was on the south. I pumped my legs, working my knees hard against the frigid iron that was the denim. I searched my mental map for a ford, a shallow. Hadn't there been a BLM road downstream before the Wedge? Yes, I was certain: There was a private inholding along the riverbank at a place called Fuller Bottom. Would I find a friendly human there? Or Ray, a faster swimmer, waiting for my approach? I might find a ranch, a corral, or less. Worse yet, I knew, I might stumble right inside the nest where Brother Nephi sowed his hungry seed.

I whisked through the brush, weighing speed of motion against the level at which I made too much sound. I shook my head, cold to the point of whispering to myself, reasoning my way through my predicament. The rifles Ray and I had seen on the cliff top had come on foot from the west or south within minutes of Manti's call. Was their compound near, or had Nephi deployed them from his truck? Fuller Bottom was east, and perhaps safe. But no, it had those roads, big graded roads, over which Nephi's truck could roll quickly, and he might meet me there. I hastened my pace.

Where *was* Ray? I could not sense his presence. Had a bullet found him? Or had he found himself westward, toward help?

I glanced overhead, watching for the needle shapes of rifles above the upper banks, taking quick bearings from the stars. The river was snaking, I knew, winding between the banks in sinuous curves as it hastened to the east. I calculated a doubling of the distance of Ray's swimming over my scramble through the brush, if I continued to follow the bank.

Cold was seeping into my shoulders. "I've got to keep moving," I whispered to myself. "I have to find him." *Have to help him. I got him into this. My lie. The one I told myself. That I could do this, fix this, solve the crime and win his favor, my freedom, his admiration.*

Another twig scraped my face, raising a bloody weal. I let the sting keep me conscious, distract me from the cold. I fed on the pain, met it with a lover's heart. Rain pelted my face. I considered scrambling above the bank, where I could move faster, make better headway, make fewer oscillations from the straightest track. Knew that above this bank, on open ground, they'd pick me off like skeet.

I wondered what time it was, wondered when Not Tom would send in searchers, helpers, friends with better rifles. *But he won't know where I am. He knows the way to Sherbrooke's site, at least by road and trail, but that would take an hour and put him there by foot. The emergency transmitter on the helicopter is dead, and even if it were live, it's sitting in the bottom of a narrow slot, where line-of-sight radio surveillance will miss it. A search plane can do no good before daylight, and then it will find only rubble.* I hurried onward, doggedly, thinking now about the chances missed. *What if I'd accepted Ray's blessing? Might I then live? Might he?* I thought of the fear that had kept me from joining that gathering, fear of change, the unknown, the unseen. So foolish that now all seemed.

I pressed on, breaking here and there into the corridor between the upper bank and the tamarisks, ready to dodge back into their cover if I needed it. *I'll find help at Fuller Bottom. Ray will be there; I'll fish him from the waters and warm him with my sorrow, my apology, my . . . love. We'll climb the ramp to the Wedge. There'll be helpers there, nice people with cell phones, a warm fire, hot chocolate. . . .*

The night wore onward, punctuated only by the shifting patterns of stars and clouds, the whispering of the wind, and the yelps of distant animals, a coyote here, another call there that sounded like a child pretending to be a bird. Now a dog barking in the distance, and another answering it. I listened for trucks, saw another airplane fly high overhead, followed the far arc of a satellite barely bright enough to see. Could it find me? Could it hear my heart beat, smell the harshness of my breath? I was the daughter of a technological world, running scared through endless halls of brush and dens of animals, running, hurrying, into the quiet, too quiet, perhaps a trap—

I trudged onward. Fatigue wrapped me in its heavy cloak. As my stride slowly shortened, I heard voices in my mind, heard again Ava's uncertain welcome, Katie's chiding challenge. *We saw you coming*, the voices told me. *You live outside God's love, in the lie. You're not of us. Loneliness is a lie; don't you hear us? Follow your heart. Find Ray. Bring him home to us.*

Now Nina's voice swam through me, rushing to the rhythm of my breath; *We'll be together in the Kingdom. George awaits us; Heavenly Father loves us. Stay beside me; let me love you. Drop that armor from your heart.*

My feet flew along the sands of the riverbank, spanked down on mud that shone with starlight. Numb, leaving tracks. Didn't care now, had to make the distance before the sun rose—

"I'll find him," I panted, speaking to nobody and everybody. "I'll bring him back, I swear it."

I watched continually for a crossing, for shallow waters to break my trail should the dogs find it, a way across to climb to the Wedge. I could not see through the thicket of the brush. It waved now with the lashings of a growing wind. I stopped, looked westward. Clouds befriended me, deepening my cover, but rain again was wetting me, and the breath of the wind was cold. I stumbled onward, almost fell into the cut where the road sliced down from the bank.

I had stumbled into Fuller Bottom before I expected. I'd been waiting for the crosscut of sandstone, the Entrada, a brown band on one map, a cliff on another. I had toyed with these outcrops in my mind, wondered if they might afford a cleft or a cave that might hide me, an aerie from which to watch the river, to watch for Ray. I had missed it, and Ray? Where was his voice in my mind?

My mind was dead, my body lost to feeling.

I ran one clawlike hand across my face, tried to force clarity into my mind. Ray was a man of motion, not of words. I caught that idea and held it, followed it down into a wordless place, followed the tracer of his heat—

With surprise, I felt him now, but where?

Listen, my mind told me. *Feel.*

The soft voice of a child cut through the darkness startingly close. "I can do it," the voice said. "I can pull this trigger. Kill the Satan. I can do it."

Stiff with fear, I cocked my head, tracking the voice toward its source. Up above me and to the right.

I eased backward under the blackness of the cliff, lay down on the bank of the river, and thought. *If I slide into the river, he'll hear me. Shoot me. And then yet one more life will be on my hands, a child's future ruined by the ugly fact of having killed.*

I could not let that happen. For that matter, I could not let these children face the war that could arrive any time now from the air, or from the roads. If cornered, I knew that Nephi would sacrifice every last one of them. I had heard it in his voice—"The *least* of my spawn."

I eased up again, slowly rising until I could see the outline of the child. I heard a heavy thump in the darkness. The shifting of a cow, a sound I knew from a hundred nights searching for calves with my father. Sliding down again, I picked up a handful of gravel, took aim, and hurled it beyond the child at the cow. The cow bawled. The child gasped, swung suddenly around and shouted, "Brother?" Under the cover of this diversion, I slithered back into the water. Felt for the bottom with my hands. Floated gently, facedown, my

hands walking me down the eddy, my spine stiff with anticipation of a bullet, the cold bleeding my hands into stumps,
letting my body trail like a log, head raised up to keep my
lips above the water. I sent a blessing to the rain god that had
sent the cover of clouds to snuff the glistening stars out, and
floated onward, around one more bend, two, three, thanked
the river god for wider banks here, for shallow waters—

I rolled out on the north bank and stared up into the blackness of the clouds. Lightning bloomed high up in them, sound-
less, a cloud-to-cloud acrobatic of electric heat.

Heat. Where was Ray?

I heaved myself into a sitting position, dragged myself up
under the brush, began the slow drudgery of ejecting my sodden clothes. Wrung them out. Struggled back into them, my
legs as stiff as tree trunks.

Ray. I could feel him almost as a physical presence, as if
the last heat of his body was guiding me. Over here—he
pulled me like the needle on a compass. Over here—

I lurched back onto my feet and stumbled along the riverbank, following the pull I felt deep inside. Lost the sense,
paused, closed my eyes, then felt it again, moved toward it.
Stronger now. One hundred feet farther along the bank, I
found Ray, lying on the gravel, facedown. I rolled him onto
his back and pressed an ear against his neck, listening for a
heartbeat, forcing back the sobs that surged up my throat.
Thump.

He was alive, but cold as the waters. His breath came thinly.
He opened his eyes and stared at me, tried to smile. His face
twitched with the cold.

I grabbed him by the wrists and pulled, dragging him up
the bank into the brush, where I settled him on a bed of dried
leaves, and began to skin away his clothes. His jacket was thin,
although lined with flannel. I wrung it dry, pulled off his shirt,
found another layer beneath it, pulled.

"N-n-no," he whispered.

"Got it," I whispered back. I'd heard of Temple garments, but never seen them. I smiled ruefully. "Angel suits," some called them, the Mormon armor against an unsheltering world. I said a silent prayer that they were not cotton but polyester, that they might warm him.

Working quickly against the freezing fingers of the coming storm, I replaced his jacket with my own. His wrists jutted from the sleeves, but the zipper met in front with some tugging. I emptied the water from his shoes, squeezed his socks as dry as possible—*Wool; good*, I noted, *they'll hold some heat*—undid his pants and peeled. His legs were moving now, slowly, like an old man's. He pushed feebly, trying to free himself of the embrace of wet denim. I wrung the pant legs, pressed the pockets free of each loose drop.

I whispered, "Ever been camping before, Eagle Scout?"

Ray's teeth glowed faintly from below me. "Never was in scouting. Is there a merit badge for hypothermia?" he asked, taking my arm by the wrist and pulling me down. He was shaking now, shivering hard from toes to crown, and needed my added warmth. I extracted my emergency kit from the pocket of the jacket and unfolded it. Hurriedly, I spread it out and wrapped it around us both so the heat from my body would stay with him. If the fates were against us, the Mylar would reflect the lightning, the stars, and the headlights of Brother Nephi's truck, but the chance had to be taken. I shucked off my clammy jeans and lay down on top of him, exhaled against his neck, sending my heat into his brain, shifted until our bodies met with greatest contact. I fed his arms up inside my—his—jacket, wrapped my arms around his sides and rubbed. Minutes passed. I breathed against his scalp, his cheeks. At length, his shivering subsided from racking tremors to a slight vibration, and his breath came more easily. His arms melted from rigid to relaxed, then tensed again as he hugged me tightly.

Then he kissed me, a long, searching kiss, a kiss of passion, thanksgiving, and friendship, but not of sex. We were both still too cold for that.

I ran a hand through his hair, savoring its stiff, springy texture. He was warming quickly now. If I lay with him much longer, I would be taking advantage of him in his weakest moment. He had made his vow of chastity, and it held meaning for him. It wasn't my place to help him break it. I thought how much better it might be to be this man's friend first, and see where friendship led. I smiled, feeling a warmth of affection for him, regardless of his stubbornness and complexities. Ava was correct: love was a verb, not a noun.

Ray had saved my life, and now I had saved his. But we had also lost lives, and it was time to save others. We had crossed to the far side of the river, away from the hunters, and dawn was coming. With the dawn would come greater vulnerability, but also search planes, and someone—either more pilots or one of these children out here—would get hurt. "Time to go," I said.

23

THE FIRST VELVET ROSE OF DAWN SMUDGED THE EASTERN
sky as we threaded our way carefully through the forest of
junipers and piñon pines that graced the great rampart of canyon rim called The Wedge. The storm had blown past us, its
waters spent, and it had been a long, slow job scaling the
curving face of the Navajo Sandstone, once we'd finally found
it where the river cut down into the Little Grand Canyon. Bats
had wheeled curiously about us, and we had taken our time.
Our clothes were almost dry, and we were warming quickly
with the exertion, but the cold and fatigue had weakened us.
And it wouldn't do to hurry; the drops were too sheer, too
dangerous, and besides, the night was magic now, a cloak
within which we could savor this time together.

Wordlessly, we knew what waited at the summit of our
climb: reality, a test too great for most.

I heard a thudding from the north. A helicopter. A big one.
I hurried to break the waterproof matches out of my pocket
and fumbled with the downy duff of inner bark I had collected
a half hour earlier from a piñon pine. I huddled to the ground,
struck a match. The first one splintered in my hand. Ray
watched as I selected another and struck again. This time, the
match caught, and the tiny flame leapt quickly to the kindling.

I worked to tease more dry duff from the bark. "I could do this faster if you hadn't confiscated my pocketknife," I commented wryly.

Ray smiled and handed me the twigs that he had gathered. "Tough girl," he said.

The fire spread and flared as I held it to the dry brown needles we had stacked on the lowest branch of a small dead piñon tree. Ray fanned the flames with his jacket as I pressed more dead branches against it. In two minutes, we had the tree ablaze, our own burning bush in the desert, and Ray pulled the Mylar sheet out of his other pocket and let it catch puffs of smoke like an Indian signal blanket. "Like this?" he asked.

"Just like a real Eagle Scout," I answered. "Another merit badge for you. So why didn't you join scouting? I thought all Mormon males did that."

"Dad was too sick. They needed me at home."

"Oh." I kept to the smaller issues, didn't ask about the rest of it, such as how he'd known how to find me and help me find him; I didn't have to. I'd had the experience now myself, but it was as yet fragile, and I didn't want to touch it, for fear it might shatter.

Just as we had planned, the fire drew the attention of the approaching Huey, and it wheeled, dipped, and settled toward us. Ray waved and pointed, leading it toward the clearing we had selected. As it descended, bounced, and settled onto the stony soil, I kicked the piñon over and stacked rocks and soil on it, extinguishing the flames and making certain that the wind from the rotors didn't scatter sparks. Then I hurried to the landing place.

The side door of the Huey opened and a man appeared: Not Tom Latimer, in a helicopter again, despite his deepest anxieties. He grinned, jumped down onto the ground, and, keeping his head down, hurried to where we were and led us far enough from the rotors that we could hear more easily.

Another figure appeared by the open helicopter doorway, a slight person swathed in the army green of a fatigue jacket, wispy blond hair flying out from beneath her flight helmet. Nina. When she saw me, she smiled and waved, and at the direction of a National Guardsman, she hopped down, ducked her head, and hurried out to join us. "Thank the Lord you're all right!" Nina said, clutching my hands to her breast.

"And you!" I replied. "But what are you doing here?"

Nina bowed her head like a little girl caught filching cookies. "I had to come. I was afraid you'd . . . get hurt. When I got home, no one was there, and I was really worried. Then Mr. Latimer came and knocked on the door with some friends of his." She beamed at the FBI agent. "Mr. Latimer said your helicopter had gone missing and that I could help find it. Remember, I'm a good finder, and—" She waved a hand across the landscape with stately pride. "I know it like the back of my hand."

I said, "I'm sure you do."

The FBI agent interrupted these musings. "Where in hell have you been all night, and where are the rest?" he demanded.

Ray shook his head.

Not Tom's eyes widened in alarm. "Crashed?"

"Shot down," I said. "But listen, you got to do this some other way. You can't go in like this; all you'd find is a bloody fight. They have kids down there armed with high-powered rifles, spread all over the place and scared of devils. The armament I saw close-up looked like an AR-seventeen. They move like guerillas over this land, and you can't risk yourselves *or* them. They're children. And they're her family."

Nina buried her face in my jacket and hugged me.

Not Tom nodded. He returned to the airship, plugged his headphones back in, and spoke to an unseen listener. When he was done talking, he returned to us, gave us each a blanket, and said, "Okay, you got it. Plan A was rescuing you. Let's go to plan B."

"What's that?"

"Pull back, seal the roads, and wait. We don't want another Waco."

I took Nina's face in both my hands and said, "You know all the good hiding places out there where Brother Nephi has one of your brothers or sisters waiting with a rifle. Can you point those places out from here?"

Nina searched my eyes wistfully, as if contemplating a lost love. In a few seconds, she aged from the child who had stepped excitedly off the helicopter to a woman, full of cares and responsibilities. But she said nothing.

I ran a hand over the crown of her head and willed her toward her wisdom. "Nina, Brother Manti has killed your beloved. And he killed the woman who was flying my helicopter. And Brother Nephi killed a policeman. They won't be allowed to stay here after that. What does the Bible say about that kind of killing?"

" 'Thou shalt not.' George showed me that. When he taught me to read."

Thank God for George, I thought. "What would George do now, Nina?"

She closed her eyes and took a deep breath, then turned to the agent, and she said, "You take this machine away and bring me back over the road in a truck. Drop me a ways north of the river. I'll find my brothers and sisters, and our mothers, and I'll bring them to you, one by one." Her smile flickered with uncertainty for a moment, and she added, "But, um, you have to promise again that you'll treat them nicely and give them hot meals, and, um, could you please be the one to go to the house and talk to Brother Nephi?"

The agent nodded soberly. "Okay. But are you sure? I'm

not sending you in there if anyone is going to mistake you for the enemy."

Nina released her grip on me and said, "The risk is mine to take. This is my family." She smiled. "And I'm *good* at keeping away from Brother Nephi and Brother Manti." Then she took my hand again briefly and gave it a squeeze, as if to comfort me, then turned to Ray and said, "Please thank Ava for me. It was rude of me to leave without saying thank you."

Ray smiled. "I'm sure she understands. You come visit again as soon as you can."

To the FBI agent, she said simply, "We should go now," then turned and marched off toward the helicopter, a good soldier.

I wanted to run after her and stop her. I wanted to protect her, not just from the risk she was facing but from the pain of full adulthood that lay before her. She would be spared from the full lash of the law, but those older than her would not. As I watched her slender form climb up into the helicopter, I suspected that I was watching the new leader of her clan ascending. I sensed a sea of sadness for the struggles that would fill her future.

The FBI agent was speaking to Ray. "Okay, we're out of here. You coming with us, or can you make it the rest of the way up the hill here? It's not real warm in this crate." He pointed up the hill. "There's a dirt road near the edge of the canyon. You'll find campsites. We have a man stationed there with a camper. Yellow truck, white shell, Colorado plates. About a half mile, no farther."

I knew that our resources were nearly exhausted. We needed hot meals and hotter baths, and a good long sleep. I opened my mouth to say so, but Ray tipped his head toward the hill, grinned, and said, "We can make it."

So much for his merit badge in hypothermia.

Not Tom puckered up his lips and smiled saucily. "Catch you later, then." He gave a quick thumbs-up and turned to go, then turned back and said. "Oh, and one more thing."

"What?" I asked.

"You two look like drowned rats. Ray, your jacket shrank and you need a shave. Where's your pride?"

"I don't have any," I said.

Ray just continued to grin. I decided I'd at least give him a consolation badge for wilderness couture.

We backed into the trees. The helicopter lifted off and veered toward the north, ascended, and thudded into the distance.

Before we climbed higher, we checked to make sure the fire was completely extinguished from our piñon beacon, then turned our faces toward the red glow of the coming sunrise. The dance of fire across the horizon brought to mind the image of a house on fire in the desert, the millennial conflagration of a dying siege that had existed within the mind of a man who had lost his soul and beckoned others to follow him. I prayed that Heavenly Father, or whatever God's name or visage was, might grant Nina the strength she needed to outwit her earthly sire. And I sent a special one, too, for Not Tom Latimer, who had agreed to face him for her.

Ray and I walked side by side, breathing in the morning. At length, we found a road, two tracks along the brink from which countless travelers had taken pictures of the stunning beauty that spread before us: the Grand Canyon in miniature, now touched by the first warm fingers of the rising sun.

We stayed in the trees, well away from the cliff edge, still watchful in case our enemy had spread this far from the west.

Another turn, a bend in the trail, and there was the camper van. Parked next to it was a car, a big sedan with Utah plates. Ray blinked, surprised. He smiled and turned toward me. "Hot chocolate," he whispered into my ear. "That's Mother's car."

I felt a laugh wriggle free from my heart. *Welcome home to Innocence,* I told myself. *We'll be baptized in chocolate and reborn.* I took a step toward the car, but Ray caught me and pulled me back out of sight behind the cover of the trees. There, he took me in his arms and gazed questioningly into my eyes. He swallowed hard. "Em," he began.

As I looked up into his eyes, my mind sped ahead of us, in search of possibilities and truths. I needed a moment to draw myself inward. I snuggled my arms up around his firm, wonderful torso and pressed my face to his stubbly throat. "Ray."

"Em, what about us?" He sighed, his breath caressing my ear.

"What *about* us?"

He pulled his head back. "Look at me."

I did so.

"Come to Salt Lake," he said. "You could get a job there, I'm sure of it, and—"

I let his invitation tickle through my consciousness, let my heart be open. "No," I said. I'd never make a Mormon; I knew that. But I *had* found Ray in the darkness. This experience was true; irreproducible, untestable by the five senses, but true. Perhaps someday science would explain it, but for now, I felt the light of Divinity warming my soul. "No, I have a job and a life waiting for me in Denver. You need to visit me there, and see what you think."

Ray's eyes widened with fear. "But if you go back there, you'll—"

"Shh." I raised one hand and put my fingertips across his lips and felt their warmth. They were only inches from mine, close enough that I could see tiny flaws where the ravages of the night had chapped the splendid skin. Yet somehow, the deep, inner sense of what he had felt like as he had drawn me through the night was even more real. I was going back to Denver, and I was going to take this one small experience of the magic between souls with me, and I was going to find out for myself where it fit with the rest of my thoughts, feelings, and faith. I was tempted to tell him yes, and stay. But I needed also to say, Don't make me your crisis of faith, or the victory of your beliefs. That crisis belonged to his heart alone, just as it visited each of us, in its own time. Softly, I said, "Ray, I'm going to be too busy for a while discarding some of my own beliefs to consider yours. You give me a few weeks or a month, and then come visit me, okay?"

Ray's deep indigo eyes slowly closed, and as his lips moved closer, seeking my own, he said, "I will."

I kissed him with my eyes open, mapping the curves and colors of his face, fearful that this closeness would live only in my memory. Tears filled my eyes and spilled down my cheeks. His hands moved across my back, through my hair, and to my face. When he felt my cheeks grow wet, he pressed his face against my neck and himself wept.

When the moment came to let go, I took off his jacket and handed it to him. He nodded and did the same with mine. I smoothed his hair, and he kissed mine. Then he took my hand and led me on around the grove of trees and up the road to where Ava now waited outside her car, smiling a welcome as she unscrewed a thermos full of cocoa and readied our cups.

I accepted her gift of warmth and sweetness gratefully, nodded to Ray, and, alone, took my cup to the edge of the canyon to watch the sun bless its deep interior with light and warmth. In such moments lie a magic of understanding and proportion. I loved the earth, and now felt its love for me; felt it in the pull of gravity, smelled it in the scent of pine, tasted it in the pleasure of chocolate, heard it in the sigh of the breeze, and saw it in every tint and hue of color that played across the rock. In the act of caring for it and all its passengers, my universe had widened and grown deeper. For in its beauty lay a depth and perfection of history I could not describe. And in this truth lay revelation, and hope.

Author's Note

Anyone interested in conspiracies will enjoy the story of how this book came to be written. It began as I was attending the 1997 meeting of the Geological Society of America (held that year in Salt Lake City). Utah State Geologist M. Lee Allison buttonholed me and said, "You ought to write a book about fossil theft and set it in Utah. Just think of it—you can have a dinosaur on the cover, and the book will sell like hotcakes."

Lee is a smart man. In an era of dwindling fiscal support for even such essential government agencies as the Utah Geological Survey, which Lee heads, he had grasped the fact that in order to do his job, he must communicate with the public he serves—that is, inform them of what he has done for them lately. The more people he can hornswoggle into doing this work for him, the better. "Here's my E-mail address," I told him. "Send me your ideas."

Lee delivered. He provided me not only with the virulent germ for the plot of this book—the Sue *T. rex* case—but also with most of its red herrings and the murder weapon. And Lee didn't stop with E-mails worth framing. He introduced me to a host of key sources, first and foremost among them David D. Gillette, Utah's State Paleontologist.

The next event in the conspiracy occurred a month later, when Sonoma State University department chair Tom Anderson invited me to teach the "Dino" course during the 1998 spring semester. I thought, Great, I'll get paid to research the book. But I thought I would learn about dinosaurs, not people.

About halfway through the semester, a visiting lecturer gave an interesting talk. I must expurgate specific references so I don't get sued, but I can diagrammatically state that the lecture was based on physical evidence that had recently been discovered by foreign researchers. When I asked this American how he'd gotten his evidence, he said, quite matter-of-factly, "I had a photograph smuggled out of [their country]." The man smiled proudly, and added, "And I scooped them. Got it on the cover of [a famous magazine] before they got their story in [another famous magazine]." The sound that immediately followed was the thud of my chin hitting the floor. This man had just blithely admitted that he had committed theft. A moment later, as I began taking notes on his speech patterns, I noticed that the string of coincidences leading toward this book was getting unusually long. And it got a whole lot longer.

The mystery writer as mystic.

I have long been fascinated by the systems of belief—perceptions of truth—we humans construct and live by. A mystery about people who study dinosaurs seemed a good arena in which to examine these beliefs. Being confronted by the evidence of dinosaurs' bones, we are compelled by the machinery of our imaginations to construct theories about them. And because dinosaurs grew to fabulous sizes but left few clues other than scattered bones from which to construct our beliefs about their origins and fates, they epitomize the mysterious and unexplained.

I had an agenda in writing this book. Scratch that—I had

several. First, I wanted to vent my spleen regarding the propagandistic and often paranoid blather that has been leveled at me (and countless colleagues) by certain creationists who know nothing more about me than that I am a scientist. I say "certain creationists," because most appear to believe I am entitled to my constitutional right to believe whatever I believe, so long as I don't infringe on their rights to peace, freedom of religion, and reasonable things like that.

I respect all who are conscious of what they believe. Consciousness does not come easily.

My goal and agenda in writing this book, beyond constructing a few hours of entertainment for the reader, was the more personal pursuit of examining the similarities and disparities between scientific and religious beliefs and practices. Approaching this task with the habits of a scientist, I gathered evidence, stated a theory (the two are more similar than dissimilar), and set out to test it. I was immediately at odds with myself, and therefore knew I was on to something. I must state that this method of testing my hypothesis was entirely unscientific, guided not by any empirical testing but, instead, by that within me which I shall identify as the artist's gut sense of accuracy. To explain that any better would fill a book on its own, so forgive me if I just move along with what I learned from this exercise.

Outwardly, I discovered that laypeople know little of the mechanics of the scientific method. By extension, I fear that likewise they know little of the mechanics of their own religious belief system, even if their central belief happens to be the null hypothesis, which simply stated is, God does not exist. To illustrate what I mean by that, let's consider how many people who believe that: "If God existed, God would not allow the terrible things that happen in this world to happen." The logic behind this statement is self-serving. The subject first sets a definition of God (all-powerful), then delegates all responsibility to God and has the temerity to erase God's existence basd on performance of this impossible job. Anyone who's ever worked in management knows that when accepting responsibility, one must also demand commensurate authority to define the job; even then, one must put up with endless criticism from underlings who, due to lack of experience, cannot perceive the true nature of the job. To believe that God does not exist, the subject of the belief has first defined for himself what God must be like.

As I learned about dinosaurs by teaching about them, the students in my dinosaur class became research subjects for my deeper agenda. I announced to them that I was teaching a certain system of beliefs, and that if they did not agree, I would respect them for that, but I wanted them to understand something about the research techniques, intuitive practices, and deductive logic that go into constructing the theories and proofs that embody the scientific method. I said, "I don't care if ten minutes after you walk out of my final exam you forget every polysyllabic dinosaur name I teach you. What I care about is that the next time you watch a program about dinosaurs or any other scientific matter on TV, you have a clue whether the people interviewed are presenting carefully researched deductions, or simply bullshitting you."

This agenda struck most of the students in the room as somewhat unusual. Some of them smiled, some played hooky, some snoozed, and some whispered who knows what to the kid in the next seat. To my horror, most who spoke up wanted to know what isolated facts they must memorize in order to pass the next test. But one came to me about halfway through the term and asked to interview me for a paper he had to write for his English class. It quickly emerged during our conversation that he had been raised in a fundamentalist system of beliefs and was trying to come to some sort of accommodation between this foundation and what he wanted to build on it.

He wanted to depart from his parents' conservative idea of training as a dentist and instead take the more uncertain, more artistic path of becoming an architect. He wanted to know how I juggled the rationalist thinking of scientific training with the extrarational experience of the spirit which I encountered in writing.

It was clear to me that this young man was entering a crisis of faith. I was impressed that he'd found his way there so young, and I told him that, in my experience, creative work requires that one be willing to embrace such ambiguities as he was noticing and follow them through to the truths hidden within them. I told him also that because he was asking the questions he was asking, I had no doubt he would be successful. God only knows what that success may hold.

Ambiguity is a seed from which great understanding can grow. The ambiguity between scientific and religious beliefs is young. A mere century and a half ago, most scientists were, in fact, clergymen. Consider Gregor Mendel, the father of genetics, a humble monk. It is only since the time of Darwin, a heretic who suggested that change occurs through time within living populations, that an argument has arisen between those who believe in this change (evolution) and those who believe that the stories of the Bible are literally true (special creation). What is true? And are we deterred from uncovering truth by what we believe?

Carol Mapes, one of my advisers on matters Mormon, listened with great interest to what I was struggling to understand through constructing the plot of this book. I led her through the story, then said, "I'm surprised to find that it's a book about a liar. Also, I'm having trouble understanding where the Mormon church stands on certain beliefs, such as the origin of the earth." I went on to describe the trials and travails of Nina, whom I felt had a lot to tell me. I thought that the pressures of emerging into the "real" world might push Nina to a crisis of faith. Carol said no, that Nina would be "a good girl" and go right back home. I stared at Carol rather blankly, because my own mind is wired more for defiance than compliance.

Carol said, "Sarah, you don't understand what blasphemy is, do you?"

I thought I did, and said so, but Carol said, "No, it's clear to me that you don't. Let me explain. Suppose you adhere to the beliefs of a religion. You have given up something—made a personal sacrifice—to do this. Say sex, or certain other pleasures or comforts. Then someone comes to you and tells you that it's all a sham. You react emotionally. You feel that your beliefs have been blasphemed. You get it? It's like a betrayal."

It took me a while, but the more I thought about it, the more I knew that she was right, and that the fact of how blasphemy works stood at the center of this book and of what I was struggling to understand by writing it; that when people have adhered to a belief on the strength of blind faith alone, they feel betrayed, and, worse yet, humiliated by the very idea that what they have sacrificed to support that belief is in vain. Note that I am not talking about the *definition* of blasphemy—an irreverence or deviling of God or anything else held sacred—but about how it *functions*.

My realization of the way blasphemy functions led me to a partial disproof of my theory that scientific and religious faith and practice are similar. Scientists may hotly disagree when their beliefs are challenged, and can grow quite emotional, but they do not accuse one another of blasphemy. Scientists do not accuse each other of blasphemy because in the practice of science, it is assumed that the truth is not known, and efforts are directed toward uncovering it. This is done by forming theories—false gods, if you will—and trying to disprove them. The scientific method is, in fact, a system that encourages blasphemy—or shall I say heresy, which is a more dignified form of challenge—through an institutionalized testing of beliefs. At its best, the scientific method leads us to the discovery of truths, or at least closer to them, and often toward a profound perception and admiration of the Divine (read Albert Einstein, or Stephen Hawking). At its worst, the scientific method grows stodgy and collapses into a sheltered workshop for poorly socialized intellectuals.

Many religions, by contrast, grow up around truth and accompanying rules revealed through an adept (Jesus, Mohammed, Joseph Smith), and, as the religion becomes institutionalized, the object becomes to accept on faith these truths and rules and adhere to them. At its most benign, surrender of individual wills to a religious ideal or leader leads toward enlightenment. At its worst, it becomes contorted and precipitates wars, or implodes into mass suicides, as happened in Jonestown. Before I enrage my readers with these generalizations, let me hasten to point out that I speak of religious practice, as contrasted to spiritual practice. Spiritual practice, more like scientific practice, usually leads the devotee through a process of refinement and clarification toward a perception of ever larger and more universal truths.

The scientist as mystic.

Much that fuels the plot of this book springs from the gentle fact that scientists believe their colleagues are telling the truth as they know it. Scientists do not like being told they're wrong, and much less do they like to face the public humiliation of having it proved to them. They are no different with regard to the emotions behind these reactions than a member of any other culture, religion, or sports team. But because they presume everyone is playing the same game by the same simple rule—tell the truth as you know it—they do not gore each other with ancient jawbones over such humiliations; instead, they bear up, examine the evidence, draw their own conclusions, and take their medicine when the time is ripe. They do not consider challenges to their beliefs to be blasphemous, simply because, as with spiritual devotees, their faith lies more in their process than in their beliefs.

My husband once told me about scientific experimentation that apparently demonstrates that the human brain is hardwired to construct a context of logic—for example, a cause-and-effect linkage—about every experience it encounters. I think this is an important theory to consider, because it would mean we are compelled to interpret every experience we have, regardless of how incomplete or even misleading the data, and regardless of how sorely we are limited by the facts of who and what we are. The consequences of such an urge to interpret our experiences would impact every system of belief we have, be it scientific, cultural, religious, or even spiritual. The authors of the U.S. Constitution must on some level have known this when they guaranteed a separation of church and state.

I am pleased to live in a country where each one of us has a chance to have his or her own thoughts, and follow his or her own heart to a place of truth.

With best wishes for a happy new millennium,
Sarah Andrews

.